Praise for Paula Graves

"Wonderfully romantic and beautifully written…
exciting and tense…"
—*CataRomance* on *Case File: Canyon Creek, Wyoming*

"Sizzling chemistry and plenty of action
keeps the plot moving, and readers on their toes,
in this fantastic read."
—*RT Book Reviews* on *Smoky Ridge Curse*

"Paula Graves delivers a chilling,
thrilling cocktail of suspense and romance."
—*New York Times* bestselling author Jayne Ann Krentz

"For a small town, there's plenty of crime and action
in Bitterwood, and Graves' second installment in
the series doesn't disappoint, neither in action nor
in the secrets buried deep in the Smokies."
—*RT Book Reviews* on *The Secret of Cherokee Cove*

"She yanks the reader into the story
as the first bomb explodes, and she
doesn't let go until the final page."
—*USATODAY.com*'s *Happy Ever After* blog
on *Major Nanny*

"The tension and romance kept me reading."
—*Fresh Fiction* on *Murder in the Smokies*

PAULA GRAVES

Alabama native Paula Graves wrote her first book, a mystery starring herself and her neighborhood friends, at the age of six. A voracious reader, Paula loves books that pair tantalizing mystery with compelling romance. When she's not reading or writing, she works as a creative director for a Birmingham advertising agency and spends time with her family and friends. She is a member of Southern Magic Romance Writers, Heart of Dixie Romance Writers and Romance Writers of America. Paula invites readers to visit her website, www.paulagraves.com.

PAULA GRAVES

Case File:
Canyon Creek, Wyoming

and

Chickasaw County Captive

◆ **HARLEQUIN**® INTRIGUE CLASSICS

Recycling programs
for this product may
not exist in your area.

ISBN-13: 978-0-373-60654-2

CASE FILE: CANYON CREEK, WYOMING/CHICKASAW COUNTY CAPTIVE
Copyright © 2014 by Harlequin Books S.A.

The publisher acknowledges the copyright holder
of the individual works as follows:

CASE FILE: CANYON CREEK, WYOMING
Copyright © 2010 by Paula Graves

CHICKASAW COUNTY CAPTIVE
Copyright © 2010 by Paula Graves

Printed in U.S.A.

CONTENTS

CASE FILE:
CANYON CREEK, WYOMING

For my brother Dennis,
who taught me how to fish, and whose
wild imagination always sparked my own.

CHAPTER ONE

THE FLASHING BLUE light in the rearview mirror came out of nowhere, cutting through the cool shadows of the waning afternoon. Hannah Cooper glanced at the rental car's speedometer needle, which hovered just under sixty. The speed limit was sixty-five on this stretch of Wyoming's Highway 287, so she wasn't speeding.

Maybe he just wanted her to move aside to make it easier to pass her on the two-lane highway. She edged the Pontiac toward the narrow shoulder, but the car behind her slowed as well, making no attempt to go around her. The driver waved out the window for her to pull all the way over.

Damn it. She released a slow breath and looked for somewhere to pull to the side. The highway shoulder barely existed on this stretch of winding road, the grassy edge rising quickly to meet the dense stand of pines lining the highway. Hannah spotted a widening of the shoulder a few yards ahead. She slowed and pulled over, cutting the engine.

Tamping down a nervous flutter in her belly, she lowered the window with one hand while pulling her wallet from her purse with the other. Outside the window, footsteps approached. She turned to face the lawman. "Is something wrong?"

She got a brief glimpse of weathered jeans and a

shiny silver belt buckle before the man's hand—snugly tucked into latex gloves—whipped up into the window and sprayed something wet and stinging in her face.

Her gasp of surprise drew a spray of fiery heat into her mouth and throat, and her eyes slammed closed, acid tears seeping from between her lids. *Pepper spray,* she realized, gagging as fire filled her lungs with every wheezing breath. Coughing, she tried to reorient herself in a world turned upside down.

She felt a rough hand on the back of her neck, pushing her forward toward the steering wheel with a sharp thrust. She threw herself sideways, avoiding all but a glancing blow of her cheekbone against the steering wheel. The shock of pain faded quickly compared to the lingering agony of the pepper spray. Panic rose as she felt the man's hand groping for her again.

Don't ever let them get you out of the car.

The warning that filled her foggy mind spoke in her brother Aaron's voice. Aaron, the cop, who never let pass any opportunity to give her advice about personal safety.

If they get you out of your car, you're dead.

The man's hand tangled briefly in her hair then retreated. A soft snapping sound outside the car made her jerk her head toward the open window, and she forced her eyelids open, blinking hard to clear her blurry vision. Through a film of white-hot pain, she saw her assailant's right hand sliding something black and metallic from a side holster.

Gun.

It snagged coming out of the holster, giving her the distraction she needed. Spotting his left hand resting on the car-door frame for balance, she rammed her elbow on to the back of his hand, crushing his fingers against the door. Something hard and metallic cracked against her elbow bone—a ring? It sent pain jarring up her arm, but she ignored it as he spat out a loud curse and pulled his hand free, just as she'd hoped.

She turned the key in the ignition. The rented Pontiac G6 roared to life and she jerked it into Drive, ramming the accelerator pedal to the floor.

The Pontiac shimmied across the sandy ground, the right back wheel teetering precariously along the edge of the dipping shoulder, but she muscled it back on to the highway and pointed its nose toward the long stretch of road ahead.

She groped on the seat next to her for the bottle of water she'd picked up from a vending machine at a gas station a few miles back. Grappling with the cap, she opened the bottle and splashed water in her eyes, trying to wash out enough of the burning spray to help her see as she drove. It helped the stinging pain in her eyes but did nothing to stop the burning on her skin and in her nose and throat.

Think, Hannah. Think.

She felt for her purse, which held her cell phone, but it must have fallen to the floorboard. She couldn't risk trying to find it. Though she could barely see, barely breathe, she didn't dare slow down, taking the curves at scary speeds. There had to be civilization somewhere ahead, she promised herself, shivering with shock and pain. Just another mile or so....

She peered blindly at the rearview mirror, trying to see if the car with the blue light was following. She'd rounded a curve that put a hilly stand of pines between her car and the waning daylight backlighting the Wyoming Rockies. Behind her, night had already begun to fall in murky purple shadows, hiding any sign of her assailant from view. Maybe she'd bought herself enough time.

She just had to keep going. Surely somewhere ahead she'd run into people who could help her.

She wiped her watering eyes, trying to see through the gloom. More than once over the next endless, excruciating mile, she nearly drove off the road, but soon the highway curved again, and the mountains came back into view, rising with violent beauty into the copper-penny sky. And just a mile or so ahead, gleaming like a beacon to her burning eyes, a truck stop sprawled along the side of the highway.

She headed her car toward the lighted sign, daring only a quick glance in her rearview mirror. She spotted a car behind her, a black dot in the lowering darkness. It seemed to be coming fast, growing larger and more threatening as the distance between her and the truck stop diminished.

Heart pounding, Hannah rammed the accelerator to the floor again, pushing the Pontiac to its limits. It shuddered beneath her, the engine whining, but the distance to the truck stop was yards now, close enough that she could make out men milling in the parking lot.

Behind her, the pursuing car fell back, as if he realized the foolishness of trying to overtake her so close to a truck stop full of witnesses. Shaking with relief, she aimed her car at the blurry span of the truck-stop driveway.

The sun dipped behind the mountains just as she made the turn, casting a sudden shadow across the entrance. The unexpected gloom, combined with her blurred vision, hid a dangerous obstacle until it was too late. Her right front wheel hit the rocky outcropping that edged the driveway and sent the car lurching out of control.

Fighting the wheel, she managed to avoid a large gas-tanker truck parked at the far edge of the truck-stop parking lot, but a scrubby pine loomed out of the darkness right in her path. She slammed on her brakes, but it was too late.

She hit the tree head on, and the world went black.

IN CANYON CREEK, WYOMING, night had long since fallen in cool, blue shadows tinted faint purple by the last whisper of sunset rimming the ridges to the west. With sunset had come the glow of streetlamps lining Main Street, painting the sidewalks below with circles of gold.

From his office window on the second floor of the Canyon Creek Police Department, Deputy Chief Riley Patterson had a bird's-eye view of the town he protected, though few people remained in town at this time of night. Most of the stores had shut down a couple of hours earlier, though a light still glowed in the hardware store across the street. After a moment, even that light extinguished, and Riley spotted storekeeper Dave Logan locking the store's front door, his dog Rufus waiting patiently by his side.

Riley turned from the window and sank into his desk chair, his gaze lifting to the large, round clock on the wall. At seven-forty on a Tuesday evening, Riley was one of four people left in the building, but up here on the second floor, he might as well be the only person. The quiet was like a living thing this time of night, unbroken for the most part, though a few minutes earlier he'd heard the fax go off in the chief's office. He'd check it before he left for home.

He worked late most evenings, in part because he liked the quiet time to catch up on the paperwork that took up most of his time these days, but mostly because the alternative was going home to his empty house.

He worked his way through a handful of reports the day-shift officers had left on his desk, making notes on interviews that needed follow-ups and putting them in the outbox for his secretary to file in the morning. Then he leaned back in his chair and stared at the ceiling, willing himself to grab his jacket and keys and head home before he started worrying himself the way he knew he'd begun to worry his friends and colleagues.

His desk phone rang before he could move, shattering the quiet. He dropped his feet to the floor and checked the number on the caller ID display. It was Joe Garrison, his boss and lifelong friend. Riley grabbed the receiver. "I'm about to head home, I swear—"

"Just got a call from the Teton County Sheriff," Joe interrupted briskly. "Attempted abduction on Highway 287 late this afternoon. Female victim, mid-twenties."

Riley felt a twinge of unease. "Deceased?"

"No, but I don't know any more details yet. It's Teton County's jurisdiction, but the sheriff gave me a courtesy call. His department should be faxing the details over any minute."

"The fax rang a minute ago. I'll check." Riley put Joe on hold and walked into the chief's office. He grabbed the handful of sheets from the fax tray and scanned them on the way back to his office. Standard BOLO— Be On Lookout—notice, short on details. The victim apparently hadn't gotten a good look at her attacker.

Riley reached his desk and picked up the phone. "Still there?"

"For the moment, although Jane's giving me come-hither looks that are getting a little hard to resist," Joe answered, laughter tinting his voice. "Anything on the BOLO we need to worry about?"

"According to the victim, the assailant was driving a police car, although she doesn't seem sure whether it was a marked car or not. The guy had a blue light on the roof, but it might have been a detachable one." Riley scanned further. "Not much in the way of a description, either, beyond what he was wearing."

"Odd," Joe said.

The next words Riley read made his blood go cold. A faint buzzing noise filled his ears as he read the information again.

"Riley?" Joe prodded on the other end of the line.

Riley cleared his throat, but when he spoke, his voice still came out raspy and tight. "She was pepper-sprayed. In the face."

There was a brief silence on the other end of the line while the implications sank in for Joe. A second later, he said, "I'll be there in ten minutes." He hung up without saying goodbye.

Riley put down the phone and stared at the BOLO, rereading the passage one more time to make sure he hadn't misread. But the words remained unchanged—oleoresin capsicum found on the victim's face, clothing and in her mucus and saliva.

He sank heavily into his desk chair, his hand automatically reaching for the bottom drawer to his right. He pulled it open and took out a dog-eared manila folder, the only thing that occupied the drawer. He thumbed through the familiar pages inside the file folder, searching for the three-year-old Natrona County coroner's report. His breath caught when he read the decedent's name—Patterson, Emily D.—but he dragged his gaze away from the name to the toxicology report on the pages stapled behind the death certificate.

Oleoresin capsicum. It had been found in her eyes, nose, throat and lungs, preserved, ironically, by the plastic sheeting her killer had wrapped her in before sinking her body in a lake off Highway 20.

He heard footsteps pounding up the stairs outside his office. Joe burst through the doorway, his wife, Jane, right behind him. Joe grabbed the fax pages from Riley's desk while Jane crossed to put her hand on Riley's shoulder, her green eyes warm with compassion. "You okay?" she asked.

He nodded, putting the coroner's report back into the file folder and sliding it into the open drawer.

"This is six," Joe said, settling on to the edge of Riley's desk with the fax pages in his hands.

"Six that we know of," Riley added grimly. "And we're not sure about a couple of them." The plastic sheet wrapped around the bodies of two of the victims hadn't protected them from the water where their bodies had been dumped.

"The plastic sheeting was enough of an MO for me," Joe said firmly. "If this one hadn't gotten away, she'd have shown up in a lake or river somewhere around here, wrapped in plastic, too. Maybe this time, the FBI will finally see the pattern."

The FBI didn't want to see the pattern, Riley knew. He'd tried to get the feds involved the minute he'd started piecing together the murders three years ago, when Emily had become one of the killer's victims. They hadn't been interested. "The connection was too nebulous" or some such B.S.

"I'll give Jim Tanner a call in the morning," Joe said, referring to the Teton County Sheriff. "He owes me a favor."

Jane put her hand on Riley's shoulder again. "Come home with us for dinner," she said. "It's nothing much— just some leftover barbecue, but we have plenty of it."

"Even with her eating for three," Joe added with a smile.

"Two," Jane corrected with a roll of her green eyes, "although one of us is half cowboy, so you may have a point."

Riley tried to smile at the banter, but it stung a little, even though he was happy as hell that his old friend had finally found a little happiness in his roller-coaster of a life. Seeing Joe and Jane so clearly happy, so clearly in love, was a reminder of all he'd lost three years ago when Emily had died.

"Actually, I think I'm just going to head home and try to get some sleep so I'll be fresh in the morning," he lied, even as a plan began to form in his restless mind. He gave Jane a quick kiss on the cheek and nodded toward the door. "Let's get out of here and I'll talk to you both tomorrow."

He could see a hint of suspicion in Joe's expression as the three of them walked out to the parking lot, where Joe's dark-blue Silverado was parked next to Riley's silver one. But his friend just gave a wave goodbye as Riley slid behind the truck's wheel and backed out of the parking lot.

He drove west, toward the small farmhouse located

on the last parcel of what used to be his family's cattle ranch a couple of miles outside the Canyon Creek town limits. But he passed the house and kept driving west.

HANNAH WOKE TO SILENCE, her heart pounding. She lay in an unfamiliar bed, the unmistakable smell of antiseptic surrounding her. Her eyelids felt heavy and swollen, but she forced them open.

The room around her was mostly dark, only a faint sliver of light peeking under the door. A darkened television sat on a wall mount in one corner of the room. Curtained windows lined the wall beside her bed.

She was in the hospital, she remembered. She'd been attacked on the roadside and crashed while escaping. The memories returned in bright, painful fragments.

She lifted her hand to her face. The touch of her fingers to her raw skin hurt a little, though not as much as the dull ache settling in the center of her forehead. She touched the left side of her head and found a bandage there. From the wreck or from the man's attempt to slam her head into the steering wheel? Pressing lightly, she felt a sharp sting.

And how had she gotten away? She couldn't remember—

The door to the room opened, admitting a shaft of light from the hallway and the compact frame of a woman in blue scrubs. The woman crossed to her bed and pushed a button on the wall. The room filled with gentle golden light, giving Hannah a better look at her visitor.

She looked to be in her late forties, short and muscular, with sandy-brown hair and large blue eyes. A badge clipped to her belt read Lisa Raines, LPN. She smiled at Hannah as she reached for her wrist to check her pulse. "How're you feeling, Hannah?"

"Head hurts," Hannah croaked, her throat feeling raw.

"You took a bit of a bump. You have a concussion." She said it with a slight chuckle.

"You've told me that before, huh?" Hannah shifted into a sitting position, groaning a little as the room spun around her.

"Yeah, you had a little short-term memory loss when you first got here, so you kept asking the same questions every few minutes." Lisa slipped a blood-pressure cuff over Hannah's arm. "You're going to be fine, though. We didn't find anything seriously wrong. We're just going to keep you overnight for observation." Lisa checked her blood pressure and took her temperature, jotting notes on her chart. "Everything's looking normal. You must have a hard head."

"Has anyone called my family?"

"You didn't have any emergency contact information in your belongings. I can make a call for you if you like."

Hannah started to shake her head no but thought better of it. She'd told her mother she'd call once she reached Jackson Hole, just to check in. If her mother didn't hear from her soon, she might send half of her brothers north to Wyoming to find her. "Could I make the call myself?"

"Sure." Lisa smiled and waved her hand toward the phone by the bedside. "I'll be back in an hour to check on you again, but if you need me before then, just push the call button."

Hannah waited for Lisa to leave before she picked

up the phone and dialed her parents' number. Her father picked up after a couple of rings.

"Hi, Dad, it's me. I'm in Jackson." Her voice came out much hoarser than she had intended.

"Hannah?" Her father sounded instantly suspicious. "What's wrong with your voice?"

She couldn't lie, now that he'd asked a direct question. "I had an accident."

"Are you okay? Where are you calling from?"

"The hospital, but I'm okay. I promise. Nothing broken. Just a concussion, but the nurse just told me I'm doing great and I'll be getting out of here in the morning. Can I speak to Mom a moment?"

A moment later, Beth Cooper took the phone. "Tell me everything that happened."

Settling back against the bed pillows, Hannah told her mother about the attack and her escape, trying not to make it sound too alarming. But by the time she was finished, her mother was making plans to fly to Wyoming immediately.

Tears stinging her eyes, Hannah fought the unexpected urge to agree. "Mom, there's no need to come up here. I'm okay, I promise. No real harm done, except to my rental car, and that's insured. I'm going to finish out my vacation just like I planned and I'll be home by Sunday evening."

"That's crazy. You get on a plane tomorrow and come home."

The temptation to do what her mother asked alarmed Hannah. The youngest of seven, and the only girl, she'd fought hard to assert herself, to prove she could take care of herself. The last thing she needed to do now was slink home to hide beneath her family's wings. She'd done enough of that over the past four years.

"No, I'm staying here, Mom. I need to do it."

Her mother was silent for a moment before she answered. "Okay. You're right. But you'll call me every night. Fair enough?"

Hannah smiled. "Fair enough."

"You're a brave woman," her mother said, her voice tinted with admiration.

"I had a good role model." Hannah blinked back hot tears. She heard the door handle to her hospital room rattle. The door started to open. "Looks like the nurse is back, so I need to go." She rang off and hung up the phone, turning back to face the nurse, ready to make a joke about how hard it was to get any sleep in a hospital.

But she stopped short as her visitor entered the soft cocoon of light surrounding her bed, revealing a pair of long, jean-clad legs and a shiny silver belt buckle.

Her heart rate doubling in the span of a second, she opened her mouth and screamed.

CHAPTER TWO

AT THE SOUND of Hannah Cooper's scream, Riley whipped around to look behind him, half-certain he'd see a crazed maniac with a gun. But all he saw was a nurse run into the room, alarm in her eyes. She pushed past Riley to her patient's side.

"Who is he?" Hannah asked the nurse, gazing at Riley with wide, frightened eyes.

The nurse looked at him over her shoulder, her expression wary. "What are you doing here? Visiting hours are over."

"I'm sorry. I should have announced myself at the nurses' station." He hadn't done so, of course, because he didn't want anyone to tell him he couldn't see Hannah Cooper. "I'm Riley Patterson with the Canyon Creek Police Department. I wanted to talk to Ms. Cooper about what happened to her this afternoon."

"The police have already spoken to her." The nurse lifted her chin, looking like a she-wolf guarding her young.

"That was the Teton County Sheriff's Department," Riley said, not ready to give up until he'd talked to the victim alone. "I want to talk to her about a similar case in my jurisdiction." That was stretching the truth a bit; none of the murders he'd been looking into over the past three years had actually happened in the Canyon Creek jurisdiction. But if nobody else in Wyoming gave a damn about connecting the dots, he was happy to make it a Canyon Creek priority.

"What do you want to know?" Hannah Cooper spoke in a raspy drawl, her voice a combination of honey and steel. Her green eyes remained wide and wary, and she hunkered deeper into the pillow behind her as he approached, but her jaw squared and she didn't turn away when he reached her bedside.

"I'm going to reach into my pocket and show you my badge first." He kept his voice low and calm. "So you'll know I am who I say I am."

She remained wary as he showed her his credentials. "The guy who attacked me was driving a cop car." Her gaze lifted defiantly to his. "You'll forgive me if I'm not particularly impressed by your badge."

Of course. He should have considered that possibility. Sliding the badge into the back pocket of his jeans, he did his best to soften his expression. "I'm sorry. I know you've been through a terrible ordeal. If you want to call the Canyon Creek Police Department, they can verify my credentials—"

"That's not necessary." Anger flashed in her eyes, although he got the feeling she was angrier at herself than at him. She pushed her hair away from her face, taking a deep breath. When she spoke again, she was calmer. "It's okay, I don't mind talking to him for a minute," she told the nurse.

The nurse slanted a look at Riley, as if she wanted to argue, but after a short nod, she left them alone.

"I apologize for barging in without any warning." Riley pulled a chair next to her bed. "How are you feeling?"

"Like I've been kicked in the head and dipped in acid."

"Pepper spray's nasty." He'd been exposed a few times, mostly in his police training. "And so's a concussion. I took a hit my senior year playing football. Kept asking the trainer what had happened every other minute for a solid half hour."

His confession elicited a tiny smile from her, the effect dazzling. Bandages, blotchy skin and red-rimmed eyes disappeared, revealing how pretty she was beneath her injuries. Her eyes were a mossy-green, her pupils rimmed by a shock of amber—cat's eyes, bright and a little mysterious. Her small, straight nose and wide, full lips might have been dainty if not for her square, pugnacious jaw. She was a scrapper. He'd known a few scrappers in his life.

Her smile faded, and he felt a surprising twinge of disappointment. Her chin dipped when she spoke. "You said there was a similar case in your jurisdiction?"

He cleared his throat. "Actually, there are a handful of cases I've been looking at over the past three years. Similar MO's—women driving alone on the highway, incapacitated by pepper spray." He didn't add that they usually ended up dead, wrapped in plastic sheeting in some river or lake not far from the highway where they disappeared.

Her expression darkened. "How many got away like I did?"

He licked his lips and didn't answer.

She nodded slowly. "I'm lucky, aren't I?"

"Yeah, you are."

She took a deep breath, coughing a little from the aftereffects of the pepper-spray attack. Her lower lip trembled a moment, but she regained control, her gaze lifting to meet his. "He tried to pull me out of the car, but I kept hearing my brother's voice in my head. 'Don't let him get you out of the car.' So I smashed my elbow against his hand where it was sitting on the window frame and I drove off as fast as I could."

"That was smart and brave."

"I don't know about that," she said faintly. "I just didn't want to die today."

The simple emotion in her voice tugged at his gut. Had Emily felt that way, trapped by a monster on the highway out of Casper? He knew from the autopsy that she'd fought him—her fingernails had been ripped in places, and there was some pre-mortem bruising from the struggle. Had the pepper spray incapacitated her more than it had Hannah Cooper? Had she lacked the opening that Hannah had to fight back and get away?

He rubbed his forehead, struggling against the paralyzing images his questions evoked. "I saw your statement to the Sheriff's Department. You didn't see your assailant's face?"

"No. I barely saw his midsection through the window before he hit me with the pepper spray. I didn't see much of anything after that. Just blurry images."

"You mentioned a silver belt buckle. Can you remember what was on it?"

Her brow furrowed with tiny lines of concentration. "I just know it was silver and there was a pattern to it, but I can't remember what it was. Maybe I didn't get a good look."

Though his instinct was to push her to remember more, he held his tongue. As frustrating as it was not to have all the answers right now, he reminded himself how lucky he was to have a living, breathing witness to the killer's MO. Maybe she'd remember more as the effects of the trauma wore off.

"You look tired," he said.

"Gee, thanks," she muttered, and he smiled.

Behind them came a knock, then the door opened just enough for the light from the corridor to silhouette the shape of a man. The hair on the back of Riley's neck rose. On instinct, he moved to put himself between Hannah and the visitor.

"Sorry to interrupt. I'm with hospital security. The nurse thought I should check and see if everything's okay here." The security guard remained in the doorway, his shoulders squared and his hands at his side, close to the unmistakable outline of his weapon holster.

"Everything's fine," Hannah said firmly. "Thank you."

With a nod, the security guard closed the door behind him.

"Did the Teton County Sheriff's Department offer to post a guard outside your door?" Riley asked.

"Why? The guy who attacked me didn't know me. I was—what do y'all call it? A target of opportunity?"

She was right, but leaving her alone here in the hospital didn't sit well with him. The staff had shown they had her best interests at heart, but he couldn't shake the idea that the wily killer he'd been looking for over the past three years wouldn't be happy leaving behind a live victim. The more time Hannah had to remember details from the attack, the more valuable she was to the police—and dangerous to the killer.

He pushed to his feet, sensing she was running out of energy. She needed her rest, and they could pick up this conversation in the morning. "I'm heading out now. You get some sleep and don't worry about any of this, okay?"

She nodded, her eyelids already starting to droop.

He slipped out of the room and headed down the hallway toward the nurses' station, where the nurse he'd met previously was making notes in a chart behind the desk. She looked up, her expression turning stern. "You didn't stress her out, did you?"

"Is there a waiting area on this floor?" he asked.

The nurse pointed out a door a few feet down the corridor.

Riley entered the room, which was mostly empty, save for a weary-looking woman stretched out across an uncomfortable-looking bench in the corner. Riley grabbed a seat near the entrance, where he could keep an eye on the door.

He hadn't wanted to worry Hannah Cooper, but it had occurred to him that, target of opportunity or not, she'd seen the killer and lived to tell.

The son of a bitch wouldn't like that one bit.

ONE OF THE DIRTY LITTLE secrets of hospitals was how shoddy hospital security was, especially in a place like Jackson, Wyoming. Jackson Memorial Hospital had a single security camera trained on the main entrance and a few guards scattered throughout the hospital in case trouble arose. If you looked like you belonged and knew where you were going, nobody gave you a second look.

That's how it worked in institutions of all sorts.

He wasn't on duty that evening, but it was a piece of cake to enter right through the front door, wearing his work garb, without anyone lifting an eyebrow. Now, he had just one more job to do to cover his tracks, and then he'd finish what he'd come here to do.

He slipped inside the empty security office and closed the door behind him.

SHE DREAMED OF HOME, with its glorious vista of blue water, green mountains and cloud-strewn skies. The lake house where she'd spent her first eighteen years of life had been built by her father's hands, with lumber and stone from right there in Gossamer Ridge, Alabama. Though she'd lived on her own for almost eight years, the lake house remained home to her, a place of refuge and a source of strength.

She didn't feel as if she was dreaming at first, the setting and companions as familiar and ordinary as the sound of her own voice. Out on the water, her brother Jake was taking a fisherman on a guided tour of the lake's best bass spots. Nearby, her brother J.D. worked on the engine of a boat moored in one of the marina berths, while his eleven-year-old son, Mike, shot a basketball through the rusty old hoop mounted on the weathered siding of the boathouse.

She basked in the sun on her skin and breathed in the earthy wildness of the woods and the water from her perch on the end of the weathered wooden pier. Her bare toes played in the warm water, drawing curious bluegills close to the surface before they darted back down to safety near the lake bottom.

Suddenly, the pier shook and creaked beneath her as footsteps approached from behind. She turned to look up at the visitor and met a pair of brilliant blue eyes gazing out from the chiseled-stone features of Riley Patterson.

"Wake up," he said. "You're in danger."

The dream images shattered, like a reflection in a pool displaced by a falling stone. She woke to the murky darkness of a hospital room filled with alien smells and furtive movements. A shadow shifted beside her in the gloom, and she heard the faint sound of breathing by her bed.

She froze, swallowing the moan of fear rising in her throat. *It's a nurse,* she told herself. *Only a nurse. In a minute, she'll turn on the light and check my pulse.*

But why hadn't the nurse left the door to the hallway open?

She felt the slightest tug on the IV needle in the back of her hand. Peering into the darkness, she caught the faint glint of the IV bag as it moved.

The intruder was putting something into her IV line.

Panic hammering the back of her throat, she swallowed hard and tried to keep her breathing steady, even though her lungs felt ready to explode. Slowly, quietly, she tugged the tube from the cannula in her right hand until she felt the cool drip of liquid spreading across the bed sheet under her arm. She had no idea where the nurse call button was, but it didn't matter anyway. She was too terrified to move again. The last thing she wanted to do was let the intruder know she was awake.

Instead, she focused on her breathing, keeping it slow and steady. In and out. Her heart was racing, her head was aching, but she kept breathing until she felt the intruder move away from her bedside. A moment later, the door to her room opened and the silhouette of a man briefly filled the shaft of light pouring inside. But he was gone before she got more than a quick impression of a solid, masculine build.

The door clicked closed and she jerked herself to a sitting position, groping for the nurse call button that hung by a cord from the side of her bed. She flicked the switch that turned on the bedside light and frantically pressed the call button.

A few seconds later, a woman's tinny voice came through the call-button speaker. "Yes?"

"Someone just came into my room and tried to put something in my IV line," she said, her voice shaking.

After a brief pause, the nurse's voice came through the speaker again. "I'll be right there."

A few seconds later, the door opened and a nurse hurried inside. She hit the switch by the door, flooding the room with light. Her brow furrowing, she looked at the tube Hannah had extracted from the cannula. "Are you sure someone was in here?" she asked, checking the IV bag.

"He was standing right there. He put something in that port thing." Hannah pointed toward the bright orange injection port positioned a few inches below the IV bag.

The nurse's frown deepened.

The door to the room whipped open and Riley Patterson entered, his tense blue eyes meeting Hannah's. "What's going on? I saw the nurse run in here—"

Hannah watched him close the distance between them, unsettled by how glad she was to see the Wyoming lawman again. The memory of her dream, of his quiet warning, flashed through her mind, and she felt the sudden, ridiculous urge to fling herself in his arms and thank him for saving her life.

Instead, she murmured, "I thought you went home."

"You thought wrong," he said drily. "What happened?"

She told him what she'd just experienced, watching with alarm as his expression darkened. "I wasn't imagining it," she said defensively.

He looked at her. "I didn't say you were."

"I'll call security," the nurse said, heading for the door.

"I think we should call the Teton County Sheriff's Department, too." Riley reached for the phone.

"So you believe me?" Hannah pressed.

"Any reason I shouldn't?" He started dialing a number.

Hannah sank back against her pillows, reaction beginning to set in. She tried to hold back the shivers, but it was like fighting an avalanche. By the time Riley hung up the phone and turned around, her teeth were chattering wildly.

He sat beside her on the bed and took her hands in his. "It's okay. You're going to be okay."

His eyes were the color of the midday sky, clear and brilliant blue. They were a startling spot of color in his lean, sun-bronzed face. He seemed hewn of stone, his short-cropped hair the rusty color of iron ore, his shoulders as broad and solid as a block of granite. His lean body could have been chiseled from the rocky outcroppings of the Wyoming mountains. He had cowboy written all over him.

Aware she was staring, she looked down at his hands enveloping hers. They were large, strong and work-roughened. A slim gold band encircled his left ring finger.

She tugged her hands away, acutely aware of her

own bare ring finger. "I should have screamed. I let him get away."

"There are probably security cameras around. He took a big risk coming after you here."

"He was so calm." She gripped the bed sheets to keep her traitorous fingers from reaching for his hands again, though she felt absurdly adrift without his reassuring touch. "His actions were furtive, but he didn't seem nervous."

"Did you see anything about him?"

"It was too dark. I saw his outline when he slipped out the door—definitely male."

"My size?"

She let her gaze move a little too slowly over his hard, lean frame. Chiding herself mentally, she shook her head. "Heavier. More muscle-bound or something. Probably your height, maybe an inch or two taller." She pressed her lips together to stop her chattering teeth. "I should have made noise, gotten the nurses in here—"

"If you're right about what you saw, the man came here to kill you. Making a noise only would have made it happen faster." He briefly touched her hand where the cannula remained, unattached to the IV tube. "You got that tube out. You saved yourself, and nobody could expect anything more."

He was saying all the right things, but she heard disappointment in his voice. Clearly, finding the man who'd attacked her was more than just another case to him.

She'd always been insanely curious—nosy, her brothers preferred to call it—but something kept her from asking any more questions of Riley Patterson. She sensed that pushing him for more information would make him back off. She couldn't afford for him to back off.

A man had tried to kill her twice in one day, and she had a feeling Riley Patterson might be the only person who could stop him if he tried it a third time.

JOE GARRISON ARRIVED not long after the Teton County Sheriff's Department detectives. Riley caught his boss's eye as he entered Hannah Cooper's room, motioning him over with a twitch of his head. Joe met him in the corner, his gaze wandering across the small room to where Hannah Cooper sat in a chair by her empty bed, her green-eyed gaze following the activity of the evidence techs who were processing the scene.

"The Teton County Sheriff's Department wants her in protective custody, but she's refusing," Riley said. "She said she'd rather go home early tomorrow and forget all about this."

"You don't want her to leave."

Riley met his friend's understanding gaze. "She saw the guy. Maybe she didn't see his face, but she's the only living witness, and she's about to fly back home to Alabama."

"You can't keep her here against her will."

Riley pressed his hands against his gritty eyes. "I can't let her leave."

Joe's answer was dry as a desert. "So kidnap her and hold her hostage."

Riley slanted a look at his boss. "Did you drive all the way here to give me a hard time or are you going to help me figure out how to keep her in Wyoming?"

"Do you want me to arrest her or something?"

"Could we?" Riley glanced at Hannah, only half-joking. She looked calm now, more curious than worried, her slim fingers playing absently with the hem of her hospital gown, tugging it down over her knees.

"Maybe you should tell her why you're so desperate to solve this case."

Riley looked back at Joe. "Tell her about Emily?"

Joe nodded.

Riley looked at Hannah again and found her returning his gaze. After a couple of seconds, she looked away.

"Maybe if she knew how many victims we could be talking about, and the way they were killed..." Riley said softly.

"You want to scare her into staying?"

"Maybe she'll want to help."

Joe arched one eyebrow. "At the risk of her own life?"

Riley sighed. "You're just a wellspring of optimism."

"You want a yes man, you called the wrong guy." Joe thumped Riley on the arm. "But maybe you're right. The Teton County Sheriff's Department doesn't know what we know about these murders. They're not giving her the whole picture. I guess you could lay the truth on her and let her make an informed choice." Joe's gaze shifted as the hospital-room door opened and a tall, rangy lawman entered. "There's Jim Tanner."

As Joe left Riley to greet the Teton County Sheriff, Riley crossed to the chair where Hannah sat. She looked up at him, a dozen questions swirling behind her eyes. He smiled slightly and crouched beside her. "Three-ring circus."

"I'll be glad to be out of it," she admitted. "I get the feeling the police aren't taking me very seriously. I think they think I'm just paranoid."

"It shouldn't take that long to find out what the guy put in your IV tube. I heard them say the lab is working on it right now."

"They just want to prove it was nothing so they can pat me on the head and tell me it was just a dream."

Riley had a feeling she was right. "I don't think it was just a dream."

She shot him a look of pure gratitude. "I wasn't asleep. I know what I saw. And all that's supposed to be in that IV is saline, so there's no reason for anyone to put anything else into it."

"You don't have to convince me."

She lowered her voice, eyeing the technician standing nearby. "Nobody in the Teton County Sheriff's Department said anything about multiple murders."

He couldn't hold back a little smile. "Yeah, I know."

"But you disagree?"

He lowered his voice, too. "I've been tracking a series of murders, one or two a year, for the last three years. All across Wyoming, east to west, north to south. Women driving alone, disappearing en route from one place to another. Their bodies are later found wrapped in plastic, dumped in a lake, river or other body of water. Three of the six showed traces of pepper spray around the mouth, nose and eyes. The other bodies had too much weather exposure to take a sample."

Hannah's face went pale, but she didn't look away. "If I hadn't gotten away—"

He didn't finish the thought for her. He didn't need to.

The door to the room opened, and a woman in a white coat entered, carrying a file folder. She crossed to speak to Jim Tanner, whose brow furrowed deeply the longer she spoke. Joe looked across the room at Riley, his expression grim. Riley's stomach twisted into a knot.

Joe and Sheriff Tanner crossed to Hannah's side. Riley stood to face them.

"The lab report on the IV tube is back," Tanner said.

"And?" Hannah asked.

His expression grew hard. "There was enough digoxin in that tube to kill you in a matter of minutes."

CHAPTER THREE

THE BUZZ OF urgent conversation surrounding her seemed to fade around Hannah as she took in Sheriff Tanner's quiet announcement.

Her attacker had tried to kill her. Again.

It had to be the same guy, right? It wasn't likely two different people would go after a nobody tourist like her. But why? She hadn't even seen him, really. She could remember almost nothing about him. Why did he consider her a threat?

She looked around for Riley Patterson, the closest thing to a familiar face in the room. His ice-blue eyes met hers, his expression grim but somehow comforting. He crouched beside her again, one hand resting on her forearm. "You okay?"

She nodded quickly, forcing her chin up. "I just want to know how he could get to me so easily."

"So do we," Sheriff Tanner assured her. "I've sent a man to check with hospital security. But I don't have much hope. This is a small hospital, and Jackson Hole's a pretty laid-back place. There's not much security in place here."

"He thinks he's invincible," Riley said softly. "He's gotten away with everything so far."

"Joe tells me you two think this attack is connected to other murders in the state," Sheriff Tanner said.

Riley glanced at Hannah. She could tell he didn't want to talk about this in front of her. He hadn't given her many details about the other cases he'd been investigating, though what he'd told her had been horrifying enough.

"I've made file folders full of notes," he told Sheriff Tanner. "I don't mind sharing. The more people looking for this guy, the better."

The Teton County sheriff studied Riley, his eyes narrowed, then turned his gaze to the lanky, dark-haired man Riley had introduced as his boss, Joe Garrison. "You vouch for this, Garrison?"

Joe nodded. "Riley's right. This guy has struck before, and he'll do it again if we don't stop him."

Sheriff Tanner didn't look happy to hear Joe's affirmation. "Okay, send me copies of your notes, and I'll put a detective on it. See if we can't tie it to any open cases we're working on."

"Cold cases, too. I've only been keeping notes since three years ago, but I think it could go back further," Riley said.

"Why three years ago?" Hannah asked.

Joe and Sheriff Tanner both turned to look at Riley, but Riley kept his eyes on Hannah, his expression mask-like.

When he didn't answer, she rephrased the question. "You said you've been keeping notes for only three years. What happened to make you start?"

Riley held her gaze a long moment, then looked down at his hands. He flexed his left hand, the ring on the third finger glinting as it caught the light. He spoke in a soft, raspy voice. "Three years ago, the son of a bitch murdered my wife."

Riley's words felt like a punch to Hannah's gut. No wonder he seemed personally involved in this case. "I'm sorry."

He acknowledged her condolences with a short nod, his mouth tightening. "I want this guy caught even more than you do," he added softly, as if the words were meant for her ears alone.

She swallowed hard, remembering how just a little while ago, she wanted nothing more than to catch the next plane home to Alabama. A part of her still did.

She'd done a lot of running home over the last four years.

But knowing what she now knew, could she really run away? She was possibly the only living witness who could identify a cold-blooded murderer.

A murderer who'd killed Riley Patterson's wife.

"Excuse me?"

Hannah turned at the sound of a new voice. The doctor who'd treated her in the Emergency Room when she arrived at the hospital stood nearby, his expression concerned.

"I'd like to check on my patient," he said firmly.

Riley stepped between the doctor and Hannah. "Mind if I see your ID?"

The look on the doctor's face almost made Hannah laugh. "Mind if I see yours?"

Riley had his badge out before the request was finished. The doctor's mouth quirked. Once he'd studied Riley's credentials, he held out his name tag for Riley's inspection. "James Andretti," he said aloud. "I've been working here for ten years. Ask anyone."

"He treated me in the E.R." Hannah touched Riley's arm. He retreated, though he didn't look happy about it.

"I'd like to check on my patient," Dr. Andretti repeated, giving Riley a pointed look. "Can you clear the room?"

"It's a crime scene," Riley said.

"It's also a hospital room."

Sheriff Tanner stepped in. "The techs have processed the areas around the bed. We'll step out a few minutes and let the doctor do his business. When he's done, I'll be back in to talk to you, Ms. Cooper."

Hannah gave a nod, darting a look at Riley. She found his gaze on her, his expression impossible to read. But when the other police personnel left her room, he followed, leaving her alone with the doctor.

Dr. Andretti pulled out his stethoscope and bent to listen to Hannah's heart through her hospital gown. "Heart rate's a little elevated, but I guess that's to be expected. How's your head feeling?"

"Better, actually," Hannah admitted. The headache that had plagued her earlier in the evening had faded to nothing.

He had her follow his fingers as he moved them in front of her face. "No double vision, no more memory lapses?"

"Nope."

"Good. Looks like we'll spring you in the morning. But I think we should move you to another room so you can get some rest."

"Do I really need to be here at all?" she asked.

"That's how we usually handle a concussion."

"But I'm not symptomatic anymore, right? You only kept me for observation and you just said I'm doing fine."

The doctor shot her a questioning look.

"Somebody's already gotten to me here tonight. I'm not that comfortable hanging around to let them have another shot."

"I can have a security guard posted at your door."

"You don't know one of your guards isn't behind this. Or even another doctor or nurse," she pointed out.

Dr. Andretti bristled visibly. "That's not likely."

Hannah sighed. "Maybe not. I just want to get out of here. I don't have to have your permission to check out, do I?"

"No—"

"Then arrange it. Please."

"What are you going to do when you leave? It's four in the morning. No motels worth staying in are going to let you check in at this hour. Assuming you can even find a room available."

"I just want out of here." A tingle of panic was beginning to build in the center of her chest. The thought of staying in this room until the next day was unbearable.

"Why don't I go get the nice police officers to tell you why leaving right now would be a very big mistake?" Dr. Andretti suggested, making a final note in her chart and tucking it under his arm. "You stay put."

He left her alone in the hospital room, which now looked like a war zone, thanks to the handiwork of the evidence technicians. She tucked her knees up to her chin and closed her eyes, feeling as tired as she could ever remember. But she couldn't afford to fall asleep.

Not in this place, surrounded by people she didn't know and couldn't trust.

"SIX MURDERS DON'T SEEM like much over three years," Jim Tanner said, passing Riley a cup of lukewarm coffee from the half-empty carafe on the break-room hot-plate. "I thought serial murderers tend to escalate, but this guy's pretty steady at two a year."

"Well, Hannah would have been three this year." Riley grimaced at the taste of the stale coffee.

"So he's escalating...slowly?" Tanner looked skeptical.

"There may be others. These are the ones I've been able to glean from relatively public sources."

"You'd think the feds would be all over this."

"Some of the links are nebulous," Joe said, refusing Tanner's offer of coffee. "We've only linked three of the murders to pepper-spray attacks. Two years ago there were two instances, and one last year. And what happened to Hannah."

"All six of the murder victims were wrapped in plastic sheeting and dumped in bodies of water," Riley pointed out. "All six were killed by ligature strangulation."

"That's not an unusual mode of murder. Same ligature used each time?"

"No," Riley admitted. "I think he uses weapons of opportunity."

"Victims of opportunity, weapons of opportunity—" Tanner shook his head. "Yeah, I could see the FBI needing more."

Riley glanced at Joe. Did his old friend secretly agree with Jim Tanner and the FBI about the scarcity of connections between the cases? Was he simply humoring Riley out of loyalty?

Tanner put his cup down on the Formica counter. "You know what? You clearly believe the cases are linked, and I'm not one to blow off a fellow cop who's having a hunch. I'll put one of my guys on the cold cases in our jurisdiction, see if any of them match any of your criteria. Maybe it'll help flesh out the body of evidence. You never know."

Riley gave the Teton County chief a grateful half smile. "I appreciate it."

"Sheriff Tanner?"

Riley turned and saw Hannah's doctor approaching, a frown creasing his forehead.

"Can I help you?" Tanner asked.

"Ms. Cooper is asking to leave the hospital early. Now, in fact. She feels uncomfortable remaining here."

Riley's stomach tightened. "Did you leave her alone?"

"I posted a guard outside, but—"

Riley didn't wait for the rest of his sentence, pushing past Joe and heading back to Hannah's room. He didn't see a guard outside her door, or any other door lining the corridor.

His heart rate climbing, Riley pushed open the door to Hannah's room and almost bumped into the guard standing just inside. He was a slim man in his early twenties, with crow-black hair and sun-bronzed skin. He was laughing as he turned to look at Riley.

Riley pushed past him, putting himself firmly between the guard and Hannah. "Are you okay?" he asked her, keeping his eyes on the guard, whose brow furrowed at Riley's question.

"I'm fine. Charlie was just introducing himself, since he was going to be my babysitter." Humor and annoyance tinted Hannah's whiskey drawl. "I was just telling him I'm thinking of digging a tunnel out."

Riley arched an eyebrow at the guard. "Shouldn't you be frisking me or something? Checking my ID?"

Charlie looked suitably crestfallen.

"He's messing with you," Hannah said. "Riley, leave him alone."

"Go stand guard outside and don't let anyone in without checking ID," Riley told the younger man, his tone firm. Charlie quickly obeyed.

Riley turned to look at Hannah, who still sat in the chair by the window. Her knees were tucked up against her chest, her chin resting atop them as she gazed at him with sleepy green eyes. He felt a funny twisting sensation in his gut. "You look wiped out."

"Always with the compliments," she said around a yawn.

"Your doctor says you want out of here."

"Ya think?"

He managed a smile at the crack. "There won't be any flights out before 8:00 a.m. What do you plan to do, camp out in the airport where you don't know a soul?"

"I'm camped out in a hospital where I don't know a soul. At least at the airport I wouldn't be wearing a cotton smock with an open back."

There was a quiet knock on the hospital-room door, and a moment later, Joe Garrison and Jim Tanner entered, followed by one of the Teton County evidence technicians holding a notebook computer.

"Trammell here has a copy of the only security-camera footage available," Tanner said, motioning for Trammell to set up the notebook computer on the over-bed table at the foot of the hospital bed. "I want you to watch and see if anyone looks familiar."

"I didn't get a good look at him either time."

"You can at least eliminate people by body type. It can't hurt."

Riley and Joe gathered around the computer as Trammell hit play. Riley felt a prickle of warmth down the left side of his body and turned to find Hannah sitting closer to him, like a kitten curling up next to a heat source. The mental image amused him.

He reached behind her to grab the blanket wadded near the foot of the bed and caught a glimpse of golden skin peeking out the back of her hospital gown.

She smiled her appreciation when he tucked the blanket around her, then turned back to the computer. "What are we looking at?" she asked Trammell.

"This is the front entrance." Trammell pointed to a pair of glass doors center frame. "We asked for everything from about an hour before you arrived to the time you called the nurse's station around 1:00 a.m." He pointed to another button. "Click that button and it'll fast-forward the images. Click that one and it'll pause the image."

It was easy to fast-forward the video; about half the visitors could be eliminated by their sex, others by age or build. Hannah stopped the video three times, but each time she shook her head. "I don't think so."

Riley frowned, something on the video catching his eye. "The hell?" He reached across and hit the pause button, then touched another to reverse the video.

"What is it?" Hannah asked.

"I'm not sure—" He saw the flicker again and hit pause.

"Oh," Hannah said, her voice tinted with surprise.

On the screen, the tip of one dark boot was visible

just past the edge of the mottled carpet in front of the lobby door.

"Well, hell." Tanner grimaced at the screen.

"Someone tampered with the recording." Riley looked at Joe, whose blue eyes had darkened.

"Son of a bitch," Jim Tanner growled.

"How did he manage that?" Hannah asked.

Riley laid his hand on her shoulder. She gave a little trembling jerk, turning her head to look up at him. He gave her shoulder a squeeze and felt her relax under his touch.

Tanner released a deep sigh and turned to look at them. "Inside job?"

Joe nodded. "Probably. It's where I'd start looking for sure."

"But why would someone who worked here want to hide his image? It's not like it would raise an alarm," Hannah said.

"Unless they tampered with the image to throw us off," Riley countered. As convoluted as that possibility sounded, he wouldn't put it past their target to be just that devious.

"I'll get a list of all the personnel, then. Security, medical staff, sanitation, the whole lot." Tanner clapped his technician on the shoulder. "Trammel, I want the original footage sent to the crime lab in Cheyenne. See if those fellows can get anything out of it."

Trammell nodded, grabbed his computer and left.

Tanner looked at Hannah. "I think you're right, Ms. Cooper. It's not a good idea for you to stay here tonight. I can set you up in protective custody here in Jackson—"

Hannah turned and looked at Riley. "You said I'm the only one who ever got away."

"That we know of," Riley agreed.

"I'm the only one who's seen him." Her voice softened even more. She moved away from them, toward the window, her arms wrapped around her as if she felt a sudden chill. The movement spread the back of her hospital gown even wider, baring more of the golden skin on her back and the sweet curve of her bottom beneath the cotton of her pale-blue panties.

Riley felt a flutter low in his belly and clamped his teeth together, surprised by his body's traitorous response. He cleared his throat and glanced at Joe and Jim Tanner. Both men were looking at him rather than Hannah's pretty backside, which made him feel like even more of a slug.

"Have you talked to her doctor?" Joe asked Tanner in a faint murmur. "What are the chances of her getting back more memories of the attack?"

"Nobody knows," Tanner admitted. "Head injuries are unpredictable. She might never remember anything more than she's told us."

"There might not be anything more to remember," Joe said grimly. "I hoped when we learned there was a living witness—"

"We know a lot more than we did," Riley pointed out, glancing at Hannah again. She'd turned and was watching them whisper among themselves, her eyes slightly narrowed.

"I'm still here in the room," she said aloud, making the other men look at her as well. "Since I'm pretty sure you're talking about me, why don't y'all tell me what's on your minds?"

Riley walked toward her slowly. "We were discussing what you do and don't remember about the attack."

"Not much," she admitted, her voice apologetic. "I'd hoped that I'd remember more once the symptoms of the concussion passed, but I come back to the same thing. I didn't get a good look at him when he pulled me over. I remember jeans and a silver belt buckle. He seemed fit—muscular, or at least that's the impression I got before he sprayed me in the face with pepper spray. It happened so fast."

Riley touched her shoulder again. "You told us he posed as a cop. That's something we didn't know before, and I think it could be important." If nothing else, it suggested the man might have some law-enforcement experience, or at least more understanding of police work than the average citizen.

"What if it's not enough?" Hannah asked. "What if I fly out of here tomorrow and nothing changes? What if he goes on killing people?"

Riley frowned, not following. "We keep looking for him anyway."

She looked up at him suddenly, her green eyes bright with an emotion he couldn't identify. "I'm the only living witness. If I leave—"

She didn't finish the sentence, but Riley finally understood what she was getting at. "If you leave, it could hamper the investigation," he admitted aloud.

Her head lowered, her back slumping as if it suddenly bore a terrible weight. Riley felt a rush of pity for her, for he had some idea of what she was feeling. It was a horrible thing, carrying the burden of six unsolved murders, knowing that it fell on you to bring them justice and closure.

"I can't leave Wyoming, can I?" she asked softly.

He didn't answer, knowing it was a question she had to answer herself.

Her tongue ran lightly over her lips and he saw her throat bob as she swallowed. When she looked up at him again, her gaze was solemn but direct. "I have five more days left of my vacation. I can't stay forever, but I can give you those five days. Maybe it'll be enough."

"We can put you in protective custody," Jim Tanner offered.

"She needs to go somewhere the killer doesn't expect her to be." Riley glanced at Joe.

"Somewhere small and off the beaten path?" Joe asked, his voice faintly dry.

Riley shrugged and turned back to Hannah. "Canyon Creek is about an hour and a half from here, in ranching country. I have a place there. Plenty of room. Great view."

Hannah's brow creased. "You want me to stay alone with you? I don't even know you."

"You don't have to know me. You just have to trust me."

The room fell silent as Hannah considered his words. The walls seemed to close in around them, every molecule, every atom focused on her words.

He wasn't sure what he wanted her answer to be, now that he'd made the offer. He'd lived alone for three years, his home both a refuge and a prison since Emily's death. He'd found a certain familiar comfort in his loneliness, Emily's absence so powerful it became a tangible thing he could hold on to when the nights were dark and long. He hadn't let anyone intrude on his solitude in a long time.

Hannah would change that. How could she not?

Hannah released a long, deep breath and looked up at them. "Okay."

Riley felt as if the ground was crumbling beneath his feet.

"Let's do it," she said, her chin high. "Let's go to Canyon Creek."

CHAPTER FOUR

"JOE SHOULDN'T HAVE dragged you out of bed to do this." Hannah took the blanket Jane Garrison handed her, feeling terrible about putting a stranger—a pregnant stranger—through so much trouble.

"I wasn't asleep. I'm not used to my husband being called to Jackson in the middle of the night." Jane's expression was a mixture of ruefulness and besottedness. Clearly, she was madly in love with Canyon Creek's Chief of Police.

"I guess it's usually quiet around here, huh?" Hannah had dozed a bit on the drive from Jackson, drained from the last eventful hours, but she'd awakened long enough to see that Riley Patterson's small ranch house was located smack dab in the middle of Nowhere, Wyoming. He had assured her there was a town a few miles to the east, with stoplights and everything, but they were clearly in ranch country, where the closest neighbors— the Garrisons, as it turned out—were six miles down a narrow one-lane road.

"Quiet?" Jane's lips quirked. "Mostly, yes. But we do have our moments, now and then." She crossed to the corner, where an old-fashioned woodstove sat silent and cold, and started to pick up pieces of firewood from a nearby bin.

"Let me do that." Hannah quickly intervened.

"You have a concussion," Jane protested.

"And you're pregnant," Hannah countered firmly.

Jane gave her an exasperated look. "It's not a disease."

Hannah laughed. Jane's lips curved and she finally gave into laughter as well.

"Joe treats me like I'm suddenly made of glass when he knows damned well I'm tough as old leather," Jane complained as she opened the door to the stove so Hannah could throw some wood inside. "I've lived through the Wyoming winter for two years now. Having a baby's nothing compared to that."

"I wouldn't say it's nothing." Hannah put the last piece of wood on the fire and stepped back. "How does this thing work? We're more into air-conditioning where I live."

Jane took over lighting the woodstove. "You're from Alabama?"

Hannah sat on the end of the bed, watching Jane's deft hands strike a match to the kindling she'd piled atop the stack of wood inside the iron stove's belly. "Yeah. It's a little town called Gossamer Ridge, up in northeast Alabama. It's pretty small. My family owns a few hundred acres on Gossamer Lake. We run a marina and fishing camp there. Most of my brothers and I work there in some capacity."

"You have a lot of brothers?" Jane stepped back from the stove, holding her hands out to warm them from the radiant heat.

"Six. I'm the youngest and the only girl."

"Wow. Six brothers." Jane settled carefully in a rocker next to the bed, rubbing her hand over her round belly. "I'm an only child. Joe had a brother, but he died."

For a second, Jane's expression grew bleak, her eyes dark with pain. She took a deep breath and seemed to physically shake off the sadness. "Riley's an only child, too. It can be lonely."

"He seems lonely." Hannah kicked herself mentally the second the words spilled from her lips. The last thing she should be doing was psychoanalyzing the man who'd made himself her guardian angel. She should just accept his offer of protection for what it was and try not to get any more involved.

She'd already made the mistake of falling for a guy who was hung up on another woman and lived to regret it. She had no intention of making the same mistake again.

But Jane wasn't ready to drop the subject, apparently. "He's a complicated guy."

"I know about his wife's death." And understood his thirst for justice better than he might have imagined. Her own brother, J.D., whose wife had been murdered several years ago, was still waiting for justice as well.

She wondered if either man would get what they wanted.

Jane gave her a sidelong look. "I didn't know Emily. She had died about a year before I met Joe. He tells me Riley used to be very different. Clowning around, always the one to crack a joke—" She stopped herself. "Like I said, complicated."

Hannah resisted the temptation to push for more information. She was here for only a few more days, and her focus needed to be on remembering the lost details of her ordeal with the fake cop, not on Riley Patterson's tragic past.

She quickly changed the subject. "Is this your first child?"

"Yeah." Jane rubbed her belly. "Joe keeps talking about lots of kids. I told him he can carry the rest of them."

Hannah grinned, deciding she liked Jane Garrison. She wasn't what you'd call pretty, exactly, with her freckle-spotted face and unruly brown curls, but her emerald eyes were full of life and laughter, and when she smiled, Hannah couldn't help smiling back.

"I missed my mother's pregnancies, being the youngest. But my brothers tell me stories that would curl your hair."

Jane chuckled. "Scooter here has been pretty good for most of the pregnancy, but now that I'm nearing the goal line, he's started kicking up a storm—"

"And you love it."

Riley's deep voice from the doorway drew Hannah's gaze. She felt suddenly, intensely aware of him as he entered the room, his boots thumping against the hardwood floor with each step. He'd shed the leather jacket and dress shirt for a dark-blue T-shirt. A sizzle of pure attraction shot through Hannah's body, settling low in her belly. It simmered there, spreading warmth through her veins.

She tamped it down ruthlessly. The last time she'd let her heart and hormones lead her head, she'd ended up heartbroken and humiliated.

"Joe's on the phone with Jim Tanner," Riley told Jane, holding out his hand to her. "He said to round you up and head you in the direction of the front door. You're supposed to be resting like a good mama-to-be."

Jane rolled her eyes. "See what I have to put up

with?" But she let Riley help her from the rocking chair, and the look of affection she gave him when he ruffled her curls made Hannah smile. Jane waggled her fingers at Hannah. "Call if you need anything. Riley has our number."

"I will," Hannah agreed, though she didn't plan on imposing on the Garrisons or Riley if she could avoid it.

While Riley walked to the front of the house with Jane, Hannah pulled her suitcase onto the bed and started unpacking. The closet across from the bed was empty, save for a couple of extra blankets piled atop a high shelf. Hannah filled several of the bare clothes hangers with her sparse collection of blouses and sweaters. Jeans, T-shirts and underwear went into the small chest of drawers by the door.

Her toiletries she kept in the bag she'd packed them in, since she'd be sharing the house's only bathroom with Riley. She couldn't quite bring herself to store her deodorant next to his on the sink counter.

Riley tapped on the open door, making her jump. "Do you have everything you need?"

She looked up to find him leaning against the door frame, his arms folded over his chest. His direct gaze made the skin on the back of her neck prickle, but she refused to look away. If they were going to be sharing this house for the next few days, she was going to have to control her rattled nerves. Now was as good a time to start as any.

"I'm taking the rest of the week off from work," he told her, pushing away from the door and walking farther into the room. His broad shoulders and muscle-corded frame seemed to crowd the room, leaving Hannah feeling small and vulnerable. She stood up, thinking it would put them on more equal footing, but rising only brought her closer to him. Up close, he seemed bigger than she'd thought, solid, hard and masculine. He smelled good, a tangy combination of pine needles and sweet hay. He'd gone with Joe to check on the horses in the stable, she remembered, while Jane helped her settle in.

Taking a step backwards, she forced her thoughts back to what he'd just said. "Don't take time off on my account."

His lips quirked. "I have to. Since I'm supposed to be protecting you."

"I should be safe enough here by myself. The guy who attacked me doesn't know where to find you, does he?"

"I wouldn't think so. But I don't think we should take chances. I'm not really going to be off. This is police business." To her relief, he backed away, settling in the rocker where Jane had sat earlier, his long legs stretched in front of him. "Joe's going to tell everyone he forced me to take vacation. They'll believe it. I haven't been off in a couple of years."

She arched her eyebrows. "Workaholic?"

His expression closed. "I just like to work."

She knew a warning flag when she saw one. She shifted the subject. "The doctor told me before I left that I could get back some of the memory that's hazy right now. About the day of the attack, I mean. Maybe I'll remember more about what the man was wearing— the belt buckle, what kind of shirt he had on."

"It's possible," he conceded. "Meanwhile, Jim Tanner is looking into the backgrounds of the hospital personnel."

"I don't know that just anyone would know how to tamper with a security camera." Hannah sat down cross-legged on the end of the bed, tucking her feet under the blanket Jane had given her. A cold wind had picked up during the night, blasting the valley with a bitter autumn chill that the little woodstove couldn't quite combat.

"There are a few ways it could have been done. The tech guys in Cheyenne will be able to tell us more." Riley shifted in his chair and pulled a cell phone from his pocket. "I want you using this to make all your calls. It's my personal cell phone. I can use my work phone. I don't want you to use your own phone while you're here in Wyoming."

She frowned. "Why not?"

"We don't know how much this guy knows about you now. If he's a hospital employee, he could have accessed your hospital records, which would give him a hell of a lot of personal information at his fingertips. If he has your cell phone number, he could possibly have a way to trace its use."

Hannah's stomach gave a little flip as she took the phone from him. "Are you trying to scare me or something? Believe me, it's not necessary."

"I just want you to be on guard every moment. Think about the things you do and say, who you talk to. I assume you'll want to call your family to let them know where you are?"

Hannah rubbed her head. She hadn't even thought about what she was going to tell her parents about what she'd decided to do. "I don't know what to tell them."

"It's up to you. Tell them as much or as little as you think they need to know."

"If I tell them too much, there'll be eight Coopers on the next flight to Wyoming."

"Tell them you met a nice doctor at the hospital and he's taking you skiing in Jackson Hole." Riley's lips quirked. "A nice rich doctor. Don't mothers love to hear stuff like that?"

"My mother can sniff out a lie faster than a bloodhound on a 'possum."

He grinned at that. "So tell her you met a nice cop who took you home and has you locked in his spare bedroom."

She rolled her eyes. "That's *so* much better."

His soft laugh caught her by surprise. It was a great laugh, musical and fluid, though it sounded a bit rusty, as if he hadn't used it in a while.

Maybe he hadn't.

"Just tell her the truth," he suggested, his laughter dying. "But don't make it sound too scary. I'm pretty sure the guy who attacked you hasn't yet connected you to me, so that should keep you safe while we see if we can put together all the pieces to our puzzle."

Hannah glanced at the clock sitting on the bedside table. It read 5:30 a.m. "Is that clock right?"

Riley checked his watch. "Yes."

It was an hour later in Alabama. Her parents would be up by now. She flipped open the cell phone he'd handed her and dialed her parents' number.

Her mother answered, sounding sleepy. "Hello?"

"Hey, Mom, it's me."

"What's wrong?"

Hannah smiled at her mother's immediate leap to the worst possible conclusion. "Everything's okay. I just wanted to let you know what's happening."

She caught her mother up to date on all that had happened, pausing now and then to allow her mother to catch her father up on all that she was saying. Feeling Riley's gaze on her, she looked up to find him studying her with slightly narrowed eyes. His hands rested on the arms of the rocker, his fingers drumming softly on the polished wood, but it seemed more a nervous twitch than a sign of impatience.

"You need to be on the next plane instead of holed up under police protection," her mother said firmly.

"I have almost a week left of my vacation, Mom. If I stick around, maybe something will trigger my memory—"

"You can trigger your memory in the safety of your own home," Beth Cooper insisted. "Mike, talk to your daughter."

"Mom—don't...Hi, Dad."

"You mother wants me to tell you to come home." Her father's gruff voice held a hint of weary amusement. "Of course, I know damned well you're going to do whatever you want, just like you have since you were six years old. Can you just promise you'll be careful?"

"I promise I'll be careful."

"Good. Now, can I talk to the policeman? Is he there with you now?"

Hannah's eyes widened with alarm. "Come on, Daddy, you don't need to talk to him—"

Across from her, one of Riley's eyebrows ticked upward. "Your father wants to talk to me?"

"Is that him?" Mike Cooper asked. "Hand him the phone."

With a deep sigh, Hannah held the phone out to

Riley. "I'm sorry," she whispered, "but trust me, it's easier just to talk to him and get it over with."

Riley's lips twitched as he took the phone from her. "Hello, Mr. Cooper."

Hannah could hear the low rumble of her father's voice coming from the cell phone receiver, but she couldn't make out any words. There was no telling what he was telling Riley. She'd been present for enough pre-date lectures to know there was no way to predict what her father might say if he thought her welfare was at stake.

"Yes, sir, I absolutely will," Riley said a few minutes later. His eyes flickered up to meet hers. "Yes, I'm beginning to realize that."

"What did he just say about me?" she whispered, mortified.

"No, sir. I won't." Riley's smile spread slowly. "Oh, absolutely. You can count on me."

"Won't what? Count on you for what?" Hannah reached out for the phone. "Give that to me."

"Here she is again, sir." Riley handed over the phone, grinning. "Didn't get many second dates?" he whispered.

"No," she whispered back, before putting the phone to her ear. "Dad, I hope you didn't embarrass me."

"I just made sure your cowboy cop knows that we expect you back in Alabama by the end of the week alive and in one piece."

"I can do that by myself. Give Mom a kiss for me and I'll call back tomorrow." To her horror, she felt tears burning the back of her eyes. "I need to get some sleep. Bye!"

She wiped at the tears with the back of her hand, but

they just kept coming. She turned her face away from Riley, hating that one stupid little call home had made her turn into a blubbering baby.

She heard his boot steps moving out of the room and down the hall, no doubt to give her a little space to have a good cry without an audience. But a few seconds later, she heard him return. The bed shifted as he sat down next to her.

"Here." He thrust a small white handkerchief into her hand. "It's clean."

She laughed and used it to wipe her eyes. "Thank you. I'm sorry to act like such a baby."

"It's okay," he assured her. "Listen, it's been a long night, and I bet we both could use a little sleep. I'm going to make sure we're locked up tight and then I'll get a little shut-eye myself."

She twisted the handkerchief between her fingers. "I bet you don't usually lock up, do you?"

He looked at her. "No. Not usually."

"I don't lock up at home much, either. I guess that's craziness in a world like this, huh?" She tried to smile, but inside, she felt as if something small and innocent had died.

The bleak understanding she saw in his eyes was cold comfort. "I guess it is." He gave a brief nod and left the bedroom, closing the door behind him.

RILEY SLOWLY CIRCLED the ranch house, checking doors and windows to make sure they were secure. The place was all that was left of his family ranch—the house, the stable and enough acres of land for the horses to graze and roam. His parents had wearied of the bitter Wyoming winters and the struggle to make a cattle ranch thrive when family ranches were a dying breed. So they'd retired to Arizona.

They'd offered to let him keep more of the land, to turn the place into a guest ranch, like so many places in the state had become, but he liked his work as a cop, and Emily was dedicated to her nursing job. Plus, they'd been talking about starting a family. They couldn't have given any time to running a dude ranch.

So much had changed since then. His whole life, really.

He wandered into his bedroom and sat on the edge of the old four-poster bed Emily had found at a flea market in Thermopolis. It was solid oak, battered by time and use, but she'd loved it. He was a man, and it was a bed, so he'd loved it, too.

He'd loved her in it.

He released a weary breath and pulled his boots off, letting them drop to the floor with two heavy thuds. Stripping off his T-shirt, he lay back on the bed and closed his eyes, trying to will himself to sleep.

For the moment, Hannah Cooper was safe with him. Only a handful of people knew where she was going when she left the hospital—Joe, Sheriff Tanner and him. Tanner had agreed not to tell anyone else on the Teton County force.

But secrets had a way of getting out, no matter how carefully you tried keeping them, he knew. About a year earlier, he'd seen how easily a bad man with determination and the right connections could find the person he was looking for. Joe and Jane had nearly died as a result.

He didn't want Hannah Cooper to die because he was sleep deprived and off his game. He was so close to finding the bastard who'd killed Emily and destroyed his life.

He couldn't make any mistakes.

He pushed himself up from the bed and grabbed a fresh change of clothes from the bureau by the bed. Maybe a shower would help him relax. He started out into the hall, then backtracked to grab the Ruger pistol in its holster by his bed.

He paused in the bathroom doorway, listening for sounds from the guest room. Everything was quiet.

Too quiet?

He shook off the paranoid thought and entered the bathroom. He turned on the shower to let the water warm while he undressed, then stepped into the hot spray. The drumbeat of water felt good on his tense muscles.

Unbidden, an image popped into his mind. Hannah Cooper's bare back, smooth and golden-brown, peeking through the ribbons of her hospital gown. The thin cotton had done little to hide her curvy hips or the soft swell of her breasts.

He closed his eyes and pressed his head against the shower tiles, reaching down to turn the cold tap.

HANNAH HEARD THE SHOWER cut on and wished she'd thought of it first. She'd managed a sponge bath in the hospital, but a nice hot shower seemed like sheer bliss at the moment.

And maybe it would help her fall asleep, because lying here staring at the ceiling wasn't getting it done.

She sat up, lifting her hand to her brow as the room spun a little. Her equilibrium settled and she padded barefoot out of the bedroom to the kitchen just down the hall. She found a tumbler in the cabinet next to the sink and filled it with water from the tap. Leaning against the counter, she drained it quickly and turned back to the sink for a refill.

Behind her, she heard the rattle of a door lock. Her whole body jerked with reaction. The glass slipped from her nerveless fingers and shattered in the sink.

The door opened behind her with a creak. Cool morning air drifted inside, scattering chill bumps along her bare legs. Down the hall, the shower cut off.

Reaching into the sink, Hannah grabbed the bottom of the broken tumbler and whirled around to face the intruder, holding the jagged glass in front of her.

A tall, slim man with raven-black hair and dark eyes stared back at her, his mouth open with what looked like genuine surprise. "Who the hell are you?"

"Don't take another step!" Hannah said firmly as he started toward her.

He held up his hands and froze in place.

Down the hall, the bathroom door opened, slamming back against the wall. Riley burst into the kitchen, wearing nothing but a dark-blue towel and carrying a Ruger. He swept Hannah behind him and turned to face the intruder.

"Geez, cowboy, dial it down a notch," the dark-haired man drawled.

Riley's shoulders slumped, and he dropped the Ruger to his side. "Jack."

"Jack?" Hannah asked.

"Jack." The dark-haired man peeked over Riley's shoulder and waggled his fingers at her.

Riley laid the gun on the counter and stepped aside.

He waved at Jack. "Hannah, this is Jack, my brother-in-law."

Jane had told her that Riley was an only child, so Jack must be…

"Emily's brother," Jack added, slanting a look at Riley.

Riley's lips pressed to a thin line. "I thought you were in Texas these days."

"Yeah, well, Texas had about all of Jack Drummond it could handle." Jack smiled wickedly at Hannah, flashing a pair of dimples Hannah was sure had broken more than one heart in Texas. Then he looked at Riley, his smile fading. When he next spoke, there was a dark undercurrent in his voice. "So, Riley—you've moved on, I see."

Riley looked at Hannah, his eyes dark with pain. "Had to happen some time. This is Hannah Cooper. My new girlfriend."

Hannah dropped the broken glass she'd been holding.

CHAPTER FIVE

"DON'T MOVE," RILEY said quickly, putting out a warning hand toward her. "You're barefooted."

She met his urgent gaze, trying to regain her mental balance. Had he really just stormed in here, wearing nothing but a blue towel, and told his brother-in-law
that she was his new girlfriend?

What the hell was he thinking?

A droplet of water slid down the side of his neck and
pooled briefly in the hollow of his throat before trickling over the muscles of his chest. Hannah licked her
lips and dragged her gaze away to meet Jack Drummond's dark scrutiny.

Now that her initial panic had subsided, she saw that
Riley's brother-in-law was only a little older than she,
no more than thirty. His sun-bronzed skin was smile-
lined, as if he laughed a lot, although at the moment, the
pained look in his eyes made her stomach hurt.

"I guess I shouldn't have just sprung the news on you
like that, Jack. I wanted to be a little more sure where
things were heading—" He shot Hannah a look full of
pleading, as if begging her to play along with his story.

She cleared her throat. "I told him he should call
you and give you a heads-up." Her tone was more tart
than she'd intended. "Small-town gossip. Things get

around fast. But you know how he likes to do things his own way."

Jack crossed slowly to the kitchen table, his boots crunching over the shards from the glass she'd dropped. He sank into the nearest chair. "How long has it been going on?"

Hannah shot Riley another look. How was she supposed to answer that? They didn't have their stories straight yet.

"Let me get a broom and sweep this up." Riley disappeared down the hall, returning with a broom. He swept up the glass around her feet, clearing a path to the door. "Go get dressed and get some shoes on. I'll let Jack in on what's going on." He moved so close that she could feel the steamy heat of his damp skin. He smelled good, like fresh air and a hint of pine. Her hands curled into fists.

She tamped down the urge to bury her nose in his neck to breathe in more of that heady scent. "And then you'll let me in on it?" she added under her breath, soft enough that Jack couldn't hear.

He answered with an apologetic look and a quick gesture toward the guest bedroom.

She scurried down the hall to get dressed, keeping an ear cocked to follow the conversation going on in the kitchen as she pulled on a pair of jeans and a warm sweater.

There was a soft tinkle of glass—Riley sweeping up the glass she'd broken. "Out of minutes on your cell phone?" he asked drily.

"You and Emily never used to care if I called ahead." There was a petulant tone in Jack's voice that Hannah had not expected. She dropped her estimate of his age by a couple of years. "'Drop by anytime, Jack. We love to see you, Jack.'"

"You were her only family."

"And now you're my only family," Jack shot back. "At least, I thought you were."

Hannah paused in the middle of tying her shoe, the pang of sorrow in Jack Drummond's voice catching her by surprise. He sounded so sad. It made her appreciate her big, rowdy family even more.

She heard Riley dumping the broken glass into a trash bin. "Don't be a baby, Jack."

Hannah winced.

"What's with the bandage on your girlfriend's face?" Jack asked after a few seconds of silence. Hannah finished tying her shoe and padded down the hall to the kitchen.

"Car accident," Riley answered. "She knocked her head a bit, but she's going to be fine."

"I thought she was gonna cut me." Jack's voice was tinted with a smile. "I bet she'd be tough in a bar fight."

"I don't get into bar fights," Hannah said from the doorway.

Riley turned to look at her. She gazed back, not hiding her irritation. He shouldn't have sprung this crazy girlfriend cover story on her without warning her. And he shouldn't have been so harsh with his brother-in-law, who was clearly hurting from the loss of his sister just as much as Riley was hurting from the loss of his wife.

She looked away from Riley and smiled at Jack. "Have you had breakfast? I could probably make an omelet or something."

"I grabbed something at the diner in town," Jack answered, returning the smile. "Riley told me about your accident. I hope you're feeling better."

"We were up most of the night at the hospital," Riley answered quickly. "The doctors said she had a mild concussion, but they cut her loose this morning."

"Wow, I bet you're beat, then. Look, I can go find a place in town or something—"

"I started a fire in the woodstove," Hannah said quickly, darting a glance at Riley. He started this mess, so now he'd have to live with it. "The bed's made. I put a few of my things in there because Riley's closet is full, but there's plenty of space for you to put your things."

The look of alarm in Riley's eyes made her smile. *How's that surprise thing working for you now, big guy?*

"Are you sure?" Jack directed the question more toward Riley than Hannah.

He hesitated only a moment, genuine affection in his eyes. "Of course I'm sure," he said. "You're family."

Jack's grin made Hannah's stomach twist into a knot. The poor guy looked like a grateful puppy, happy he didn't get kicked out of the house once the new kid came along. "Can I do something around here?" he asked Riley, pushing to his feet. "I bet you two were too tired to check on the horses this morning—want me to go let 'em out into the pasture?"

"Would you? That would be great." Riley latched on to the idea quickly, no doubt wanting to get Jack out of the way so he and Hannah could finally get their stories straight.

"I'll be back in a bit." Jack winked in Hannah's direction, grabbed his hat from where he'd laid it on the counter by the door, and headed out the back, the screen door slamming behind him.

The ensuing silence made Hannah's skin prickle. Riley turned slowly to look at her. "Go on, say it."

"Your girlfriend?"

"What else was I supposed to say? He walks in on you in your robe, me in a towel—"

Her gaze fell on the towel, which had slipped down his body a notch to reveal the hard, flat plane of his lower belly. She swallowed hard and forced her gaze back up to his face.

"We can't tell people why you're really here," he said.

She sighed. "How long do you think he'll be here?"

"I don't know. This is the first time he's been here since Emily died." He started to sit, until he apparently realized that he was wearing only a towel. He nodded toward the hallway, as if asking her to follow.

After a quick detour to the guest room to grab a few things she'd need, they went down the hall to Riley's bedroom. She waited outside, standing with her back against the wall while he entered his bedroom to dress. "I guess we should get our stories straight. But I should warn you, I'm not a good liar."

"So we keep it simple and as close to the truth as possible. Why did you come to Wyoming in the first place?" His voice was a bit muffled.

Trying hard not to picture a T-shirt sliding over his lean, muscular chest, she swallowed the lump in her throat. "Some friends invited me up to fish on their private lake, and then I planned to do the tourist thing at Grand Teton and Yellowstone."

Her friends, David and Julie Sexton, had a small ranch with a very good trout lake nestled in a valley in the Wind River Mountains. She'd spent the first four days of her vacation with them and their two school-age daughters.

If only she'd stayed there instead of deciding to do the typical tourist thing and visit the national parks—

"So we stick with that. You came here to go fishing, and we met by accident—"

She heard the sound of a zipper. Squeezing her eyes shut, she sighed. "And immediately started shacking up? I'm not that kind of girl."

"Hey, you're the one who gave Jack your room."

She glared at the opposite wall. "You started it with the girlfriend thing."

"Enough. Clearly, since you're not that kind of girl and I'm not really that kind of guy, we met months ago." He emerged from the bedroom dressed in jeans and a fresh T-shirt. "Maybe we met online."

If she'd thought a fully dressed Riley Patterson would be less distracting than a naked one, she'd been gravely mistaken. The T-shirt only emphasized the broadness of his shoulders and the powerful muscles of his chest, and the well-worn jeans fit him like a second skin.

Stop looking, Hannah. Looking leads to touching and touching leads to getting your heart shattered in a million pieces the day before your wedding—

She cleared her throat. "Where online?"

"I don't know. I don't go online much." Frustration lining his lean features, he headed toward the kitchen.

She followed. "Do you fish?" she asked.

He turned to look at her, leaning against the sink counter. "What is with the fishing thing?"

"My family runs a marina and fishing camp. I'm a fishing guide, among other things." She shot him a wry smile. "You're looking at the Crappie Queen of Gossamer Lake."

His lips quirked. "Okay, we met on a fishing Web site."

"Which one?"

He reached for the coffeemaker. "You tell me. You're the Crappie Queen."

Over coffee, they quickly outlined their cover story. They'd met online on Freshwater Expeditions, a fishing forum that put avid freshwater fishermen together with fishing guides all over the country. Hitting it off immediately, they'd formed a friendship that became something more, and Hannah had combined her planned fishing trip to Wyoming with the chance to finally meet Riley face-to-face.

"One thing led to another, and..."

"And now we're sleeping together." Hannah's forehead wrinkled as she finally realized the full implications of offering the guest room to Jack. She pushed away her unfinished cup of coffee and rubbed her tired eyes. "Mama's right. My temper always gets me in trouble."

"I've got a sleeping roll I can put on the floor."

She shook her head. "It's your bed. I'll take the roll."

"I've slept outdoors on the hard, cold ground before, plenty of times. Snugged up next to the woodstove will be a luxury." He carried their cups to the sink. "So we're set? Is our cover story close enough to the truth for you to handle?"

"I think so. But we should make a pact—we share whatever we tell Jack separately. There's a lot of room to mess up."

The rattle of the back door cut off any response he might have made. He grabbed his gun from the counter.

Jack entered the kitchen, his dark hair windblown and his cheeks bright with exercise. Riley relaxed, tucking the gun in the waistband of his jeans.

Jack's earlier glum mood was gone, replaced by a mischievous light in his dark eyes. "I took Jazz out for a run. He cut loose—you haven't been riding him much recently?"

"Not as much as I should," Riley admitted.

Hannah almost asked how many horses he had, then wondered if that was something they'd have discussed online. She slanted a quick look at Riley and found him looking a bit unnerved.

"Do you ride?" Jack asked Hannah.

"Yeah, though not as much as I'd like. In fact, we've been thinking of buying some horses and offering trail rides in the spring and fall up Gossamer Mountain."

"Gossamer Mountain?"

"It's in Alabama," Riley interjected. "Hannah's family has a fishing camp up there. That's how we met."

"You met at a fishing camp in Alabama?" Jack looked at Riley with a confused expression. "When did you go to Alabama?"

"No, we met online. On a fishing forum," Riley said.

"You go online?" Jack's eyes widened further.

"Not a lot," Riley said defensively, as if his brother-in-law had accused him of being a nerd.

Hannah stifled a grin. "It's a forum called Freshwater Expeditions." She checked out the forum from time to time herself to keep up with what avid anglers were talking about. It was good for business. "We hit it off right away."

"And when Hannah made plans to visit some friends here in Wyoming, we decided to finally meet in person."

"And here we are." Hannah hoped her smile didn't look as brittle as it felt. Playacting wasn't one of her talents. It was nerve-racking, wondering if Jack Drummond was buying the load of bull she and Riley were selling.

Not to mention the way her rattled brain kept returning to the realization that she and Riley Patterson would be sharing a bedroom come nightfall.

"SHE SEEMS NICE."

Riley looked up from the case folder he was reading to find his brother-in-law's dark-eyed gaze on him. He set the folder on the coffee table. "I know this has been a kick in the teeth for you, Jack. I'm sorry we sprang it on you like that."

Jack pushed the rocking chair closer and propped his socked feet up on the coffee table. "Three years is a long time to be alone. I get that."

Pain settled over Riley, down to the bone. "I haven't stopped loving Em. I never will."

"But we both know she wouldn't want you to live the rest of your life alone," Jack said solemnly.

Lying to Jack about his fake relationship with Hannah was worse than Riley had anticipated. Each fib felt like a bitter betrayal of Emily and the love they'd shared. His skin prickled, as if the truth was trying to seep through his pores and shout itself to the world.

He wasn't over Emily! He hadn't moved on.

He never would.

"You look a little beat, Riley. You were up all night with Hannah at the hospital, weren't you?"

"Yeah," he answered, relieved to finally say something that was true. "It was an eventful night."

"Where'd she have her wreck?"

"Just outside of Whitmore—on the road toward Jackson."

"Isn't that way past here?"

Hell. "Yeah. She wanted to drive into Jackson to do some shopping." Women liked to shop, right? Emily always had.

"How'd the wreck happen?"

Riley tamped down his irritation. Jack's question wasn't unreasonable, and if he and Hannah weren't lying through their teeth, it wouldn't even matter. "Nobody's quite sure—Hannah doesn't remember much of what happened around the time of the wreck. The police think she might have been run off the road."

"Hit and run?"

"Something like that."

Jack cocked his head. "I'm surprised you're not out there hunting down the jerk who did it."

"There aren't any leads. And I'm more interested in taking care of Hannah." That was true, at least. His voice rang with conviction.

Jack smiled, although Riley still detected a hint of sadness in his eyes. "I like her, I think. I mean, what I've seen of her. She seems very down to earth. Emily would approve."

Pain sliced through Riley's chest at Jack's words. He took a couple of shallow breaths and looked away.

"I'm sorry if the way I acted this morning made you feel bad or anything." Jack leaned forward, laying his hand on Riley's arm. "You were a good husband to Emily. You deserve to be happy again."

Riley managed a smile, but inside, an ache had settled in the center of his chest. He pushed to his feet. "I'm going to check on Hannah. Make yourself at home."

Jack responded with a silent nod, his expression bemused.

Riley headed down the hallway to his bedroom, opening the door quietly. Hannah lay curled on her side beneath a plaid woolen blanket, her back to him. Walking softly so as not to wake her, he settled into the armchair by the window and watched her sleep. Early-afternoon light filtered through the curtains, bathing her face with shimmering rose color. She looked weary and battered, her face a roadmap of scrapes and bruises. But beneath the imperfections was beauty that even his shuttered soul couldn't miss.

He wondered if Jack was right. Would Emily have liked Hannah Cooper? If this charade were the truth instead of a necessary lie, would Emily approve?

He wasn't sure he wanted to know the answer.

THE AFTERNOON HAD WANED while she slept, cool blue shadows of twilight encroaching on the bedroom where she lay. She heard the sound of footfalls, boots on the hardwood floor. Riley, perhaps, coming to wake her for dinner.

She was warm and comfortable. She didn't want to move. Perhaps if she pretended she was still asleep—

As she started to close her eyes, something shimmered in the low light. She made out a curve of silver, complex shapes and shadows.

A silver belt buckle.

The breath left her lungs in a shaking hiss. She tried to stir, to escape the cottony cage of twilight slumber, but she was paralyzed. The bootfalls came closer, and she heard him breathing. Slow, steady and deadly.

Riley, she thought. *Where is Riley?*

She opened her mouth and tried to scream. Only a hoarse croak emerged. Her vision narrowed to the silver belt buckle moving inexorably closer.

A hand caught hers, tugging her up. She tried to fight, her movements sluggish and flailing.

"Hannah!" Riley's voice tore through the fabric of her nightmare, dragging her into consciousness with shocking speed. Her whole body buzzed with adrenaline, making her tremble.

Riley's hands cradled her face, his gaze intent. "Are you okay? You were crying out."

She dropped her head against his shoulder, pressing her nose into the curve of his neck. She breathed deeply, filling her lungs with his tangy scent. "I'm okay," she said, her voice muffled against the collar of his T-shirt.

He brushed her hair off her cheek. "Nightmare?"

She nodded, hoping he wouldn't pull away. It wouldn't hurt to cling a moment, would it? At least until the shivers eased.

He edged over, sliding onto the bed beside her. Tucking her against him, he waited patiently for her to relax. The silence between them was comfortable, she found to her surprise. She had not thought of him as someone who could provide much comfort, no matter how good his intentions.

"I'm okay," she repeated a little while later, afraid she'd tested his patience too long. She sat away from him, brushing her hair back from her damp face.

"Do you remember what you dreamed?"

She didn't really. Only the nagging sense that she'd seen something important lingered with her.

"You cried out as if you were afraid."

"I was," she admitted. "I just don't know why."

She couldn't tell if he was disappointed or not. He was good at hiding his feelings. He had turned on the lamp by the bed, casting a warm glow on the shadowy room. She must have slept most of the day, for outside the window the sky was dark and the room had grown uncomfortably chilly.

Riley crossed to the woodstove in the corner and added wood and kindling. The dying embers flickered to life.

When he turned back to her, the wary look in his eyes drove away the memory of their earlier ease. Though she couldn't read his thoughts in his shuttered expression, there was no softness there, only a tense watchfulness that made her skin prickle.

He sat beside her on the edge of the bed, his gaze searching hers, as if he wasn't sure she was telling the truth about not being able to remember. The silence between them became anything but comfortable, the air in the small bedroom crackling with electric awareness.

Looking away, she swallowed hard and tried to remember whatever it was that was hovering just on the outer edges of her memory. There had been fear. Darkness.

A glimmer of metal, curves and recesses...

"A snake," she said, her voice faint.

"A snake?"

She looked up and met his quizzical gaze. "The man who attacked me. I remembered what was on his silver belt buckle. It was a rattlesnake."

CHAPTER SIX

"She thinks it's in the shape of a rattlesnake, or some sort of snake." Riley spoke softly into his cell phone, intensely aware of his brother-in-law moving around in the guest bedroom just down the hall.

"That's not exactly a unique design," Joe warned.

"It's more than we had," Riley said. "Can we put someone on it, get some pictures for Hannah to choose from?"

"Needle in a haystack," Joe said tightly.

"More than we had," Riley repeated.

"I'll put Jane on it. She's been wanting to do something besides sit home waiting for the baby to come, and it's safer than the patrol job she's been trying to talk me into."

"Thanks."

"How's it going now that Jack's in town?"

"A little harder than I'd planned. But so far, so good."

Of course, he still had a long night alone with Hannah in his bedroom to look forward to.

Hearing the sound of footsteps coming down the hallway, he rang off with Joe and turned to find Hannah standing in the kitchen doorway, her dark hair tousled and her eyes soft with sleepiness. Though her gray sweats hid her tempting curves, she still fired his blood in a way no woman had since Emily's death.

What the hell was going on with him? Why her, why now? He couldn't have chosen a worse situation—or woman—to rediscover that he was still a living, breathing, healthy male.

She hovered in the doorway. "I could fix something for dinner," she suggested, her raspy voice sending a shiver of pleasure skating down his back. "I mean, I'm not a great cook or anything, but I'm pretty good with a can opener."

Her wry smile made her green eyes sparkle, and Riley had to look away.

"You're still recuperating." His voice came out gruff.

"I'm not sick." She sounded defensive in response.

He looked up, annoyed with himself and the way this whole situation was spiraling out of control. But before he had a chance to apologize, Jack walked up behind Hannah and put his hands on her shoulders.

She gave a start, but Jack calmed her quickly with a gentle squeeze. "How about I handle dinner?" he suggested, guiding her into the kitchen. "I've been dying to try out a chili recipe I got from a saucy little *señorita* I met down in Laredo." He winked at Hannah, grinning broadly.

Riley squelched an unwelcome rush of irritation at his brother-in-law's easy familiarity with Hannah. "I don't know if you'll be able to find chili fixings here. I haven't done a lot of grocery shopping recently."

"I drove to town while you two were resting." Jack arched an eyebrow at Riley, grinning when Riley scowled in response. He crossed to the cabinet and pulled out a large canvas bag full of his purchases. "You know, that little place on Canyon Road has a really good fresh-produce stand. I had to pay a pretty penny, but it'll be worth it." He turned to Hannah. "How are you with a chopping knife, gorgeous?"

Hannah smiled, clearly pleased to have something to do besides lie in bed. She took the knife Jack handed her and went to work chopping onions and peppers.

Riley watched her deft hands make short work of the vegetables. "You're good with a knife."

She looked up with a start, her knife slipping and nicking her knuckle. "Damn it!" She sucked her knuckle between her lips, her forehead wrinkling.

"I'm sorry—" He grabbed a couple of paper towels from the dispenser and ran them under the tap. Taking her hand, he dabbed at the blood to check how badly she'd cut herself.

"It's nothing," she said. But she didn't pull her hand away as he applied a little pressure to the shallow nick.

"I'll get a bandage." Jack set aside the beef tips he was seasoning and headed toward the bathroom.

"I told you I wasn't much of a cook," she said, her cheeks flushed and her lips curved with a rueful smile.

"I startled you." They stood so close he could smell the apple soap she'd used when she'd showered earlier. The scent reminded him of spring—fresh, crisp and full of promise.

Her green eyes darkened. "I guess I'm still jumpy."

His blood simmered, slow and hot in his veins. He'd forgotten the feel of fire licking low in his belly and pulsing hunger drumming in his chest.

"Here we go." Jack returned to the kitchen with the first-aid kit Riley kept in the bathroom. He eased Riley aside and pulled out a tube of antibiotic ointment.

As Jack bandaged Hannah's hand, Riley crossed to the back door and pushed aside the faded curtain, looking out into the deepening blue of nightfall. A chill wind rolled down the mountains, rattling the door. He was tempted to step outside, into the bitter breeze, and let it cool his burning thoughts.

How was he going to make it through a night alone with Hannah Cooper without losing his mind?

Once bandaged, Hannah finished her task of chopping vegetables. She and Jack worked together with enviable ease preparing the chili, while Riley kept a watchful distance. With Jack, Hannah laughed, she joked, she sparkled like a jewel set incongruously in the middle of his plain, utilitarian kitchen.

This was the real Hannah Cooper, Riley realized. The one unencumbered by fear. The woman she must have been when she arrived in Wyoming, before a killer had tried to make her his next victim. She didn't have to think about clues or harsh memories with Jack. She could just be Hannah, the woman from Alabama who'd come to Wyoming to go fishing and see Old Faithful and the Grand Teton mountains.

Jack was right, Riley realized with some pain. Emily would have loved Hannah.

Despite her long nap that afternoon, Hannah didn't make it through dinner without breaking into yawns.

"We're boring her already," Jack teased.

She gave a rueful laugh. "I promise I can stay awake long enough to help with the dishes."

"No, you don't." Riley broke his silence. "You go on and get to bed. Jack and I can handle a few dishes."

She gave him an odd look, then pushed herself out of her chair and offered them both a soft good-night.

After she'd gone down the hall, Jack looked at Riley. "You were quiet during dinner."

"I figured you and Hannah had conversation covered," he replied drily, immediately kicking himself for the irritation in his tone. He was acting like a jealous jerk.

Ironically, it worked in his favor. "I'm not moving in on your girl, Riley. I know I've got a reputation as a player, but you're family. I wouldn't do that to you."

Riley made himself laugh, although inside his guts were in a tangle. "I know."

"And you know, you guys don't have to be all proper and formal around me. It's not going to kill me to see you kiss the girl." Shooting Riley a pointed look, Jack got up and started putting away the leftover chili.

The image Jack's words evoked made Riley's mouth grow dry. What would it feel like to kiss her? To feel her soft curves settle against his body as if she'd been made exactly for him? The need to know was suddenly overwhelming.

He had to get out of the house. Now. Go take a ride, work off some of the restless energy tormenting him. But before he could act on the impulse, there was a knock at the back door.

Riley made sure his Ruger was tucked firmly in his waistband, ignoring Jack's curious look. He crossed to the back door and edged the faded curtains away from the inset window.

Joe and Jane Garrison stood outside, stamping from foot to foot against the cold night air.

Riley unlocked the door and let them inside, giving Joe a warning glance. He'd already told his friend about Jack's unexpected arrival and the charade he and Hannah had to keep up in front of his brother-in-law.

Joe and Jack knew each other from way back, but

Jane hadn't yet met his brother-in-law. Joe handled the introductions, and Jane immediately engaged Jack in conversation, giving Joe a chance to show Riley the file he'd brought over.

"Jane spent the last couple of hours online, tracking down all the snake-shaped belt buckles she could find. She printed them out and they're all in here. I thought you'd want to see them as soon as possible, while the dream is still fresh in Hannah's mind." Joe handed over the folder. "Also, I've asked Jim Tanner to fax me the personnel files of the hospital security staff as soon as he gets access to them. His people will run the background checks, but I figure it won't hurt to put both departments to work on it."

"Good idea," Riley agreed. "If you do get them, I'll bring Hannah to the office. Give her a chance to get out and take in a little fresh air." Maybe, with people around, he wouldn't find himself thinking about the softness of her skin or wondering what she tasted like.

Because if he didn't get control of his treacherous body soon, the next four days would be the longest of his life.

A WAXING MOON HUNG LOW in the eastern sky, spreading cool blue light across the mountain in the distance. Beyond, the night was alive with stars, millions of them, more visible than Hannah could ever remember. She had grown up in one of the more remote areas of Alabama, where there weren't enough city lights to obscure the stars in the night sky, but even at home, she had never seen quite so many stars as this.

She couldn't orient herself, an odd feeling. She knew the window of Riley's darkened bedroom faced east, or she couldn't have seen the moon from this vantage point. But what was east when you didn't know where you were in the first place?

She had always prided herself on being aware of her surroundings, of picking up on the nuances of her settings that most people never even noticed. She was as skilled a tracker as any of her brothers, as good a boatman, as successful a fisherman and she was the best night hiker in the family.

She didn't like feeling so up-ended. It reminded her too much of that moment, four years ago, when she watched her future shatter into a million pieces.

She leaned her forehead against the cool windowpane, feeling the vibration of the night wind rattling the glass. In a little while, Riley Patterson would walk through the bedroom door behind her and they'd close themselves into this small, intimate room for the night. The thought gave her a sense of safety, the knowledge that in this place, with Riley watching over her, nothing outside could hurt her.

But with that sense of safety came another, more complicated feeling of reckless anticipation. Riley would be there soon, so close she could hear him breathing, and she could hardly wait.

It was crazy. He was still clearly mourning a wife he'd never stop loving, and their acquaintance was supposed to be businesslike and short, spanning no more than the next few days. She'd been around other attractive men before without feeling like a schoolgirl trembling with a crush. Far more suitable and available men.

Or was that the appeal? Her brothers always teased her about her competitive streak. Did she think she had a fighting chance at winning his heart away from the other woman this time?

Go for it, Hannah. Maybe you've got a better shot against a dead woman.

Idiot.

She pushed her hair back from her face, wincing as her palm brushed against the scrape on her forehead. She had to get control over herself before she did something stupid.

A soft knock on the door behind her made her nerves twitch. The door swung open, spilling light from the hallway into the darkened bedroom. Hannah turned to look at Riley as he entered, her heart suddenly hammering against her breastbone.

He paused in the doorway a moment, a tall, lean silhouette against the light. She couldn't see his eyes in his shadowy face, but she felt his gaze like a touch. She felt suddenly naked, despite the warm flannel enveloping her from chin to ankle.

He reached for the light switch.

"Don't," she said. She wasn't ready to come into the harsh light of reality yet.

He hesitated a moment, then dropped his hand to his side and closed the door behind them, plunging the bedroom into darkness again.

Hannah turned back to the window, leaning her hot cheek against the cold glass pane. "You can see the mountain better without the light on."

Warmth washed over her as Riley edged close to the window, just behind her. Though he didn't touch her, she felt him as surely as if he had. "That's Sawyer's Rise."

"The mountain?"

"Yes." He moved the curtain aside, stepping up beside her. She looked up and found moonlight painting his masculine features a cool, shadowy-blue, emphasizing the hard, lean lines of his cheekbones and the deep cleft of his chin.

In this light, he looked as if he'd been carved from the face of the mountain, solid rock with a million unexpected facets. The itch to touch him tingled in her fingertips. Would he feel like stone, cool and rough to the touch?

After a moment of exquisite tension, he spoke again. "There's something I need to show you."

He moved away from the window. A moment later, the soft glow of lamplight filled the bedroom, obscuring the moonlit landscape outside behind the reflected light in the windowpane. Hannah caught a glimpse of herself in the reflection, her hair a tousled mess, her cheeks flushed beneath shadowy eyes.

She turned away quickly, running a hand through her hair to tame the riotous tumble. "What is it?"

He was carrying a thin manila folder, she saw. He sat on the bed and opened it, patting the mattress beside him.

She took a seat where he indicated and looked at what lay inside the folder. There were photos, obviously pulled from the Internet and printed on a color printer. Belt buckles, in a variety of snake shapes.

"Jane was a busy woman this evening," he murmured. "Do any of these look familiar?"

Hannah took the folder from him and started leafing through the printouts. None of the belt buckles jumped out at her. So much about the attack on her that day remained fuzzy, whether from the aftereffects of her concussion or the sheer trauma of the ambush. The more she tried to force herself to remember, the more confused the effort seemed to leave her. "I'm not sure," she said honestly.

"Can you eliminate any of them?"

She looked again. There were a couple of designs where the snake itself was the belt buckle. She was sure that hadn't been the case with her assailant. "Not these," she said, setting those pictures aside. "And not these two, either," she added, culling out a couple that were a dark, weathered pewter rather than a soft, shiny silver.

"That helps," he said, although she heard a faint strain of frustration in his voice.

She stood up and began laying the other printouts on the bed, placing them in a grid. When she was finished, she stepped back and closed her eyes, trying to clear her mind so she could go back to the day of the attack.

She'd been driving down the highway, hoping to make Jackson before nightfall. But she hadn't been speeding—she'd checked her speedometer when she saw the blue light behind her.

"I pulled over," she said aloud. "I reached for my purse and got my driver's license. I turned back to the window, and I saw only his midsection. He had jeans on, and he was wearing a silver belt buckle—" The image in her mind came into sharp focus suddenly. It was oval-shaped, fashioned of silver with black detailing. The snake was coiled, its diamond-shaped head in the center of the buckle as if ready to strike.

She opened her eyes and looked at Riley. He was looking at the images, a deep furrow in his brow.

She looked down at the images, scanning them to see if any matched the belt buckle she remembered.

She spotted it, third from the left, middle row. As she reached for it, Riley moved forward at the same time. Their hands met over the image.

Electric tingles rippled up her arm. She looked up, surprised, to find him staring at her, a strange intensity shining in his blue eyes.

"Is that the one?" His fingers tightened over hers.

She nodded, suddenly breathless.

A triumphant grin spread slowly over his face.

"How did you know?" she asked, looking down at his hand still covering hers on top of the color print.

He let go of her hand and stood, crossing to the desk near the window. He pulled a thick file folder from the bottom drawer and brought it over to the bed. "Can you put away all of the other prints?" he asked, already thumbing through the file in his lap.

She replaced all the useless printouts in the manila folder from which they'd come and held on to the one she'd identified, looking at it more closely. It was definitely the one she'd seen that day. But if it was a popular style—

"Here." Riley held out a piece of paper.

She took it from him, wincing as she realized it was an autopsy photo. The photo showed a close-up image of a woman's abdomen, from the bottom of the breasts to the pelvic bone. A dark bruise marred the skin of the upper belly, just below the ribcage.

Riley pointed to the bruise. "Can you see that?"

She looked closer. Suddenly, the bruise started to take a recognizable shape. "Oh, my God. It's the belt buckle."

She looked up at him, surprised to find him laughing softly. He dropped the file folder on the bed and reached for her hand, pulling her up and into his arms. His laughter vibrating against her chest, he swirled her around and around until her head swam.

He set her down, finally, still laughing softly as he kept her close. "You don't know how long I've been puzzling over that bruise," he murmured against her hair, his grip tightening.

Tentatively, she moved her hands up his sides, tracing the whipcord muscles lining his ribcage. Deep in her belly, heat pooled, setting off tiny tremors that rippled up her spine. Her breathing sped up as her heart began to pound like a hammer against her ribcage.

Oh, God, it was happening again.

Riley pulled back slowly, his gaze meeting hers. His eyes went midnight dark, and she realized he'd felt the traitorous response of her body to his. His eyes darkened, but not with anger or surprise. Where her hand rested against his chest, she felt the racing of his heart. Resistance fell away, leaving only hard, ravening need.

Kiss me, she thought, her breath trapped in her aching lungs.

She nearly collapsed to the floor when he let her go.

CHAPTER SEVEN

RILEY CROSSED TO the window and gazed out, as if he could see the mountains instead of his own traitorous reflection there. His whole body was humming with awareness. He could even hear Hannah's soft, quick respirations behind him.

"This is a break in the case, isn't it?" she asked.

He took a deep, steadying breath. He could control himself, damn it. He'd become very good at self-discipline over the last few years.

He turned to look at her. "Her name was Cara Sandifer. A rancher found her body in an irrigation pond a few hours after she was killed." He crossed to the bed, keeping his distance from her, and added the printout of the belt buckle to Cara's file. "Because her body was found so quickly, the evidence in her case is probably the best we have at the moment."

"We should tell someone. Joe. You should call Joe."

Riley nodded. "He can fax a notice over to other law-enforcement agencies in the area. We'll also track down the manufacturer and see how many belt buckles we're looking at, what stores in Wyoming carry them, that kind of thing."

He glanced at Hannah and found her sitting in the middle of the bed, her knees tucked up against her body protectively, the same way she'd sat in the hospital watching the crime-scene investigators go over her bed. Compassion trumped his uneasiness, and he crossed to her side, reaching out to squeeze her arm. "This is good news. You really came through for us."

She lifted her chin, unfolding out of her self-protective tuck until she sat cross-legged. When she spoke, her voice was stronger. "I hope it helps you find him. That's all I want, you know. To find this guy and go back home in one piece."

Her tone didn't change, but Riley couldn't miss the warning in her words. She may have felt the same charge of electricity between them that he'd experienced, but she was no more interested in pursuing it than he was.

That should make things between them considerably less complicated, he thought with relief.

He should have known better.

"THERE ARE 450 STORES in 36 states that carry the Cal Reno brand buckles. Most of those have, at one time or another, carried the Rattler design. At least thirty of those stores are located in Wyoming, and God knows how many there are in the surrounding states." Joe Garrison's expression was grim.

Hannah stared at the police chief, her heart sinking. "That many?"

"We've put out a request to track the purchases, but if someone made the purchase with cash, there's really no way to identify him. We can hope he paid with a credit card." Joe looked apologetic.

"Well, maybe we'll get lucky," Hannah said, not ready to let go of optimism. She glanced at Riley. His expression was shuttered, but she was beginning to figure out how to read him. It was all in his eyes. He couldn't hide his feelings in those expressive blue eyes.

Right now, he was feeling wary. Afraid to hope but, like her, not ready to give up yet. She felt an odd sense of camaraderie with him, as if the two of them were pitted against the rest of the doubting world.

Unfortunately, camaraderie with Riley Patterson wasn't really what she wanted to feel. If last night's restless attempt at slumber had proved anything, it was that all her good intentions, and all the hard lessons of her past, made poor preventatives against her attraction to the man.

Just the sound of his slow, steady breathing had been enough to fire her fantasies, and she'd tossed and turned all night, trying to fight their potent allure.

He wasn't even that good-looking, she had tried to tell herself, even as her skin still remembered the feel of his body pressed so tightly against hers. His craggy features were too rough-hewn to be considered conventionally handsome, his rusty hair close-cropped, almost military style, and worthless for running one's fingers through.

Except she kept finding herself imagining the crisp texture of his hair sliding beneath her fingertips, and the mere thought made her whole body tingle with anticipation.

An image of Craig's face flashed through her mind. So handsome, so familiar. She hadn't been able to keep her hands off him, either.

And hadn't that worked out well?

"What about the personnel files from the hospital?" Riley asked Joe.

"Jim called this morning. He was having a little trouble working out the legal details, but he found a judge late last night who'd sign the court order for access to the records. Only he can't share them outside his jurisdiction, so we'll have to wait for his people to work through the list," Joe said.

"That could take forever," Riley protested, running his left hand over his jaw, clearly frustrated.

Morning sunlight slicing into the room between the kitchen window curtains reflected off the slim gold band on his ring finger, catching Hannah's attention. She let her gaze linger on the ring as it provided a much-needed reality check.

Riley Patterson might be sexy. He might be the kind of rugged, masculine man that made ordinarily sane women consider moving to Wyoming and roughing it through long, harsh winters just to sleep at night in such a man's arms.

But in the ways that mattered most, Riley Patterson was a married man. His love for his wife drove him, day in and day out, to find an elusive killer who'd left few clues to follow. His body might respond like a man when he was around a woman, just as he'd responded to being close to her last night. But his heart was strictly off-limits.

"I know it's frustrating that we can't get all the answers immediately," Joe said, giving Hannah something to think about besides her alarming attraction to Riley. "But this is pretty significant movement on these cases. That's good news."

Riley nodded. "I know you're right. It's just—" He looked at Hannah.

"So maybe you should spend your time trying to

concentrate on what else Hannah can remember," Joe suggested.

Footsteps on the back porch heralded Jack Drummond's return from the stable. Joe stuffed the files he'd been sharing with them in his briefcase and rose from the table as Jack walked into the kitchen. "Hi there, Jack."

Jack shook hands with Joe. "Back so soon?"

As Joe responded, and their greeting turned into small talk, Riley leaned toward Hannah, his voice lowered. "I think Joe's right. We need to concentrate on helping you remember more of what happened the day of the attack."

"Every time I try to concentrate on it, I just become more confused," she said softly. "I don't even know what would help at this point."

"I have some thoughts—"

Jack cleared his throat loudly. "Can't even leave these lovebirds alone for five seconds before they've got their heads together, whispering sweet nothings, Joe. What am I gonna do with them?"

"Short of hosing them down?" Joe responded, shooting a wink at Hannah.

"Well, they'll have themselves a little free time today, because I'm heading into town to see if I can stir up a little trouble." Jack held his hands up toward Joe. "Strictly legal, of course."

"Of course." Joe patted Jack on the back and turned to Riley. "I'll let you know if I hear anything about that case I was telling you about. Enjoy your time off."

"Thanks." Riley walked Joe out, while Jack settled into the chair his brother-in-law had vacated.

"You could ditch Riley and come to town with me,

you know," Jack said with a wicked grin. "I'd show you places in Canyon Creek Riley probably doesn't even know about—"

"I heard that," Riley shot over his shoulder as he closed the door behind Joe. "And you'd be surprised the places I know about in Canyon Creek, son." He crossed to Jack's side and clamped his hands on his brother-in-law's shoulders. "Like where to bury a body so nobody can find it."

"Okay, okay, I'm going!" Jack said, laughing. He headed down the hall toward his room.

"He's right about one thing," Riley said, holding out his hand to Hannah. "Let's get out of this house."

THE MORNING WAS TURNING out to be unseasonably mild for October in Wyoming, the bright, late-morning sun warming the cab of Riley's pickup truck. Hannah laid her head back against the headrest and closed her eyes, enjoying the light on her face and the slow, bluesy strains of a Tim McGraw song playing on the truck's radio.

If it weren't for Riley's steady stream of questions, she might even be able to pretend it was a carefree outing.

"What had you been doing before you headed west on 287?"

She opened her eyes, releasing a soft sigh. "I'd spent longer on the lake at my friends' place than I'd intended. The trout were biting great, so we decided to eat some of our catch for lunch. I'd planned to be on the road before lunch, but I couldn't pass up the fresh fish, so I didn't get out of there as early as I'd hoped."

"You were about twenty miles southwest of Grand Teton State Park when you were pulled over, right?"

"That's what Sheriff Tanner said. I don't know for sure."

Riley's brow creased. "Would you be able to recognize where you were pulled over if you saw it again?"

"I don't know. Maybe. I know it was fairly isolated, and there was no shoulder of the road to speak of. I pulled over just past a crossroad, because there was finally a little bit of a rocky shoulder to pull over on." She turned to look at him, wincing a little as her seatbelt pressed against her still-sore body. "Would it help to find the place?"

"I suppose the Teton County Sheriff's Department has already looked for it, but—yeah. I think it would help. Maybe it would jog your memory, if nothing else."

"If we're lucky," she agreed, although the thought of recreating the nightmare of that day held little appeal. Still, if it helped Riley get closer to stopping a killer, she'd do it.

"Where do your friends live?"

"It's a small ranch in the Pavillion area."

He nodded. "I know the area. Do you think you could find it again?"

"You want us to go there? Today?"

"I want us to start where you started, when you started. The more directly we duplicate your drive, the better." He reached into his pocket for his cell phone and dialed a number. "Hey, Joe, it's Riley."

As Riley outlined the plan over the phone with his boss, Hannah turned her gaze back toward the landscape unfolding ahead of them. They were driving east, toward Canyon Creek. The plan had originally been to stop for lunch in town, just to give Hannah a chance to get out of the house. The countryside outside of town was mostly ranch acreage, punctuated by scrub grass and the occasional small lake or winding creek. Horses and cattle dotted the grassy pastureland, although Riley had told her that the grazing season was mostly over for the year.

"Anything new from Jackson?" Riley asked. His lips pressed to a line as he listened to Joe's response. "Yeah, I know I just talked to you a half hour ago. Yeah. Bye."

"Still nothing?"

He shook his head. "Jackson has this stuff on rush, which is really all we could hope for, given we haven't definitively made the connection between your attack and the murders."

"But the belt buckle—"

"The state lab guys will look at what we sent them. But they have other cases."

Hannah slumped against her seat, frustrated. It was a lot easier to be patient with the snail's pace of forensic science when you weren't the one whose life had been upended, she supposed. And she knew the Wyoming authorities were probably working as quickly as they could.

"So, are we still going into town?" she asked aloud.

"Yeah. You left your friend's place in Pavillion when?"

"Around two in the afternoon."

"Good. We've got time to grab lunch and a car and still get to your starting point by two."

"A car?"

"You were driving a Pontiac G6. I can probably talk

Lewis at the used-car place into letting us borrow something similar."

They reached town within ten minutes. Other than a distinctive western feel to the town's buildings, and the sprawling blue Wyoming sky spreading out for miles beyond the town's small cluster of business and in-town residences, Canyon Creek, Wyoming, was not that different from her own hometown of Gossamer Ridge, Alabama. The friendly waves from pedestrians and drivers alike as they drove down Main Street were something she encountered daily at home. Everybody knew everybody else in a small town.

Which meant, of course, that she attracted plenty of curious looks as people realized that Riley Patterson wasn't alone in his Chevy Silverado.

"Same story as we're telling Jack?" she asked aloud as he pulled into the parking lot of a small used-car lot.

He looked at her, his brow furrowed. "Same story?"

"People will want to know who I am."

His brow creased further. "Ah, damn. You're right."

"We can pretend I'm a cousin or something—"

"No, it's okay. Now that Jack knows you're here, it's not like he's going to keep quiet about it. People will probably be so thrilled to see me out with a woman, they'll bend over backwards to leave us be." There was a bitter edge to his voice that made Hannah's stomach hurt.

Yet she understood what he was feeling, more than he knew. "Everyone keeps waiting for my brother, J.D., to fall in love again," she said. "And it's been almost eight years for him."

He stopped with his hand on the door handle. "Eight years since what?"

"Since his wife was murdered."

THE WORKSHOP IN his mother's root cellar was small but private, just as he required. She'd become too arthritic to handle the rough wooden stairs a few years before she died, making the cellar solely his domain for almost a decade now. Besides the house access, the cellar also had an outside entrance built into the ground. Its wide double doors accommodated easy loading and unloading from the Crown Vic parked in the side yard, and the extra insulation he'd added a few years back made the room virtually soundproof.

He sat on the work stool, polishing his tools and reviewing the last two days in his mind, determined to fix what had gone wrong not once but twice in the past forty-eight hours. There was no way to candy-coat the truth. The girl had caught him by surprise. She'd kept her head, despite the pepper-spray ambush, and managed to get away. She'd almost drawn blood, he thought, looking down at the light scrape on his pinky finger where the ring had been the day before.

Worse, she'd thwarted his careful plan to mop up his mess. He should've known she was awake. He should have heard her breath quicken, seen her furtive movements to undo the IV cannula. He'd gotten sloppy, and things were now worse than before. The cops were putting the pieces together, after all he'd done to spread out his kills in different jurisdictions and different years. He'd overheard the cops talking about the kills at the hospital. Three years of murders, they'd said.

He smiled with the first real satisfaction he'd felt in two days. Three years wasn't even close.

His first kill had been almost ten years ago. A neighbor girl, not a half mile down the highway. She'd been seventeen. He'd been twenty.

It had been sweet. So very sweet.

He laid down his knife and reached across the work-table for the folder that he'd compiled after his earlier visit to the Teton County Sheriff's Department. It had been so easy—stop by to see an old friend from his prison-guard days who'd made the move to real police work. He'd just kept his eyes open, grabbed the file when his friend wasn't looking and stuck the folder under his coat. So easy. A quick trip to the copy shop down the street and a return trip to the sheriff's station on pretense of leaving his cell phone behind, and he'd had everything he needed.

Nobody had suspected a thing. And now he had his own file on Hannah Jean Cooper of Gossamer Ridge, Alabama.

It didn't do much to tell him where she was at the moment, but quick phone calls to her home number and work number had, at least, given him hope that she had not yet left Wyoming. He still had time to tie up that loose end.

Meanwhile, he thought, turning to look at the woman lying gagged and bound on the worktable, he had work to do.

"YOUR BROTHER'S WIFE WAS murdered?" Riley's stomach muscles clenched.

She nodded, her expression grim. "Eight years ago next February. She was abducted from the trucking company where she worked—she'd worked late and her car battery had died, stranding her alone. By the time anyone realized she was missing, it was already too late."

"I'm sorry." The words seemed inadequate.

"My brother was devastated. In some ways, he still is." Moisture sparkled on her eyelashes. She sniffed back the tears. "So, you see, I know it's hard to deal with people who think you can just get over it and move on. I've watched my brother deal with it for years."

"Did the police ever find out who killed her?" As soon as he asked the question, Riley realized he didn't want to know the answer. Three years without answers had been a living horror. The idea of eight years of not knowing who'd upended his whole world was almost more than he could stand.

"J.D. hasn't stopped searching, either," Hannah said, her voice small and strangled.

"Then you understand," he said grimly.

She nodded, sniffing again. She took a deep breath, squared her jaw and turned to look at him. "You do whatever makes you comfortable. Tell people whatever you want. I'll go along with it."

He wished it were that simple. But Jack's arrival had complicated everything. Once Riley blurted the first thing that had come to his mind to explain Hannah's presence, the die had been cast. He'd have to go on with the charade.

"We could tell Jack the truth," Hannah said, as if reading his mind.

He shook his head. "No, we can't."

"Don't you trust him?"

He rubbed his jaw, wishing he could say yes without hesitation. "Jack's a good guy. He wouldn't hurt you or me on purpose for the world. But he's also the kind of guy who thinks Saturday nights are made for drinking himself under the table, and I know from experience that he can't keep his tongue when he's drinking."

Her brow furrowed. "I see."

"We have to go on with what we've started." He began to open the truck's driver's-side door, but Hannah stayed him with a hand on his arm.

She tightened her grip on his forearm. "I'll wait here in the truck."

"That's only delaying the questions. It won't make them go away," he warned.

"I know. But look at it this way—when I'm finally out of here, you can just pretend things between us didn't work out, and then you'll get a reprieve while you get over our failed romance." She smiled at him, her eyes sparkling with amusement at figuring out a way to turn their uncomfortable charade into a plus.

Her humor was infectious. He felt his own lips starting to curve with a smile. "You're devious. I like that."

She laughed at that. "Six older brothers will do that for you."

He smiled again, surprised how much he enjoyed having someone to conspire with again. It had been one of the things he'd enjoyed most about his marriage to Emily—someone to keep secrets with, to cocoon himself with against the often cold and indifferent world outside.

But as he entered the used-car lot's office and answered the greetings of the staff, it occurred to him that getting comfortable around Hannah Cooper could turn out to be a very dangerous proposition.

CHAPTER EIGHT

"It's SORT OF like truth or dare without the dare part. Or strip poker, without the stripping." Hannah cut the deck of playing cards she'd talked Riley into picking up at the service station where they'd stopped for gas and a couple of deli sandwiches. "My brothers Jake and Gabe made it up. Come to think of it, there might have been a dare aspect to it early on, but I think Mom ended that after the tree-house incident."

He looked at her skeptically as he gathered up the remains of their lunch and set them aside to drop in the trash can later. "Why do you call it popsmack?"

She grinned. "I'm pretty sure it's because my brothers ended up in a huge punching match by the end of every game. They're cretins." She lightened the insult with affection; her brothers, for all the irritation they'd been over the years, were good guys, and she loved them all dearly.

"Couldn't we just play strip poker instead?" Riley flashed her a leering grin, but she saw the nervousness behind his eyes. He was clearly a private kind of guy, and what she was asking him to do had to be pretty daunting.

"It's just a getting to know you kind of thing," she assured him, dealing half the cards to him atop the weathered picnic table, dealing the other half to herself.

They'd arrived early in Pavillion, since they hadn't stopped to eat in town, so they had a couple of hours to pass before they could head toward Jackson to recreate the events leading up to the event. Talk had been sparse during the drive, Riley sinking into a sort of contemplative silence for most of the way. No doubt going over all the facts of the cases he was investigating. He was nothing if not single-minded.

But their discussion about Jack and his relative trustworthiness had convinced Hannah that she and Riley needed to get their stories straight if they were going to spend much more time in Jack's company. Riley's brother-in-law was good-natured and mostly benign, but he wasn't stupid. They had to be convincing as lovers, and that included knowing a little more about each other than just their names. She'd hoped popsmack would prove a fun way to make that happen.

"It's very simple—you play your cards one at a time. The person with the highest card wins."

"Which means?"

"Which means the winner gets to ask any question he or she wants, and the other person has to answer that question honestly."

The wary look in his eyes deepened. "What if it's a really personal question?"

"Jack thinks we're sleeping together. I think that means we should know a few really personal things about each other."

His shoulders squared and the muscles in his jaw twitched tight. "Okay, let's go."

She picked up her half of the deck and dealt the top card. A three of clubs.

Across the table, Riley smiled. When he dealt a ten of hearts, his smile widened. "So, I can ask you anything?"

Hannah's stomach tightened. He looked entirely too pleased with the idea. "Yeah, anything."

He thought for a minute. "What's your favorite color?"

"Blue," she answered quickly, torn between relief and disappointment. If they both got cold feet about asking the hard questions, this game would go nowhere.

She dealt another card. Queen of spades. He dealt a five of clubs and gave her a narrow-eyed look.

"What made you decide to be a policeman?" she asked.

His expression eased. "I didn't want to be a rancher, and Joe was my best friend. So when he decided to become a police officer, I thought it sounded like my kind of adventure."

"And was it?"

He quirked an eyebrow. "I don't remember follow-up questions being part of the game rules."

As he started to deal another card, she put her hand over his. "Seriously. Do you like being a cop?"

He looked down at her hand on his. She started to pull it away, but he reached out and trapped it with his other hand. "If we're supposed to be lovers, I think we should probably get used to touching each other."

Her heart turned an erratic little flip. He was right, of course, but her mind hadn't stopped with just holding hands. Would Jack expect to see them embrace? Even kiss?

"Should we be playing spin the bottle instead?" she muttered nervously.

His grip on her hand softened into something alarmingly like a caress. His thumb moved slowly over the back of her hand. "Probably."

He's still married in his heart, she reminded herself silently. *He still loves his wife.* She eased her hand from between his and reached for her deck.

"I do like being a cop," he said before she could deal her next card, his blue-eyed gaze direct. "I haven't been in a position to enjoy the investigative aspect of the job that much in a place like Canyon Creek, but I like being one of the go-to guys in town. People trust me to protect them. Make sure justice is done. I like being useful."

She smiled. "You sound like my brother, Aaron. He's a deputy sheriff back home."

"What about your older brother—the one who lost his wife?"

She toyed with the stack of cards in front of her. "He was in the Navy awhile—he worked in ship maintenance. When he left the service, he came back to the marina to help my parents run the place. They'd been wanting to offer on-site service to our slip renters, and now J.D. does that full-time. He likes tinkering with things, making them work."

Riley flipped the top card of his stack on to the table face up. "Five of spades."

She dealt a card. "Nine of diamonds."

He smiled slightly. "Your turn."

She was beginning to wish she'd never started this game. The more she learned about him, the more she liked, and she had a feeling he'd be a lot easier to resist if she didn't like him quite so much.

"What's your favorite food?" she asked finally.

His mouth quirked. "Lost your nerve?"

"It's better than 'what's your favorite color?'" she shot back with a roll of her eyes.

"Fair enough." He rubbed his chin as if giving her question some thought. "Would steak and potatoes be too much of a cliché?"

"Not if it's the truth."

He smiled. "I do like a good steak, but I guess my favorite food is barbecue ribs."

"My brother Jake makes the best ribs," she said, her mouth watering at the thought. "Slow cooked, slathered with his homemade sauce—yum. He cooked some for Labor Day."

"I make my own barbecue sauce, too," he said. "Actually, it's Emily's recipe—"

The air between them grew immediately colder. Riley sat back from the table, his fingers tapping the stack of undealt cards in front of him, moving them forward toward her.

"I wish I could have met her," Hannah said. She immediately regretted her words when she saw the flash of pain cross Riley's face.

"We should probably get on the road." He looked away.

She scooped up the cards and put them back in the pack. "Okay." She scooted off the picnic-table bench and started toward the Ford Taurus Riley had borrowed from the used-car lot.

He caught her halfway there, his hand encircling her elbow. "You should drive from here on. I'll get you to the starting point, then you can take it from there."

She took the keys he held out and unlocked the Taurus's driver's door. She adjusted the seat and buckled herself in while he climbed in the passenger side.

"Just head northeast on this road and you'll come to Highway 287."

Hannah pulled the Taurus out of the rest area and back onto the main road, stealing a glance at Riley. He'd donned a pair of sunglasses and was gazing forward at the road, although he wore a slight smile that made her own lips curve in response.

A moment later, he cleared his throat. "I think Emily would have liked you."

Her smile faded. Forcing herself not to analyze that statement, she headed for Highway 287.

HE HAD TO STOP LETTING the mention of Emily's name paralyze him, he thought as he watched Hannah drive west on Highway 287. If not for himself, then for Emily. She'd be horrified to know he was trapped in her memory like a bug in amber. He'd never known a woman more alive, who'd found more joy in just living, than Emily, and she would hate what he'd become, almost as much as she'd loved him in life.

It was just—Hannah. Hannah made him feel things. Not just physical attraction. That was biological. He hadn't stopped being a man when Emily died. But those kinds of urges were no different than his stomach growling when he was hungry or yawning when he was sleepy.

Hannah made him laugh. She made him want to know more about her. She had the same sort of vibrancy, the same curiosity, the same enjoyment of the simple pleasures of life that had drawn him to Emily.

She was dangerous to him in the way that a simple biological response to a beautiful woman could never be.

She's leaving in less than a week, he reminded himself. There wasn't much point in trying to learn more about her or let himself worry about where their relationship was going to go.

Maybe that was as good an excuse as any to stop worrying and just enjoy what she was making him feel. Like a limb coming back to life after being asleep for a while, the worst of the painful tingles had begun to pass, and he was starting to feel a hum of energy that reminded him he wasn't dead after all.

He was thirty-four years old, in excellent health, with years of life ahead of him. It was time to start living again, wasn't it?

He knew what Emily would tell him.

"I got gas at that station," Hannah said, pointing to a Lassiter Oil station coming up on her left. Behind the station, a small herd of Appaloosas grazed on a dwindling patch of pastureland. "I'd forgotten about that. I filled up about fifteen minutes before I was pulled over."

"Are you sure this is the station?"

She nodded. "I remember the Appaloosas."

"Then we should stop here, too."

Hannah slowed and turned into the gas station, parking near the front. She shut off the engine. "I know I didn't go in. I paid at the pump. I think I got a couple of bottles of water out of one of those vending machines." She pointed to a pair of machines standing against the wall of the station's food mart.

Riley glanced at his watch. It was after three. According to the case report, she'd wrecked her car at Big Mike's Truck Stop, which was about ten miles down the highway.

"It takes about three or four minutes to fill up a tank. Did you talk to anyone?"

Her brow wrinkled as she considered the question. "I'm not sure—I don't really remember much about stopping here, except the horses. If there was someone else here filling up, I might have made small talk, but—"

He sighed. Her memory was still spotty from the concussion. Her doctor had admitted that she might never remember some of what happened that day.

"Let's get back on the road," he said after three minutes had passed.

She started the car, but paused a moment before putting it into drive. "I think there was someone at the pumps. I kind of remember asking about the roads to Yellowstone—whether there'd been any closings yet. I don't remember the answer."

"It's okay," he assured her. "It probably doesn't have anything to do with what happened to you."

Still, he made a note to mention it to Joe. They could check the station's receipts from that day, maybe find out who else bought gas around the time she had.

They drove a little farther west. Riley tried to pay particular attention to the surroundings, as they should be coming up on wherever the attack had taken place any time now.

"Hmm," she murmured.

He looked up to find her brow furrowed. "What is it?"

"That road we just passed on the right. I think that may be where he was waiting."

Riley looked back toward the small dirt road they'd just passed. "You think he was waiting?"

"I check my mirrors regularly. Old habit my father drummed into me when he was teaching me to drive." She glanced at the mirror just then. "I think it was right about here when I looked into the rearview mirror and saw the blue lights."

He looked around them. There was no shoulder on the right to speak of; where the road top ended, the ground rose steeply up a craggy hillside.

"I couldn't pull over here," she said softly, her eyes narrowed as she followed the curve of the road. He noticed her breath was coming in short, fast little clips, even though her chin was up, her jaw squared with determination.

It was getting to her, being here.

"I was looking for—there." She pointed toward a turnoff ahead, where the shoulder widened enough to accommodate a vehicle. "That's where I pulled over. It happened there."

She slowed suddenly, whipping the Ford off the highway on to the side road. Braking at the road's edge, she jammed the Ford into Park and bent her head forward, her breath coming in short, shallow gasps.

He reached across and unbelted her. "Just breathe," he coaxed, rubbing her back. "Take a big breath and hold it for a count of ten."

She squeezed the steering wheel hard, breathing in and holding it while she counted to ten under her breath. She exhaled, then repeated the deep breath. Twice. Three times. One more deep breath and she looked at him, her eyes dark with humiliation. "Sorry about that."

"Don't be." He slid his hand up to her neck, gently kneading the tight muscles bunched beneath his fingers. He kept his voice calm and comforting. "Just take a minute to breathe."

After another minute, she was visibly calmer. But she couldn't quite bring herself to look him in the eye when she next spoke. "Any chance we could find tire tracks on the shoulder where he pulled me over?"

"I'll take a quick look, but we should probably call the Teton County Sheriff's Department. It's their case, officially. They'll want to call in the crime-scene investigators." He pulled his cell phone from the pocket of his jacket as he got out of the Ford and crossed to the highway to take a closer look at the shoulder.

What he found there made his heart sink.

There weren't any tire tracks at all. In fact, the sandy shoulder looked as if it had been raked clean of any marks either car might have made upon pulling over.

Son of a bitch was always a step ahead.

HANNAH RESTED HER HEAD against the back of the seat and watched the crime-scene investigators at work in her rearview mirror. They seemed to be taking soil samples, despite Riley's grim pronouncement earlier that someone had already tampered with the scene to remove any sort of tread marks that the police might have been able to preserve from the scene.

He'd sat with her awhile as they waited for the Teton County deputies to arrive but jumped from the car as soon as they drove up, no doubt as horrified by her humiliating bout of hysterics as she'd been.

She saw Riley moving away from the detectives overseeing the evidence collection. He opened the driver's door and held out his hand. "I'll drive home."

She took his hand and let him help her out of the

car, her skin burning with embarrassment. He probably wasn't holding her weakness against her, she knew, but that didn't ease her own sense of shame. She was a Cooper, for God's sake. Coopers were made of tough stuff, and just because she was the only girl didn't mean it was okay to go all weak-kneed and neurotic.

"I'm not a wuss," she muttered aloud as she buckled herself into the passenger seat.

Riley turned to look at her. "I know that."

She slanted a look at him. He seemed to be sincere. "We don't have to leave now if you don't want to. I know you'd probably rather be back there with the other detectives."

"They're not going to find anything," Riley said with a brisk shake of his head. "They haven't found anything at the turn off down the road where you thought he might have lain in waiting, either. I think he covered his tracks." He gave a nod toward the western sky, where gunmetal rain clouds had started to gather. "Rain's coming. Let's not get stuck driving home in it." He took off his jacket, tossed it in the backseat of the borrowed car, and slid behind the wheel.

She settled back against the seat, willing herself to relax. Now that her brief panic attack had passed fully, the ebb of adrenaline had begun draining her body of energy. All she wanted to do at the moment was close her eyes and let the last of the tension melt away.

Riley fiddled with the radio dial until he found something soft and slow playing on a country station out of Jackson. The quiet music blended with the hum of the Ford's motor until the vibrations seemed to take over her weary body. Her limbs felt heavy and numb. The rain clouds blotted the afternoon sun from the sky, casting gloom across the Ford's dark interior, drawing her deeper into her own mind.

He was nearby. She felt him, like a chill in the air around her. She struggled to open her eyes, certain that if she looked in the side mirror, she'd see him lurking behind them, waiting to make his move.

She tried to warn Riley, but her voice came out in a soft, voiceless cry. Her arms and legs felt paralyzed, and a growing hum filled her ears.

He was closer. She could smell him, the fetid stench of hate and malice, stronger than the sting of pepper spray that still seemed to linger in her nose. Was he right outside her window? If she opened her eyes, would she find him staring back at her, from a face she had struggled for two days to picture? Or would she see nothing but those hard, cruel hands, reaching for her, determined to finish what he'd started two days ago?

Hard hands grabbed her from behind and squeezed her throat, trapping her breath in her chest. Her head started pounding, and the world around her swirled into a spiral of darkness.

Oh, my God he's here, he's in the car, I'm going to die—

"Hannah!"

The fingers lost their grip. Air rushed into her lungs, and she lurched forward, her paralysis gone. Her surroundings swam into focus. The dashboard in front of her. Fast breathing beside her.

She had to get out.

Fumbling with the seat-belt buckle, she managed to free herself just as someone grabbed her arm. She jerked away, plucking at the door handle, a soft keening sob escaping her lungs as she missed on the first try.

On the second attempt, the door opened and she flung herself out of the car into the driving rain, scrambling over the rocky shoulder.

"Hannah!"

She kept moving, though her sluggish brain tried to process how the killer knew her name. And what was he doing in the car?

She heard swift footsteps on the ground behind her, and her heart rate soared. Hands caught at her, missing at first but finally trapping her in their hard grip. She struggled to get away, but strong arms wrapped around her, pulling her tight against a warm, solid body.

"Hannah, it's Riley. Stop fighting me."

She fought a few seconds longer until his words seeped into her sleep-addled brain. She twisted around to look at him, needing to see his face, to be sure.

Rain dripped off the brim of his hat, falling against her cheek. Beneath the brim, his anxious blue eyes bored into hers. "Are you okay?" His voice shook.

Relief flooded her body, knocking her off balance. She grasped his arms, her fingers digging in just to keep herself from sliding to the ground.

He caught her up against him. "You were trying to scream in the car," he said, his voice rough.

"I thought he was here." Her voice came out in a croak. "I thought he was trying to kill me."

Riley's eyes closed as he took a couple of quick, deep breaths. "I didn't know if you were having some sort of seizure or something. I pulled over and then you just went wild."

He had parked the Ford off the side of the road, she saw, on a narrow shoulder not far from the exit to the rest area where they'd eaten lunch and played that silly game of popsmack. She must have slept longer than she realized; they'd been back on the road for almost an hour and a half.

"It felt real," she said, tears stinging her eyes. She'd felt the man's anger. His hate.

"Nobody's out there," he assured her, pushing her wet hair out of her face. His hand lingered against her cheek, his touch warm and firm, full of strength tempered by gentle concern. Her breath hitched, catching somewhere in the middle of her chest. She gazed up into his shadowed eyes, where something glittered, fierce and white hot, stealing the air from her lungs. His fingers tangled in the hair at her temples, trapping her.

He was going to kiss her. And she was going to let him.

As she rose to meet him, his mouth descended, hard and hungry against hers.

CHAPTER NINE

THOUGH A COLD wind whipped around them, and the rain
drenched them to the skin, all Hannah could feel was
Riley's mouth over hers, hard and relentless, drawing
out of her a feverish passion she thought she'd buried
somewhere so deep inside it could never be found again.
She dug her fingers into the muscles of his arms, holding on tightly as he dragged her closer to him, until her
breasts pressed flat against the hard wall of his chest,
until she could feel his heartbeat galloping wildly along-
side her own.

Slowly, he ran his hand over her jaw, down the curve
of her neck, his thumb settling on the hollow of her
throat. His mouth softened, coaxing her to relax against
him. His tongue slid lightly over her bottom lip, seduc-
ing her until she opened up to him, letting him deepen
the kiss.

Their tongues met briefly, a gentle thrust and parry,
and a low moan escaped her throat.

The sound seemed to catch him off guard. He went
still, his mouth resting briefly against hers, then letting
go. His hand dropped from her neck and away from her
body altogether.

Released from his hold, she had to struggle to keep
her feet, her breath coming in short, raspy pants.

"I'm sorry," he said, his voice tight.

She didn't know what to say. Was he sorry for kissing her in the first place? Sorry for pulling away and leaving her breathless and stunned?

"You scared me," he added, immediately wincing as if he knew it was the wrong thing to say.

The sudden tension between them was almost painful. She pressed the heel of her hand against her suddenly aching forehead. "Let's get back in the car, okay? We're soaked."

He gave a brisk nod and guided her back to the car. He opened the door for her, letting her settle in before he shut it and went around to the driver's side. He cranked the engine and turned up the heat, pulling back out on to the highway.

The next hour passed in near silence, the beat of the windshield wipers and the patter of rain taking up the slack.

They reached Canyon Creek near nightfall, stopping at the used-car lot to switch vehicles. On the short drive back to Riley's place, he broke the silence only to make a phone call to the office. "He's not in? Do you know where he went?"

After listening a moment longer, he rang off, gazing ahead at the road with his brow furrowed.

"What is it?" Hannah asked.

"Joe left the office about four hours ago, headed for the Grand Teton National Park. He didn't leave any message for me."

"Maybe it's not related to my case?"

He shook his head. "Grand Teton is way out of our jurisdiction. Why would he be going there?"

Hannah had a sinking feeling they'd find out sooner rather than later.

JACK'S TRUCK WAS NOWHERE in sight when Riley pulled the Silverado up the gravel-packed drive to his house. He frowned, wondering where his brother-in-law was off to in this storm.

As Hannah started to get out of the truck, he put his hand out to hold her in place. "Let me go get an umbrella for you."

She stared at him as if he'd lost his mind. "I'm already drenched to the bone. I'm not going to melt." She slid out of the car into the rain.

He hurried to catch up with her, unlocking the door and guiding her to the narrow mudroom just off the kitchen. He took her jacket and shook off the water, hanging it to finish drying on a hook on the wall. He did the same with his own jacket, trying to ignore the tense silence that had fallen between them.

What the hell had gotten into him, grabbing her up like that, kissing her with all the finesse of a cowboy hitting town after weeks on the trail? Jack, for God's sake, would have handled her with more gentleness, and he was a damned bull rider and an unrepentant player.

Hannah crossed the kitchen to stand near the woodstove. Inside the chamber, the embers were dying, but it still gave off a soft stream of heat. Riley joined her there, holding his hands out to warm them from the damp chill.

"Hannah, I wanted to say—"

"Do you think Joe might have left a message on your answering machine?" she interrupted, looking up at him with anxious eyes.

That should have been the first thing he thought about, he realized with some chagrin. He went down the hall to his bedroom to check, acutely aware of Hannah's soft footsteps moving down the hallway behind him.

There was nothing on his answering machine, and when he tried calling Joe's cell phone, he got no answer.

"Something's wrong, isn't it?" Hannah's voice was right behind him. He turned to find her standing quietly, her eyes dark with worry.

"I don't know," he admitted, touching her arm, needing that contact to ground him, somehow.

She laid her hand on his chest, right over his heart, her touch gentle and questioning. He put his own hand over hers, pulling her into a gentle, undemanding embrace.

They stood there a long time, wrapped in each other's arms, her head resting against his shoulder. Outside the house, darkness fell, painting the bedroom with shadows. The only light came from the glowing embers of the woodstove in the corner, yet Riley couldn't seem to rouse himself to release Hannah and go turn on the overhead light.

"I'm sure he's okay," she murmured against his shirt.

"It's unusual for him not to answer his phone."

"Maybe it's out of cell-tower range or something."

That was certainly possible. There were plenty of places in the Wyoming hills and valleys where cell-phone towers didn't reach. And had Joe left Riley a message, telling him he might be out of pocket for the afternoon, he probably wouldn't give it a second thought.

"Should I call Jane and see if she knows where he is?"

"No," Hannah said quickly, pulling her head back to look at him. "You'd just worry her without really knowing anything. Give Joe time to get home and try him again later." She let go of him, backing out of the embrace, though this time she didn't seem uncomfortable to be around him. "Let's get out of these wet clothes and then see what we can rustle up for dinner. I bet you'll hear from Joe by the time we're finished."

She was almost right. Riley had just walked into the kitchen, dressed in a dry pair of jeans and a warm sweatshirt when a knock sounded on the back door. A second later, Joe stuck his head through the door. "Riley?"

"Come on in," he answered, turning as Hannah came into the kitchen from the hallway. She'd dressed in a loose-fitting pair of yoga pants and an oversize T-shirt, and still he found himself wanting to pin her up against the kitchen wall and finish what he'd started out on that rain-washed highway.

He dragged his gaze away as Joe let himself into the kitchen, rain dripping from his Stetson to the floor of the entryway. He gave them both an odd look as he ducked into the mudroom briefly to hang up his wet coat, then returned to the kitchen where they waited.

"I heard you went to Grand Teton," Riley said, trying not to sound impatient.

Joe nodded. "I got a call from Jim Tanner. A hiker found a body up there."

Next to Riley, Hannah moved sideways, dropping into one of the nearby kitchen chairs. Riley slanted a look at her to make sure she was okay. She looked a little pale, but her gaze was steady as she waited for Joe to elaborate.

"They found pepper spray on her skin. She was wrapped in a plastic sheet and dumped in a creek just inside the park, east of Moran. She's been dead less than a day. Maybe as little as a couple of hours. M.E. thinks the hikers found her within minutes of her being dumped."

Riley shook his head. "Our guy's not that sloppy."

"Who else could it be?" Hannah asked. "It can't be a copycat, since none of that stuff is common knowledge, right?"

Riley looked at her, then back at Joe, not yet sure what to think. Their guy wasn't the sloppy type, so if this was him, something in his MO had changed.

"He could be escalating, beyond his normal control," Joe suggested. "Maybe he couldn't handle the failure of letting Hannah slip through his fingers not once but twice in the last two days."

It was possible, Riley supposed, but something about that theory just didn't feel right. The guy had been able not only to escape capture for the last three years but escape detection as well. Riley had been the first law-enforcement officer in Wyoming to connect the dots, and even he'd had doubts at first. Was a guy as wily as that really going to lose control and start getting sloppy because one of his targets got away?

"Maybe it's not escalation," Hannah said. Riley looked at her and found her gazing back at him, her green eyes dark with horror. "Maybe it was a message. To me. What he'd have done to me if I hadn't gotten away."

Riley pulled out the chair beside Hannah and sat down, reaching across to close his hand over hers where it lay on the table. "Don't you start blaming yourself for this."

Joe sat across from them. "Riley's right. Whatever

this bastard does, it's his own doing. You haven't done a damned thing wrong."

Riley squeezed her hand. "What were you supposed to have done differently—let him kill you?"

"No, of course not," she said, releasing a deep sigh. "I just think he's trying to tell us we can't stop him. I mean—he killed her and dumped her in a national park where hikers found her probably within minutes. That's bold."

"And risky, too," Joe pointed out. "If he starts thinking he's invincible, that's good for us. He'll start making mistakes, and we'll have him."

"Are we going to be in the loop on this investigation?" Riley asked Joe. "I need to see the reports."

"They're faxing everything they get. As soon as they know something, we'll know something. I'll bring by copies when they're ready." Joe shot a comforting smile at Hannah. "Don't let this get to you, Hannah. You just stay safe here with Riley and do what you can to remember more about the attack. That's all you can do."

Riley walked him to the door when he rose to leave. "Do you think she's right? Is it a message?"

"I think you and Hannah need to keep working on her memory lapses," Joe responded. "If she knows anything at all about the attack she hasn't yet remembered, it could be the break we need. If this guy is willing to kill someone just to let us know he can, nobody's safe."

Riley closed the door behind Joe and looked back at Hannah, who still sat at the table, gazing at him with wide, worried eyes. "Why don't we rustle up some dinner?" he suggested.

"I'm not hungry."

He sighed. He wasn't, either, even though lunch had

been a long time ago. He wished he knew where Jack was. It had been a real help to have him around for the past day, especially since the horses didn't just feed themselves every day. He should have asked Joe to take over stable duties that night, but Joe had a very pregnant wife at home, and with a murderous bastard out there killing women—

"I should call Jack," he said aloud, reaching into his pocket for his phone. "I'm not sure whether he fed the horses or not."

"We could do that, couldn't we?" Hannah stood, flexing her arms over her head. "I wouldn't mind the exercise."

Or the distraction, he suspected. "You sure? It's cold and wet out there."

"I go fishing in December in the rain all the time," she said firmly, her square little chin lifting. "I'm not fragile."

He didn't remind her of how she'd damned near fallen apart earlier that afternoon. Post-traumatic stress could fell big, tough, well-trained men. Then again, considering what she'd been through, she was holding up pretty well.

"Okay," he agreed. He grabbed their coats from the mudroom and led her out to the truck.

THE HARD RAIN HADN'T SEEMED to affect the hard-pressed dirt track to the stable, Hannah noticed. Perhaps the ground had been too dry for the rain to have made much impact, or maybe it was mostly rocky soil to begin with. There was a lot about Wyoming that seemed almost as alien to her as a foreign country, from the craggy mountains to the thin, dry air.

Amazing, then, how familiar Riley seemed to her after such a short time. Though she knew so little about him, beyond the handful of facts she'd gleaned over the past two days, she was more convinced than ever that she'd made the right choice that night in the hospital when she'd made the leap of faith and put herself under his protection.

He put her to work, showing no signs of trying to coddle her. She was grateful for the show of confidence. After the way she'd acted during their trip west that day, he'd have been justified in thinking she was weak and unreliable.

She brushed the mud off the chestnut mare's coat and held her bridle while Riley picked the dirt out of her hooves. "What's her name?" she asked.

"This is Bella. She was Emily's." Riley stood up and patted the mare's flank. "The black gelding is Jazz. And those two—" he pointed to the paint gelding and the buckskin mare they'd already settled for the night "—are Lucky and Lady. Joe bought them last year after he and Jane married. He doesn't have a stable on his land, so we share feed costs and vet bills, and he pays me for boarding them. He and Jane used to come daily to ride, too, before Jane got pregnant."

"I mentioned we've been thinking about building a stable on our land back home, to offer trail riding up the mountain as part of our services, didn't I?" Hannah put the brush back on the tack table and turned to look at Riley. "We all know how to ride well, and I think my brother Luke might consider coming back home to run the stable if we ever got around to doing it. He's the best horseman among us."

"I thought all your family was together back home in

Alabama." Riley put Bella in her stall and added food to her feed bowl.

"We mostly are. Sam and his little girl Maddy live in the Washington, D.C. area—he's a prosecutor—but he's been talking about moving back to Alabama so Maddy can grow up around her grandparents and her cousins. If he comes back, the only one missing will be Luke. He retired from the Marines last year, but so far, he's still hanging around San Diego." She couldn't hide a little frown.

Riley picked up on it immediately. "That worries you?"

"A little," she admitted. She turned to look at Bella over the stall door. The mare was crunching her feed contentedly, her dark eyes soft and calm. "Luke has always been a bit of a loner, which is hard to do in a family as big as ours, but after his last tour of duty, it's—worse, somehow. He hardly ever calls, and when we call, he keeps it short."

"Is he married? Or maybe has a girlfriend keeping him busy?"

She smiled. "I wish. I think I'd relax more if that's what I thought it was. There's just—I don't know. It almost feels like he's brooding about something."

"Do you think something happened to him that he's not telling you?"

She wasn't sure. She knew he'd done a tour of duty in Kaziristan right before he returned stateside, but that had been nothing but peacekeeping. Kaziristan's civil war had been over for a couple of years now, and the small Central Asian republic was mostly stable. Compared to some of his previous tours of duty, the one in Kaziristan should have been a cakewalk.

"I just want him back home where I can keep an eye on him," she answered finally.

Riley smiled. "All your ducks in a row."

"Exactly." She laughed self-consciously. "I can't believe I just told you all that about Luke. I haven't even talked to my parents about it."

"Maybe it's easier to tell things like that to a stranger."

Except he didn't feel like a stranger, she thought. She looked up at him, realizing just how much she was going to miss him when she had to go home.

And every day took her closer to that moment.

"What if I don't remember more about who attacked me?" she asked aloud.

The sound of boots on the hard-packed barn floor made them both turn in surprise. Jack Drummond stood in the doorway, his hat and jacket glistening with rain. He looked from Hannah to Riley, his expression dark and suspicious.

"Someone attacked you?" he asked.

Hannah and Riley exchanged looks. He gave a little shake of his head, clearly not ready to let Jack in on their secret.

"We were wondering where you'd gotten off to," Hannah said quickly, ignoring Jack's question. "Did you have fun in town?"

Riley stepped up behind her and slipped his arms around her, clasping his hands in front of her stomach and resting his cheek against her head. "*You* were wondering, baby," he said in a low growl that seemed to make her bones liquefy.

"Don't try to distract me." Jack strode into the stable, his eyes darkening. "You said something about an attack, Hannah." He reached inside his jacket and pulled out a folded section of newspaper. "Funny—I read something about an attack in the newspaper just this afternoon."

Riley's arms tightened around Hannah's waist. His tension radiated through her where their bodies touched, making her stomach clench painfully.

"Seems a woman was attacked on the road to Moran the other day. No identity given, but police sources say the assailant got away, and other sources mentioned a possible second attack in a Jackson hospital." Jack handed the paper to Hannah. "Page three."

She opened the paper to the page he mentioned. There it was: *Tourist attacked on highway; hospital security breach?*

"What makes you think that's me?"

"The timing. Your injuries. The complete impossibility of Riley meeting someone online, much less someone he'd invite to stay with him after just one meeting."

Riley dropped his hands away from Hannah, backing away. Cool air replaced the heat of his body, and she shivered.

"Nobody can know Hannah's connected to that story. Nobody, Jack. Understand?"

Jack's lips tightened to a thin, angry line. "You lied to me. *Me,* Riley. I didn't deserve that."

"You drink too much, Jack. You party too much. You don't keep your tongue when you're drinking."

Real pain etched lines in Jack's face. "That's what you think of me?"

"Tell me it's not true."

"It's not true," Jack said angrily. Then he lowered his voice. "Not anymore."

Riley's expression grew thoughtful. "When did that happen?"

"Last year. I got drunk in Amarillo and lost the best thing that ever happened to me." Jack removed his hat and ran his fingers briskly through his thick black hair. "I guess you wouldn't have known about that."

"And why's that, Jack? Because you haven't been back here since Emily died?"

"I couldn't."

Hannah felt like a voyeur, watching the two men deal with their private pain. She eased away from them, retreating to the horse box near the back, where Lucky quietly chewed what was left of the night's feed. She ran her hand down his brown spotted neck. He rewarded her with a soft nicker of pleasure.

"Why did you bring her here to stay with you?" Jack asked, apparently not caring that she was right there in the stable with them. "She could have stayed with Joe and his wife, or, hell, the Teton County Sheriff's Department could've found her a safe place to stay. Why was the first lie you came up with about sleeping with her? Have you given that any thought?"

"Stop it, Jack! This is all about Emily," Riley said, his voice rising with emotion. "Everything I've done since the day she died is about making sure the son of a bitch who murdered her gets what's coming to him. Don't you dare question that."

Hannah felt a sick, hot pain in the center of her chest. She turned her back to them, pressing her face against the gelding's warm, silky neck.

What's the matter, Hannah? You knew what was what. You knew it all along.

"Okay, so nobody can know why she's here," Jack said. "What's next?"

Hannah looked over her shoulder at Riley, wondering what he'd answer. He paused, as if at a loss for an answer, and slowly turned to look at her, his expression impossible to read.

"A lot of people have already seen us together," he said, his gaze remaining locked with hers. "The few who've asked, I told the same story I told you, Jack. It's probably all over town by now. We can't shift gears now."

"I can move back to the guest room," she suggested, pleased that her voice came out calm and pragmatic, considering how much she wanted to go find a quiet corner and cry.

"Then I guess I should go," Jack said.

"No," Hannah said quickly, moving toward him. The last thing she could bear was driving Jack away from what was apparently the only home—and family—he had.

And the last thing she needed was to spend the next few nights alone in the house with Riley.

CHAPTER TEN

QUIET TENSION SETTLED over the scene, punctuated by the drumming of rain on the stable's metal roof. Hannah's pulse drummed in her ears as she waited for Jack's answer.

Jack looked at Riley, a question in his eyes. Hannah looked at Riley, too, wondering what he'd say.

"It's your home," Riley said. "You're Emily's brother."

She released a soft breath and laid her hand on Jack's arm. "You keep the guest room. I'll bunk on the sofa."

"I'll take the couch. You're still recuperating." Jack patted her hand, the tension in his muscles easing. "Dinner's on the table. I grabbed takeout from Haley's Barbecue—best beef ribs west of the Mississippi."

The thought of food made her feel ill, but she managed a smile. "Why don't you drive me back to the house and I'll brew up some old-fashioned Southern sweet tea to go with it? Riley can finish up here."

"Wait and let me drive you back," Riley countered.

"Don't you trust me?" Jack shot him a pointed look.

Riley frowned. "Fine. But don't mess around. Go straight home and lock up when you get there."

Jack laid his hand on Hannah's back, gentle pressure guiding her out with him. They dashed through the rain to his battered Ford F-10 and hurried into the cab.

Jack paused with his hand on the starter. "I know I'm being a big baby about all this. It's just—Riley was the best thing that ever happened to Emily. It's hard even imagining him caring about anyone else the way he loved her, you know?"

Hannah smiled, genuinely this time. "I do understand. And for the record—I think Emily was the best thing that ever happened to him, too. I know he thinks so."

The gratitude in Jack's eyes made her want to cry. "I wish you could have known her."

"I do, too," she admitted.

Emily Patterson must have been one hell of a woman, to have left such a big hole in the lives of men like Jack Drummond and Riley Patterson.

HANNAH HAD THOUGHT SHE'D be relieved by having a room to herself after so much togetherness with Riley over the past couple of days, but she'd found it hard to fall asleep. Every bump, rattle or moan of the wind kept her on edge for most of the night. She fell into a restless sleep around 3:00 a.m., waking around seven thanks to the sound of bootfalls outside her door. Her headache was back, though she suspected the culprit was her sleepless night rather than her concussion, and sometime in the night the fire in her woodstove had died away, leaving the room icy cold.

She dressed in jeans and a dark green sweater, thankful she'd done her homework and packed for the cooler mountain climate. Back home in Alabama, early October was still warm enough to walk around in short sleeves and sandals most days.

She followed the smell of bacon and coffee to the

kitchen and found Jack alone at the stove, cobbling together an omelet. "Good morning," he said over his shoulder.

She mumbled a response and poured a cup of coffee, stirring in a teaspoon of sugar from a canister by the coffeemaker. The brew was hot and strong, just like she liked it. She took her cup back to the table and let it warm her up.

"Want an omelet?"

Now that the coffee was doing the trick, her appetite was kicking in. "Yes, please. Where's Riley?"

"Joe came by early this morning. I think they're out with the horses." Jack flipped an omelet onto a plate and placed it in front of her. "Dig in."

The omelet was excellent, and she told him so.

"Don't sound so surprised," he said mildly.

"I just figured a rodeo cowboy wouldn't have much time to hone his culinary skills."

"Oh, there's plenty of downtime. And rodeo pay is pretty unpredictable, so you learn to get by without a lot of the perks." He finished off his double omelet quickly, downing it with two cups of coffee. "I'm getting too old for it."

"Thinking about settling down?" she teased, expecting him to quickly deny it.

But he didn't. "I've lost too much time with people I love while I was chasing rodeos around the country. Maybe if I'd been here—"

She reached across the table and covered his hand with hers. "From what I understand, there's not much anyone could have done, except stop the killer first."

He turned his palm up, squeezing her hand with a

grateful half smile. "You're right. I know you are. I just—"

He fell quiet when the kitchen door opened and Riley entered, Joe Garrison bringing up the rear.

Riley's eyes narrowed slightly as he saw Hannah's hand in Jack's. Hannah ignored the urge to jerk her hand away, letting Jack remove his hand first.

"Anything new?" she asked, directing the question to Joe. Riley crossed silently to the coffeemaker and poured a cup.

Joe sat next to her, laying a thick folder on the table. "Maybe. We're not sure." He opened the folder and handed her a photocopy of a driver's license. "Does this man look familiar?"

The man in question was Dale Morton, age 44, with a home address in Moran, Wyoming. He had sandy-brown hair and, according to the information on the license, brown eyes, though it was hard to tell that from the photo. He was average-looking, maybe a little on the beefy side.

She shook her head. "But I didn't see his face."

"As far as you remember." Riley had remained standing to drink his coffee, leaning against the counter. He continued to watch her through narrowed eyes.

It was starting to annoy her.

"Who is this guy?"

"He's a security guard at the hospital. He was on duty the night you were admitted, but he was off duty earlier in the day. He also worked at the hospital in Casper where Emily was working when she was murdered," Riley answered.

Jack reached across the table to take the photo

from Hannah's hands. "You think this is the guy who killed Em?"

"We don't know," Joe warned quickly. "We were looking for links, and that one turned up."

"It's the only link between the two hospitals among the Jackson Memorial security staff," Riley added.

"What if it wasn't someone in security?" Hannah asked. "I mean, we don't know that it wasn't someone on the medical staff. Whoever it was sure seemed to know his way around an IV tube."

"We started with security because of the tampered surveillance recording," Joe said. "We're looking at the medical staff, too."

"Joe just wanted to pass this one by you, see if he jogged your memory at all."

She looked up at Jack. He handed her the photo again, and she gave it another look. "I think the build could probably fit." Though she'd seen little more than the man's midsection, he'd been on the bigger side. Not overweight, exactly, but thick waisted and on the burly side.

"I'll tell Sheriff Tanner. Maybe we can connect him to some of the other crime scenes." Joe took the photo from her and put it back in the file.

"Nothing yet on the belt buckle?" she asked.

"No, but we've got people from three different agencies out there looking," Joe assured her. He picked up the file and stood. "I've got to get to the office. I'll call later if anything new comes up." He let himself out.

"There's an omelet for you in the pan on the stove," Jack told Riley.

Riley made a grunting sound in response and grabbed a clean plate from the drying rack by the sink.

He transferred the omelet to the plate, took the seat Joe had vacated and started eating without a word.

Jack caught Hannah's eye, lifting one eyebrow.

She shrugged.

"If you're going to talk about me, do it aloud," Riley said, setting his fork down by his plate.

"Bad morning out at the stable?" Jack asked innocently.

"No, everything's fine. I just didn't sleep well."

"I didn't, either," Hannah admitted. "The coffee helped."

Riley looked at her, his expression softening. "You didn't have to get up so early."

"I don't want to sleep away what time I have left here in Wyoming. I feel like I haven't accomplished anything."

"You have," he assured her. "We may not find the guy before you leave, but you've already given us leads we didn't have before."

"I wish I could remember more details. Maybe something about the car, or his voice or—something."

Riley finished his omelet and washed it down with the rest of his coffee. "Actually, I thought about that while I was trying to go to sleep. I think we may have been doing the wrong things to try to jog your memory."

"What do you mean?"

"The only thing you've really remembered was the belt buckle. And that happened when you weren't actually trying to remember, right?"

She nodded, her cheeks growing warm as she remembered the intimacy of that moment, alone in Riley's bedroom. He'd been sitting there watching her, close enough to touch.

"It gave me an idea." Riley's voice took on a dark, warm color that left her with no doubt that he also remembered that moment between them. He held out his hand, his gaze challenging her to take it.

She put her hand in his and rose from the table.

"Jack, you don't mind cleaning up, do you?" Riley didn't wait for an answer, closing his fingers around Hannah's and leading her to the back door. He reached into the mudroom and grabbed their jackets off the hooks, letting go of her hand just long enough to help her into her coat.

Taking her hand again, he led her outside.

"Feel like a little exercise?" he asked, waving toward a wooden post to the right of the door, where Jazz and Bella stood, saddled and a little restless, breath rising from their nostrils in wispy curls of white.

She grinned, her mood immediately lightening. "We're going riding?"

"You bet." He handed her Bella's reins, and she pulled herself up in the saddle. The chestnut mare nickered softly, her muscles twitching as if eager for a good run.

Riley mounted Jazz and took the lead, guiding the horses through an open gate toward the pasture beyond the stables. Once they were out in the pasture, he gave Jazz a swift nudge in the side and the shiny black gelding sprinted ahead, hitting a full, joyous gallop in a matter of seconds.

Excitement flowing like blood in her veins, Hannah urged Bella into a run and flew across the pasture in pursuit.

"THAT DOES IT," SHE SAID LATER, watching the horses grazing a short distance away, their coats glistening with a light sweat after the morning run. "We're definitely adding trail rides to the Cooper Cove Outdoor Experience."

Riley had led them to the upper reaches of the pasture, where the grassland met the foot of Sawyer's Rise. Flat, wide boulders dotted the area, providing a dry place to sit after the exhilarating ride.

"You're a good rider." Riley settled next to her on the boulder rather than finding his own seat on one of the nearby rocks, though her choice of seats was barely big enough for two. She didn't know whether to be glad for his warmth or worried by the sudden acceleration of her pulse.

"I'm no cowgirl." She smiled to cover her sudden nerves. "Bella's a great horse."

"She likes you." He reached up and combed his fingers through her tousled hair. "We need to find you a hat."

She closed her eyes, trying hard not to lean into his light touch. She might as well stop kidding herself— she was halfway over the moon about this guy, and all the self-lectures in the world wouldn't do a damned bit of good.

So what if they'd be parting ways forever in just a few days? People had vacation flings all the time. Would it really be so wrong to enjoy whatever there was between them, even if she knew it could never last? Once she got home, she could file it away as a nice memory, to take out now and then and remember with fondness.

Couldn't she?

Riley's fingers crept lower, moving gently against

the muscles of her neck. "How's your head? Any more pain or dizziness?"

"No," she answered. The headache she'd awakened with was long gone, banished by the invigorating ride. She felt better than she had since the attack. "You don't have to treat me like an invalid anymore. I really feel fine now."

He shifted until his legs were on either side of her and added his other hand to the neck massage. "I wouldn't have brought you riding with me if I didn't know that."

Giving up her resistance, she relaxed back against his chest and gave herself permission to enjoy being close to him.

"Too bad we don't have a deck of cards with us," he murmured in her ear. "We could play another game of smackpop."

"Popsmack," she corrected with a chuckle. "We don't need cards—we could just take turns. You can start. Ask me anything."

"Anything?"

She nodded. "Except how much I weigh."

"I already know. I peeked at your hospital chart."

She groaned. "Completely unfair."

He tugged at her hair. "Can I ask a question or not?"

She sighed and settled back against him. "Shoot."

"Does the Crappie Queen have to wear a crown?"

She nudged him with her elbow. "Smart aleck."

"And maybe one of those—what do you call it— sashes?"

"It wasn't like I was in a pageant or anything," she protested. "I'm just the best crappie fisherman on Gossamer Lake. I know where all the little suckers are hiding, no matter what time of year."

She felt his lips nuzzle her earlobe. "Do you wear little shorts when you fish?"

"Only in the summer," she murmured, moving her head to make it easier for him to keep doing whatever amazing thing it was he was doing to the side of her neck. "And that's two questions."

"Sorry. Your turn."

She pondered what to ask, not wanting anything to shatter this perfect moment of contentment. She could keep it light, she supposed, like he had. Something he could answer yes or no, so he wouldn't have to remove his lips from the side of her neck for long.

Before she had a chance to speak, however, Riley's cell phone rang. Relaxation was over; Riley stood, stepping around the boulder as he answered. "Hey, Joe, what's up?"

As he listened to Joe's response, his expression darkened. He shot a quick look at Hannah. "We'll be right there."

"What's happened?" she asked when he rang off.

His expression went grim. "Someone's leaked your name to the press."

THE FIRST FLUSH OF ALARM had passed quickly on the ride back to the house, settling into a low-level sense of tension by the time she and Riley found Joe waiting in the den.

Joe didn't waste time on the niceties. "A reporter from a Casper TV station who works out of Jackson Hole broke the story. They have your name and some of the details of the attack."

"How?" Riley asked tersely.

"He says an anonymous source, but it almost has to

be someone from the hospital. I think Jim Tanner runs too tight a ship for it to be anyone from his department."

"Could have been an EMT," Riley suggested. "They were first on the scene, had access to her driver's license. Someone could have greased somebody's palm."

"Why is it even a story?" Hannah asked, torn between anxiety and confusion. "I'm nobody famous. I didn't even get hurt that much."

"You're a tourist," Joe answered. "If someone's out there attacking tourists, this close to two national parks—"

"It's news," Hannah finished for him.

"How much do they know about the attack?" Riley asked.

"Less than we do. No mention of the cop-car angle, and of course, nobody's connected it to any of the other murders, although I'm beginning to think it's only a matter of time before someone puts two and two together and realizes that the murder at Grand Teton is connected."

"That's odd, isn't it?" Something tugged at the back of her mind. "The anonymous source didn't think to add the part about the fake cop car. I mean, that would be a pretty sensational detail to omit."

"Maybe the leaker didn't know that detail," Joe said.

"Or he didn't want the press to know," Hannah replied.

Both men turned to look at her.

"What if the killer is the one who leaked the information?" she asked.

Riley's expression darkened. "To flush you out?"

"Using the press to do it," Joe added.

"Half the town knows Hannah's here by now," Riley said in alarm. "We need to move her somewhere else."

"No," Hannah said firmly. An idea was clicking into place in her brain, perfect and terrible.

"No?" Riley looked at her as if she'd lost her mind.

"He wants to flush me out, right?"

"Looks that way," Riley agreed warily.

She lifted her chin. "Then let him."

CHAPTER ELEVEN

RILEY TURNED ABRUPTLY toward Hannah, ceasing his rapid pacing. The stubborn set of her jaw, which he generally found appealing, had started to get on his nerves over the last half hour, as he and Joe had tried in vain to talk her out of her dangerous, hare-brained idea. "That's it. You're not doing it. Discussion over."

Next to him, Joe took a deep, swift breath. He gave Riley a warning look that Riley ignored.

"You're not my keeper," Hannah retorted, crossing closer and coming to a stop in front of him. Her eyes blazed with green fire. "You don't order me around."

Riley looked over at Joe, completely at a loss. "Tell her it's a bad idea."

"I've spent the last thirty minutes doing just that," Joe reminded him. "But she's right. It's her choice. Even if it's wrong," he added sternly, giving Hannah a look of pure frustration.

"I don't have a lot of time left to help you catch this guy, and I don't know how I'm supposed to go back to my nice, safe life in Alabama if I don't do everything I can to stop that monster from killing another woman." Her expression softened, her green eyes pleading with Riley to understand. "Emily would do the same thing, wouldn't she?"

He pressed his lips together, biting back a harsher

retort. "That's below the belt, Hannah." He slanted a look at Joe, who got the message and headed out of the den to give them some privacy.

Her expression softened more. "I'm sorry. I just need you to understand."

He closed his hands around her arms, desperate to make her see what she was asking of him. "I understand. But I don't think you do."

"I lost Emily three years ago this week," he said, trying not to let too much of his emotion spill over into his words. He wasn't looking for her pity. He wanted her to understand the stakes. "She wasn't doing anything crazy, just driving home from work, and suddenly she just wasn't there anymore. Everything we'd built together was gone, in a heartbeat."

She lifted her hand to his face, her palm warm and soft against his jaw. "I'm sorry."

"I don't want you to be sorry. I want you to see that I don't need this bastard to kill someone else I care about."

Moisture pooled in her eyes. "I don't think it has to be that risky," she answered. "Listen—we already know he's taking more risks than he usually does, or he wouldn't have killed the woman near Moran. I'm the one who got away, and it's driving him crazy."

She took his hand in hers, drawing him with her to the sofa. They sat together, silent for a minute, as if they'd mutually agreed to let their passions cool so they could talk more reasonably.

She folded his hand between hers, her grip gentle but firm. "He's the one who's out of control. If he really did tip off the press, he's the one taking a risk. The reporter he talked to knows who he is."

"He's not going to burn his source."

"It doesn't matter. It was still a risk, and the killer took it because he can't stand that I'm the one who got away. I'm the one who was smarter than he was. That's how he sees it. He can't let that stand."

"What makes you think we can do this thing safely?"

"We hold all the cards. We know he's after me. We're on alert. He's the one taking stupid chances."

Riley pulled his hand away from hers and stood. "No. It's not worth the risk." He paced away from her, a bleak resolve stiffening his back. No way in hell would he let her put herself in the kind of danger she was talking about. There was only one choice left. One he hated more than he ever imagined he would. But it was the best way to keep her safe.

He turned and took in the sight of her slowly, thoroughly. Committing her to memory. When he spoke, his voice was tinged with regret but full of calm resolve.

"It's time for you to go home, Hannah."

"YOU'RE GOING TO LEAVE A MARK." Jack took the grooming brush from Hannah's hand and patted Bella's side. They were alone in the stable; Joe and Riley were back at the house, talking about new strategies for going after the killer without Hannah's involvement.

She'd made her escape to the stable soon after Riley's calm announcement that her time in Wyoming was over, using the horses as an excuse to get away from him before she said something she'd regret.

"He's not trying to get rid of you, you know."

She knew. She'd seen the regret in Riley's eyes. Somehow that only made things worse.

"And for what it's worth, I think you're right about

talking to the press." Jack handed the brush back to her. "If we have a chance to catch that monster—"

Hannah touched his arm, knowing that his need to catch the killer was even greater than her own.

"What are you going to do now?" A thoughtful look darkened Jack's eyes.

"I don't know," she admitted, trading the grooming brush for a mane comb. "I don't have a death wish, but I don't have a lot of time left here. I just don't think I can leave without doing all I can to help stop this guy from killing again."

"I'll help you, if you want to do it." Jack's dark gaze met hers. "I know a guy with the paper in Jackson. I can set up an interview with him. He's a good guy—he won't take advantage. He'll agree to whatever precautions we think are necessary to keep you safe."

"Riley will be furious with you."

"I'm a big boy. Besides, I'm faster than he is. He'd have to catch me."

Hannah chuckled softly. "How quickly could you set it up?" Time was too short as it was.

"I can call him right now." Jack pulled his cell phone from his pocket. "You want to do it?"

She nibbled her lip, doubts creeping in now that the moment of decision was at hand. Was Riley's idea the better choice? Should she grab the next flight out of Wyoming and return home to the safety of her family, even if it meant turning her back on the best chance to catch Emily's killer that might ever come Riley's way?

The thought of Riley Patterson spending the rest of his life entrapped by his need for justice made the decision for her. "Let's do it," she said, meeting Jack's questioning eyes. "Call your friend."

"YOU'RE NOT SAYING YOU THINK she's right, are you?" Riley whipped around and gave his friend a look of disbelief.

"No, that's not what I'm saying." Joe held his hands up defensively. "At least, not exactly."

Riley slumped into the armchair, frustrated. If it were anyone but Hannah, would he be trying to stop her? On the merits, her idea was solid. The killer *was* getting bold—and therefore sloppy. There had probably never been a better time to take the offense against him.

But the thought of letting that bastard near Hannah, even if it made him a sitting duck, made his blood run cold.

Losing Emily had almost killed him. If Hannah died, too...

"How about a compromise?" Joe asked. "No making her a target—but she sticks around for the rest of her vacation."

"She's too easy to trace to me."

"So take her out of town. She wanted to see Grand Teton—I'll get Jim Tanner to book you a couple of rooms in Jackson Hole and you can do the tourist thing. Maybe she can relax a little, remember something new—"

"That just puts her closer to the killer's hunting grounds."

"Are you in love with her?"

Riley looked up sharply. "What kind of question is that?"

"It's not a crime to fall in love again." The gentleness in Joe's voice only made Riley angrier.

"Hannah Cooper is here only because I hoped she would remember something else about the attack on her," Riley said with a firmness he didn't feel. "I think she's remembered all she can, so it's time for her to go home."

"Good to know," Hannah said quietly from the doorway to the den. She met Riley's startled gaze with moist green eyes.

"Hannah—"

She turned and walked down the hall toward her room.

The look Joe gave Riley was as hard as a punch. "Who are you trying to impress with your loner act, Riley? Emily?" Joe stood and paced angrily to the doorway, turning to deliver one last shot. "Emily would hate what you're becoming." He walked out without another word.

Riley leaned forward in the armchair, resting his aching head in his hands. He hadn't cried since Emily's funeral, but hot tears gathered in his eyes right now, stinging painfully. He blinked them back, refusing to give in to the weakness. Anger, not grief, was what kept him upright these days. He couldn't afford to fall apart.

Not now, when he was closer than he'd ever been to finally catching the man who'd stolen the best part of his life.

"HE DIDN'T MEAN IT LIKE it sounded." Jack took the shirt out of Hannah's suitcase and put it back on the bed with the other shirts stacked there. "I've known him longer than you have. I know when he cares about someone. He cares about you."

She snatched the shirt back from the stack and shoved it into the suitcase. "I know he cares about me. But not enough to keep me here."

"Are you in love with him?"

She glared at Jack. "I'm not stupid."

"That's not an answer."

"Yes, it is." She punctuated the statement by slamming a pair of socks into the suitcase.

"It's not stupid to love someone."

She slumped to the bed. "It is if that someone is in love with someone else."

Jack cocked his head, his eyes narrowing. "We're not talking about Riley anymore, are we?"

"Not entirely," she admitted.

Jack leaned back on the bed, propping himself up with his elbows. "So tell Dr. Jack all about it."

She rolled her eyes at him, not wanting to be amused. But his humor was contagious, and her lips crooked slightly in response. "A week ago, this was all just a pitiful memory I was mostly over," she started. "I mean, it was four years ago, and it ended the way it was supposed to end—"

"With some other woman getting the guy?"

"He was always hers. She was his first love, and neither of them really got over it. I thought I loved him enough for both of us." She buried her face in her hands, mortified by the memory of her foolishness. "I was such an idiot."

"I've seen bigger idiots, trust me." Jack looked at her with sympathy. "How far did it get?"

She flushed with embarrassment. "The bachelor party."

Jack winced. "That far, huh?"

She lifted her chin, finding the steel at her center even though her heart was breaking a little. "I know Riley's not going to suddenly get over Emily just because he met me. I'm not going to fool myself into thinking otherwise. Does that answer your question?"

"No," he said with a smile. "But, that's not even the most important question anymore. Are you going back home?"

She shook her head. "I have three more days of vacation left, and I have an interview with a reporter."

"That's the spirit."

"But I am leaving here," she added, reaching for the stack of shirts again.

"I don't think you should."

"Riley's decided I should leave."

"I'm asking you to stay," he countered stubbornly. "You can stay as my guest."

"It's Riley's house."

"He'll cool down and see reason," Jack said confidently. "As long as you don't tell him about the press interview."

"You think I should lie to him?"

"I think you should just not tell him." Jack reached into the suitcase and started removing the clothing she'd already packed. "Mark Archibald's meeting us at Kent's Steakhouse at five. I'll tell Riley you need time to cool off and I'm taking you out for dinner. That's not a lie, right?"

Hannah had to smile a little at that, remembering how Riley had tried to keep the lies they were telling Jack as close to the truth as possible. They were more like brothers than either of them realized. "No, it's not a lie," she agreed. "We are going to dinner and I do need time to cool off."

And maybe, once the plan was in action, Riley would see why it was the only real choice she'd had.

THE INTERVIEW WITH THE reporter went as well as she could have hoped. Mark Archibald was friendly, funny and sympathetic. He asked good questions, which she answered as honestly as she could, while keeping a few of the details to herself, like the silver belt buckle and the fact that the killer had worn latex gloves when he attacked. She knew the police liked to keep some things back, in case they got a call from someone claiming to be the killer.

She made it clear, however, that there was more she remembered that she wasn't telling. She hoped Mark would make that fact just as clear in his article. She had to make herself as tempting to the killer as possible.

"It'll be in the paper tomorrow morning," Jack said on the drive back. He seemed jittery and energized, as if the cloak and dagger game they were playing had brought him to life. That definitely wasn't how Riley had reacted to lying, she remembered. Maybe he and Jack weren't so alike, after all.

"You need to calm down or Riley will know something's up," she suggested.

He grinned. "I know. I just—I think it's going to work. I think it's going to smoke this freak out and get a little justice for Em."

"And for the other women, too," Hannah added soberly.

His grin faded. "For the other women, too." He parked his truck next to Riley's in the yard. "I'm going to go feed the horses. You go on in."

"Coward," she said, but lightly, because it probably wasn't a good idea for Riley to see Jack as wound up as he was right now. Riley would wonder what his brother-in-law was up to.

She went into the house alone, not certain what she'd find. The kitchen was empty, though he'd left the light on over the sink so she wouldn't be entering into darkness. The hallway was dark, but a light shone in the guest room.

She entered her room to find Riley sitting on the bed, holding the sweater she'd left lying on her bed when she'd changed clothes for dinner with Jack and the reporter.

He looked up at her, his expression calm and regretful. "I didn't tell Joe the truth," he said.

She stopped at the rocking chair near the woodstove and sat, folding her hands on her lap. She held his gaze, waiting for him to elaborate. She wasn't sure what she wanted to hear from him—the blunt, harsh truth or some half-baked pointless apology. Either way, it was going to hurt.

"I'm not just using you to find Emily's murderer. I do care about whether or not you get hurt." He bent forward, his forearms resting on his knees. He looked as bone-weary as she felt. "The last three years have been hard."

"Sounds like an understatement," she murmured.

His pain-darkened eyes lifted to meet hers. "I used to be a very different man. I wasn't driven, I wasn't focused. I just enjoyed life as it came. Rode out whatever happened, not worrying too much about it. I had my health, I had my friends, I had Emily."

She didn't want to think about how much his description of his former life matched her own. Despite the broken heart she'd told Jack about, her life had been pretty good. Pretty easy. She'd done well in school, never having to struggle to achieve. Surrounded by a loving, happy family and the friends she'd grown up with, she'd gone to college just as planned, took a job at the Marina because it was what she'd always assumed she'd do.

What in her life had ever been a struggle before now?

"I sometimes think Joe just sticks around out of stubbornness. I'm a terrible friend to him. He and Jane were in a dangerous mess a couple of years ago, and I barely managed to pull my head out of my backside enough to give them a hand right about the time it was all over." He looked away, his face flushed with shame. "My other friends gave up a long time ago. I keep telling my parents I'm fine, but they know. They just don't know what to do about it."

"It's hard to know what to say to someone who's hurting," she said, thinking about her brother J.D., who was, at least, lucky enough to have his two kids to keep him putting one foot in front of the other every day.

"It's not their fault. It's mine." He briefly pressed his palms against his temples, then dropped his hands to his knees. "I've pushed people away because it took all the energy I had to keep going, keep focusing on finding out who killed Emily and those other women. I can't—I can't let other things matter."

His voice faltered, the words trembling on his tongue. She wanted to go to him, pull him into her arms and share the burden, but he clearly wasn't ready for that.

Might never be ready.

"But you matter," he said finally, so softly that she almost missed it. He looked up at her, his eyes blazing blue fire. "You matter."

He lurched off the bed, towering over her for a long, breathless moment, then bent and put his hands on the rocking chair arms, leaning close enough that she felt his breath warm on her cheeks. "You can't put yourself at any further risk. Do you understand? If something happened to you—"

Tears burned her eyes and spilled down her cheeks as he pulled her to her feet and into his embrace. His mouth descended on hers, fiery sweet and urgent. She wrapped her arms around his neck, pulling him closer, needing the heat of him against her trembling body. Guilt mingled with desire as she struggled to find the center of her suddenly upended world.

He edged her toward the bed, turning and falling until she lay beneath him, her back against the mattress. He drew back long enough to cradle her head between his hands and gaze down at her with a question in his eyes.

Her body screamed for him to keep touching her, keep kissing her, to fill the aching, empty places inside her. But her mind was dark with regret, because she'd already set into motion something that would put her in much more danger, the one thing he'd just begged her not to do.

"Stop," she said softly as he bent to kiss her again.

Riley went still, gazing at her with suddenly wary eyes. She felt the rapid drumbeat of his heart against her chest.

"I talked to a reporter tonight," she confessed.

CHAPTER TWELVE

RILEY FROZE, HANNAH'S admission washing over him like ice water. His arms trembled as he hovered over her, trying to process what he'd just heard.

"I told him some of what happened to me." The words spilled from Hannah's lips in an inflectionless rush. "I held back most of the details—the belt buckle, the latex gloves. But I mentioned that my attacker posed as a cop. And I made it clear that I remembered more than I was telling the reporter."

He rolled away from her, sitting up with his back to her. Cold, hard fear settled in his gut as a dozen terrifying outcomes rattled through his brain like a horrible slide show.

What had she done?

"I'm sorry," she said, regret threaded through her voice. "I thought I had to do something to push things forward. I have so little time left before I have to go back home."

If she even made it home alive, he thought bleakly. "You shouldn't have done that." His voice came out hard and strangled.

She didn't answer.

"How did you get in touch with a reporter?"

She couldn't answer that question without implicating Jack. She hedged instead. "Does it matter? It was my choice to do it."

He looked inclined to probe deeper, but to her relief, he just sighed and asked, "Can we stop it?"

"No. He was writing and filing the story as soon as he got back to the office. It's probably already on the press."

He pushed to his feet, not ready to give up. He pulled out his cell phone. "Who was the reporter?"

"I don't even remember the paper—it's a daily out of Jackson. The reporter's name is Mark Archibald." She caught his arm, tugging him around to look at her. "I don't think we should stop it, Riley."

Her chin was up, her jaw squared. A sinking feeling settled in his gut, and he shook off her hand. "Like hell." He flipped open the phone and dialed the number for Teton County Sheriff Jim Tanner.

Tanner answered on the second ring. "Jim Tanner."

"Sheriff Tanner, it's Riley Patterson." Not waiting for the chief's response, he tersely outlined what Hannah had told him about her meeting with the Jackson reporter. "Can you get the story killed?"

After a brief pause, Jim Tanner answered, "No."

"Why the hell not?"

"The First Amendment comes to mind," Tanner answered in a dry drawl. "Also, we're doing a disservice to the communities we serve by holding back on this any longer."

Riley couldn't believe what he was hearing. "This article will put Hannah Cooper's life in greater danger."

"And not running it will put the lives of women all over Wyoming in greater danger," Tanner countered firmly. "Hannah Cooper has a cop playing bodyguard for her twenty-four hours a day. Those other women don't even know the flashing blue light in their rear-view mirrors could mean their lives are over."

Riley slumped against the bedroom wall, reason starting to gain on the galloping fear eating away at his insides. They'd only sat on the story this long to give Hannah time to remember more before they went public. But the women of Wyoming were sitting ducks with no idea what might be lurking out there to snuff out their lives. They didn't know what to look for or how to protect themselves.

He closed his eyes. "Okay. It runs."

He heard Hannah release a slow, shaky breath. Opening his eyes, he found her watching him with eyes bright with tears.

"I should probably schedule a press conference once the story breaks," Tanner added, a hint of weary resignation tinting his voice. "Want to be part of it?"

"Hold on a sec." Riley covered the mouthpiece. "Is the reporter going to say anything about where you're staying?" he asked Hannah.

"No," she answered. "The idea for this story was to get the killer's attention and get him thinking about me again, instead of going on the hunt for another woman."

He saw the fear lurking like a vulture behind her eyes, but the brave determination in her voice inspired his admiration. He might be mad as hell that she'd put her life on the line, but he had gained a new respect for her courage.

"Keep me out of it," he told Tanner. Having him there might provide the killer with a clue where to look for Hannah.

"Okay," Tanner agreed. "I'll see if I can get an early

look at what the paper's going to run with. If I can, want me to fax you a copy?"

"Fax it to the police department." He gave Jim Tanner the station's fax number. "Joe will get it to me."

He rang off, shoving his phone in his pocket. "Tanner thinks it should run," he told Hannah.

"What do you think?" she asked.

He released a long, slow breath, trying to answer with his head instead of his gut. "I think the women of Wyoming should know there's someone out there pretending to be a cop, pulling them over, abducting and killing them."

The corners of her lip twitched briefly, though the relief didn't quite make it to her eyes. "I'm sorry I blindsided you with it."

"I'd have been more blindsided if I'd opened the paper in the morning and found you on page one," he admitted. "I appreciate the heads-up."

Uncertainty flitted across her face, but he didn't know how to reassure her. He wasn't sure he even wanted to. The danger surrounding her was about to grow exponentially thanks to one small newspaper story, and he found himself wanting to retreat, to save himself from the torment he knew might be coming.

What if he couldn't keep her safe?

He was already half a man, thanks to losing Emily. If something happened to Hannah, would there be anything left?

"I need to go lock up for the night. We'll talk in the morning." He rose to go.

Behind him, he heard her take a quick breath, as if she had something to say. But he didn't turn back to look at her, and she didn't speak, so he closed the door behind him and went out to wait for Jack.

THE WOMAN STARING AT HANNAH in the mirror looked like crap. Purple shadows bruised the skin beneath her eyes, dark against her pale cheeks. Her body still buzzed with unsatisfied hunger, but her heart felt as hard and cold as a rock.

Riley had left the bedroom only moments ago, but he'd distanced himself from her long before he closed the door. She'd watched it happen, saw his expression shutter and the light in his eyes blink out.

He'd had too much pain in his life already. And she'd just asked him to take a chance on a whole lot more.

No wonder he'd walked away.

It was bittersweet, knowing that Riley really did care about her. Maybe not enough to build a relationship on, but she supposed it was something she could take home with her, like a secret souvenir, to bring out now and then to remember what it was like to be wrapped up tight in Riley's arms.

But would that be enough? Could she go home, never to return, and be content with nothing but a memory?

WHEN JACK CAME BACK FROM the stable, Riley was waiting for him. Jack didn't even have time to say hello before Riley pushed him against the door.

"You went behind my back and called a reporter in."

Jack's expression went from puzzled to guilty. "Hannah told you."

"No, but *you* should have."

He sighed. "I'm sorry. But someone needed to do something, and you were about to pack Hannah off to

Alabama rather than listen to what she was trying to tell you. She *wanted* to talk to Mark."

"Because she feels guilty about being the one who got away. You know how that feels, Jack."

Jack blanched, and Riley felt a little ashamed of himself. But it was the truth, however harsh. One of the things that tied him and Jack together, now that Emily was gone, was good old-fashioned guilt.

He was a cop, Jack was a rodeo cowboy. They were the ones with dangerous lives, not Emily, who'd been the nurturer. The healer. And yet, she'd been the one to go too early. Either one of them would have traded places with her in a heartbeat.

Jack gave Riley a little push out of his way. "I know something else, Riley. I know what it feels like to need to make things right." He crossed to the kitchen sink, fiddled with the cups drying on the rack, and finally just rested his hands on the counter, his head dropping to his chest. "Hannah's time here is almost over, and she feels she hasn't done anything to get you any closer to catching that bastard. It's been eating her up."

"You think I didn't notice?" Riley challenged, growing angrier by the second.

Jack turned slowly to look at him. "Did you? Sometimes I think the only thing you see these days is your own pain."

Riley flexed his fingers, longing to drive his fist into the stubborn set of Jack's square jaw. He forced himself to stay where he was, needing distance to get a grip on himself.

"It's not me you're angry at," Jack added.

"Wrong," Riley snapped. "It's not just that you set

up the meeting, though that's bad enough. It's that you didn't have the guts to be a man and tell me about it."

"You would have stopped it."

"That's an excuse for lying?"

"I did what I thought I had to do," Jack answered. "For Hannah—and for Emily."

A thread of dark pain turned Riley's anger into weary resignation. "I trusted you with Hannah's safety and you put her in danger. How am I supposed to trust you after that?"

Jack looked as if Riley had slapped him. "I guess you can't." He turned on his heel and headed out of the kitchen.

Riley followed him into the den. "I have enough to deal with, just keeping Hannah safe, and what the two of you did is only going to make things harder." He realized Jack was starting to pack his bag. "Going somewhere?"

"I don't stay where I'm not wanted."

Riley sighed. "Where would you go?"

Jack glared at him over his shoulder. "I didn't come here to mooch. I came here because this was Emily's home. I have enough money to rent a motel room for a few days."

"Then what?"

"That's my business." Jack stuffed the last pair of jeans into his bag and started past Riley.

"Jack—" Riley went after him, catching his arm at the door. Down the hallway, the door to Hannah's room opened, and she stepped halfway into the hall, her eyes meeting his.

"Is something wrong?" she asked.

Jack set his bag on the floor and walked toward her. "I'm heading out."

Hannah looked down at the bag, her brow wrinkling with dismay. "You're leaving?"

"Just like a tumbleweed, sweetheart." Jack patted her cheek. "It's been great meeting you, Hannah Cooper. If I'm ever in Alabama, I'll look you up."

Hannah followed him into the kitchen, with Riley on her heels. "What's going on?"

"Riley's had his fill of me, I think."

"That's not what I said," Riley insisted.

"If this is about the reporter, that was my doing, Riley!" Hannah grabbed his arm, desperation in her eyes. "Jack did what I asked him to do. Please—"

"I didn't tell him to leave," he said weakly.

"Did you tell him to stay?" she countered, her eyes flashing with fire. "If anyone leaves, it should be me. It was my idea. I'm the outsider."

"Stop it, Hannah." Jack put his hand on her shoulder. "It's time. This just gives me an excuse to make a dramatic exit." When he looked up at Riley, his dark eyes were warm with understanding. "I'm just hiding out here anyway because I don't want to face what I left behind in Texas."

If Riley knew his brother-in-law at all, what he left behind in Texas was a broken heart.

"I need to see if I can fix what I broke," Jack added softly.

That was a first, Riley thought. Maybe the kid really had started to grow up this time.

"I'm not kicking you out," he said aloud, not because he thought it would soften the resolve he saw in Jack's eyes, but because it needed to be said.

"I know." As Hannah stepped aside, Jack stepped forward and held out his hand.

Riley took it, giving it a firm, warm shake. "At least stay the night. Where are you going to find a motel that'll take you in this time of night?"

"You'd be surprised." Jack grinned wryly. "But don't worry—I ran into an old friend yesterday while I was out. He said I could come visit whenever, so I'm taking him up on it."

"Need any money?"

Jack laughed softly. "No, but thanks for offering."

Riley glanced at Hannah, who still looked upset. He wished he could reassure her that everything was okay, but it would take forever to try to explain the complexities of his relationship with his brother-in-law. He settled for an apologetic smile and put his hand on Jack's shoulder. "I'll walk you out."

Hannah remained inside as they walked out to where Jack's truck was parked. Jack tossed the bag into the passenger seat and turned to Riley. "Take care of yourself, man."

Riley pulled Jack into a hug. "You, too. I hope you can fix whatever you left broken down in Texas."

"I hope you can fix what you've broken here." Jack stepped back and gave Riley a smile. "You've got three more days, man. She could change your life."

Jack climbed into the truck, shut the door and cranked the engine. He gave a short wave as he backed down the gravel drive, then he was gone.

Riley walked slowly back to the house, Jack's parting words still ringing in his ears. *She could change your life.*

That was the problem wasn't it? His life had already

changed, irrevocably. Since Emily's death, it had become twenty-four hours a day, seven days a week of trying to cope with a world that no longer made any sense.

Yes, Hannah Cooper had been the first person in three years who'd broken through that haze and made him feel something good again. But how much of that was just two young, healthy bodies doing what young, healthy bodies do? How much of what he felt for her was wrapped up in the fact that she was his best break in the case that had haunted him for three years?

She deserved more. She deserved better.

And yet, when he found her waiting there in the kitchen for his return, her green eyes sympathetic, it took all the control he had not to sweep her into his arms and carry her into the nearest bedroom.

"It wasn't his fault."

Riley crossed to the refrigerator and opened it, though he wasn't the least bit hungry. Anything to drag his gaze away from Hannah. "Jack and I are okay. I promise."

"Then why'd he leave?"

"Because I think he realized staying here was just an excuse to hide from his problems." Riley closed the refrigerator, empty-handed.

He supposed the same thing could be said about his own life for the last three years. God knew, he'd buried himself in this investigation as an escape from his own pain, though he couldn't really say he'd been successful.

"I've been hiding here, hiding behind you, for too long," Hannah said. "I have three days left of my vacation, and what have I been doing? I haven't remembered anything new since the belt buckle. I haven't even really tried." She slammed her hand against the table, the sudden sound putting his nerves on hard alert. "I have to do something, Riley."

"You already have," he said, knowing it wasn't going to appease her.

The look she gave him proved him right. "I think I need to do more interviews. Maybe play up the tourist in jeopardy angle. It would get plenty of play, wouldn't it?"

"And draw the killer right to you." The thought made his stomach hurt.

She crossed to stand in front of him, her eyes shining with a manic light. "Exactly."

He shook his head. "No way in hell."

"We could come up with a way to lure him in. Police would be everywhere. I'd be safe."

Everything inside him rebelled. "Hannah, that's crazy. You're letting your frustrations overcome your good sense."

"You're letting your fears overcome your cop instincts," she countered passionately. "If it was you, you'd do it."

"That's different."

"Because I'm a woman?"

"Because I can't—" He bit off the rest of the thought, not ready to say it aloud. Not even to himself.

She took his hand and threaded her fingers through his, gazing up at him with a warm, soft gaze. "Why don't we do this? Let's table the discussion for tonight. We can wait and see how things go tomorrow when the article comes out."

"Okay." He grabbed the reprieve, weary of arguing with her when all he really wanted to do was hold her close, to bury himself in her soft warmth and make the hard, dark world outside the two of them disappear.

"Let's just have a nice, quiet evening, okay?" She tugged his hand, pulling him down the hall to the den. She let go long enough to drop on to the sofa and pat the cushion beside her. "Let's see if we can find a movie on TV. Something funny."

He handed her the remote, content to let her choose. She found something old, in black and white. Cary Grant, Katharine Hepburn and a leopard. He paid little attention to the story, content to listen to Hannah's peals of laughter and the feel of her warm and solid beside him.

Three more days alone in this house with Hannah was a lifetime.

And not nearly long enough.

THE ARTICLE IN THE JACKSON paper was exactly what Hannah had hoped for, although she could tell from the grim look on Riley's face that he thought she'd gone too far.

"Look at it this way," she said as they walked down to the stable after breakfast, "if it grabs the killer's attention, then maybe he won't be out hunting for another woman to kill just to prove a point to us."

"Yeah, he'll just be looking to kill you."

"And you'll be there to stop him," she said firmly, refusing to allow the little knot of terror tap dancing in her belly to win the battle.

"It doesn't always work that way." The stricken tone of Riley's voice caught her by surprise.

"I know," she relented, stopping halfway to the stable to take his hand. He turned to look at her, his eyes shadowy beneath the brim of his hat.

"I've been after this guy for three years. God knows how many more years he's been killing women that we don't even know about." Riley's fingers tightened around hers. "I couldn't stop him from killing those other women." His voice grew a notch fainter. "I didn't stop him from killing Emily."

"How were you supposed to do that?" Hannah asked, torn between wanting to hug him and wanting to shake him. "Drive her to work every day? God, Riley, you sound just like that guy at the gas station!"

Riley's brow wrinkled. "What guy at the gas station?"

Hannah blinked, surprised by the question, until she realized she'd never mentioned the man she'd run into at the gas station on Highway 287. In fact, until this moment, she hadn't remembered him at all. "He was at the other pump—at that station on 287. He was filling up his car, and he saw the rental-car plate. Said I was brave to drive around all by myself in a strange place. Only, I could tell he really meant I was stupid to be traveling alone."

"Did he say anything else?"

She shook her head. "I don't think so. He finished by then and drove off."

"Did you get a good look at him?"

"Not really—there was a pump between us, and he had a hat on, and sunglasses." She frowned. "You think he might be the guy who pulled me over?"

"I don't know. Was he in a car or a truck?"

"A car." It had been a dark sedan, but beyond that, she couldn't really remember anything. "I guess it could have been the same car. I really don't remember much but the flashing blue light, to be honest."

He laid his palm against her cheek. "It's something new. Joe's got someone going through the receipts from the gas station. If he paid with a credit or debit card, we'll know who he is soon." He dropped his hand and headed for the stable.

She followed, her mind reeling. Had she actually spoken to the killer that day at the gas station?

Had that one simple exchange marked her for death?

CHAPTER THIRTEEN

"WE FOUND HANNAH'S credit-card receipt from the Lassiter station, and a few others sprinkled through the day, but nothing right around the same time." Joe Garrison gave Riley an apologetic look. "Guy must've paid cash."

"Damn it," Riley growled, slanting a look at Hannah, who sat in one of the armchairs in front of Joe's desk. She'd been so hopeful on the drive into town, but now she looked as if Joe had kicked her right in the teeth.

"What if it was him?" she asked faintly. "I can't even tell you what color hair he had, or what shape his face was. Why didn't I pay more attention?"

"Because you weren't expecting some nosy guy at the gas station to track you and try to kill you," Joe said sensibly.

"And we don't even know if it's the same guy," Riley added, laying his hand on her shoulder. He soothed her tense muscles beneath his palm and turned back to Joe. "Has Jim Tanner held his press conference yet?"

Joe glanced at the wall clock. "It's supposed to start in about twenty minutes."

More waiting, Riley thought. Hannah's growing impatience was contagious.

"What about security video?" Hannah asked suddenly. "Don't most places like that have cameras trained on the gas islands to discourage gas theft?"

"The Lassiter station's security video hasn't worked in over a year," Joe answered. "Population is so low in Wyoming, people here don't take the same precautions you find in other states. It's just not a big problem, most of the time."

"I bet he knew it, too," Hannah said glumly. "This guy seems to be a step or two ahead of us."

"He's clearly a local," Riley agreed.

"He wore gloves, so no fingerprints. He moved fast before I even got a look at his face, so I can't ID him. Even at the gas station, I never got a good look at him. Now that I think about it, he was careful not to turn his face toward me." She looked up at Riley. "Maybe he was already in hunting mode."

It was possible, he conceded. "Did anybody find out who was working that shift at the Lassiter station? Maybe he'd remember if our guy hung around longer than usual."

"We've got the cashier's name. I have Prentiss tracking the guy down to see if he remembers anything from the day of the attack." Joe picked up the television remote and hit the power button. The small television on the credenza near the window flickered on, the volume low.

No press conference yet, just a syndicated talk show, Riley noted. He turned back to look at Hannah. Her green eyes met his, shining with a mix of excitement and dread.

He knew just how she felt. He'd never been as close to finding the killer as he was now, yet he wasn't sure he was really prepared for the uncertainty that lay ahead. What if, despite all efforts to keep her safe, Hannah ended up hurt—or worse? How could he live with such an outcome?

And what if they actually found her attacker, and it turned out Emily hadn't been one of his victims after all? Could he start from scratch, devoting more years of his life to nothing but cold, comfortless vengeance?

"Here we go," Joe said suddenly, and he turned up the volume on the TV.

As Sheriff Tanner laid out the basic details of the pepper-spray attack, Riley found his gaze drawn to Hannah. Emotions played across her face as she listened, a battle of fear and hope. As much as he had riding on this case, she had more. It was her life in danger, and she'd stayed here to help in spite of that fact, when a lot of other people would have gone home.

She was one hell of a woman.

I'm going to keep you safe, sweetheart, he vowed silently. *Whatever it takes.*

On television, Tanner had finished his statement and was taking questions. Most were utterly predictable. Did they have a suspect? Were other women at risk? Was Ms. Cooper going to make herself available for questions?

"What is he going to say when they ask if there's a connection to the murder in Grand Teton State Park?" Riley asked Joe, knowing the question was coming.

Before Joe could answer, a reporter asked just that question. Joe nodded toward the television.

"We aren't certain, but we're proceeding as if there's a possibility," Tanner answered carefully. "That's why it's important for women traveling alone to be especially careful. Local and state agencies have agreed that no law-enforcement officer driving an unmarked vehicle will attempt a traffic stop in Wyoming. So if such a vehicle attempts to pull you over, do not stop. Call nine-one-one and drive to a public place. Do not stop in an isolated place for any reason."

"What if you have car trouble?"

"Lock your doors, call for help if you have a phone. I know cell service doesn't work in all areas, but the people of Wyoming are friendly, helpful people. The Wyoming Department of Safety and several corporate partners are making distress signs available for motorists. These can be placed in windows to alert other drivers to your need for assistance."

He motioned to his right and a uniformed officer brought out a long banner with the words "Assistance Needed—Call 911" printed in block letters across the length.

"Please remember—if you see this sign, it is not a good idea to stop and give aid yourself. Please contact the local authorities and alert us to the problem."

"They're afraid the killer might use this to lure in unsuspecting good Samaritans," Hannah murmured.

"It's possible," Riley agreed.

The rest of the questions were little more than rewording of previous questions. Tanner put an end to the questions and left the stage, and the station returned to the local news anchors in the studio.

Joe turned off the television and looked at Riley. "That went okay, don't you think?"

It could have been a lot worse, Riley had to concede. God knew he was relieved to have information about the killer in front of the public.

Joe's phone buzzed. "Boss?" Over the intercom came the tinny voice of Bill Handley, the day-shift desk sergeant. "Sheriff Tanner from the Teton County Sheriff's Department on line one."

Joe exchanged a quick look with Riley and picked up the phone. "Garrison." He listened a moment, glancing at Hannah. "Yes, they're both here. I'm putting you on speakerphone."

He pushed a button and Jim Tanner's voice came over the line. "Good morning, Patterson. Ms. Cooper."

"Hello, Sheriff Tanner," Hannah murmured.

"Tanner," Riley added gruffly, his stomach knotting up.

"I'm just going to get straight to the point," Tanner said. "I have an idea to go on the offense on this case, but it requires your help, Ms. Cooper."

"No," Riley said firmly.

Both Joe and Hannah looked up at him, startled.

"What do you have in mind, Sheriff?" Hannah asked.

"I want you to give an interview to one of the TV stations and let them know that you're seeing a psychiatrist here at the hospital in Jackson—someone who's helping you recover some of the memories you lost thanks to the concussion."

"You want to set her up as bait," Riley interpreted.

"In a controlled way. I have already discussed the idea with one of the hospital's staff psychiatrists, and she's willing to go along with the plan."

"I'll do it," Hannah said swiftly.

"No, she won't," Riley said, glaring back at her when she once again turned angry eyes toward him.

"When do you want me in Jackson?" Hannah asked, her gaze doing fierce battle with Riley's.

"I need time to set things up, but I think we'll want to shoot for the local evening newscast," Tanner answered.

"Give them a day to promo the interview, make sure our guy knows to watch. So, if you could be in Jackson tomorrow morning, we can get the ball rolling."

"Set it up," Hannah said firmly.

"Hannah, no," Riley pleaded softly. "It's too dangerous."

"Call Chief Garrison when it's set," she added, her eyes softening. "He'll pass the information along to me."

"Thank you, Ms. Cooper. You're doing a brave thing." Admiration rang in Tanner's voice.

"I just want this man caught," Hannah replied.

Tanner rang off and Joe hung up the phone. He looked at Riley, sympathy in his eyes, then spoke to Hannah. "If you want to back out at any point, don't feel obligated to go through with this plan. I know Sheriff Tanner will do all he can to keep you safe, and I'll make sure I'm in on things, too, but nobody can promise you that there's no danger."

"I'm not trying to be a hero," Hannah said. "I want to be able to go back home and sleep at night knowing I didn't chicken out on a chance to catch a really bad guy who's hurt a lot of people." The look she gave Riley made his heart hurt.

"If you're doing this for me—"

"For you, for me, for that woman in the national park and all those other women you told me about." She leaned over and took his hand. "For Emily."

He lifted her hand, pressed his lips against her knuckles. The arguments he wanted to make died in his throat.

Joe cleared his throat. "I guess that's it for now."

Riley didn't let go of Hannah's hand as he turned to

look at his friend. "I want you in on everything. Every bit of the planning. Can you stay on Tanner, make sure he's covering all the possibilities?"

"Of course. But don't you want to do that yourself?"

Riley looked at Hannah again. "No, I'm going to spend the next twenty-four hours talking her out of this crazy idea."

So, she was remembering, he thought, replaying the sheriff's press conference in his head.

Jim Tanner hadn't said it in so many words, but clearly he was holding something back, something that put that smug half smile on his face throughout the entire press conference.

So far, he hadn't had much luck finding out where the girl was hiding out. His friend at the Sheriff's Department didn't know. He'd even made a point of running into Mark Archibald, the reporter who'd managed the first interview with Hannah Cooper, but he wasn't dropping any clues about the woman's whereabouts.

No need to panic yet. Whatever the woman remembered, it wasn't enough to implicate him. She'd never gotten a good look at him; he'd been careful, wearing nondescript clothing and his hat low over his face. She might have seen his belt buckle, but that wouldn't hurt him. He wore it only when he was hunting, and it had been a hand-me-down, not a purchase.

Still, he'd feel better when he finally tracked her down.

Hannah cocked her head, watching Riley flip the steak on the grill. He looked over his shoulder and smiled at her, fueling her suspicion that he was playing some sort of game with her. On the up side, at least she was getting a steak dinner out of it. But she couldn't help wondering why he wasn't trying to talk her out of playing bait for the killer.

Driving home from the Canyon Creek Police station, he hadn't said a word about Sheriff Tanner's plan. On the contrary, he'd taken the scenic route, detouring along lightly traveled side roads winding through open range, where horses and cattle grazed on the last good grass before winter arrived. He was a charming tour guide, telling her all about the local legends from a time when cowboys were kings.

"Just north of here," he had told her, "lies the Wind River Indian Reservation. Northern Arapaho and Eastern Shoshone. Emily's mother grew up there."

Which explained Jack's coloring.

"Emily's mother died when she was little—not long after Jack was born. They grew up with their dad, so they never really knew much about their mother's side of the family. She always regretted that." Riley's voice had gone faint, as it often did when he spoke of his late wife.

He'd changed the subject, and the conversation for the rest of the ride home had been light and inconsequential.

Certainly no mention of Sheriff Tanner's plan to put her in the killer's crosshairs.

"Are you sure I can't help you with something?"

"Got it covered," he assured her. He closed the grill cover and came to sit next to her on the rough, wooden bench set against the back wall of the house. He edged closer, enfolding her cold hands in his. "Are you sure you want to wait out here with me? Your hands are like icicles."

She leaned against him, happy for his body heat. Though the house blocked some of the wind whipping down from the north, the sun was already beginning to set, robbing her of its waning warmth. "And miss watching you play chef? Not a chance."

He wrapped his arm around her, pulling her closer. "Better?"

He smelled like wood smoke and grilling steak. Her stomach growled, and she chuckled inwardly. Tasty, indeed.

"Somebody's hungry." His low, growly baritone rumbled in her ear, turning the statement into a nerve-melting double entendre. She looked up to find him watching her, his gaze restless.

She swallowed hard, her heart fluttering wildly. "Yes."

He bent his head to nuzzle the side of her neck. His lips traced a shivery path up to her ear. "Me, too."

So, this is what he's up to.

Resistance was impossible, even though she was onto his plan of distraction. By the time his mouth slid over the curve of her jaw, she was far beyond protest.

His lips found hers, moving lazily. She lifted her hands to his head, his crisp, short-cropped hair rasping against her palms, making them tingle. She pulled him closer, ready for the next course, but he gave her only a quick taste, his tongue brushing lightly over hers, before he pulled back. The kiss was an appetizer, only whetting her hunger.

"Don't want to burn anything," he murmured, pulling away and returning to the grill.

He grabbed a set of tongs and flipped the steaks. The smell wafting toward her made her mouth water.

At least she told herself it was the smell.

"You haven't given up on talking me out of the plan, have you?" she asked.

He glanced over his shoulder at her. "Did you think I would?"

She shook her head slowly. "It's not going to do you any good. You can't wine and dine me out of this."

He smiled slightly, his eyes dark with determination. "I wasn't expecting food to change your mind."

Oh, my. The unspoken promise of that statement sank in, spreading heat over her throat and down her back. The fleece coat she wore to fend against the evening chill felt suddenly heavy and constricting.

"And I'm out of wine," he added. "Afraid we'll have to go into this sober."

She unzipped her jacket, grateful for the cool rush of air. "I don't like wine anyway. Makes me sleepy."

"Exactly." He turned back to the grill.

Warning bells rang frantically in her brain, but walking away seemed beyond her. Instead, she scrambled mentally for a safe topic to cool down the heat rising between them. "I called my parents earlier. I told them what I had decided to do."

He looked over his shoulder again. "What did they say?"

"Not to do it, of course."

"Mom and Dad know best."

She pressed her lips into a tight line. "If they were in my position, they'd do what I'm doing. Where do you think I learned it from?"

His answer was to flip the peppers charring on the grill.

"I just hope they don't call my brothers and let them know what's up. I'm surprised Aaron hasn't called me already. He's the cop," she reminded him. "Chickasaw County's finest."

He closed the top of the grill again and turned around to look at her. "What would Aaron the cop tell you?"

"Not to do it," she answered.

"Seems to be the consensus." He walked slowly toward her, every step a seduction, whether he intended it to be so or not. She tried to look away, but her muscles seemed paralyzed.

A fly in a spider's web, she thought faintly. Then he sat beside her again, lifting one hand to cup her cheek. What was left of her rational side curled up and whimpered.

He had large hands, rough with work. He ran the pad of his thumb lightly across her bottom lip. "You have a beautiful mouth. Has anyone ever told you that?"

The memory his words evoked helped her gather up what was left of her self-control. "Yes."

His thumb stopped moving. "Whoever he was, he was right."

"He liked kissing me." She forced the words from her mouth, not because she wanted to talk about that painful time in her life, but because it was her best defense against Riley's potent seduction. "But he loved someone else."

Riley dropped his hand to his lap. "What happened?"

"He married her, not me."

Riley breathed deeply, bending forward to rest his forearms on his knees. "When was that?"

"About four years ago." She hadn't planned to tell him more, but the gentle encouragement in his eyes made her open up about Craig, their whirlwind romance, the wedding plans and the terrible moment when, at the bachelor's party, he confessed to Hannah's brother Aaron that he was still in love with another woman. "Aaron made him tell me the truth." She smiled wryly. "Craig's lucky. Aaron was really ticked."

Riley took it all in silently, his expression solemn. Surely he couldn't miss the parallels between then and now, between Craig's lingering feelings for his old flame and Riley's unending passion for his dead wife.

"I think I knew long before he told me." Shame burned the back of her neck. "I just thought I could change his mind. But you can't will a man to get over the woman he loves."

"No." Riley moved restlessly away from her and opened the top of the grill. The smell of grilled peppers and steak filled the light breeze, but she'd lost her appetite.

Apparently, he had as well. Turning off the grill, he transferred the meat and peppers to a couple of plates, but he returned to her side without bringing the food. He turned toward her on the bench, reaching out to take her chin in his hand. He lifted her face, making her look up at him.

The intensity of his gaze made her stomach tighten into a hot, tight knot. "I don't want you to go to Jackson tomorrow."

"I know."

"I don't know how to stop you. You've already said wining and dining won't work."

She had to laugh at that, and his lips curved in response, but he soon grew serious again.

"I can only tell you that I came damned near losing my mind when Emily died. I don't think I've gotten all of it back yet." He cradled her face with gentle strength. "If something happened to you, I don't think there'd be anything left of me."

Tears trembled on her lashes and tumbled down her cheeks. She blinked them back, fighting for control. "You hardly know me," she said, trying to be reasonable. But even as she spoke the words, she knew they were inadequate. In a few, brief days, she'd shared more about herself with him than she'd shared with most of her family. He knew the fears that hid behind her bravado, the longing she buried beneath her outward contentment.

He didn't have to contradict her. She saw in his eyes that he knew the complexity of their relationship went far beyond a few days of acquaintance. *Soul mates,* her traitorous mind whispered, and she couldn't disagree. But the truth didn't make Riley any less in love with his dead wife.

She closed her eyes and drew away from him, needing breathing room to gather the scraps of reason still left in her rattled brain and try to figure out what to do.

She wanted him. She couldn't have denied that truth if her life depended on it. And she also knew the futility of letting her desire become anything more demanding. They might have a deep and special connection, but that was no guarantee of happily ever after.

Could she settle for happily right now?

"Please don't go to Jackson tomorrow," he said.

She forced her eyes open, letting the tiny flicker of

anger licking at her belly grow into a slow burn. "I told you my decision," she snapped. "You're going to have to respect it."

She stood and entered the house, leaning against the door for a second to calm her jangled nerves. She listened through the door for any sign that he intended to follow, but all she heard was the clatter of plates and cutlery.

A sudden crash made her jump, and she peeked through the small window set in the top of the door and saw Riley crouching by the grill, piling up pieces of a broken plate with swift, jerky movements.

She went to the guest room, closing the door behind her, and sat on the bed, hating herself for breaking the peace between them. He'd just opened up to her, sharing feelings she suspected he hadn't shared with anyone since Emily's death, and she'd rewarded him with a temper tantrum.

Nice, Hannah. Way to make sure the rest of your time in Wyoming is a living hell.

RILEY TOSSED THE PIECES of broken plate into a trash bag one by one, grimly enjoying the sound of each thunk. As irritated as he was at the moment, he found a strange sort of pleasure in the feeling. It had been a while since anyone had inspired in him a powerful emotion outside of grief.

He understood her frustration with his stubborn insistence that she back out of Jim Tanner's plan, but what choice did he have? He'd sacrificed a normal life in his quest to find Emily's killer, but he wasn't going to sacrifice Hannah.

Which was also a new sensation—caring about someone more than he cared about revenge.

He set the trash bag in the bin by the door and went back to the grill to gather up the food and take it inside.

Hannah was nowhere to be found. He glanced down the hall and saw the door to her room closed.

So she was hiding. Trying to stay mad? He knew she wasn't as angry at him as she wanted to be. But anger was better than vulnerability. He knew that better than most people.

He found a pair of clean plates and split the steaks and peppers between them. Going back to the drawer for flatware, he glanced down the hallway again. The door was still closed.

He waited until after he'd poured ice water in two glasses before he went down the hall to knock on the door. "Hannah?"

She didn't answer, but he could sense her listening just behind the door.

"If you don't answer me, I'm going to assume something bad happened to you and bust the door down," he warned.

The door opened and she stood on the other side, looking up at him with flashing green eyes. He took a step forward before he could stop himself.

She put her hands up, almost defensively, but when her fingers touched his chest, they curled into the fabric of his shirt, pulling him closer.

His heart rate soared as their bodies made contact. He couldn't have stopped his physical response if he'd wanted to.

She rose to her toes and pulled his head down, slanting her head back and fitting her mouth against his. He drank in her sweetness, fire building low and slow in his belly.

"I don't want to fight," she whispered, sliding her lips across the edge of his jaw.

He felt himself falling into her, the last shred of resistance gone. Pushing her back toward the bed, he fell atop her, shifting so that her body cradled his. Her thighs parting to welcome him, she tugged urgently at his shirt, her eyes glazed with hunger.

"Hannah—" he began, needing to be sure she knew what was about to happen between them, but she silenced him with her mouth, drawing him down to her with strong, determined arms.

There was nothing he could do but follow her into the sweet, desperate madness.

CHAPTER FOURTEEN

SHE ROSE BENEATH him, her strong fingers digging into the muscles of his back. The sound of her whispered endearments seemed as familiar as his own voice. Her body opened to him, soft and furnace hot, drawing him into a web of pure pleasure that left his body weak but his soul as strong and enduring as the Wyoming mountains. She clung to him, raining kisses over his cheeks, his jaw, down the side of his neck.

He raised his head to look at her, her name trembling on his lips.

But the face gazing back at him wasn't Emily's.

He woke with a small start, gazing up into darkness, his heart pounding wildly in his chest. At eye level, the pale blue light of an alarm clock displayed the time. 5:30 a.m.

Tucked into the curve of his body, Hannah's body was soft and warm. He could feel her slow, even breathing and knew she was still asleep.

The memory of their night of passion blurred with the dream that had wakened him, until he wasn't sure what was real and what was imagination. Was this really her body, fitted to his so perfectly it seemed they'd been chiseled from the same stone? Had their bodies found, instinctively, that perfect rhythm that lovers knew, the ebb and flow of control and submission that usually came from years of intimacy?

Had it been Hannah's face gazing back at him in his dream?

Carefully, he edged away from her. She stirred briefly but settled back into a deep, quiet sleep.

He rolled from the bed, grabbing his discarded boxers from the floor, and padded down the hall to the bathroom. He looked into the mirror over the sink, gazing curiously at the man who stared back at him in the glass.

He looked rested, he realized with surprise, despite the early hour and the exertions of the previous night. Stress lines that had creased his forehead had almost disappeared, only faint shadows marking the skin as a reminder of what had once been. His eyes looked clear, his gaze steady, devoid of pain for the first time in three long years.

About a year after Emily's murder, when his self-imposed isolation had begun to make him crazy, he'd gone to Jackson for a weekend, just to be around people who didn't know who he was or what he'd lost. It hadn't been hard to find a woman as uninterested in happily-ever-after as he had been. Trips to Jackson had become a regular thing for him, once or twice a month. Just to take the edge off.

The other nights, the other women—all had left their mark. But always for the worse. Never the better.

He turned off the light and went out into the hallway, pausing outside the bathroom. What should he do now? Go back to the bedroom, where Hannah lay warm and naked between his sheets? Or to the kitchen, to get an early start on figuring out how to talk Hannah out of her crazy, dangerous plan?

She made the decision for him, emerging from the guest room wearing nothing but his shirt.

She gave him a tentative smile. "Good morning."

Her hair was a dark tangle, framing her sleep-softened face. Her lips were pink and swollen from their kisses, and the skin of her throat was bright red from the rasp of his beard against her skin.

His body quickened in response, and he had nowhere to hide.

A slow, naughty smile spread over her sleepy face. She walked slowly down the hallway, her gaze locked with his. She stopped in front of him, lifting one hand to his chest.

"It's cold out here in the hallway." She slid her hand slowly down his belly, until her fingers tangled briefly in the waistband of his boxers, then dipped lower. "Why don't we go back to bed?"

He couldn't have said no if he wanted to.

THEY TOOK TURNS SHOWERING a couple of hours later, oddly hesitant to share that particular bit of intimacy. Maybe it was tacit acknowledgement, on both their parts, of how transient their intimacy really was.

Hannah went first, and by the time Riley emerged from the bathroom, dressed in clean jeans and a fresh, blue chambray shirt, she'd already brewed a pot of hot, strong coffee and was cracking eggs in a skillet on the stove.

"Two eggs or three?" she asked over her shoulder, trying not to picture the long, lean body hidden beneath the clothing. If she didn't get her mind out of the bedroom, how was she going to pull off her part of Sheriff Tanner's plan?

She couldn't afford to be off her game today.

"Three." Riley reached into the breadbox to pull out a loaf of wheat bread. "I'm making toast—want a piece?"

"Please." She cracked two more eggs into the pan and let them cook sunny side up. "Sheriff Tanner didn't call last night, did he? I didn't hear the phone ring."

"I checked while I was dressing. No messages." He sounded relieved.

"I'm sure he'll call soon." She said it gently, not wanting to sound defensive. She hadn't really expected a night of lovemaking to change Riley's mind about the plan to lure the killer into a trap. If anything, it probably made him even more determined to keep her out of danger.

It had certainly made her think twice about risking her life. The closeness to Riley she'd felt, far beyond the passion and pleasure, had shown her that she could still open herself to the possibility of love.

At least, she could with Riley, she amended silently. There was no guarantee she'd find this feeling again with another man. What if Riley were the one for her, the man she'd thought she'd found in Craig before reality proved otherwise?

It would be just her luck, she thought bleakly, to fall for a man who'd forever be in love with his dead wife.

Her appetite drained away, although she forced herself to work her way through the eggs and toast on her plate. Across from her, Riley ate with gusto, his gaze playing lightly over her face. Whenever their eyes met, he smiled, tempting her to believe he might not be as out of reach as she thought.

Fortunately, the phone rang before breakfast was

over, dragging her back to sober reality. Riley answered, his expression immediately going grim. He held out the receiver. "Jim Tanner for you."

Hannah took the phone. "This is Hannah."

Jim Tanner got right down to business. "I've arranged for McCoy Edwards from Channel Twelve to interview you for the five o'clock news. You're to meet him at the station around 11:00 a.m. to pretape the segment. Can you be there?"

"Of course." She glanced at Riley. He watched her with stormy-blue eyes.

"In fact, have Patterson bring you to my office by ten-thirty. That way I can deliver you to the station myself. Riley can come along if he likes, but not in any official capacity. We don't want word getting around that you're under the protection of a Canyon Creek policeman."

"Will do," she agreed, and rang off soon after.

Riley hung up the phone for her and returned to the table, dropping into the chair across from her. "So, you're really going through with it?"

"Yes," she answered simply.

He sighed deeply, signaling his disagreement, and proceeded to finish breakfast in silence.

RILEY'S STOMACH WAS A SERIES of knots by the time they arrived at the television studio in Jackson. Sheriff Tanner had briefed Hannah on what to say and what not to say, and now the three of them piled out of the sheriff's Ford Bronco and entered the studio, where the television reporter, McCoy Edwards, was waiting to greet them.

Edwards was in his early fifties, with sharp, green eyes and thick, slicked-back dark hair edged with silver. He greeted the sheriff as if they were old friends, a feeling the sheriff clearly didn't share, and then pulled Hannah aside with a gentle tug once the introductions were over.

Riley watched them go, keeping his eye on Edwards as he led Hannah to a pair of chairs in front of a textured gray wall of a news set and settled her in with care. Riley could hear the murmur of their low conversation but couldn't make out any words. He turned to Tanner. "Are you sure you can trust him?"

"We need to get the story out to make this work. Edwards is the guy who can make it happen."

Not exactly the answer he'd hoped for, Riley thought, his gaze finding Hannah again. She looked in his direction, a tentative half-smile on her face. He knew she couldn't see much past the lights shining on her, but he smiled his encouragement anyway, even though his gut felt twisted inside-out.

Once they settled down to the interview, Riley could hear their words more clearly. To his credit, Edwards asked smart questions, and his follow-ups suggested he'd done his homework beyond reading Mark Archibald's article in the Jackson paper.

Finally, he got to the question Riley knew Hannah had been waiting for. "Do you think you'll ever remember everything about the event?"

"I don't know. But I'm going to see a doctor at Jackson Memorial tomorrow morning. She's a certified therapeutic hypnotist. I'm hoping we can work through some of the memory blocks so I can help the police even more."

Riley's heart clenched. With that one answer, she'd

set the trap. Nothing left to do now but see it through to the end.

He just hoped Hannah was still standing when the smoke finally cleared.

"You still think I'm making a mistake." Hannah stirred in Riley's arms, turning to face him. She couldn't see more than the shadowy outline of his face in the darkened bedroom, but she felt the tension build in his body at her words.

"I don't think it was a safe choice," he answered.

Such a careful response, she thought with as much affection as frustration. "I know it's not the safe choice. That doesn't mean it's not the right one."

His big hand found her face in the dark, his fingers tangling in her hair as he gave her a soft, slightly clumsy caress. "Depends on who you ask."

She twined her fingers with his and leaned in to kiss him. His mouth was hot and soft beneath hers, and the low simmer of heat in her belly flickered into flame. "I have to do this," she breathed against his lips.

"If you're doing it for me—"

"I told you already, it's as much for me as for you." She lay back against the pillow, closing her eyes.

"What if nothing happens?" he asked quietly. "What if he doesn't take the bait?"

Pain nipped at her heart. "Then I go home as planned."

"And I keep looking." He rolled on to his back until they lay side by side, no longer touching.

In the morning, Hannah thought, *I'll pack my bags so I'll be ready to catch the afternoon flight out of Jackson Hole. I'll be home tomorrow night, back in my lit-*

tle house by the lake with my crazy, enormous family surrounding me.

But where would Riley be?

"If the plan works, and we catch him—what then?" she asked aloud. "What will you do?"

He didn't answer right away, though she could almost hear him thinking. After a moment, the bed shook as he gave a small shrug. "I don't know. I've never thought that far ahead."

She slipped her hand into his. "I hope you have to start thinking about it."

His fingers curled around hers, and she smiled sadly in the dark.

FROM HIS POSITION NEAR the front entrance, he spotted Sheriff Jim Tanner entering the hospital first. The clock on the wall over the information desk read 10:49 a.m.

Right on time. He'd checked the shrink's schedule earlier that morning, before she arrived, and found Hannah Cooper's name pencilled in at eleven.

Dressed in jeans and a denim jacket, the Teton County Sheriff was indistinguishable from the other visitors milling about the hospital lobby. Most people there probably didn't realize he was the sheriff.

But I'm not most people, he thought with a grim smile. Ever since the newscast the night before, he'd been expecting something just like this to happen.

As if he was stupid enough to fall for so obvious a setup.

He could imagine the sheriff's reasoning. *He's escalating. Time is running out to get to her. He'll be desperate enough to take a big risk.* All that psychobabble cops pulled out of their backsides when they didn't know what would happen next.

He'd applied to the FBI a while back. He knew all about that sort of thinking, the tricks the G-Man types pulled to make people think they were smarter than they really were.

But they hadn't been smart enough to hire him, had they?

Movement to his right caught his eye. His heartbeat kicked up a notch. There she was, as expected, walking slowly toward the entrance. A few feet in front of the glass doors, she hesitated, just a moment. A surge of pure pleasure rushed through him at the sight of her unease.

I'm in your head, aren't I, sweet baby?

As he watched, her chin came up, her shoulders squared and she entered the hospital lobby. Her renewed resolve did nothing to dampen his enjoyment, however. He liked a challenge.

She walked past where the sheriff sat, not even giving him a glance. Heading straight to the elevators, she punched the up button.

As she disappeared inside, the new guy, Sanchez, strolled up next to him. He smiled pleasantly. "Boss sent me down here to learn the ropes, would you believe? Like I've never walked security before. I worked county lockup, for God's sake."

So had he, though not in Teton County. He'd put in his time as a prison guard in Natrona, a few years back.

Sanchez nodded his head to the right, his meaty brow furrowed. "Hey, is that the sheriff?"

He just smiled.

"I ADMIT, THIS IS ONE OF MY stranger moments as a therapist." Dr. Janis Templeton smiled at Hannah across her wide, oak desk. "I've never been part of a police sting before. I can't decide if it's exciting or nerve-racking."

Hannah smiled back, though her stomach had been in knots all morning. "If it makes you feel better, neither can I."

"How long before you know if it worked?"

"I'm supposed to stay the hour. Then I walk through the hospital alone and meet the sheriff downstairs in the lobby." Hannah glanced at her watch. She'd been in Dr. Templeton's office for only ten minutes. It had felt much longer.

Dr. Templeton sat back in her chair, crossing her legs. She was only a little older than Hannah, maybe in her early thirties. She was pretty in a natural sort of way, with minimal makeup and a short, unfussy hairstyle that suited her. Her suit was simple but well cut, showing off her slim swimmer's build. Hannah wondered if she had much chance to swim in a place like Jackson, Wyoming.

"I suppose while we're here, it wouldn't hurt to talk to you a bit about your memory loss. Has anything come back at all?" Dr. Templeton asked.

"A few things. I don't know what I'm at liberty to tell you, though."

Dr. Templeton nodded. "Of course. I was just wondering if you'd seriously considered hypnosis to recover some of the missing pieces."

"Not really." Hannah gave her an apologetic look. "One of my brothers is a prosecutor, and he's not a big fan of hypnotherapy as a means of recovering repressed memories."

"He's thinking as a litigator—what can be used in court. I'm talking about a relaxation technique to let your mind do its job without any interference." Dr. Templeton picked up a pencil on her desk and ran it between her slim fingers. "You clearly want to remember more or you wouldn't be here risking your safety. Maybe you should consider contacting a hypnotherapist when you get back home."

"I'll think about it," Hannah said, although she wasn't comfortable with the idea.

"Meanwhile, we might as well enjoy the next twenty minutes," Dr. Templeton said with a smile. "Why don't you tell me more about yourself?"

"DO WE HAVE A MASTER LIST of the personnel on duty this morning?" Riley asked Jim Tanner as they settled into chairs in the hospital lobby. Joe Garrison sat nearby, within earshot.

"The hospital administrator sent it by fax this morning." Tanner opened his briefcase and pulled out a printed spreadsheet. "Since the five o'clock news aired, seven employees called in sick. Two nurse's aides, one orderly, a cafeteria worker, a doctor and two nurses."

"Nobody in security?" Joe asked.

"Everybody reported as scheduled." Tanner passed a sheet of paper to Riley. "I typed their names up for you, since I know you think security is the weak link."

Riley scanned the list of names. "This is a new one," he said, pointing out one of the names near the bottom.

"Yeah, Mike Sanchez. He's a retired county-jail guard. He wasn't ready to be put out to pasture, so I vouched for him here at the hospital." Tanner raised his eyes and gave the lobby a quick scan. "He's a little on the husky side these days. Doesn't fit your girl's description."

My girl, Riley thought with a pang. They'd certainly spent the last two nights wrapped up in each other like lovers.

He glanced at his watch. "It's nearly noon. She'll be coming down any minute." Every muscle in his body felt like a rubber band stretched taut, ready to snap. He forced himself to breathe slowly and evenly, trying to regain control. The Ruger tucked into the holster hidden beneath his leather jacket felt heavy against his hip.

He knew there were two undercover Teton County deputies on the third floor, where the psychiatrist's office was located. One of them had been assigned to follow Hannah into the elevator for the ride down to the lobby. He, Joe and Jim Tanner were in charge of getting her safely out of the lobby.

He should be hoping for the killer to make a move. With so many officers on the lookout, the guy would be a sitting duck.

But Riley couldn't wish Hannah danger. He'd rather spend the rest of his life chasing the bastard.

With a soft ding, the nearest elevator opened and Hannah emerged. A moment later, the sandy-haired undercover deputy came out behind her. The deputy locked gazes with the sheriff and gave a slight shake of his head.

The plan had failed.

Hannah walked up to where they sat, slumping into the empty seat by Riley. "No luck, it seems."

Riley slid his arm around the back of her chair. "Depends on who you're asking," he murmured.

The look she gave him was a blend of disappointment and affection. "So, I guess the next stop is the airport."

His heart sank. They'd packed her bags and put them in the truck before leaving the house that morning. Her flight left the Jackson Hole airport around three, so there'd be no time to return to the house.

This was it. His last hours with her.

Sheriff Tanner stood up, cuing them to do the same. Riley settled his hand at the small of Hannah's back and walked out with her as she followed Tanner and Joe outside to the parking lot. He stayed alert crossing the lot to their vehicles, in case their unidentified suspect decided to make one last play to take Hannah down.

But the walk was uneventful.

At the truck, Tanner turned to Hannah, holding out his hand. "It's been a pleasure meeting you, Ms. Cooper. You have a safe trip home, and I'll be in touch if anything comes up on the case." He nodded to Riley and Joe and headed for his Bronco parked a few slots over.

Hannah turned to Joe. "Thank you for all your help, Joe. And please tell Jane again how much I appreciated her help when I arrived. She promised to e-mail me when the baby gets here. You make sure she does, okay?"

"I'll do that. Have a safe flight." Joe gave her a quick hug and met Riley's gaze over her shoulder, a thousand questions in his eyes.

Questions Riley couldn't have answered if he wanted to.

After Joe left, Hannah turned to look at Riley, her expression as bleak as a Wyoming winter. "We'd better hit the road. Jane said it's a bit of a drive to the airport."

He helped her into the truck cab and went around

to the driver's side. "It's a little ways," he agreed, "but we'll have a good view of the mountains."

She buckled herself in. "I'm sorry the plan didn't work."

"I'm not," he said, and meant it.

She turned her head and gazed at him with moist eyes. "I just wanted this to be over for you. It doesn't feel right to be going home and leaving you here still searching for answers."

Then stay, he thought. But he couldn't say the words aloud. What he could offer her, at best, was half a man, and she deserved so much more than that.

They stopped for burgers on the trip to the airport, eating in silence, each knowing that everything that could be said between them already had. They didn't speak again until he parked in the short-term parking at the airport and carried her luggage for her to the check-in area.

She turned to look at him, her green eyes dark with sadness. "I won't make you go through security just to see me off. It'll just make me all weepy and stuffed up for the flight, and who needs that at thirty-thousand feet, right?" She managed a watery grin.

He cradled her face between his hands. "You have my phone number. Call when you get home so I know you got there safely."

She nodded, still smiling through her tears.

"Are you sure you don't want me to contact the local authorities to give you some protection?"

"My brother's a deputy. Two of my other brothers are auxiliary deputies. I have a rifle of my own. I'll be fine. Besides, he's not likely to follow me all the way back to Alabama, is he?"

Tamping down his fears and regrets, he brushed his lips to hers, not daring anything more, and then crushed her against him, holding her tightly. "Thank you for everything," he murmured into her ear.

He let her go and stepped back, his heartbeat playing a slow dirge against his ribcage. He wanted to say more, to explain to her how much he regretted seeing her go, but he'd long ago learned the difference between what he wanted and what had to be. So he gave her a quick smile that he hoped conveyed how much he was going to miss her and turned toward the exit.

Reaching the door, he looked back one more time to find her standing where he'd left her, her heart in her eyes.

Mustering all the strength he had, he turned and walked out the door.

CHAPTER FIFTEEN

HER TIMING WAS lousy all the way around.

If she'd gone to Wyoming in the spring, she could have returned to a wildly busy office to take her mind off everything she went through on her vacation. The past week would have been a whirlwind of fishing-camp bookings, clients looking to schedule guided fishing trips, and several of her brothers running in and out of the office between fishing trips and maintenance calls.

But by late October, the season was coming to an end, and the phone calls slowed to a trickle, leaving her too much time to think about Riley and the way things between them had ended.

Maybe it would have been easier if their brief fling had blown up in a huge, dramatic fight. At least there would have been passion, tears and the chance to get good and mad. But watching him walk away, knowing with every cell in her body that he felt the same connection between them that she did, had been a sort of quiet, relentless torture she hadn't yet escaped.

She pushed back her desk chair and crossed to the filing cabinet on the pretense that there was something in the office she hadn't filed in the week since she returned home. But the cabinet was immaculately organized, thanks to her desperate attempt to keep her mind off Riley for the past seven days.

Admitting defeat, she slammed the drawer shut and turned around to look at the empty office.

The phone rang, an unexpected reprieve. She hurried to answer it. "Cooper Cove Properties."

"Hey, Skipper, it's me." It was her brother Aaron, using her much-hated childhood nickname because he liked to hear her growl. But this time, her heart wasn't in it.

"Hey, what's up besides the crime rate?"

"You're funny," he retorted. "It's down, for your information."

"In spite of you?" she teased, knowing how much he prided himself on his job as a Chickasaw County Sheriff's Deputy.

"Because of me, naturally." He took the teasing with good humor. He was the youngest, except for her, which had often made them natural allies over the years. "But that's not why I called. Have you talked to Mom yet?"

From the excited tone in his voice, she guessed it wasn't bad news. "No—what's going on?"

"Sam's moving back home."

"Officially?" She grinned. "When?"

"He got the job he wanted in the Jefferson County District Attorney's office."

Some of her excitement faded. "But Birmingham's an hour away. We won't ever get to see Maddy."

"The job is an hour away, but he's going to commute. He's already got his eye on a house on Mission Road in town. Nice place—I swung by to take a look for him. Nice big yard, easy drive to the lake. It's perfect."

"Tell him to take it!" The more brothers to distract her from her miserable life, the better.

"I plan to." Aaron's voice softened. "So, how are you really doing?"

The concern in his voice made tears prick her eyes. She blinked them back. "I'm good. The concussion was nearly two weeks ago."

"I'm not talking about the concussion. It had to be unnerving to be on a serial killer's hit list."

"It was, but I'm home now, safe and sound, and if there's any justice, the cops in Wyoming will have him behind bars any day now."

"They haven't got him yet."

She frowned at the phone. "And you'd know that how?"

"I might have given the Teton County sheriff a call this morning," he admitted.

She couldn't decide if she was relieved or disappointed that he hadn't called Riley instead. "But they're still on it, right?"

"Absolutely. And the sheriff thinks you should be perfectly safe now that you're home."

"Good to hear." The office door opened and Mariah entered, waggling her fingers at Hannah. "Listen, Mariah just got here, and you need to get back to work. Great news about Sam. Now if we could just get Luke home, I'd have all my ducks in a row."

She winced a little, mentally, at her choice of words. Riley had said something very like that to her, at a time that now felt like a lifetime ago. She ruthlessly shoved the memory out of her mind and rang off. "That was Aaron," she told Mariah.

"He told you about your brother coming home, no?" Mariah laid her backpack on her desk and smiled at

Hannah. "Jake told me the news. I can't wait to meet him."

"That's right, you haven't met him or Luke yet." Mariah and Hannah's brother Jake had met less than a year earlier, and eloped to Gatlinburg a couple of months after that. At the time, Hannah had secretly questioned whether a marriage based on two months' acquaintance was a good idea, but after almost eight months, they seemed to be working out well.

And after Wyoming, she didn't have much room to talk.

Mariah smiled at Hannah again, but as always, the smile didn't quite overcome the sadness always present in her coffee-colored eyes. She'd been a widow with a small child when she met Hannah's brother Jake, and it seemed even her obvious love for her new husband hadn't quite erased that sense of loss. "It's odd to have such a large family. Back in Texas, there were only my parents and me."

"Having seven kids is pretty odd these days, no matter where you're from." Hannah grinned.

Mariah settled behind her desk and pushed papers around the blotter, no doubt looking for something constructive to do. Hannah was about to tell her to use her time doing homework or reading ahead for her next class when Mariah looked up shyly, a faint blush staining her olive skin.

"I've been thinking about something you told me. About the case in Wyoming." Her lightly accented English had a musical quality that Hannah always found soothing. "You said you saw a psychiatrist in Wyoming—a hypnotherapist?"

"Right—when we tried to set the trap for the guy,

the cover story was that I was seeing a hypnotherapist to recover missing memories." Hannah smiled. "It reminded me of you and your hypnosis tricks."

Mariah's smile was tinged with thoughtfulness. "It is not so much a trick, actually. It is a way to let your mind relax and open. Perhaps you really should try it."

The thought still gave her the willies. She took such pride in her self-control that losing it, even a little, was frightening. But courage was about doing the right thing, even in the face of fear, wasn't it?

She didn't want to think of herself as a coward.

"What do you need to do it?" she asked aloud. "Can we do it right here and now?"

Mariah's eyebrows notched upwards, but she gave a quick nod. "I think I can find something—" She dug through her desk drawer until she emerged with a yellow pencil. "This will work. Come, let's go to the conference room."

Hannah followed Mariah to the small sitting room that served as the booking office's conference room. Mariah motioned for her to sit in the cozy armchair, while she took a seat on the sofa across from her.

"The main thing I want you to do is breathe. In and out, slow and steady." As she spoke, Mariah tapped the eraser end of the pencil rhythmically on the coffee table.

Dr. Pendleton had done something very similar when Hannah was talking to her in her office, she remembered. Had it been an attempt to ease Hannah's obvious tension?

"Close your eyes, clear your mind and concentrate on breathing in tempo with my taps," Mariah said.

Hannah did as Mariah asked, focusing on the slow, steady intake and exhale of air in rhythm with the tapping pencil. After a few moments, her limbs began to feel heavy.

"You are relaxed and open. You are aware of everything around you. There is nothing you have seen or heard that you cannot access. Do you believe me when I say that?"

She did, Hannah realized. "Yes."

"Good. Because all we're doing here is answering questions. Answer them as well as you can. No pressure at all. Now, I want you to remember the day you were attacked. Was it a sunny day?"

"Yes, but it was late afternoon. The sun was dropping behind the mountains and there were shadows all around me." She saw the road spreading out in front of her, the endless wilderness on either side of the highway.

"When did you notice the car?"

"I checked my rearview mirror and there he was."

"What did the car look like?"

"It was big. A sedan. I think it might have been dark blue. I really only noticed the blue light on the roof."

"Did you see the man inside the car?"

"No. The windshield was darkened." Had she told the police in Wyoming about the tinted windows? She felt herself begin to tense up.

"Breathe, Hannah. When we are done, you can ask yourself the questions that make you anxious, but for now, the anxiety is gone. Breathe it away."

Hannah did as Mariah told her, and soon the tension passed.

"He came to your car. What were you doing as he was walking toward you?"

"I was getting my license and registration information."

"Did you glance in any of the mirrors to see what he looked like?" Mariah asked.

"No. It happened so fast—he was there within seconds."

"What did you do when you found the license and registration papers?"

"I turned to the window." Anticipating Mariah's next question, she added, "He was already right by the car. All I could see was his shirt, his midsection and his hand. I saw his belt buckle—a rattlesnake." Funny how clear it was in her head now. "His belt was brown leather. No markings."

"Was the pepper spray in his hand?"

"Yes. He was wearing latex gloves. I got a brief glimpse before—" She stopped as she replayed the moment in her head and saw something she hadn't remembered before. "He used both hands to spray the pepper spray, almost like a two-handed shooting stance. I'd forgotten that. And on his left pinky finger he wore a ring."

"You could see it through the gloves?"

"Yes. It was gold with a black stone and a small gold inset on the stone." She opened her eyes and looked at Mariah, excitement building. "I can't believe I didn't remember that. I mean, when I slammed my elbow down on his fingers to get away, I felt the ring crack against my funny bone."

Mariah put the pencil down on the table and regarded her solemnly. "Do you remember what the gold inset was?"

Hannah broke into a broad smile. "It was a horseshoe."

NEARLY 30,000 FEET BELOW, Missouri looked like a tiny relief map, crisscrossed by rivers and streams snaking west from the Mississippi River. He was still a few hours away from landing in Nashville, but from there, the drive to Gossamer Ridge, Alabama, would take less than three hours. He planned to stay overnight in Nashville and get an early start on the road.

He had to get to Gossamer Ridge for a morning rendezvous.

She'd been quite helpful, really, telling the newspaper reporter all about her life in Alabama. The family marina, running the booking office, even her quirky little side job as a fishing guide. He supposed she did that alone, too.

Reckless woman.

He'd used this past week not only to prepare for his cross-country trip but also to let the police—and Hannah Cooper—develop a false sense of security. They didn't expect him to go to such lengths to tie up loose ends. Wouldn't fit the profile, he thought with a smile.

As the flight attendant passed, she smiled back at him. For a moment, he imagined what it would be like to have her on his table in the basement of his mother's house. To watch her twist and writhe as her fate became clearer, to realize that her own actions had led her to that place and that outcome.

But the flight attendant hadn't earned that punishment, had she? At least, not yet. She hadn't ignored his warnings and sealed her fate.

Hannah Cooper had, however. And he wasn't one to leave things unfinished.

RILEY GAZED AT THE PAPERS spread across his desk and saw none of them. He'd spent most of the past week in this same position, hunched forward over his desk, moving papers around like pieces of a jigsaw puzzle in the pretense that his mind was still on the work and not hundreds of miles away in the hills of northeast Alabama.

New information had come in on the case, most of it eliminating suspects rather than pinpointing anyone in particular. Among the hospital security personnel, only five possibles remained. None of them looked very promising, but they still remained more likely than the other hospital staffers they'd also been looking at.

He picked up the background sheets on the possibles, trying to concentrate on finding something he'd missed the first ten times he'd looked at these sheets over the past week, but all he could see was Hannah's shattered expression when he'd turned around in the airport terminal to look at her for the last time.

He should have asked her to stay. Or hell, offered to go with her. What was keeping him here anymore, except an unhealthy craving for revenge? His parents were in Arizona. Jack was God knew where.

And Emily was dead.

But he wasn't. He may have felt as if he were a walking corpse for the past three years, but he wasn't dead yet. He still had years ahead of him, and living them as if life held no joy at all was the worst possible tribute to Emily's memory.

For the first time, he felt her censure, the full truth of the words Joe had told him just a few short days ago.

Emily would hate what you're becoming.

The buzzer on his desk phone sounded. "Riley—get in here." It was Joe, and he sounded excited.

He headed into Joe's office and found him on the phone. Joe held up a finger and finished the conversation. "Yes, I think it'll be very helpful. For sure it gives us another piece of the puzzle to help us cull suspects. I'll definitely let you know if anything comes of it. Bye, now." Joe hung up and looked at Riley, clearly excited but also exhibiting telltale signs of guilt.

"Who was that?" Riley asked, although in his sinking heart he knew the answer.

"Hannah Cooper," Joe answered, sending a sliver of pain slicing straight through Riley's heart. "She remembered something else."

Riley listened as Joe told him about how Hannah had let her sister-in-law hypnotize her and remembered a ring the killer had been wearing, but all he could think about was the fact that Hannah had called Joe and not him.

No surprise, really. After all, he'd broken her heart. He'd known it even as he was doing it. Why would she ever want to speak to him again?

Yet she'd obviously kept thinking about the case, enough to let her sister-in-law hypnotize her into remembering more.

"I need time off," he said bluntly.

Joe looked at him as if he'd lost his mind. "I just told you we got a break in the case, and you want time off?"

Riley stood, propelled by a restless urgency that grew stronger each second he remained in this office. He'd been headed toward this moment for a week, hadn't he? Every moment spent thinking about her, rewinding every touch, every conversation, every regret for seven endless, excruciating days.

"She could have gone home and not given this case

another thought," he said aloud. "After all she went through, I wouldn't have blamed her for it. But she didn't."

A slow smile of understanding spread across Joe's face. "You're going to Alabama, aren't you?"

Riley grinned back at him, suddenly feeling the urge to laugh aloud. "Yes, I believe I am."

"Well, I'm going to pass this information along to Sheriff Tanner and see if any of the Memorial Hospital staff wears an onyx pinky ring with a gold horseshoe set into it. You go book a flight and get packed."

"Call me on my cell if you get any breaks in the case," Riley said over his shoulder, already halfway out the door.

He found a flight leaving around 4:30 p.m. from Casper arriving in Birmingham before midnight and booked a room for a night at a motel not far from the Interstate. Packing in a rush, he was on the road to Casper by noon.

In twenty-four hours, he'd be with Hannah again. And if he was lucky, and she was forgiving, he wouldn't ever be without her again.

HANNAH WAS LOCKING UP at the booking office late that afternoon when the phone rang. She glanced at the caller identification display, ready to blow off anyone she wasn't in the mood to talk to. But the number had a Tennessee area code. Might be a client. She answered. "Cooper Cove Properties."

"Hi, there." The voice was male and friendly, with a neutral accent Hannah couldn't place, though it sounded vaguely familiar. "My name is Ken Lassiter, and I was hoping you might have an opening in your schedule tomorrow morning for a guided crappie-fishing tour."

She pretended to grab her book, although the truth was, hardly anyone was fishing for crappie on Gossamer Lake this time of year. No matter—she knew good spots to fish any time of the year. "I have an availability first thing in the morning. Can you be here by 6:30 a.m.?"

"I certainly can," Lassiter answered cheerfully. "Are you the one who'll be taking me?"

"That's right." She braced for a change of heart. Some men didn't like being guided by women.

"Do I need to bring my own tackle?"

She relaxed. Apparently, Mr. Lassiter wasn't one of those men. "Not unless you want to. We provide all the tackle and gear as part of the service." She named a price. "That will get you a full day on the lake. Half a day, half price. You pay up front at the bait shop by the docks. I'll be here when you arrive."

"Let's go with half a day. I'm betting we can get the job done by then," Lassiter said. "I didn't get your name—"

"Cooper. Hannah Cooper."

"I look forward to fishing with you, Ms. Cooper. I'll see you at six-thirty." Lassiter rang off, and Hannah wrote the appointment down in the book.

As she finished locking up the office, she found herself looking forward to getting back on the lake. If anything could take her mind off Riley Patterson and Wyoming, it was a day of crappie fishing on Gossamer Lake.

HE HUNG UP THE PAY PHONE outside a store within sight of the Metro Riverfront Park. The late afternoon was pleasantly mild for October; he was glad he'd thought to pack clothes for a warmer climate. Around him, locals and tourists mingled along the city sidewalks, heading for their cars parked along the busy streets or for the bus stop near the river.

Nobody gave him a second look, which was why he'd chosen this place, miles from his motel room, to make his call to the Cooper Cove Marina.

Hearing her voice had been an electric shock to his system. The week he'd given her to relax her guard had been harder on him than he'd realized. While he prided himself on his self-control, he'd never really been one to deny himself necessary pleasures.

And seeing Hannah Cooper again would be a pleasure, indeed.

CHAPTER SIXTEEN

SATURDAY MORNING TURNED out to be sunny and mild, warm for mid-October. Hannah would have preferred to be out on the lake by sunrise, but today she was on the clock for a paying client, so she played by his rules.

She brewed a pot of coffee at home and poured it into a sturdy thermos in case the client needed a little caffeine to get him going in the morning. She'd packed her boat with all the necessary rods and tackle the night before, and her father had culled out four dozen minnows, ready to stow in the boat's bait well in case the client wanted to fish with live bait.

Her parents were already at work at the bait shop when she arrived. "Are you sure you want to take this one by yourself?" her father asked her, worry in his eyes. "It's so soon after—"

"It's a fishing trip. I've been doing these by myself for years," she assured him, giving him a quick kiss on the cheek. He smelled like Old Spice and mint toothpaste, the scents familiar and comforting, reminding her that she was safely home, surrounded by a loving, fiercely protective family.

"I went ahead and put the minnows in the bait well for you," he said. "And J.D. gassed it up for you last night, so you should be ready to go."

Car headlights sliced through the early-morning gloom outside the bait shop.

"Must be your client," her mother said.

Anxiety slithered through her belly at the sound of footsteps crunching the gravel outside. She wrestled it into submission and pasted a welcoming smile on her face as the sandy-haired man in his early thirties entered the bait shop and flashed them a friendly smile.

"Ms. Cooper?" The man held out his hand. "Ken Lassiter."

She shook his hand firmly. "Good morning, Mr. Lassiter."

"Ken, please. I can call you Hannah?"

"Of course." She walked around the counter to the cash register. "We can take all major credit cards, or cash. We don't take checks from out of state."

"Cash is fine." Reaching into his pocket, he pulled out a folded stack of bills and placed them on the counter. Hannah rang up the service and thanked him.

"How long have you been guiding?" he asked once they had boarded her small, sleek Triton TC 17 and settled in for the ride across the lake to one of her favorite fall crappie spots.

"Since I got my boating license about twelve years ago," she answered, raising her voice above the roar of the Mercury outboard. "I grew up on the lake, so I've been fishing since I could hold a cane pole."

Ken flashed her a quick smile, then looked back out over the lake. "Quiet this morning."

"A lot of the boats are already out this time of day."

"Are we going to be rubbing elbows with a lot of other fishermen, then?" he asked, looking a little disappointed.

"Not where I'm taking you," she assured him.

The wind was brisk and cool as they skimmed the green waters of Gossamer Lake, but she knew it would warm up once they dropped anchor and started trolling for the quirky little speckled-white fish they were after this morning. Meanwhile, the loamy smell of the lake and the rosy glow of the morning sky gave her a giddy feeling of well-being, the first glimpse of her normal self since she returned home from Wyoming.

She should have come out fishing sooner. It had always been her favorite way of centering her world.

Maybe she'd get Riley Patterson out of her heart yet.

RILEY'S CELL PHONE RANG around 7:00 a.m., while he was in the motel bathroom about to shave. He fished the phone out of the pocket of his jeans. It was Joe's cell number. "Yeah?"

"Where are you?" The tension in Joe's voice set Riley's nerves immediately on edge.

"Budget Suites Motel in Birmingham." He headed out of the bathroom, shaving forgotten. "What's going on?"

"How long will it take you to get to Gossamer Ridge?"

"Hour and a half, I think—what's going on?"

The brief pause on the other end of the line made Riley's empty stomach cramp. It was almost a relief when Joe spoke. "I think we've found the killer."

Riley dropped heavily on to the bed. "Who?"

"Guy named Kyle Layton. Six-one, early thirties, sandy-blond hair, gray eyes. A security guard at Memorial Hospital."

"Someone recognized the ring," Riley guessed.

"He wears it on his left pinky finger, like Hannah said."

"Can we connect him to our other cases?"

"We can connect him to at least one, I'm pretty sure," Joe answered grimly. "He was working as a prison guard in the Casper area when Emily was killed. He was one of the ones in charge of taking prisoners to the hospital where she worked when they couldn't handle their injuries or illnesses at the prison infirmary."

"Son of a bitch." Riley curled his hand into a fist as bleak rage poured into his gut like acid. "Tell me you have him in custody, Joe."

"He boarded a plane out of Casper yesterday morning around 9:00 a.m.," Joe answered. "Headed for Nashville, Tennessee."

"Tennessee?" It took a moment for Riley to get it. "Oh, hell."

"It's less than a three-hour drive to Gossamer Ridge. We've been able to ascertain that he spent the night at the motel in Nashville, but none of the staff has seen him this morning, and he's not in his room."

Riley lurched off the bed, swiping his keys and his holstered Ruger off the dresser. He shrugged on his jacket, snapped the holster to the waistband of his jeans and grabbed his hat on his way out the door. He took the steps down to the rental car two at a time. "I need you to get the Chickasaw County Sheriff's Department on the phone. Ask for—" He grimaced. What the hell was the brother's name? "Ask for a Cooper. I can't remember the name."

"I'm on it."

"If you get him, tell him to find his sister and keep her in one place until I can get there. And give him my cell number." Riley rang off and jerked the rental car into gear, startling a maintenance staffer who was out picking up garbage in the cool of the early morning.

Punching the number of Hannah's cell phone into his cell phone as he sped up the on-ramp to I-59, he muttered a fervent prayer that she'd answer. But her voicemail connected after two rings. "Hannah, it's Riley. If you get this, find your parents or one of your brothers and stick with them until I get there. I'm in Birmingham but I'm heading your way. Do not go anywhere alone, do you hear me? We've found the killer. His name is Kyle Layton." He rattled off the description Joe had given him. "He's on his way to Alabama."

The voicemail beeped, cutting him off. He cursed and considered calling back but decided he'd been able to record enough to warn her to stay put. He tried directory assistance next and got the phone number for the Cooper Cove Marina booking office, but voicemail kicked in at that number as well. He left a similar message and rang off, a slow, sick terror rising like bile in his throat.

Where the hell was she? Was he already too late?

He was somewhere just past Gadsden, about five miles from the Gossamer Ridge exit and driving as fast as he dared when his cell phone rang. He grabbed it, not even checking the display. "Riley Patterson."

"This is Aaron Cooper. Hannah's brother." The voice on the other end of the line was low and tense. "Joe Garrison gave me your number."

"Tell me Hannah's with you right now," Riley demanded.

"She's not. She's out on the lake with a client."

The knots in Riley's stomach twisted into new knots. "A client?"

"I talked to my parents. She and a fishing client left around six-thirty this morning. Guy named Ken Lassiter."

"Six-one, sandy-blond hair, gray eyes?"

On the other end of the line, Aaron let loose a stream of profanities. "It's him, isn't it?"

"Yes. Do you have any idea where she'd take him?"

"One or two. I'm about ten minutes away from the lake. I'll call my brothers. They're probably already on the lake with clients. How far away are you?"

"I'm taking the Gossamer Ridge exit now," he said, jerking the rental car hard right and down the off-ramp.

"You're only a couple of miles from the turnoff to the marina. Take a left and watch for the sign on your left. You may beat me there, but wait for me!" Aaron rang off.

Though bleakly certain it was a futile gesture, Riley tried Hannah's cell number again. Voicemail again. He snapped the phone shut with a growl and took a left at the bottom of the ramp, shooting through a yellow light and hoping like hell there weren't any speed traps between him and the marina.

Hannah was on the lake with a killer, and he might already be too late.

HANNAH SLOWLY STEERED the Triton with the stick, watching her client twitch the jig around the edge of the sunken pier. This was one of her favorite fishing holes, but so far Ken Lassiter wasn't having much luck. He lacked the smooth, instinctive rhythm of an experienced crappie fisherman, but so far he'd refused her suggestion that he switch to live bait.

"Where are you from, Mr. Lassiter?" she asked, bringing the boat to a stop and unreeling the anchor until she felt it thump lightly on the muddy lake bottom.

"Idaho." He flashed her a rueful smile. "Not a lot of crappie fishing up there, I'm afraid."

"I was next door in Wyoming a couple of weeks ago," she commented, watching him cast the jig toward shore. "Good trout fishing there."

"Yes." He glanced at her. "Vacation or work?"

"Vacation," she answered, wishing she hadn't brought up Wyoming. It reminded her of Riley, and she was supposed to be putting Riley out of her head.

"Nice country, Wyoming. Where'd you go—Yellowstone? Did you see Old Faithful?"

"Didn't quite make it there."

"Do you go out by yourself like this all the time?" he asked over his shoulder.

"Usually. It's a small boat. Not a lot of room for extra passengers."

"You must be brave. It's a dangerous world out there."

The sound of his voice echoed in her head, drawing out a memory. A man's voice, neutral and low. Familiar. *"It's a dangerous world out there. You shouldn't be driving all by yourself. Anything could happen to you."*

Blood rushed loudly in her ears, making her feel lightheaded. She gripped the seat of her chair and stared at Ken Lassiter's back, the horrible truth sliding relentlessly through the fog of first panic.

Ken Lassiter. Like the Lassiter Oil station where a

mysterious man warned her not to travel alone, then punished her for not taking his advice.

She fought to remember what the man had looked like, desperate to convince herself that everything unfolding before her now was just some crazy coincidence. But her fishing client was the right height, the right build, and as far as she could remember, the right coloring. Today, just as he had that day at the gas station, he wore a baseball cap low over his forehead.

Just then, he lifted the spinning rod, giving her a close-up view of his left hand. A pale band of skin circled his pinky finger between the second and third knuckles, contrasting sharply with the rest of the tanned skin of his hand.

It was him. That's where the onyx ring went, the one he'd been wearing the day he'd attacked her.

In the back of her mind, a terrified voice was shrieking with panic, trying to drown out her attempts at logical thought. She beat it back with ruthless determination, taking advantage of the man's distraction to gather her wits.

She mentally raced through her options, not liking any of them. If this man was the killer, anything she did out of the ordinary, like ending their fishing trip abruptly, might spur him into action sooner. Trying to subdue him alone wasn't smart, either. He outweighed her by a lot, and there would be little room to maneuver on the boat to seek any sort of advantage.

And she didn't know how long she had before he decided to make his move. She wasn't sure why he hadn't made it already.

"Why don't we try another spot?" she suggested. "Maybe we'll have more luck there." She tried to keep the fear from her voice but wasn't sure she was succeeding.

"Let's stick here a little longer," he said calmly.

Hannah darted her gaze around the boat until she spotted her open tackle box. Beneath the upper trays, she had a nice big fillet knife stored, but getting to it would cause too much of a clamor and might draw his attention. However, if she could get to her jacket, which she'd shed when the temperature had risen with full sunup, she could sneak out the sturdy pocketknife she always carried when she fished.

She stepped lightly to the middle of the boat and picked up the jacket, slipping it on.

Her movement caught Ken's attention. "Cold?"

"Just a little. The breeze has kicked up a bit." She snugged the jacket around her, sticking her hands in her pockets. She palmed the pocketknife, trying not to notice how small it felt.

If she could get him out of this secluded cove, she could track down Jake or Gabe at one of their favorite bass spots, she realized as the small comfort of the knife helped clear her mind a little. Both of her brothers were on the lake with fishing clients this morning. If she could reach one of them, she'd be safe. Then she could set the local cops on Ken Lassiter.

"Are you sure you don't want to head for another spot?" she asked again.

"Very." Lassiter turned around to look at her. "I have to say, Hannah Cooper, you're a hard woman to kill."

A CHICKASAW COUNTY SHERIFF'S cruiser sat in the parking lot of the Cooper Cove Bait Shop when Riley pulled in, his rental car kicking up gravel as he skidded to a stop. He rushed past the empty cruiser and entered the bait shop.

At the front, an older couple and a uniformed deputy turned to look at him.

"I'm Riley Patterson," he announced. "You're Aaron?"

The dark-haired deputy nodded. "These are my parents, Beth and Mike. We've tried calling my brothers on the lake, but they usually forward their calls to voicemail when they're fishing with clients. I was about to grab a boat and head out myself."

"Is that man really here?" the woman asked. Riley gave her a closer look, his heart clutching as he saw how much she looked like her daughter.

"Yes, ma'am. But we're going to stop him."

"I'm going with you," the older man said.

"No, Dad, you need to stay here with Mom." Aaron didn't say the rest of what he was clearly thinking. If Kyle Layton managed to kill Hannah, he might come back to the bait shop to tie up the rest of his loose ends.

"You're right," Mr. Cooper agreed, fear and rage battling it out in his expression.

"My boat's here." Aaron's terse, impatient voice drew Riley's attention back to the deputy. "You coming?"

Aaron led him on a weaving race through a maze of narrow docks to a mid-sized powerboat near the end of one of the piers. He jumped in, and Riley followed, settling into the passenger seat. He pulled the Ruger from his holster and checked the clip. He had a second clip in his jacket pocket.

He hoped he wouldn't need either.

"Her phone's set to go automatically to voicemail,"

Aaron called over the roar of the outboard motor. "But I think I know where she'd have started fishing."

Assuming Kyle Layton let her get that far before making his move, Riley thought grimly.

"Hey!" Aaron suddenly started waving wildly at another boat. Riley followed the direction of his gaze and saw a bass boat skimming across the lake. The driver apparently spotted Aaron's signal and throttled down, easing the bass boat across the water until he came up beside Aaron's boat.

A tall man in his early thirties sat behind the steering wheel, a quizzical expression on his face. Another brother, Riley realized, seeing the resemblance to Hannah.

"What're you flagging me down for, doofus?" He nodded to a slightly sunburned man watching curiously from the passenger bench behind him. "I've got a client."

"Hannah's in trouble, Jake."

Jake's expression immediately shifted. "Where? What's happened?"

"That guy from Wyoming who attacked her—we think he's with her, posing as a client."

Jake scowled. "I saw her about an hour ago, heading toward Papermouth Cove." He looked at Riley as if noticing him for the first time. "Who're you?"

"The cowboy," Aaron answered for him, throttling up the motor. "Let's go!" he called back to his brother.

The other boat kept pace with them as they flew east, snippets of Jake's explanation to his passenger rising over the roar of the motors and the wind. Apparently, even the client knew about Hannah and her Wyoming ordeal. Small towns were small towns, whether Wyoming or Alabama.

"We're close," Aaron told him. "Just around that bend."

Riley just prayed they'd be in time.

"So, I WAS RIGHT." Hannah was surprised by how calm she felt, now that the moment of confrontation had arrived. Maybe it was the feel of the knife in her right hand. She whispered a silent prayer of thanks that she'd been conscientious about keeping the hinge oiled; the blade had easily and silently opened for her with just a flick of her fingers.

"I certainly gave you enough clues," the man who called himself Ken Lassiter said with a soft chuckle. He reached into the tackle box beside him and pulled out a yellow, nylon fish stringer.

Hannah eyed his hands as he started wrapping the end of the stringer around one hand. One loop. Two.

"No blitz attack?" she asked aloud. "No face full of pepper spray?"

He shook his head. "You'd be expecting that. I like to keep an element of surprise."

"Your name isn't Ken Lassiter."

"No, it's not." He smiled more broadly. "Nice clue, though, wasn't it? Ken Lassiter, Lassiter Oil—you do remember that, don't you?"

Hannah ran her finger over the flat side of the knife blade, clinging to the steady calm she'd so far managed to retain. "Is this really all about proving me wrong?"

"You didn't listen to my warning."

"I didn't realize that was a killing offense."

His smile faded. "You never think about the people

whose lives you destroy with your recklessness. What about your parents, waiting at home for your return? What if you'd had a husband or children?"

"You'd have made sure I didn't get back to them, if you'd gotten your way." She felt panic and anger battling in the pit of her stomach. She tamped down both emotions. "What's your real name?"

"Kyle Layton." He answered the question as if he was swatting away a bug. His face reddened and his voice rose. "I didn't get my way. You chose your own path. You tempted fate." His voice dipped to a disgusted growl. "You all do."

It was a little harder maintaining her calm when he was starting to unravel in front of her, but she forced herself to react as if he was rational, knowing that if she could stall for time, someone would eventually wander by the cove and she'd have a better chance at a clean escape. She kept her voice steady as she asked, "You know a lot of women who've tempted fate?"

"My whole life," Layton answered, his voice softening to an almost childlike tone. "He told her not to go to Laramie. He could've made ends meet by himself. She didn't need to take a job so far away."

Somewhere behind her, Hannah heard the sound of motors nearing the opening of the cove. She'd have a narrow window of opportunity to get their attention, but she didn't dare telegraph her plans to the man coming apart in front of her.

"Are you talking about your mother?" she asked him.

He looked up, his gaze swimming into focus as if he'd forgotten she was there with him. "Yes. My mother."

"What happened to her?" she asked, trying to keep her voice sympathetic.

"She was working late at the store. That bastard she worked for had her close up alone." The little boy timbre of his voice grew more pronounced, tinged with a childlike anger and hurt. "Daddy told her not to take the job, and he was right!" Layton turned a wounded animal gaze on her. "She did this to us! She didn't listen, and she did this to us!"

Oh, my God, she realized, her blood chilling to an icy crawl. *He's been killing his mother, over and over again.*

Behind her, nearing the cove's mouth, the sound of motors grew louder. At least two, running close together. It was odd enough to distract her for a moment.

Long enough for Layton to grab the heavy, metal tackle box and swing it at her head.

She ducked at the last minute, and the tackle box grazed her temple. It hurt like hell, but she didn't see stars or lose her balance. As he started to swing again, she pulled out the knife and slashed at his arm.

He roared in pain and rage, body-slamming her in response. They both toppled from the boat into the lake.

The shock of the cold water almost made her gasp, but she was half submerged, and the last thing she needed was a lung full of water. She rose back to the surface and drew a long breath, struggling to free herself from Layton's flailing grip.

Suddenly, something pressed against her throat, pulling tight. Black spots dotted her vision as she tried to stay focused. He was using the fish stringer as a makeshift garrote. She felt the rough nylon digging into her throat.

She tightened her grip on the knife, fighting the on-

slaught of darkness and silence. Her entire consciousness seemed to narrow to the cold, hard feel of the knife
clutched in her fist.

With the last of her strength, she jabbed hard behind her and felt the blade connect with something soft.

The grip on the fish stringer loosened, and the world
rushed back in a firestorm of colors and sounds.

Water, cold as the tomb, swallowing her whole. The
bubbly sound of Kyle Layton's gasps for air behind
her. Boat motors, shrieking at full throttle, filling her
ears with white noise before the engines idled down to
a low hum.

Kyle Layton released her, and she kicked away from
him, racing for the rocky shoreline thirty yards away.
She didn't care who was behind her or what happened
to Layton. She just wanted to get as far from him as
possible.

She reached the bank and scrambled over the rocks
and mud to the grassy edge beyond. Once there, she
tried to stand, but the world around her went into a
swirling taildive. Her knees buckled beneath her and she
pitched forward into the grass. She lay still and willed
her head to stop spinning long enough for her to enjoy
the simple pleasure of still being alive.

AARON COOPER DROVE HIS BOAT into the mouth of Papermouth Cove just in time for Riley to witness Kyle Layton's blitz attack. He yelled in horror as the tackle box
made contact with the side of Hannah's head.

Aaron poured on the speed. "Hold on!"

They were within fifty yards when Layton tackled
Hannah and they both flew into the water with a booming splash.

The next thirty yards seemed to take forever to traverse. Guiding the boat closer, Aaron howled out a stream of profanity that would put even a roughneck cowboy to shame.

The struggle continued in the water, until Hannah suddenly broke free and started racing toward the shore, her swimming strokes growing increasingly sluggish and erratic as she neared the bank. In the water, Kyle Layton started paddling away from the crappie boat, his movements jerky and slow.

For a moment, Riley couldn't take his eyes off the man, all the rage and grief of three long years focusing like a laser on the man's feeble escape attempt. The urge to grab his Ruger and end the struggle was almost more than Riley could resist.

Then, out of the corner of his eye, he saw Hannah make it to shore and immediately crumple to the ground. All thought of Layton, of the sweet siren call of revenge, dissipated like smoke in the wind.

"Hannah!" A hissing stream of fear ran through his mind like a litany, threatening to drown out rational thought.

"I'll get Layton," Aaron shouted.

Riley threw off his jacket and jerked at his boots, cursing when one stuck. It finally came free. He tossed it aside and plunged into the cold lake water.

He covered the remaining distance to the shore in a few frantic strokes and pulled himself on to the bank, his heart pounding like a bass drum in his chest. Scrambling over the rocks, he reached her still, crumpled form. He felt for her carotid pulse, praying silently.

At his touch, she jerked away. Her eyes opened,

wildly fighting for focus. It took a second for her to react to what she was seeing.

"Riley?" Her voice, raspy and weak, rang with surprise.

He found himself laughing at her shocked expression, so grateful she was alive that the whole world suddenly seemed like a bright, beautiful place.

She didn't resist when he grabbed her up and crushed her to him, pressing kisses over her cheeks, in her hair, and finally hard and sweet against her lips.

The fingers feebly clutching his arms tightened, their grip strengthening. Beneath his mouth, her lips moved, parting with invitation.

He threaded his fingers through her hair, holding her face steady as he poured into the kiss all his pent up fears, longings and hopes. When he finished, he drew his head back and gazed into her beautiful, liquid gaze.

"Why aren't you in Wyoming?" she asked.

"Because I love you," he answered with a laugh.

A glorious smile curved her kiss-stung lips. "I didn't think you'd ever figure that out on your own, cowboy," she drawled, running her thumb over his bottom lip.

He dragged her closer, heat flooding his belly. "Cowboys always need a sidekick, darlin'." He tangled his hand in her hair, drawing her head back to give him access to the bruised skin of her throat. Anger coiled like a rattler in his chest, but he killed it. There'd be time to sort out justice later.

Right now, he wanted Hannah to know just how damned much he loved her.

A long, thorough kiss later, they came up for air. "Just to be clear," he murmured against the curve of her ear, "you love me too, right?"

She nipped at the tendon on the side of his neck. "From the top of your Stetson to the soles of your ratty old snakeskin boots."

When he laughed, he realized that it was the first time in three years that he felt truly, unreservedly happy.

EPILOGUE

Five months later

"PEOPLE AROUND HERE call you my cowboy," Hannah murmured in Riley's ear as he led her slowly across the pavilion that had turned into a dance floor for their wedding reception.

He tucked her hand against his heart and smiled down at her from beneath the brim of his Stetson. "Why ever would they do that, darlin'?"

"Maybe it's the boots," she murmured, reaching up to tip his hat back a notch. "Or the horse trailer hitched to your truck. Or—"

He shushed her with a kiss that would have made her toes tingle even if her feet weren't stuffed into pointed white pumps. "I'm sorry Luke couldn't make it."

She tried not to let a thread of sadness taint the happiness of her wedding day. "He'll come back, sooner or later. We all do." She looked into his happy, blue eyes. "Are you sure you're okay relocating here? Won't you miss Joe and Jane?"

Riley looked over his shoulder at his friend, who sat at one of the tables flanking the dance floor. Joe was holding his newborn son in his arms, while Jane chatted happily with Hannah's sister-in-law Mariah, who held her own little boy, Micah, on her lap. "He has his own family," Riley said with a smile. "And now I have mine. They're as close as a phone or e-mail. We won't lose touch."

She closed her eyes and relaxed into his embrace, setting aside any lingering worries. He'd miss Wyoming, even though he swore he wouldn't, but life was a series of choices with consequences. She'd make sure he never felt that trading Wyoming for Alabama was a bad bargain.

Riley cleared his throat. "There's one other thing."

She looked up, a little concerned by the frown lining his brow. "What?"

"Kyle Layton was convicted last week. They gave him life without parole."

"Oh." She hadn't thought about Layton for a couple of months. He'd pleaded guilty to assault in an Alabama court, perhaps hoping he could avoid prosecution in Wyoming, but once Joe, Riley and Sheriff Tanner had his identity confirmed, they'd been able to piece together enough physical evidence against him to bring him up on multiple murder charges in Wyoming. Alabama had waived extradition and sent him to Wyoming for trial.

"Does that mean he'll be jailed up there instead of here?"

"Yeah, that's the latest."

"Then it's really over."

He nodded, pressing his lips to her forehead. "How about we stop talking about that and start talking about what naughty, naughty things you're going to do to me when you get me alone?"

She laughed, rising up to bite his earlobe. "How

about we get the hell out of here and let me show you instead?"

He looked down at her, love and hunger shining from his blue eyes. "On the count of three. One. Two. Three!"

Joining hands, they raced off the dance floor together, the whole wide world in front of them.

* * * * *

CHICKASAW COUNTY
CAPTIVE

For Melissa, who surprises and challenges me daily.
I'm lucky to be your aunt.

CHAPTER ONE

BLUE AND CHERRY lights strobed the night sky as Sam Cooper muscled his Jeep into a tight turn onto Mission Road. Ahead, a phalanx of police cars and rescue units spread haphazardly across the narrow road in front of his house.

He parked the Cherokee behind the nearest police cruiser, his pounding heart outracing the pulses of light. Ignoring the gaggle of curious onlookers, he took the porch steps two at a time and pushed past the uniformed cop standing in the doorway.

"Sir, you can't—"

Sam ignored him, scanning the narrow foyer until he caught sight of his older brother's terrified face. "J.D.?"

J. D. Cooper turned at the sound of his name. The look on his face made Sam's stomach turn queasy flips. "Is Cissy okay?" he asked J.D. "Where's Maddy?"

J.D.'s gaze flickered back to the paramedics working over the unconscious body of his teenage daughter lying on the woven rug in the middle of the foyer. "Cissy's alive but they can't get her to respond."

Sam's heart skipped a beat. "What the hell happened? What about Maddy?"

J.D. looked at him again. "We don't know."

The panic Sam had held in check broke free, suffocating him. He started toward the stairs up to the bedroom, where he'd last seen his daughter when he kissed her good-night before leaving for his business dinner.

J.D. caught his arm, jerking him to a stop. "She's not up there. We looked."

Sam tugged his arm away. "Maybe she's in another room—"

J.D. gestured at the obvious signs of a struggle. "Cissy didn't just fall down and hit her head, Sam! Someone did this to her! Someone took Maddy."

Sam shook his head, not willing to believe it.

A pair of detectives moved toward them, their badges hooked to their waistbands. All that broke through the haze of Sam's panic was the sympathy in the man's eyes and the complete lack of expression on the woman's face.

The female introduced herself. "Kristen Tandy, Gossamer Ridge Police Department. This is Detective Jason Foley. You're the home owner?"

"Sam Cooper." He bit back impatience. "My daughter's missing."

"Yes, sir, we know," Detective Foley said.

His sympathetic tone only ramped up Sam's agitation. "What else do you know?"

"We've searched the house and the property, and we have officers questioning neighbors, as well," Detective Tandy replied. Her flat, emotionless drawl lacked the practiced gentleness of her partner, but it better suited Sam's mood. He focused his eyes on her face, taking in the clear blue of her eyes and the fine, almost delicate bone structure.

Damn, she's young, he thought.

Foley took Sam's elbow. "Mr. Cooper, let's find somewhere to sit down—"

"Don't handle me," Sam snapped at Foley, jerking his arm away. "I'm a Jefferson County prosecutor. I know how this works. My four-year-old is missing. I want to know what you know about what happened here. Every detail—"

"We're not sure of every detail," Detective Foley began.

"Then tell me what you think you know."

"At 8:47 p.m. your brother J.D. called to check on your niece Cissy to see how she and your daughter were doing," Foley answered. Behind him, his partner wandered away from them, moving past the paramedics and out of view. Sam found his attention wandering with her, wondering if she knew something she didn't want him to know. Something bad.

Foley's voice dragged him away from his bleak thoughts. "When your niece didn't answer her cell phone, he tried your landline, with no luck. So he came by to check in person and found the front door ajar and your niece on the floor here in the foyer, unconscious."

Movement to their right drew the detective's attention for a moment. Sam followed his gaze and saw the paramedics putting his niece onto a stretcher. His chest tightened with worry. "How badly is she hurt?"

"She's been roughed up a little. There's a lump on the back of her head." Foley looked back at Sam. "There's some concern because she hasn't regained consciousness."

Pushing aside his own fear, Sam walked away from Foley and crossed to his niece's side, falling into step with J.D. "She's a fighter, J.D. You know that."

His brother's attempt at a smile broke Sam's heart. "She's a Cooper, right?"

"Mom and Dad have Mike?" Sam asked, referring to J. D.'s eleven-year-old son. Poor kid, growing up without a mother and now facing another possible loss…

"Yeah. I'd better call 'em." J.D. headed out behind the paramedics carrying his daughter out to the ambulance.

"Mr. Cooper?" Detective Foley stepped into the space J.D. just vacated. "We have some questions—"

Sam turned to look at him. Foley's gaze was tinged with pity disguised as sympathy.

"What?" Sam asked impatiently.

"What was Maddy wearing tonight?" Foley asked.

"She was in jeans and a 'Bama sweatshirt when I left her in her bedroom with Cissy," Sam answered, the memory of his daughter's earlier goodbye kiss haunting him. "She didn't want me to leave. Tuesday is extra-story night."

"We found those clothes in the hamper outside her room," Foley said. "Maybe she'd already dressed for bed?"

"Then she's in Winnie the Pooh pajamas. Blue ones. She won't wear anything else to bed. I had to buy three identical sets." He fought a tidal wave of despair. He knew the odds against finding Maddy alive grew exponentially the longer she was missing.

"We'll put out an Amber Alert," Foley said.

Sam walked away, needing space to breathe. The thought that he might never see his daughter alive again made his knees shake and his chest tighten.

"Mr. Cooper?" The sympathy in Foley's voice was almost more than Sam could bear.

"I need a minute," Sam said.

"Sure. Take all the time you need." Foley stepped away. A few feet away, Sam saw the female detective edge toward the staircase. Her eyes met his briefly, her expression grim. Then she turned and headed up the stairs.

Sam's heart squeezed into a knot. Take all the time he needed? Time was the one thing he didn't have. Not if he wanted to find his child alive.

THE HOUSE WAS clean but lived-in, the carpet runner in the upstairs hallway slightly askew, as if someone had hit it at a run. Kristen Tandy moved past Mark Goddard, one of the two uniformed officers tasked with evidence collection, and crossed to a door standing slightly ajar. "Checked in here?" she asked.

Goddard looked up at her. "It's a storage area. Full of boxes. Didn't look like much had been touched, but I'll get to it before we leave."

She donned a pair of latex gloves. "Can I take a look?"

Goddard frowned. "Do you have to?"

But she'd already opened the door and flicked on the light.

Inside, the room was a mess. Stacks of boxes, mostly full, filled the spare bedroom. The Coopers hadn't been living here long, she guessed. Hadn't finished unpacking from the move.

"Maddy?" She stopped and listened. She heard no response, but the hairs on the back of her neck prickled. She stepped deeper into the room, squeezing between two stacks of boxes. "Are you in here?"

There was still no answer, but Kristen thought she heard a noise behind the boxes ahead. She froze in place, her head cocked. The sound of Goddard at work just outside the room mingled with a faint hum of conversation from downstairs.

"When I was a little girl, my favorite game was hide-and-seek." She formed the words from her frozen lips. "I was good at it, you see, because I was so little. I could go places nobody else could go. So they never, ever found me until I was ready to be found."

She eased forward, past a large box in the middle of the room, ignoring the tremble in her belly. "I bet you're good at hiding, too, aren't you, Maddy?"

A faint rustling noise came from the back of the room. Beyond the stack of boxes in front of her, she spotted a door. The closet, she guessed.

"My name is Kristen Tandy. I'm a police officer. I came here to help your cousin Cissy."

A faint hiccough sent a ripple of triumph racing through Kristen's gut, followed quickly by a rush of sheer dread. Taking a bracing breath, she pushed aside a box to get to the closet and pulled open the door.

Four-year-old Maddy Cooper gazed up at Kristen with tear-stained green eyes, her face damp and flushed. "I want my Daddy," she whimpered.

Kristen crouched in front of Maddy, helping her to her feet. The little girl's hands were soft and tiny, and up close, she smelled sweet. Kristen felt her knees wobble and she put one hand on the door frame to steady herself.

Do your job, Tandy.

She looked Maddy over quickly. No obvious signs of injury, she noted with almost crushing relief. "Are you okay, Maddy? Do you hurt anywhere?"

"Kristen?" Foley called from somewhere behind them.

Maddy Cooper flung herself at Kristen, her arms

tightening around her. The little girl buried her tear-damp face in Kristen's neck, shaking with fear.

"It's okay," she soothed, fighting the primal urge to push the little girl away and run as fast and as far as she could—the way she felt every time she was this close to a child. Instead, she picked Maddy up and turned to face her partner. The scent of baby shampoo filled her lungs, making her feel weak, but she clung to her equilibrium.

Sam Cooper stood by Foley, staring at her with eyes full of shock and fragile hope. "Maddy?"

At the sound of her father's voice, Maddy wriggled to get away. Kristen put her down, and the child weaved through the stacks of boxes to reach her father.

He scooped her into his arms and smothered her face with kisses. "Oh, baby, are you okay?" Sam held his daughter away to get a good look.

Kristen looked away, a powerful ache spreading like poison in her chest.

"The bad man hurt Cissy!" Maddy wailed.

"I know, baby, but the bad man is gone now. And Cissy's getting help. It'll be all right now, okay?" Out of the corner of her eye, Kristen saw Sam Cooper thumb away the tears spilling from his daughter's eyes.

"Mr. Cooper, we need to ask Maddy—" Foley began.

"Enough, Foley," Kristen said flatly, joining them in the doorway. "You might want to take her to the hospital, too, let a doctor check her over," she said to Sam. "We'll talk to you soon." She grabbed her partner's arm, tugging him with her as she headed out of the room. She couldn't stay there one minute longer, she knew.

Foley stopped in the middle of the hallway. "How the hell did you know—?"

"Kids like to play hide-and-seek," she said, moving ahead of him down the hallway.

She knew from experience.

HOSPITALS HAD A smell to them, a strange mix of anti-septic and disease that made Kristen's skin crawl. A doctor had once told her that knowing the reason behind an irrational aversion was the key to overcoming it. But knowing why she hated hospitals hadn't done much to cure Kristen of her phobia.

The doctors were still examining the two Cooper girls. Across from where she and Jason Foley stood, the girls' grandparents sat in aluminum-and-vinyl chairs backed up against the hallway outside the emergency treatment bays. The elder Coopers flanked a scared-looking boy of eleven or so—Cissy's brother, Michael.

"Why are we here?" Kristen asked Foley softly. "We should be back at the crime scene."

Foley slanted a gaze toward the grandparents before speaking in a whisper. "The girls saw their attacker."

"One of them has a cracked skull and the other is practically a baby," Kristen shot back, apparently louder than she realized, for Mrs. Cooper sent a pained look her way. Kristen took a few steps away from the family, waiting for Foley to catch up with her before she added, "We should be supervising the evidence retrieval."

"Goddard's perfectly capable of that," Foley said. "The answers are here with the girls."

Kristen stopped arguing, mostly because she knew her desire to leave had less to do with good police work and more to do with her need to get the hell out of this hospital.

The doors to the Emergency wing opened, ushering

in a cool night breeze and two men dressed in jeans and T-shirts. They were tall and dark-haired, clearly related to Sam Cooper and his brother J.D. The two men looked so alike, Kristen wondered if they were twins.

The one in the dark blue T-shirt caught sight of the elder Coopers. "Mom!" He hurried to her side and crouched by the chair. "I got your voice mail. Any word?"

Mrs. Cooper shook her head. "We're still waiting to hear. Sam and J.D. went back there with the kids. Cissy was still unconscious when she came in."

"What about Maddy?"

"She seems okay, but Sam wanted her looked over anyway."

The other man ruffled the dark hair of the young boy sandwiched between the grandparents, hunkering down until he was eye level with the child. "How you holdin' up, sport?"

Michael managed a faint smile. "I'm okay, Uncle Gabe."

The man in the blue T-shirt caught Kristen watching. His gaze settled on the back of Kristen's right hand for a second. She saw recognition as he raised his blue eyes to meet hers.

Kristen ignored the look, but Foley flashed his badge at the newcomers, so she had no choice but to follow.

Foley introduced himself. "You're the girls' uncles?"

The man in the blue T-shirt shook the hand Foley offered. "Jake Cooper. Sam and J.D. are my brothers. This is my brother Gabe." He nodded toward the man who had to be his twin.

Foley introduced her. "This is Detective Kristen Tandy."

Jake's gaze slanted toward the scar on her hand. "I know."

She squelched the urge to stick her hand in her pocket. "Detective Foley and I are investigating the case."

"So I gathered." He looked from Kristen to Foley and back. "What the hell happened at Sam's house?"

"That's what we'd like to ask your nieces."

"Mom says Cissy's still unconscious and Maddy's gotta be traumatized. Can't it wait till morning?"

"The sooner we know what happened, the sooner we find who did it and stop it from happening again," Foley said soothingly.

"Sam!" Mrs. Cooper's voice drew their attention. Kristen saw Sam Cooper coming down the hallway, his daughter perched on his hip. Maddy had red-rimmed eyes and a slightly snotty nose, but apparently she'd received a clean bill of health.

Sam locked gazes with Kristen. One dark brow ticked upward before he looked back at his mother.

As Mrs. Cooper reached for the little girl, Maddy clung to her father, tightening her grip around his neck. Sam gave his mother an apologetic look and kissed her forehead, then crossed to Kristen and Foley. "I thought you'd still be at the house."

"We were hoping to talk to the girls," Foley said.

"Cissy's still unconscious. They've called in a helicopter to take her to Birmingham." Sam's eyes darkened with anger. "If I ever get my hands on the son of a bitch who did this—"

"What about your daughter?" Foley pressed.

Sam looked at Kristen rather than Foley. "Can't it wait?"

She wanted to say yes. The last thing she wanted to do was spend any more time with Sam Cooper's little girl. But questions had to be asked, and for better or worse, she and Foley were the ones who'd been assigned to ask them. "I think the sooner we can talk to her, the more we'll get from her, while it's fresh in her mind."

He looked at her for a long moment, his expression hard to read. It softened a bit, finally, and he gave a short nod.

Foley glanced at Kristen, a question in his eyes.

"I'll talk to the family," she said. "You handle the kid."

Sam Cooper looked at Kristen through narrowed eyes, his irritation evident. "Don't like children?"

"They don't like me," Kristen answered shortly, wondering why his clear disapproval bothered her so much. "Foley has kids. He knows how to handle them."

Sam's expression darkened further, but his next words were directed at his daughter. "Maddy, this is Detective Foley. He wants to ask you some questions."

Maddy buried her face in her father's neck and shook her head. "No, Daddy!"

"Look, why don't we wait until tomorrow—" Sam began.

"The sooner we do this, the more she'll remember," Foley said. He took a step toward Maddy, softening his voice. "Maddy, sweetheart? I have a little girl just your age. Do you want to see a picture of her?"

"No!" Maddy's voice was muffled by her father's collar.

Foley looked at Kristen, his expression helpless. "You give it a try."

"No," Kristen said in unison with Sam.

Foley arched one eyebrow.

"She doesn't like kids." Sam's voice tightened.

"They don't like me," Kristen repeated, annoyed.

"Maddy, will you talk to Detective Tandy?" Foley asked, ignoring them both.

Maddy turned her head slightly, peeking out from under her father's chin at Kristen. "Her?"

Foley nodded.

Maddy pressed her face against her father's throat again, to Kristen's relief. But a moment later, the little girl nodded, and Kristen's heart sank. No way to avoid it now.

With resignation, she gestured toward the emergency room waiting area. "Let's find a quiet corner."

Sam Cooper gave her a warning look, as if he suspected the sole purpose of the requested interview was to further traumatize his daughter. She ignored his clear discomfort and led the way to the chairs tucked into the corner of the waiting room. Sam settled into one of the chairs, Maddy curled on his lap. Kristen pulled her chair around to face them. Maddy gazed back at her with solemn green eyes, her face still pink from crying. Teardrops glittered on her long lashes like diamonds.

"You saw the bad man who hurt Cissy, didn't you, Maddy?"

She heard Sam's soft inhalation but ignored it, keeping her eyes on the little girl. Slowly, Maddy nodded.

"Was he tall like your daddy?"

Maddy shook her head. She lifted one thumb to her mouth and laid it on her lower lip but didn't start sucking it. She craned her head to look up at her father.

The look of heartbroken love Sam Cooper gave his daughter made Kristen's breath catch. She looked away, a phantom pain jabbing her under her rib cage like a knife. Licking her lips, she pressed on. "So he wasn't tall. Was he short like me?" She stood up so Maddy could see her height.

The little girl considered the question for a moment, then shook her head again. "Bigger."

"Was he skinny like Uncle J. D.?" Sam asked.

"No, Daddy. Like Uncle Aaron."

Sam met Kristen's eyes over the top of his daughter's head. "My brother Aaron. You may know him—he's a Chickasaw County Sheriff's Deputy. A little taller than me, built like a bulldog. Played football at 'Bama till he blew out his knee."

"Yeah, I've met him before," Kristen said. She turned her attention back to Maddy. "So he's shorter than your daddy and about your Uncle Aaron's size. Did you see his hair color?"

She shook her head. "Had a daddy hat."

Kristen looked to Sam for translation.

He gave a helpless shrug. "I guess she means a baseball cap. That's the only kind of hat I ever wear."

Maddy looked up at her father again, her eyes welling up with new tears. "He made Cissy cry, Daddy."

Sam's eyes glittered as he stroked his daughter's dark curls. "I know, baby. That's why we need to find out who he is and make sure he doesn't ever do that again." He looked at Kristen. "I don't think she remembers much about it."

"Did you notice anything special about him? Did he have freckles or moles or scars—?" With a bracing breath, Kristen held out her right hand and showed it to Maddy. "This is a scar, Maddy. See that?"

Maddy looked solemnly at the burned skin on the

back of Kristen's hand, then up at Kristen. "Does it hurt?"

"Not anymore." She avoided Sam's gaze. "Did the man have anything like this?"

Maddy shook her head.

"What happened?" Sam's gaze lingered on the scar burned into her hand.

She looked up, surprised. He didn't know? She forced her gaze back to Maddy, ignoring Sam's question. "How did you get into the closet, Maddy?"

"Cissy told me to run so I runned." Her little brow furrowed. "I couldn't get the back door to open."

"Locked," Sam said. "She doesn't know how to unlock it."

"So I runned up to the secret place."

A chill darted up Kristen's spine, scattering goose bumps along her back and arms. Her stomach twisted, a sinking sensation filling her insides, but she pressed on. "The closet was the secret place?"

Maddy nodded. "Nobody ever finded me there."

"Cissy plays hide-and-seek with her sometimes. I guess she's so small she doesn't have any trouble squeezing in there behind the boxes." Sam's gaze moved away from hers, settling on something behind her. She turned to see J. D. Cooper coming into the waiting area, his face pale and drawn.

"Do you think you could watch Maddy a second?" Sam asked Kristen. He ruffled his daughter's hair. "Can you sit here with Detective Tandy for me, baby? I'm just going over there to talk to Uncle J.D., okay?"

Kristen wanted to argue, but the little girl had already climbed down from her father's lap and settled onto a seat beside Kristen, looking up at her with warm green eyes.

"Do you like to color?" she asked Kristen.

"Yeah, I do," Kristen answered, wishing she were anywhere else in the world.

"THEY'RE TRANSFERRING HER to Birmingham," J.D. was telling the others as Sam walked up. His voice sounded faint and weary. "They're afraid she's got some bleeding in her brain and they're not set up to handle that here. The helicopter should be here any minute."

"Is she gonna be okay, Dad?" Michael asked J.D., his eyes wide with fear.

J.D. hugged the boy. "She's going to be in the best hospital around. The doctors there are going to take good care of her, Mike. I promise." He looked at his mother. "Y'all keep Mike here, okay? I'll call with any word."

"I'm going with you," Gabe said.

"Thanks, man." J.D. turned at the sound of wheels rolling across the linoleum floor behind him. At the same time, Sam heard the first faint *whump-whump* of helicopter blades beating in the distance.

"Mr. Cooper, Life-Flight will be landing any moment." A nurse in a pair of blue scrubs stepped away from the gurney carrying Cissy and crossed to J.D.'s side. "There won't be room for you in the helicopter, so if you'd like to get a head start, we'll take good care of her until they get here."

J.D. looked at Sam. "I'll call when I know something."

Sam gave his brother a hug. "She's a fighter."

J.D. managed a weak smile and repeated the familiar old mantra. "She's a Cooper." He headed out the door, Gabe on his heels. Jake moved up next to Sam, watching them go.

"Hell of a night," Jake murmured. He looked over his shoulder at Maddy and the detective. "I see little Mad Dog has made a new friend."

Sam followed his brother's gaze to find Maddy leaning against Detective Tandy's arm. Tandy was sitting stiffly, gazing down at the child with a hint of alarm, but Maddy didn't seem to care. "Detective Tandy apparently isn't the maternal sort," he murmured.

"Can't blame her," Jake said. "She's got no reason to think much of motherhood."

Sam looked at his brother. "What do you mean?"

Jake looked taken aback. "Don't you know who she is?"

Sam shook his head. "Should I?"

"Oh, that's right—you'd already left town when that all went down." Jake lowered his voice. "Fifteen years ago, Molly Jane Tandy brutally killed four of her five children."

Sam looked across the waiting room at Kristen Tandy, his stomach tightening. The scar on the back of her hand made sudden, horrifying sense. "My God."

"Kristen Tandy was the oldest. She was thirteen. She's also the only one who survived."

CHAPTER TWO

The space behind the cellar wall was almost too small to hold her, but she squeezed through the narrow opening and pulled the loose board over the gap, trying to slow her ragged breathing. Pain tore at her insides, stronger and bloodier than the cuts on her palms and fingers, more wretched than the searing ache on the back of her hand where the hot spatula had branded her. She had pressed her wounded hands to her body as she ran, terrified of leaving a blood trail for Mama to follow.

She held her breath, lungs aching, and listened. The angry shouts had died away a few minutes ago, the only sounds in the now-still house were the soft *thud-thud* of footfalls on the kitchen floor above.

Her mind was filled with images too grotesque, too profane to process. A whimper hammered against her throat but she crushed it ruthlessly, determined to remain soundless.

She heard Mama's hoarsened voice from the kitchen above. "Kristy, I know you're still here. Nobody goes outside today. Come here to Mama."

Kristen pressed her forehead to the cold brick wall behind the panel and prayed without words, a mindless, desperate plea for mercy and help. The door to the cellar opened.

KRISTEN JERKED AWAKE, her heart pounding. She scraped her hair back from her sweaty brow and stared at the shadowy shapes in her darkened bedroom, half-afraid one of them would move. But everything remained quiet and still.

On her bedside table, green glowing numbers on her alarm clock read 5:35 a.m. She'd managed about four hours of sleep. More than she'd expected.

She switched on the bedside lamp, squinting against the sudden light. Her fingers itched to grab the cell phone lying on the table next to her, but she squelched the urge. Foley wouldn't appreciate a predawn call, and it wasn't as if she had anything to tell him anyway.

As of midnight, when Kristen and Foley called it a night, Cissy Cooper was still unconscious in a Birmingham hospital, her prognosis guarded and uncertain. Sam Cooper and his daughter were spending the next few nights at his parents' place on Gossamer Lake. The crime scene had offered up plenty for the lab to sift through but no obvious smoking gun. And Kristen had at least two more hours to wait before she could decently start following up on the few leads she and Foley had to work with.

She'd start with the ex-wife, she decided sleepily as she stepped into the shower and turned the spray on hot and strong. Sam Cooper had seemed certain the former Mrs. Cooper wasn't a suspect, but Kristen believed in playing the odds. Family members—primarily noncustodial parents—were involved in the majority of child kidnappings. And from what little Cooper had revealed during their brief discussion the night before, Kristen had gleaned that Norah Cabot Cooper hadn't seen her daughter in nearly three years.

She was in the middle of dressing around 7:00 a.m. when her cell phone rang. Stepping into a pair of brown trousers, she grabbed the phone. "Tandy."

"Sam Cooper here."

Her feet got tangled in the trousers and she stumbled onto the bed, hitting it heavily. "Mr. Cooper." She'd given him her business card, with her cell phone number, but he was the last person she'd expected to hear from this morning. "Has something happened?"

"I'm not sure," he said. "Maybe."

She tucked the phone between her chin and shoulder and finished pulling on her pants. "Maybe?"

"My secretary called from my office in Birmingham. She got in early today and found a package for me sitting in front of my office door."

"What kind of package?" Visions of mail bombs flitted through her head. Maybe an anthrax letter. Cooper was a county prosecutor, almost as good a target as a judge or a politician.

"No return address. No postal mark. Right now building security is examining it, and if they think it's a threat, they'll call the cops. But I thought you'd want to know." Sam sounded tired. She doubted he'd managed even as much sleep as she had. "I should probably go into the office, but—"

"No, stay with your kid. If it turns out to be anything we need to worry about, I'll handle it."

There was a pause on the other end of the phone. "I don't want this case mucked up by police agencies marking territory."

If that was a warning, she could hardly blame him. She'd seen her share of interagency wrangling during her seven years as a police officer. "I'll call your office when I get to work, and if I think the package is remotely connected to this case, I'll go to Birmingham and sort it out myself."

"Thank you." After a brief pause he added, "Maddy liked you. You made her feel safer last night when you talked to her. I know that was probably hard on you, considering—you know."

Her heart sank. So he did know who she was. Everybody in Gossamer Ridge knew. Oh, well, the brief anonymity had been nice while it lasted. "It's my job," she said gruffly.

"Thank you anyway." He rang off.

Kristen closed her phone and released a long breath. He was right. It had been hard dealing with Maddy. Kids in general, really. The psychiatrists had all assured her the prickly, uncomfortable feeling she had around young children would go away eventually, as her memories of that horrible day faded with distance.

Only they hadn't faded. The pain had receded, even most of the fear, but not those last, wretched memories of her brothers and sisters.

Their last moments on earth.

She arrived at work in a gloomy mood and found Foley sitting at her desk, jotting a note. He looked up with a half smile. "Ah, I was about to leave you a note. One of Sam Cooper's neighbors called, said she might have seen someone suspicious lurking around the Cooper house earlier in the evening. I thought I'd go hear her out. Let's go."

"Let me make a phone call first." As she looked up the number for the Jefferson County District Attorney's office, she told Foley about Sam Cooper's call. He arched an eyebrow but didn't speak while she waited for someone to pick up. After several rings, voice mail picked up.

"Maybe they've cleared the building, just in case?"

Kristen left a brief message, then dialed Sam Cooper's cell phone number.

He answered on the first ring. "Detective Tandy?"

"I got voice mail when I called your office."

"I know. I managed to get a colleague on his cell. They've evacuated the building and the bomb squad is examining the package. Tim promised to call me back as soon as he knew something more, but this waiting is driving me nuts."

"I'll drive down to Birmingham and check it out for you."

"I'll meet you there."

"Shouldn't you stay with your daughter?"

"Jake and Gabe took her and my nephew Mike fishing to keep their minds off what's going on with Cissy. They'll be out on the lake all morning."

"You should've gone with them."

His soft laugh was humorless. "I'd be on the phone the whole time anyway."

"Then why don't you ride along with me?" Kristen supposed he might be of use to her if the Birmingham Police didn't want to play nice.

"Okay," he agreed. "Do you know where Cooper Marina is?"

"Yeah. See you in fifteen minutes."

KRISTEN TANDY'S CHEVROLET pulled into the marina parking lot with a minute to spare. Sam didn't wait for her to get out. "Where's Detective Foley?" he asked as he slid into the passenger seat.

She cranked the engine. "Talking to a neighbor of yours. Might be a lead." She didn't sound convinced.

"I talked to my colleague again just before you arrived." Sam buckled in as she headed toward the main highway. "Bomb squad's still inside. Nobody seems to know anything yet."

"Don't imagine it's a job you'd want to rush."

He slanted a look at her. Her eyes were on the narrow road twisting through the woods from his parents' marina to the two-lane highway leading into town, her lips curved in a wry smile. He'd been too preoccupied last night to really process much about her, like the fact that she was strikingly pretty. He'd been right about how young she was, though. No older than her late twenties.

She'd shed her jacket to drive, a well-cut white blouse revealing soft curves her boxy business suit had hidden the night before. In the morning sunlight, her skin was as smooth and pale as fine porcelain and her sleek blond hair shimmered like gold. He was surprised by how attractive he found her, under the circumstances.

He distracted himself with a question. "You haven't been a detective long, have you?"

Her expression grew defensive. "Six months."

He nodded. "Big case for you, I guess."

"Not my usual petty theft or meth lab," she admitted.

"How about Foley? How long has he been a detective?"

Her gaze cut toward him. "Should we send you our résumés?"

"Would you?" he countered, more to see her reaction than any real doubt about their credentials.

She took a swift breath through her nose. He could almost hear her mentally counting to ten, he thought, stifling a grin. "Detective Foley has been an investigator for ten years. Five of those were with the Memphis Police Department Homicide Bureau. I've been an officer with the Gossamer Ridge Police Department since I turned twenty-one."

He couldn't hold back a smile. "That long, huh?"

She slanted him an exasperated look, her eyes spitting blue fire. "Anything new with your niece? Last time I checked, the hospital said there was no change."

"That's because there's not been any change," he said, his smile fading. "Better than a downturn, I suppose, but a little good news would be welcome."

"Have they diagnosed the problem?"

"She has a skull fracture and some minor bleeding in her brain. Right now they think she's got a good chance of full recovery, but I think that's based on her age and relative health more than anything they're seeing in the CAT scans."

"Damn. We could really use her statement."

He shot her a look.

Her neck reddened and her lips pressed into a tight line. "Sorry. I'm still working on my self-edit button."

"You're right," he admitted. "We could use her statement."

"I checked in with the lab before I left the station. They're comparing all the fingerprints to eliminate the ones you'd expect to find, so it's going to take time to see if there are any unidentified prints." She turned onto the interstate on-ramp, heading south to Birmingham. "I know you said last night you didn't think your ex could be a suspect—"

"She doesn't have a motive," he said bluntly. "She ended our marriage as much because she didn't want to be a mother as because she didn't want to be married to me. Maddy was an accident she couldn't deal with." He clamped his mouth shut before more bitter words escaped.

"Some women just aren't mother material," Kristen murmured.

"Some women don't even try," he shot back.

She was silent for a moment, a muscle in her jaw working. After a bit, she said, "Maybe when we get to Birmingham, we'll have the answer to who's behind the attack on your niece."

"Maybe." He doubted it, though. It wasn't likely that the guy who broke into his house, nearly killed his niece and tried to kidnap his daughter would send Sam a package that could be traced back to him.

Within thirty minutes they pulled up to the police cordon blocking traffic in front of the Jefferson County District Attorney's office. Sam directed Kristen to park in the deck across from the county courthouse, and they walked down the street to where the police had set up the barriers.

Sam spotted Tim Melton, the colleague he'd reached earlier. He crossed to Melton's side. "Any news?"

"I just saw someone from the bomb squad come out and talk to Captain Rayburn," Tim answered. He gave Kristen Tandy a curious look. "Tim Melton," he introduced himself.

"Detective Tandy," she answered.

"Oh. Right." He looked back at Sam. "How's your niece?"

"No change," he answered tersely. "Detective Tandy's investigating the case."

"I guess that package might be connected?"

"Maybe. We'll see." Kristen stepped closer to the police tape. "Any way to get me in there?" she asked Sam.

He searched the crowd of policemen and firefighters on the other side of the cordon to see if he could catch the eye of one of the handful of officers he knew by name. A few seconds later, a sandy-haired detective named Cropwell spotted him and crossed to the tape to greet him.

"Nothing like fan mail, huh?" he said with a bleak grin.

"What's the latest?"

"Perkins from the Bomb Squad said they've x-rayed it and don't think it's a bomb. They were about to open it last I heard." Cropwell glanced over his shoulder. "Rayburn'll probably be the first to know."

Kristen Tandy flipped open a slim leather wallet, displaying her badge. Sam had a feeling that Cropwell wouldn't exactly be impressed—Gossamer Ridge was small potatoes as Alabama towns went—but he had to admire her bravado.

"Kristen Tandy, Gossamer Ridge Police Department. We believe the package delivered to Mr. Cooper's office may be connected to a home invasion case we're investigating."

As Sam had expected, Cropwell looked at Kristen's badge with a mixture of amusement and disdain. "We'll let you know if anything in the package is of concern to you, Detective."

"Detective Tandy is investigating an attack on my niece, who was caring for my daughter at the time," Sam said firmly. "If this is connected, I want her in on it."

Kristen didn't drop her gaze from Cropwell's, but

Sam saw her expression shift slightly, a slight curve of her pink lips in response to his defense.

Cropwell looked at Sam, instantly apologetic. "Yes, sir."

"May I enter the scene?" Kristen asked, her voice tinted with long-suffering patience that made Cropwell flush.

"Yeah, fine." He lifted the cordon and let Kristen come under. But when Sam started to follow, he blocked entrance. "Sorry, sir," he said, his eyes glittering with payback, "but civilians aren't allowed behind the tape. Not even you, sir."

Sam nodded, acknowledging Cropwell's small victory.

KRISTEN WOULD HAVE died rather than let it show, but mingling with the Birmingham police officers busy outside the Jefferson County District Attorney's office was beginning to make her feel like the biggest rube that ever walked a city street. It wasn't that they treated her badly; most of the other policemen on the scene were polite and helpful, answering her questions and helping her get caught up as quickly as possible. But she was clearly the youngest detective there, and she could tell from the wary gazes of some of the Birmingham detectives that she'd still be wearing a uniform and driving patrol if she weren't on some hayseed rural police force.

She was waiting with the other detectives for word from the bomb squad when her cell phone rang. She excused herself, walked a few feet away and answered. "Tandy."

"I hear you're in Birmingham." Her boss's familiar voice rumbled over the phone, tinged with the same frustrated affection Carl usually showed when it came to her.

"Why do I feel like I just violated curfew?" she murmured.

"Got anything yet?"

"We're waiting for word from the bomb squad. All we really know so far is that there's not actually a bomb in the package."

"That's progress, I suppose."

"Heard anything from Foley? Did he get anything out of the interview with Cooper's neighbor?"

"A rough description of a blue van she saw circling the neighborhood a few times earlier in the day, but nothing concrete. Foley's taking her some pictures to look at, see if she can pick out a make and model but right now, he's going door to door, talking to other neighbors."

She didn't miss the slight tone of admonishment. "And you think I should be there doing that instead of being here waiting for news from the Birmingham bomb squad?"

"You said it, not me."

"You said it without saying it." Movement to her left caught her attention. "Bomb squad's coming out. Gotta go."

She rang off and returned to the queue of police officers waiting for word. A tall, sandy-haired squad member peeled away from the rest of the group and moved toward the detectives. He carried a clear plastic bag containing what appeared to be the remains of a large manila envelope.

"No bomb, no foreign substances. You're clear to examine it," he told a tall, barrel-chested man standing near the front of the line. Kristen dug in her memory for the detective's name. Raymond—no, Rayburn. Captain Rayburn. She took advantage of her small size to slip through the huddle and reach Rayburn's side just as he donned a pair of latex gloves and carefully opened the plastic bag.

He slanted a look toward her, his expression hard to read for a moment. Then his features relaxed and he gave a little half nod, as if beckoning her closer. "Reckon you'll want to see this, too, Detective."

She scooted closer. The contents were, indeed, the remains of a manila envelope. The bomb squad had apparently used a razor knife to slice it open and examine the contents.

Captain Rayburn reached into the plastic bag and delicately opened the edges of the envelope. Inside lay what looked like a small stack of five-by-seven photographs. Careful to touch only the outer edges, Rayburn pulled the stack from the envelope.

Kristen's heart plummeted.

The top photo was an image of a little girl dressed in a robin's-egg-blue shorts set, swinging on a swing at Gossamer Park.

The girl was Maddy Cooper.

CHAPTER THREE

SAM STARED AT the photographs, his stomach rebelling. There were twelve in total, five-by-sevens taken on a digital camera according to the lab tech who examined them first before releasing them back to the Birmingham detectives. Each photo depicted his daughter Maddy at play, in a variety of places, from the playground at Gossamer Park to the farmer's market on Main Street. Once or twice Sam was in the photo, as well; another time, his parents. One photo featured Maddy with Sam's sister Hannah, fishing from one of the marina's fishing piers. Maddy was holding up a small crappie and grinning at her aunt.

He looked away from the photos and rubbed his eyes. They felt full of grit.

"I called my office." Kristen Tandy's voice was toneless. He looked up at her and found her gaze fixed on the photos. "Foley's on his way to the marina now to let your parents know what's going on."

"I need to get back there."

Kristen nodded. "The detectives have agreed to send me scans of these photos." She looked up at Dave Rayburn, who gave her a nod. She and the captain seemed to have come to an understanding, Sam noted.

"So we can go now?"

"Yeah." Kristen shook hands with Rayburn and led Sam out of the office.

They didn't talk on the way to the car. Sam wasn't even sure what to say. The very notion of someone stalking his baby girl was so surreal, he spent half the drive back to Gossamer Ridge wondering if he was stuck in a nightmare.

Kristen broke the silence they'd maintained to that point, her voice uncharacteristically warm. "We're going to find the son of a bitch who took those pictures."

He looked at her. Her gaze angled forward, eyes on the road, her jaw set like stone. "He dropped them off yesterday evening," he said aloud. "Before he even tried to take her. He wanted that to be the first thing I saw the morning I woke up with my daughter gone." And he'd been sneaky, too, leaving the package outside the building after hours—but before the receptionist had left for the day. He'd probably waited around to make sure she saw the package and took it back to the office before she finished locking up for the night.

Kristen looked at him then, just a quick glance, but he saw fiery anger flashing in her blue eyes. "It doesn't matter that the security cameras didn't catch him. It won't stop us."

He hoped she was right.

At the marina, Kristen parked beside the bait shop, next to a Chevy Impala identical to the one she was driving. "Foley," she said to Sam as they got out of the car.

Inside the bait shop, Maddy sat on her grandfather's knee playing with a large cork bobber, tossing it in the air like a ball and nearly tumbling off Mike Cooper's knees trying to catch it. Nearby, Foley stood at the counter, talking in low tones with Sam's mother. All four of them looked up as Sam and Kristen entered.

Maddy's eyes lit up and she scrambled down from Mike's lap. "Miss Kristen!" she squealed, beaming up at Kristen Tandy as she ran to greet them.

Sam felt Kristen stiffen beside him. He quickly intercepted his boisterous daughter before she flung herself at Kristen's knees and hoisted her into his arms. "What? No hello for your daddy?"

"Hi, Daddy!" She patted his face affectionately before twisting in his arms to look at Kristen. "Daddy Mike's gonna let me feed the worms, Miss Kristen. D'you wanna come with us?"

Kristen looked positively green, but Sam suspected it had nothing to do with the prospect of feeding worms.

He tamped down a bit of resentment. "Miss Kristen has a job to do, baby. And I'm afraid you and Daddy Mike are gonna have to go worm feeding some other day. I've got plans for us this afternoon. Want to know what?"

"What?" She caught his face between her hands again, making his heart swell. But instead of her lopsided grin, he saw static, candid images captured in a series of still photographs. He glanced at Kristen, who was watching him, her expression for once unguarded. The look on her face was utter devastation. There was no other word for it.

He cleared his throat and looked back at Maddy. "We're going to have a movie marathon! All the princesses—as many as we can get through before bedtime."

Maddy wriggled excitedly in his arms. "Really?"

"Really."

Sam heard Detective Foley make a low, sympathetic sound behind him. Normally, Sam would agree—an afternoon and evening full of animated fairy-tale musicals were to be avoided at all costs. But this time, he could think of nowhere he'd rather be than his parents' guest cottage with his little girl tucked safely against him on the sofa, miraculously still with him to watch dancing brooms and singing mice.

"Can Miss Kristen come, too?" Maddy asked.

"I told you, Miss Kristen has to work."

"But after work, can she come, too?"

Sam started to say no, but Kristen cleared her throat behind him. "Yeah, Maddy. I can come after work."

Sam looked up at Kristen, startled. She met his gaze, sheer terror shining in her blue eyes. But her small, pointed chin jutted forward, like a soldier preparing for battle.

"Are you sure?" he asked.

"Yes," she said, unconvincingly. "Y'all are staying here for a few days, right?"

He started to tell her it wasn't a good idea, but the glee in Maddy's laughter stopped him before he uttered a word. He looked at his daughter, finding her grinning at Kristen with sheer delight, and stayed silent. "Yeah. There's a guest cottage down the hill from my folks' place."

"I can be there by seven-thirty," Kristen told him quietly after Maddy had climbed down to follow her grandfather into the back room. "I'll bring some microwave popcorn or something."

"You don't have to do this." Sam didn't miss the reluctance in her eyes.

"She goes to sleep—what? Eight? Eight-thirty?"

"Yeah," Sam agreed, not following.

"Good. Then you and I can go over a few things."

He arched an eyebrow. "A few things?"

"A few cases, actually." She stepped away from the counter, lowering her voice. "I think whoever sent you those photos may be someone you've crossed in your work. You were a prosecutor before you moved back here to Alabama, weren't you?"

"Yeah, I was an assistant Commonwealth's Attorney in Arlington County."

"Tried a few cases?"

"You think someone I prosecuted is looking for revenge?"

She shrugged. "It's worth thinking about, isn't it?"

"Okay, I'll think about it." He shot her a wary grin. "Something to do while the princesses are singing."

Her answering smile transformed her face briefly, giving him a glimpse of what she might have looked like had her tragic past not left indelible traces on her young features. Her eyes shimmered like a cloudless sky reflected in a calm lake, and the worry lines creasing her forehead disappeared as if erased.

He felt another unexpected tug of attraction, sudden and primitive, that lingered even after her smile faded into the care-worn lines he'd become accustomed to. He cleared his throat as Maddy and his father reemerged from the back room with the bait containers. "Okay, we'll see you around seven-thirty."

"Foley, I'm heading into the office to type up my report. You coming?"

"Uh, yeah." Foley's gaze moved quickly from her to Sam and back again. "Call us if you need us." He fell in step with Kristen as she headed for the exit.

"Bye, Miss Kristen!" Maddy called from behind the counter.

Kristen lifted her hand to Maddy, shot Sam an enigmatic look and left the bait shop, Foley on her heels.

"She seems like a nice girl," Beth Cooper commented, patting Sam's back as she passed on her way back to the front counter. "Too sad about what happened with her mama."

Sam dragged his gaze away from the empty doorway. "I know the basics—her mother killed her brothers and sisters and tried to kill her. But what else do you recall about it?"

His mother gave him an odd look. "That's pretty much all I remember. The news reports at the time were vague."

"What happened to the mother?"

"I don't think she went to jail. I want to say maybe the state mental hospital or something like that." Beth's gaze was quizzical. "You're awfully interested in Detective Tandy all of a sudden."

"Stop it, Mom."

Her smile faded. "Just be careful, okay? Maddy's at a ripe age to get attached to a woman in your life. She's old enough to wonder why her mother doesn't ever come around."

He'd bent over backward to make excuses for Norah to Maddy, more for his daughter's sake than his ex-wife's. But Maddy was nearing school age, and she'd soon start wondering why everyone else in her class had a mommy to take care of them. One day his excuses wouldn't be enough.

One day, he'd have to explain that not all mommies wanted to be mommies, and there was nothing she could have said or done or been to make a difference. It was going to be the hardest thing he'd ever do in his life.

No point in making it harder by letting another woman so clearly not cut out for motherhood break his daughter's heart.

"YOU CAN'T BE SERIOUS." Kristen stared at Carl Madison, shaking her head. "Carl, there's got to be someone else—"

"I could find someone else," the captain of detectives conceded. "But Foley says the child already likes and trusts you. And honestly? You need to do it for yourself."

"Don't do that." Kristen glared at her foster father, her anger festering. "You're not my father anymore."

"You never let me be," he said bleakly.

Guilt stoked her anger. "All I ever wanted was to be left alone to get on with my life. That's still all I want."

"You're not getting on with your life. You're hiding behind your badge and your attitude, avoiding anything that scares you or challenges you. I'm not talking to you as a father now," he added when she opened her mouth to protest. "I'm your boss, and this is a job I think you can do if you put your mind to it. Are you telling me I'm wrong?"

Nostrils flaring, Kristen looked away from Carl. "I don't think Sam Cooper will agree to it."

"I think he'll agree to anything that will keep his daughter safe from another attack." Carl's voice dipped an octave. "Fathers are like that."

Kristen stood up, her legs trembling with pent-up anger and a healthy dose of apprehension. "It's a terrible idea."

"But you'll do it?"

"I don't have a choice, do I?" She left his office, giving the door an extra-hard push as she shut it behind her. The slam echoed down the corridor behind her.

Foley looked up as she entered the bull pen, making a face at the sight of her scowl. "Good afternoon to you, too."

"Carl wants me on full-time babysitting duty with Maddy Cooper," she growled.

Foley's eyebrows lifted. "Really? I was betting he'd tell you not to go on your movie-night date with Sam Cooper."

She shot him a dark glare. "It's an informal interview with a crime victim at his home."

"Over popcorn and movies."

"The popcorn and *princess* movies are for the kid." Kristen crossed to her desk, grabbed her purse and headed for the door before he asked more questions.

"That kid's got a thing for you," Foley said as she passed.

"Then maybe she'll remember something new and tell it to her new best buddy," she retorted.

"That's not fair, Tandy. And you're not that cold."

She stopped in the doorway and turned back to look at him. "I have to be that cold, don't I? Especially if I'm going to be Maddy's best friend 24/7."

Foley shook his head. "I don't think that's what Carl had in mind. I know Sam Cooper won't put up with it."

She sighed, leaning against the doorjamb. "What am I supposed to do? Blow off the assignment? Do you really believe there's not going to be another attempt to grab that kid?"

"No. I think someone brazen enough to send photos to her daddy is brazen enough to try to snatch her again," Foley conceded. "But I've seen you with kids. You look like you're allergic. I keep waiting for you to break out in hives."

She pushed away from the door frame and swung her hair over her shoulder. "I'm not good with kids."

Foley's expression was full of pity. "It's not that you're not good with them, Tandy. You're afraid of them." When she didn't answer him, he added, "Are you going to do what Madison wants?"

She left without answering, her chest tight with dread.

"LET'S GET SOMETHING STRAIGHT," Sam murmured to Kristen an hour later after Maddy had squeezed out from between them to go to the bathroom. "Clearly, you're not the maternal type."

Kristen's eyes met his. The vulnerability that flashed there for a moment stunned him, but it disappeared quickly, leaving her expression unreadable. "No, I'm not."

"Then, I think from now on, we should limit your interactions with Maddy to formal visits."

Her gaze remained steady, but Sam saw a flicker of something in the depths of her blue eyes that might have been pain. Again, it slipped away as quickly as it had come. "I was afraid you'd say that," she murmured. "But—"

Maddy came back into the room and bounced onto the sofa between them. "Unpause!" she said brightly to her father.

Sam hit Play and the syrupy strains of a princess love theme filled the room, ending the conversation with Kristen for the moment. But Sam felt her gaze on his face, sensed the tension buzzing around them, as whatever it was she'd started to tell him lingered, unsaid but unforgotten.

Within an hour, Maddy's eyes began to droop, and she gave only a halfhearted protest when Sam finally stopped the DVD player and carried her off to bed. He lingered a few moments as she tossed and turned, still not used to the strange bed. She demanded a story, and he complied with a quick reading of *Horton Hears a Who.* She was asleep within a couple of minutes.

Sam put the book on the nightstand and tucked her in, lingering a moment to run his fingers over the satiny curve of her round cheek. Swaddled in the enormous old wedding ring quilt that had belonged to his grandmother, she looked tiny. So very fragile and breakable.

He felt rather than heard Kristen enter the room behind him. He turned to find her standing in the doorway, her narrow-eyed gaze fixed on his daughter as if looking for something in Maddy's soft features. Tonight she wore a pale green T-shirt and jeans, her hair loose and a little wild, very different from the buttoned-up police detective he'd spent the morning with. The T-shirt revealed even more new curves he hadn't seen before, and the snug jeans made her legs look miles long.

His whole body tightened pleasantly in response.

Kristen stepped out into the hallway, and he rose to follow, closing the door to the bedroom behind him. She faced him as they reached the living room, her tense expression working hard to kill the light sexual buzz he'd been enjoying.

"I have something to ask you." Her voice was tight, as if she'd had to force the words from her throat.

He grew instantly apprehensive. "What?"

"Carl—Captain Madison—believes there's a strong likelihood that whoever broke into your home is going to go after Maddy again. I agree with him."

"So do I," Sam conceded, though her stark assessment made his stomach hurt.

"He wants to assign someone to Maddy full-time."

Sam frowned. "Full-time? Like a bodyguard?"

"Yes."

Sam stepped away from her, rubbing his jaw. His beard stubble scraped his palm with a rasping sound. "I don't know if she'll take to some stranger coming in to play nanny—"

"It won't be a stranger," Kristen said, her voice even tighter than before.

Tension stretched in the air between them as he slowly turned to look at her, understanding dawning. Her eyes locked with his, wide and scared.

"I'll be Maddy's bodyguard," she said.

CHAPTER FOUR

WAITING FOR SAM to break his stunned silence, Kristen didn't know whether she wanted him to agree or refuse. On a purely visceral level, anything that saved her from spending every day and night with Maddy Cooper would be a welcome response. But it was also a coward's choice.

She wasn't a coward, no matter what Foley or Carl thought.

"That's the last thing I expected you to say." Sam sat down on the sofa and passed his hand over his jaw. His palm made a raspy noise against his beard stubble, and she was surprised to feel a flutter of feminine awareness in her belly.

He was an attractive man. Not handsome exactly, not by Hollywood standards. His appeal was edgier—raw male power, evident in the broad expanse of his shoulders and the lean, almost feral features that even a veneer of civilization couldn't temper.

She sat beside him, ignoring the tremble in her knees. "It wasn't my idea."

He shot her a dark look. "You don't say."

"That doesn't mean it's the wrong thing to do," she continued, ignoring his sarcasm. "Maddy may be in further danger, and I'm the best person, under the circumstances, to protect her. She seems to like and trust me. I will do anything in my power to protect her."

"My brother could do the same thing."

"He's on special assignment with the Drug Enforcement Agency. You know that." She had checked into Aaron Cooper's availability herself, during the short hour between Carl's order and her arrival at the Cooper family guesthouse.

"My sister's husband is also a deputy."

"Riley Patterson? The one who's currently in Arizona for his parents' fortieth wedding anniversary?"

"You did a background check on my whole family?"

She had, in fact. A cursory one, anyway. Standard operating procedure for child abduction cases. "He and your sister won't be back until Monday."

Sam frowned at her, his gaze intense. She could see him weighing all the ramifications in his mind as he stared her down. Could he trust her with his daughter?

Should he?

She withstood his scrutiny for as long as she could before finally blurting, "Yes or no?"

His nostrils flared briefly. "Okay. There's an extra bedroom you can use. But I don't want our lives disrupted any more than they have to be. Maddy still gets to visit with my parents and go fishing with Jake and Gabe. Understood? If I say she's safe with someone without you there you don't interfere."

Kristen nodded. The less time she had to spend alone with Maddy, the better. "I know you're probably wary about bringing a gun in here with Maddy around—"

Sam's lips curved into a grim smile. "I'm armed myself, Detective Tandy."

The deadly serious tone of his voice made Kristen's

stomach tighten. So she'd been right to see the masculinity beneath the well-cut suits and expensive ties. Despite the Italian silk and the fancy letters at the end of his name, Sam Cooper had grown up here in the hills of Chickasaw County and hardened his native strength with a stint in the Marine Corps.

She paid back his earlier scrutiny by indulging herself with a long, appraising look, smiling as he reacted to the tit for tat with a look of grudging amusement. She knew Sam Cooper had graduated from law school and passed the bar exam by the young age of twenty-four and spent the next five years working as a JAG lawyer before taking a civilian job in the District of Columbia. Sure, it hadn't been a combat assignment, but everybody in the Marine Corps had to go through boot camp, didn't they?

If the hard muscles and flat planes she glimpsed beneath his olive-green T-shirt and faded jeans were anything to go by, he'd kept up with the fitness regimen even after he'd left the service. She looked away.

"I keep wondering who'd do something like this." The vulnerability in Sam's voice caught her by surprise. "I'm not rich. I'm not a celebrity. I don't think I could scrape up a ransom payment if I tried."

"I think maybe revenge," she offered quietly. The haggard look in his eyes suggested that answer had been squirming around the back of his mind since the attempted kidnapping. "Or some other personal agenda," she added.

His eyes narrowed. "You're still thinking about my ex."

"The majority of child abductions are familial. You

have full custody of Maddy and moved her to another state recently—"

"With Norah's blessing," Sam said firmly. "She's welcome to see Maddy whenever she likes. She chooses not to."

"Why not?"

Sam's lips narrowed to a thin line. His gaze shifted toward the hallway, as if he was afraid Maddy might overhear. He nodded toward the cottage's kitchen nook, leading the way. When he spoke, he kept his voice low. "She didn't want to have Maddy in the first place. The pregnancy wasn't planned. I talked her into the marriage."

Kristen felt a cold tingle crawl up her spine. "She didn't want to have children at all?"

He flashed a bleak smile. "No. But she knew how much I did. So she agreed to marry me and have the baby, give the whole wedded bliss thing a shot." He nudged a folded dishrag across the counter with one long finger. "Didn't work out."

"How long did it last?"

"Nine months, until Maddy was three months old."

Not very long to give marriage and motherhood a chance, she thought. "And she gave you full custody?"

"Since our divorce was all about getting out of playing mommy and wife, yeah. She did."

Kristen wasn't sure how to respond. There had been a time in her life when she couldn't imagine how a woman could turn her back on her child. But that was a long time ago, before she'd seen firsthand what a mother was capable of doing to her children. She cleared her throat. "Some women just aren't meant to be mothers."

When she dared to look at him again, she was

shocked to find his expression sympathetic. She'd expected disgust.

She hardened herself against the compassion in his warm blue eyes. "I looked into your ex anyway. She's just become engaged. Did you know that?"

He looked surprised. "More background checks, Detective?"

So he didn't know about the engagement. Interesting.

"Who's she marrying?" he asked, almost as an afterthought. She wasn't sure if he was indifferent or just pretending to be.

"Graham Stilson," she answered.

One dark eyebrow notched upward. "Junior or Senior?"

"Junior. Do you know him?"

Sam turned to face her fully, resting his elbows on the narrow breakfast bar behind him. "Stilson Junior was a trial lawyer in the D.C. area before he was elected to the state senate. We crossed paths now and then. I know his father better, though. Stilson Senior is a judge."

Clearly, he didn't care much for Stilson Junior. Kristen wondered how much of his dislike was wrapped up in unresolved feelings for his ex, annoyed with herself for her curiosity. What had she expected, that he'd have lost all interest in a woman he'd once loved enough to marry?

Not that Sam Cooper's feelings were of any importance, she reminded herself. It was his ex-wife who was currently on Kristen's suspect list, not Sam.

"I asked her assistant to track her down and have her call me. Nothing yet," she said aloud.

"Norah doesn't get motivated to return calls unless

she thinks you can do something for her," Sam said with a shrug. "I left a message for her, too."

"I thought you said you didn't think she was a suspect."

"I don't," he said firmly. "But she's Maddy's mom. She should know what's going on."

Would Norah Cabot even care? She hadn't given much thought to her daughter's life so far—why would she start now?

Sam might not be indifferent to his ex-wife, but he clearly resented her abandonment of their child, and on a surface level, Kristen knew she should find Norah Cabot's actions selfish, as well. But her own mother had had no business raising children. Kristen had seen the horrible consequences. As far as she was concerned, Maddy was lucky. She had a daddy to love and protect her, and she didn't have to deal with her indifferent mother at all.

How much different would Kristen's own life have been if she'd had a father around to make sure she and her brothers and sisters were safe and cared for?

Sam interrupted her dark thoughts. "I had my office e-mail me the felony cases I've worked on since I took the job a few months ago. There are only five—they gave me a light load until I could get my bearings. I've printed them out, if you want to take a look tonight. We can see if there's anything in those files that might have set someone off."

Following him back to the sitting area, she kicked herself for not having asked him about his current case files sooner. She was letting her kid phobia take over this whole case.

Time to cowboy up. If she couldn't handle one four-

year-old poppet—and her sexy grouch of a father—her
career was in serious trouble.

SAM SAT BACK an hour later, rubbing his eyes. He'd read
through all five cases and saw nothing he could imagine enraging someone enough to come after his child.
"What if this isn't about me?" he asked Kristen.

She looked up from the case file she was reading.
"Just some random kidnapper stalking Maddy? For
what purpose?"

His stomach recoiled at the only answer that made
sense. "A pedophile?"

She shook her head. "This doesn't fit a pedophile's
M.O. They're cowards. They like targets of opportunity."

"That guy in Utah broke into his target's house and
took her out of her bedroom," he reminded her.

"That's rare."

"But not impossible."

She wrinkled her brow at him. "Do you want it to
be a pedophile?" she asked pointedly.

"God, no!" The thought was horrifying.

Her expression gentled. "Whatever pushed this guy's
buttons, it's not your fault."

How could she know that? What if he'd done something, said something or forgotten something that had
set the kidnapper off? What if this whole thing was
about payback?

What if he'd been the one who'd put his daughter
at risk?

Kristen's hand stole across the sofa and curled around
his, her grip tight. The touch felt like a jolt of electric-

ity, setting his whole body abuzz, and he was caught off guard by a flood of pure male attraction.

He'd always gone for high-octane women like Norah Cabot, with her expensive French perfume and her designer shoes. He'd worked with many beautiful, even glamorous women, and he'd always found them exciting and sexy. He'd just figured that kind of woman was his type.

So why was this quiet, no-nonsense, small-town cop making his blood run hot in a way it hadn't in years?

She let go of his hand and looked down at the files spread across the coffee table. "We should look at some of your case files from D.C. Can you get your hands on those?"

His fingers still tingled from her touch. He closed his fist and cleared his throat. "Probably more red tape than we'd like. I'll help you set that into motion. However, I keep a detailed log of all my cases—the major figures involved, whether the outcome was a conviction, an acquittal or a plea bargain, that kind of thing. It's in one of the storage boxes at home. I'll stop by and get the log, and we can go through it, as well."

"Could you get it tomorrow?"

"If you're okay with being here alone with Maddy," he said, watching her carefully for her reaction.

The line of her lips tightened a little, but she gave a nod. "Of course. It's my job."

He wasn't sure if she was reassuring him or herself. He could tell she still had doubts. He dropped his gaze to the back of Kristen's hand, where a white burn scar still marred the skin. Had she seen her mother kill her brothers and sister, or had she stumbled upon the aftermath?

Did it even matter which? Both would have been horrific.

Kristen's eyes flickered up to meet his, as if the sudden silence between them made her nervous. He felt a rush of pity he couldn't quite hide, and her expression shifted from vulnerability to a hard, cool mask of indifference. She edged away from him, readying herself to stand. "It's getting late," she began. "I need to go home and pack for tomorrow."

His cell phone interrupted, the shrill sound jolting his spine like an electric shock. He fished it from his pocket. The display showed an area code he didn't recognize.

"Cooper," he answered, slanting a quick look at Kristen, who sat very still, watching him.

A low, vibrant voice greeted him. "Hi, Sam. It's me."

Norah. He'd left a message for her to call, but he hadn't expected to hear from her tonight. "Thanks for calling back."

Kristen gave him a curious look, but before he could tell her who was on the other line, the bedroom door opened and Maddy stumbled out, her hair wild and her eyes damp with tears.

"Daddy?" she mewled.

Torn between dealing with Norah and comforting his daughter, Sam shot Kristen a pleading look. For a second, her eyes widened and she looked ready to bolt, but she regained control quickly and crossed to Maddy's side.

"Sam, are you there?" Norah's voice drew his attention back to the phone.

Sam watched Kristen crouch by Maddy and begin

talking to her in a soft tone. "Yeah, I'm here. Sorry. Maddy woke up."

"Your message said you had something important to tell me." He heard a hint of impatience in Norah's voice, probably because he'd mentioned Maddy. She didn't like to hear about Maddy. Must be easier to believe she did the right thing when she didn't have to think about a little girl growing up without her mommy.

Too bad. What he had to tell her had everything to do with Maddy. And this time, she was going to listen.

KRISTEN COAXED MADDY back into the bedroom, though she wished she could stay and listen to Sam's end of the conversation. He hadn't said the caller was his ex-wife, but Kristen could tell from his defensive body language and the immediate tension in his voice that he was talking to someone with the power to hurt him. She assumed Norah Cabot was such a person.

"Can you read me a story?" Maddy asked.

Kristen looked at the sleepy little face staring up at her from the pillows and her heart shattered. She struggled to stay focused, to keep her mind in the present as it began to wander helplessly into the nightmarish past.

Read the little girl a book, Kristen. You can do that.

She picked up the book lying on the small bedside table. Dr. Seuss. Her heart squeezed.

Seuss had been Julie's favorite. Kristen had read *Green Eggs and Ham* so often she had it memorized. Sometimes, usually late at night when she was tired and couldn't fight off the memories, the rhymes and rhythms of the child's book flitted through her mind, interspersed with the image of Julie's limp body lying at the foot of her bloodstained bed.

Kristen closed her eyes and took a deep breath, clutching the book against her chest.

"Can't you read, Miss Kristen?"

Her eyes snapped open. Maddy Cooper gazed up at her with wide green eyes full of sweet sympathy.

"I can read it for you," Maddy added, patting the bed beside her in invitation.

Kristen stared at the tiny hand thumping lightly on the pale pink sheet. Another image of Julie fluttered through her mind, surprisingly sweet. Like Maddy, her little sister had also owned a favorite pair of pajamas—bright yellow with black stripes, inspiring Kristen to nickname her Julie Bee. Julie used to "read" to Kristen, too, flipping through the pages as she recited her favorite books by memory.

Blinking back the tears burning her eyes, Kristen sat beside Maddy, releasing a pent-up breath.

The little girl edged closer, her body warm and compact against Kristen's side. She took the Dr. Seuss book from Kristen's nerveless fingers and flipped to the first page, where Horton the elephant sat in a bright blue pool, happily splashing himself with water.

As Maddy began to recite the familiar story in her childish lisp, Kristen closed her eyes and relaxed, not fighting the flood of sweet memories washing over her.

Julie had been an adorable baby, the youngest of the five Tandy kids and the one Kristen had reared almost single-handedly as her mother's break with reality had widened those last few years. Kristen hadn't shared a father with her two youngest siblings, but she hadn't cared. Her own father was long gone, and neither of the men who'd fathered baby Julie and six-year-old Kevin had stuck around long enough to see them born. It was just Kristen, the younger kids and their mother, and for most of Kristen's memory, her mother had been undependable.

Realizing Maddy had fallen silent, Kristen opened her eyes and found the little girl gazing up at her with solemn green eyes. "Don't cry, Miss Kristen." She patted Kristen's arm. "Horton will find the clover. You'll see."

Kristen dashed away the tears, forcing a smile, even as she struggled to hold back a stream of darker memories. She hadn't had a sweet thought about her brothers and sisters in a long time. She didn't want to lose it now.

Before Kristen found words to let Maddy know that she was okay, the bedroom door opened and Sam entered. His gaze went first to Maddy, a quick appraisal as if to reassure himself that she was still there and still okay.

When he shifted his gaze to Kristen, his eyes widened a little, no doubt with surprise at finding his daughter's bodyguard weeping like a baby. She looked down, mortified, wiping away the rest of the moisture clinging to her cheeks and eyelashes in a couple of brisk swipes.

Sam crossed to the bed. *"Horton Hears a Who,"* he read aloud. "Excellent choice, ladies."

As Maddy giggled up at her father, Kristen scrambled off the bed, waving for him to take her place. "Maddy was reading to me. We left poor Horton in a precarious place." She was pleased by the light tone of her voice. Maybe he'd buy that she'd been crying tears of laughter.

"But it's okay," Maddy insisted, her tone filled with childish urgency, apparently afraid Kristen was still worried about Horton and his tiny friends. Kristen felt an unexpected rush of affection for the little girl, touched by her concern.

"I'm sure Miss Kristen knows that," Sam assured Maddy, but Kristen heard a hint of puzzlement in his voice. She guessed he hadn't fallen for the "tears of laughter" attempt.

"Did your call go okay?" she asked.

He caught her meaning and gave a nod. "Let me finish reading this with Maddy and then we'll talk."

She settled against the door frame, watching Maddy cuddle close to Sam as he finished the story. By the time the jungle animals pledged to protect the imperiled Whovillians, Maddy's eyes had drooped closed. Sam bent and kissed her pink cheek, lingering a moment. Kristen had to look away, a dozen different emotions roiling through her. She'd never shared those kinds of moments with her father, who'd left the family when she was just six years old, and who'd been distant long before then.

Sam finally eased himself away from Maddy and joined her at the door. "Outside," he whispered, opening the door for her.

He guided her away from the door, stopping in the middle of the living room. "I don't want Maddy to overhear."

"Overhear what?" Kristen asked.

"That her mother's booked a flight to Alabama, arriving tomorrow," he answered grimly.

CHAPTER FIVE

"WE'RE GOING TO play a game, Maddy. Is that okay?"

Maddy looked up at Kristen, her expression curious. "But I'm coloring right now."

"I know. This is a coloring game." Kristen sat on the low stool beside Maddy's play table and pulled a blank piece of paper in front of her.

"A coloring game?" Instantly intrigued, Maddy scooted closer.

"I'm going to draw something, and you're going to help me color it in. Does that sound like fun?"

Maddy nodded, reaching for the crayons.

"I bet you have a good memory," Kristen continued, trying not to let Maddy's little girl smell distract her. She'd agreed to take this assignment to help Maddy remember more about the night of the attack. This might be one of the few moments she had alone with Maddy for a while, since her mother's impending arrival promised to be a major distraction over the next couple of days.

She took a black crayon and drew an oval. "I know this might be a little scary, but I also know you're a brave girl. Aren't you a brave girl, Maddy?"

Maddy looked up at her, a hint of worry in her bright green eyes. "Yes, ma'am."

"I want you to think about the man who came to

your house the other night. The one who scared you and made Cissy cry."

Maddy's eyes welled up with tears. "I wanna see Cissy."

The sight of Maddy's tears nearly derailed Kristen's plan, but she steeled herself against the little girl's emotions. The best way to help Maddy was to find the man who had tried to hurt her. "Cissy's with the doctor, who's taking the very best care of her. I know your daddy told you that."

Maddy nodded. "She's sick."

"That's right, but the doctor is going to help her get better. But right now, I need you to help me find the bad man so we can make sure he doesn't make anyone else sick. Okay?"

Maddy blinked away the tears and nodded.

Kristen pointed her crayon at the oval she'd drawn. "I want you to pretend this is the bad man's face. Can you pick a crayon color that matches the color of his face?"

Maddy picked through the nubby crayons and picked out a pale peach color. Caucasian, Kristen noted mentally. They'd been pretty sure that was so, but confirmation was good.

She took her black crayon and drew eyes inside the oval. "Can you tell me what color to make his eyes?"

Maddy's face crinkled with concentration. "No eyes."

"You mean you couldn't see his eyes?"

Maddy nodded.

"Was it because of his cap?"

Maddy nodded again.

Kristen drew a cap shape on top of the oval. "Can you tell me what color the cap was?"

Maddy's tongue slipped out between her lips as she studied the pile of crayons on the table in front of her. After a few moments, she picked up a dark blue crayon.

"Great, Maddy! That's very helpful. Can you color in the cap for me?"

Maddy pulled the paper in front of her and got to work, coloring in the blue cap. But she left part of the front of the cap blank, Kristen noticed.

"Why aren't you coloring that part?" she asked Maddy.

"It had ABCs on it." She beamed up at Kristen. "I know my ABCs. Wanna hear?" Maddy started singing the alphabet in an off-key warble.

Kristen steeled herself against a flood of memories. She'd taught the ABCs song to the littlest ones, Kevin and Julie, herself. By then, her mother hadn't cared much about her kids, except for sporadic bouts of manic mothering that left her younger siblings scared and confused.

"That's very good," she choked out when Maddy finished her song. "Do you think you know your ABCs well enough to tell me what letters were on the cap?"

Maddy's beaming smile faded. "Don't 'member."

"That's okay," Kristen assured her, squelching her own disappointment. Even if Maddy couldn't remember the letters, they now knew that the assailant had worn a dark blue cap with some sort of letters on the front. Possibly a sports team cap. It was, at least, corroborating evidence if they ever came up with an actual suspect.

"Miss Kristen, do you know my mommy?" Maddy's soft query caught Kristen flat-footed. It was the first question she'd asked about her mother since Sam left for the airport.

"I've told Maddy her mother's coming for a visit," Sam had told Kristen earlier that morning when she arrived to keep an eye on Maddy, "but I'm not sure she really understands what that means."

He'd told her that while Maddy had seen photos of her mother, and knew her name, she'd never spoken to Norah before, not even on the phone. Kristen wondered how Maddy was going to handle meeting a mother who was essentially a stranger to her.

Kristen pushed aside the drawing and turned to look at Maddy, who gazed up at her with worried eyes. Sam had dressed her in a pale green sundress and clean white sandals, and tamed her unruly brown curls into a ponytail at the back of her head. She looked adorable, even to Kristen's jaundiced eyes.

She wondered if Norah would be similarly impressed.

"No, Maddy, I don't know your mom," she answered the little girl's question.

Maddy slid down off her chair and crossed to Kristen's stool, tugging lightly at the edge of Kristen's denim jacket. "What if she doesn't like me?" she asked, her voice tiny.

Kristen felt a surge of sympathy for the child. "What's not to like? Look how pretty you look. And I saw your room this morning—it's nice and neat. And didn't you eat all your cereal and drink all your milk like your daddy asked you to?"

Maddy beamed at her. "And I took my vitamin, too."

"Well, see? There you go. You're a superstar."

Maddy patted Kristen's knee. "Are you afraid she won't like you?"

She grinned at the little girl. "No way. I ate all my breakfast this morning, too."

Maddy giggled and happily picked up the peach crayon, her curiosity apparently appeased. She reached for the drawing of the "bad man" and started coloring in his face.

Kristen watched her draw, trying not to let Maddy's last question nag her. It didn't matter to her whether or not Norah Cabot liked her, of course. Which was good, because the questions she had to ask Maddy's mother wouldn't win the woman's friendship. Norah Cabot might have an alibi for the night in question, but that didn't mean she didn't hire someone to take Maddy from Sam's home.

And considering what she'd learned about Norah and her fiancé the night before, she had an idea why Maddy's mother might do such a thing.

She'd have a chance to challenge Norah soon enough. Sam was due back from the airport any time now.

"You're nervous." Norah's voice was tinged with amusement.

"I'm wary," he corrected, putting the car in Park and shutting off the engine before he turned to look at her.

She looked impeccable, even after a plane ride from New York to Alabama. Her lightweight gray suit and cream silk blouse fit her perfectly, and her short, spiky hairstyle had probably cost a fortune. He wondered who she was trying to impress. Him? Or Maddy?

"I know it's been a few years, but I haven't suddenly developed a violent streak. I still don't bite." She opened the passenger door, unfolded her long legs and stepped from the car before he had a chance to circle the car and open the door for her.

He left her bags in the car, as he'd already decided before she arrived that she'd be staying in a nearby motel rather than with them at the guesthouse. "I'm surprised Graham didn't come with you," he said as he joined her on the flagstone walkway.

"So you've heard about my engagement." She flashed him a wry smile. "Graham had business back in Baltimore."

"I thought you were in the Hamptons."

"Only for a party. We were set to return home today anyway." She straightened her jacket and patted her hair as they reached the door, the first indication of nerves since he'd picked her up at the airport.

He opened the door and ushered her inside, then froze in his tracks at the sight in front of him.

Kristen was on the floor, on her hands and knees, apparently looking for something under the sofa while Maddy danced around her, shrieking with laughter.

Almost before he had a chance to blink, however, Kristen had risen to a crouch, one arm tucking Maddy behind her back while the other hand reached for the ankle holster hidden beneath the right leg of her jeans.

Sam held up his hands quickly. "We come in peace."

Kristen relaxed, dropping her hand from the hidden weapon and reaching back to swing Maddy in front of her. She pushed to her feet, straightening her blouse. A fierce pink blush washed over her neck and face. "We, um, lost a crayon."

Maddy's eyes lit up as she spotted him. "We've been drawing, Daddy!"

"So I see." Sam let his gaze slide from his daughter's

bright face to Kristen Tandy's mortified expression. He smiled, amused and a little touched by her embarrassment at being caught with her pretty little butt in the air. She managed a sheepish smile in return, and his stomach did a flip.

Maddy caught sight of Norah standing in the doorway behind him, and her broad grin faded to a tentative half smile.

Sam crossed to his daughter's side and took her hand, leading her to where Norah stood. "Maddy, this is your mother, Norah. Norah, this is Maddy."

Norah took Maddy's hand. "It's nice to meet you, Maddy."

"You're pretty," Maddy blurted, and Sam smiled.

Norah chuckled. "Thank you. You're pretty, too." She released Maddy's hand and straightened, looking around the guesthouse with a speculative gaze. "So this is the famous Cooper Cove Marina and Fishing Camp."

"Technically, it's my parents' guesthouse," he corrected lightly, trying not to let the mild disdain in her tone annoy him. "Would you like some coffee? A glass of tea?"

"God, not that sweet treacle you Southerners call tea." She shed her suit jacket, baring a pair of slim, toned arms. She hadn't been letting herself go over the past four years, he saw. She was as trim and beautiful as ever.

He took the jacket from her and hung it on the rack by the door. He turned back to find Norah looking quizzically at Kristen.

"Norah Cabot," she introduced herself, crossing to where Kristen stood beside the writing desk near the window.

Kristen shook Norah's hand. "Detective Kristen Tandy, Gossamer Ridge Police Department."

Norah's dark brows lifted. "Is this an ambush?"

Kristen's smile looked almost predatory, catching Sam by surprise. "Funny you'd jump to that conclusion, Ms. Cabot, instead of assuming I was here to protect your daughter."

Norah shot Sam a murderous look. "An hour in the car and you couldn't see fit to warn me I was walking into a trap?"

"Ms. Tandy is here to protect Maddy," he answered with a shrug, enjoying his ex-wife's discomfort a little more than he should. It was a novel experience to see Norah caught off balance. She was usually in full control of any situation, whether a heated court battle—or a marriage falling apart.

"And to ask a few questions," Kristen added firmly.

Holding back a smile, Sam decided this morning might turn out to be more enjoyable than he'd expected.

THOUGH SAM HAD spent most of the last eighteen hours fretting about how to prepare Maddy for her mother's arrival, in the end, his worries had been for nothing. Maddy didn't seem to find anything odd about meeting her mother for the first time at the age of four, and Norah didn't overplay the mommy card.

Maddy enjoyed looking at old photos Norah had brought with her, including several photos from their brief marriage. She'd even agreed with Norah that they shared the same green eyes and long fingers and toes. But she made no fuss when Norah handed her off to Sam's brother Jake and Jake's wife, Mariah, after a tour of the family property. While Jake and Mariah played tag with Maddy and Micah, Mariah's two-year-old, under the ancient oak towering over the backyard, Norah crossed the lawn to the bottom step of the deck stairs where Sam sat.

"She's lovely," Norah said with a smile, settling onto the step beside him. "You're a wonderful father. But I always knew you would be."

Sam looked across the yard at Maddy, who was laughing with glee as Jake swung her around and around. "Why did you come here, Norah?"

Norah's brow furrowed. "Our daughter was almost kidnapped. Shouldn't I be here?"

"She was hospitalized with strep throat when she was a year old. We were in the same city then, and you didn't even call to check on her."

"The police didn't leave an urgent message on my phone that time. Pretty young Detective Tandy was so insistent." Norah looked over at Kristen, who stood alone, watching Jake, Mariah and the children play. "She's very new at the job, isn't she?"

"Don't underestimate her," Sam warned. "She's tougher than she looks." Anyone who could survive what Kristen Tandy had gone through as a young teenager was made of stern stuff.

"Have you taken on a new project, Professor Higgins?" Norah shot him a pointed look. "Looking to turn Daisy Duke into a proper lady?"

Sam pressed his lips together, already growing annoyed by Norah's blithe sarcasm. He must have found her witty and entertaining once, or he'd never have fallen for her. Maybe in a different situation, when his daughter's safety wasn't on the line, he might have been amused by her sharp commentary.

But Kristen Tandy didn't deserve to be the target of Norah's verbal barbs. Especially now, when she was facing down her own demons for no other reason than to protect Maddy.

"No comment, Sam?" Norah slanted another look at Kristen.

"Not everything or everyone is fair game for your tongue, Norah." He caught Kristen's eye and gave a quick nod of his head to invite her over.

She crossed slowly to where they sat, her expression neutral. But he'd begun to understand that her eyes were the key to deciphering her moods. Right now, they were a murky blue-gray, cool as a winter sky.

She didn't like Norah. At all.

"I suppose, Detective Tandy, you have more questions for me?" Norah spoke first, her way of taking control of the conversation.

"Mostly, I'm curious," Kristen answered coolly. "After so many years away from your daughter, why show up now? I told you in my message that I'd be willing to fly up to Washington to meet you if I needed to speak in person. It seems a bit...out of character for you to hop on a plane and fly right down."

For the first time since Norah arrived, she lost her veneer of indifference. "You don't know me, Detective. You're not qualified to judge what is in or out of character for me."

The hint of gray in Kristen's eyes darkened. Sam could swear he saw ice crystals forming in their depths. "You abandoned your daughter to your husband's sole custody when she was three months old. You haven't seen her in person since then. You don't call Maddy to talk to her, not even on her birthdays or holidays. I think I'm perfectly capable of judging your behavior to be that of a woman who has excised her daughter from her life with brutal efficiency."

Sam stared at Kristen. Though he'd just warned Norah not to underestimate her, even he hadn't expected her to stand her ground with such ferocity.

Where had this little tigress come from?

This Kristen Tandy was exciting. Maybe even a little dangerous. He liked her like this, maybe more than he should, given the searing heat building low in his gut.

"The decisions I made about Maddy were for her own good," Norah said, her voice low and a little unsteady.

Kristen's lips curved slightly. "We agree on that point completely."

Norah's face reddened, and Sam saw the warning signs of a very nasty backlash. He stepped between the two women, taking Kristen's elbow lightly. "Detective Tandy, I had a thought about the files we were going over last night. Can we discuss them privately for a moment?"

Kristen dragged her gaze away from Norah and looked up at him, blue fire flashing in her eyes in place of the earlier ice. She gave a brief nod and walked with him up the steps to the deck. "What is it?"

"I enjoy a good verbal jousting match as much as the next man, but do you think you should antagonize Norah like that?"

Her cheeks grew pink. "Are you questioning how I conduct an investigation?"

"You're not investigating anything here," Sam countered. "You're angry at Norah for being, well, Norah, and you're letting that interfere with your work. You know damned well you don't get answers from people by insulting them." His voice softened with admiration. "Even if you do it magnificently."

Kristen's brow furrowed, but she gave a brief nod. "You're right. But she's such a sarcastic, snobby b—"

He pressed his fingers to her lips to keep her from saying the word. "It's half her charm," he said.

Her eyes flickered up to meet his, and he felt her lips tremble under his fingers. He dropped his hand away, the skin of his fingertips tingling once more.

"You like that in a woman?" she asked curiously.

"I guess I used to," he admitted. "Or maybe I just mistook her sharp tongue for spirit and fire." He lowered his voice even more. "I like spirit and fire."

Kristen's eyes darkened but she didn't drop her gaze. The air around them seemed warmer than before, as if the sudden tension crackling between them had supercharged the atmosphere. They'd moved very close to each other, he realized with some surprise, so close that his breath stirred the golden tendrils of hair that had escaped Kristen's neat ponytail.

She had beautiful, flawless skin, a dewy peaches-and-cream complexion that most women would kill for. He knew, without giving in to the growing temptation to touch her, that her skin would be warm and soft beneath his fingers.

He wondered if he'd be able to resist that temptation if this case lingered on too much longer.

She gave a soft sigh, her breath warming his throat. Dropping her gaze, she stepped away, looking down at the wide redwood planks beneath their feet. "Be careful, Mr. Cooper," she murmured. "Right now, Maddy doesn't really understand who Norah is to her. But she's the right age to start wondering why her mother's not around like other mothers are."

He cleared his throat. "I know. Believe me, I'm trying to be very careful here. But if Norah really does want to have a bigger presence in Maddy's life—"

"Did you know her fiancé is running for the open Senate seat from Maryland?" Kristen asked quietly.

Sam blinked. "No."

"Apparently he just announced his candidacy. He's up against a big family values candidate named Halston Stevens. Makes me wonder a bit about Norah's motive for coming here." Kristen looked toward the yard. Sam followed her gaze and saw Norah sitting in a lawn chair, smiling at Maddy, who was showing her mother something she'd picked up in the yard.

Son of a bitch, he thought. "How do you know this?"

"The Internet. It's this awesome new information tool—you should totally check it out."

He shot her a look. "Funny. Why didn't you tell me this last night when you told me she was engaged?"

She turned back to look at him. "I didn't want to poison your mind with the thought until you'd had a chance to see her interact with Maddy."

He rubbed his jaw, wondering if knowing would have made any difference. He'd been watching Norah carefully since he first introduced her to her daughter, maybe hoping to see some spark between mother and daughter that they could build on for the future. But so far, Norah's interest in Maddy had seemed little more than curiosity.

"I needed to know as much about your ex-wife as I could before she got here," Kristen continued quietly. "So I stayed up late and did some Web surfing. Her fiancé's election bid is big news in Maryland. Local blogs are all over the story."

"You're thorough, aren't you?" he asked. She really was turning out to be a smarter investigator than he'd anticipated.

The amused look in her blue eyes faded. "Someone's stalking a kid. Your kid. Damned right I'm thorough." Her cell phone rang, a muted *burr* against her side. She dug in her jacket and stepped away, answering in a soft but terse tone.

Sam looked back across the yard at Norah and Maddy, his gut twisting in a knot. Was Norah really so cynical and self-serving as to push her way back into the life of the child she'd abandoned, just to keep scandalmongers from harming Graham Stilson's Senate bid?

The fact that he could seriously entertain the question made him wonder why he'd ever fallen for her in the first place.

"Tell her no," Kristen said sharply behind him, drawing his attention away from Norah and Maddy. He turned to find her shoving her phone in her pocket, her face pinched and pale.

"Is everything okay?" he asked, taking a step toward her, his hand outstretched.

She stepped back from him, grabbing the deck railing as she stumbled a little. "Everything's fine."

But clearly it wasn't. Her knuckles were white where she gripped the wood railing, and her eyes looked huge and dark in her colorless face. Ignoring the "don't touch me" vibe radiating from her in waves, he closed the gap between them, laying his hand gently on her shoulder. "You don't look fine."

She shook her head, ducking away from his touch. "I

need to go into the office for a little while. I still want to talk to Ms. Cabot alone—do you think you could get her to the station in a couple of hours?"

"I'll get her there," he promised, his mind racing with questions he knew she wouldn't answer if he asked them.

Kristen gave a brief nod and headed down the deck steps that led out to the gravel car park at the side of the house, where she'd left her Impala parked next to his Jeep. Sam squelched the urge to follow her, instinctively aware that the harder he pressed her to tell him what the call was about, the more she'd dig her heels in and push him away.

Besides, it wasn't his business, was it? Unless it had to do with Maddy, and she'd have told him if that was the case.

Still, he had trouble dragging his mind away from Kristen Tandy's pale, shocked expression as he descended the steps to the yard and scooped his daughter up in a fierce, laughing hug.

Norah arched one perfect eyebrow at him. "Where'd Nancy Drew hurry off to?"

Sam ignored the barb, kissing the top of Maddy's head. "Maddycakes, I think I smelled some fresh cookies in the kitchen. Jake, Mariah, y'all mind taking the kids up to see if the cookies are finished? I need to take Norah to the inn to get settled into her room." He shot his brother a meaningful look.

"Ooh, cookies!" Jake coaxed Maddy from Sam's arms and swung her onto his back, where she clung like a laughing baby monkey as he followed Mariah and Micah up the steps to the deck.

Norah looked up expectantly at Sam. "You wanted

to be alone with me at the inn, Sam? I'm flattered. But I'm engaged now." She waggled her left hand, where an enormous diamond solitaire glittered on the third finger. "Remember?"

"I remember," he said with a grim smile, taking her arm in his hand and leading her toward his Jeep parked on the gravel drive. "And that's why we need to talk."

CHAPTER SIX

TILLERY PARK SAT on the outskirts of Gossamer Ridge, Alabama, less a conventional city park than a protected patch of wilderness on the side of the mountain that gave the town its name. A few picnic pavilions dotted the park, as well as an old schoolhouse that dated from the late 1800s.

Beyond the schoolhouse, the land ended abruptly in a bluff overlooking Gossamer Lake and the houses that dotted its shore. A series of long stone benches stretched across the edge, only a few feet from the drop-off. At night, it was a favorite spot of the town's teens, who considered moonlit walks spiced with the danger of walking the bluff's edge to be the height of romance.

It was one of Kristen Tandy's favorite places, too, though not for its romance. Ever since she'd been a young girl, Tillery Park had been her place of escape, first from her troubled home life, then later from the stares and whispers that followed her around town after the murders. Her notoriety never seemed to follow her here to the park, where she was just one of the handful of townsfolk who came here to enjoy the area's wild beauty. People left her alone to think in peace.

She hadn't expected to come to Tillery Park today, however. Neck-deep in the Maddy Cooper case, when she got out of bed that morning she'd planned to spend the day with Sam, Maddy and Maddy's long-lost mother. She should be there now, instead of sitting on the hard stone bench, staring across the treetops below at the sparkling blue jewel of Gossamer Lake.

But that was before Carl's phone call.

"The administrator at Darden left me a message," Carl had said, referring to the state's secure medical facility where her mother resided. "Your mother wants to see you."

Kristen rubbed the heels of her hands against her burning eyes. Why now? Why, after all these years of blessed silence, did her mother want to see her now?

Her cell phone hummed. Carl again. She sent the call to voice mail and put the phone in her pocket again.

"Do you think that's going to shut me up?" Carl Madison's gravelly voice behind her made her jump. Her foster father stood a couple of feet away, holding up his cell phone. He had shed his suit jacket to accommodate the mid-May heat and humidity, exposing the familiar Smith & Wesson 686 Plus revolver tucked into a shoulder holster. He'd never gone to a semiautomatic like most of the younger cops. She hoped crime in Chickasaw County never forced him to choose a different weapon.

"How did you find me?"

He tapped the side of his nose. "Sniffed you out like a good detective. I mean, it's not like this is your favorite place to run and hide or anything."

Sighing, she edged over on the stone bench to make room for him. "You always did have an annoying sort of radar."

He settled beside her, giving her a light nudge with

his elbow. "I'm a cop, blue eyes. It's my job to know where all the delinquents are."

She managed a smile, though her stomach was twisting and roiling. "I just needed a break from day care duty," she said, although if she were honest, she'd have to admit that watching out for Maddy was turning out to have pros as well as cons.

"Who's minding the kid?"

"Her father, her mother and a passel of extended family." Kristen couldn't hold back a soft smile. "She has them all wrapped around her finger."

"She's a cutie."

"She's a sweet kid. Sam's doing a good job raising her."

"What did you think of the mother?"

Grateful for the distraction from her own problems, she gave Carl's question the thought it deserved. "I think she's very happy with living a sophisticated, high-profile, high-power life. I don't think she sees Maddy or Sam Cooper as part of that life long-term."

"What about short-term?"

She told him what she knew about Norah Cabot's engagement to the Senate candidate. "The timing is interesting."

"You think her overture to the kid is her way of neutralizing any bad press about having abandoned the girl?"

"You know me. I'm a cynic."

"If you were really a cynic, you wouldn't be so affected by the things that happen around you," Carl said gently.

"You always think the best of me, don't you?" She couldn't hide the affection in her voice. Sometimes she wondered why she even tried. Distancing herself from Carl, the closest thing to a real father she'd ever known, hadn't worked no matter how hard she tried. He always came back for more.

"I *expect* the best of you," he corrected gently. "I know what you're capable of."

She looked away, feeling shamed and defeated. "You tried so hard to give me a normal life, Carl. But it was just too late." She ran the pad of her fingers over the knotty scar on the back of her hand. "I'm not a normal person. I'm never going to be a normal person."

"You're too hard on yourself, kitten."

Carl's use of his favorite endearment for her brought stinging tears to her eyes. She blinked them back, refusing to go soft. Not now, when staying tough was more important than ever. "I'm just honest, Carl. Too much has happened to me, you know? I don't have anything left to offer anyone."

The sad look in his eyes hurt her, so she turned away, her gaze settling on the sparkling water of the lake. Cooper Cove Marina was on the park side of the lake, just out of sight beyond the curving point of land barely visible to the east. Sam Cooper and his daughter were probably still in the backyard with Norah, trying to get to know each other again after such a long absence. "I think Norah Cabot's trying to be a mother to Maddy," she said aloud, remembering the woman's tentative overtures to her daughter. "She's just not good at it."

"You don't think her heart's in it, do you?"

"I'm not sure I'm qualified to judge."

"Sure you are. You're a cop." Carl gave her another gentle nudge. "What does that cop's gut tell you?"

"That Norah Cabot likes Maddy more than she ex-

PAULA GRAVES 311

pected to, but she doesn't feel like Maddy's mother. She probably never will." Kristen toed the dirt in front of the stone bench. "Some things you can never change, even if you want to."

Carl was silent for a long moment. When he next spoke, it was in a low, serious tone. "I think you should go to Darden to see your mother."

"YOU WANTED TO talk to me?" Norah settled into one of the armchairs in her room at the Sycamore Inn. Challenge burned in her green eyes as she waved at the seat across from her. "So talk."

Sam ignored the invitation to sit. "Your fiancé is in a tough Senate primary battle with Halston Stevens. I know Stevens well enough to know he and his handlers will be looking for any dirt they can find on Stilson."

"Graham is a puritan. There's nothing to find."

"What about his fiancée, the woman who abandoned her three-month-old child to pursue her career?"

Norah's eyes flickered at his hard words, but she shrugged. "It's not like I dropped her in a Dumpster somewhere."

This time, he was the one who flinched. "God, Norah."

"You think I came here to meet Maddy so that when someone asked, I could say, 'Oh, I was just down in Alabama last week, visiting my adorable little girl. See—this is her latest photo. Doesn't she look just like me?'" Norah leaned forward. "Does it really matter why I came? Does it change anything?"

"Did you engineer this excuse? Did you hire someone to threaten my daughter?"

"Our daughter."

"*My* daughter." Anger burned at the back of his throat. "Norah, I have never tried to keep Maddy from you. I've always said you could see her whenever you want. But so help me, if you had anything to do with what happened the other night—"

Norah's eyes grew shiny, and her lower lip trembled, catching him off guard. "God, Sam, I know I was a terrible wife and even more useless as a mother, but if you think I could do such a thing—" She stopped short, licking her lips. "I suppose you think that a woman who could turn her back on her child would be capable of anything."

"I just want to understand why you're here."

"Because I was curious, all right?" She looked down at her hands. "When the police called, and then you left a message right behind them, I realized my daughter could have died the other night, and I'd have to live with the fact that I'd never really known her. You know, a three-month-old didn't even seem like a real person, but a four-year-old—I just—I didn't want to have regrets."

Sam stared at her, not sure whether or not he could believe her. There had been a time when he'd thought he knew her better than anyone else in the world.

Clearly, he'd been fooling himself. He was beginning to think he'd never really understood her at all.

"I didn't do this, Sam. I swear that to you." Norah leaned toward him, placing her hand on his arm. Her fingers were cool and light. "But I've been thinking about it, and I may have an idea who did."

KRISTEN LOOKED UP at Carl Madison, horrified. Had he really said she should go see her mother? "No, Carl."

"You've never faced her. Not in all these years."

Though his expression was gentle, his gray eyes were hard, like pieces of flint. "I think it's time."

"I don't owe her anything."

"You owe it to yourself."

She shook her head, rising to her feet. "We're not going to talk about this, Carl. If that's why you came here—"

"I came here to see about you. Period." Carl rose and stood in front of her, reaching out one hand to tip her chin up, making her look at him. "I'm on your side, kitten. Always."

"I don't want to go see her."

"Okay." He let his hand drop to her shoulder and gave her a soft squeeze. "Let me take you to Brightwood for lunch."

She managed a real smile. "Helen would kill me if I let you step into that diner. Think of your cholesterol, man."

"She has you trained, I see." Carl slipped his arm around her shoulder and walked with her to where she'd parked her Impala. He opened the car door for her, lingering as she slipped behind the wheel. His expression grew serious. "Kristen, if you want out of this Maddy Cooper assignment, I'll arrange it. I shouldn't have pushed you into it."

She shook her head. "You were right, Carl. I need to do this. I think I can get a lot accomplished from the inside."

"Good for you." He gave her shoulder another squeeze, then stepped back, closing the door. He gave a wave as she put the Impala in gear and backed out of the parking space.

Reaching the highway, she headed south toward the

office, remembering Sam's promise to bring Norah to the station so she could question her alone. But before she was a mile down the road, her cell phone vibrated against her side. She checked the phone and found Sam Cooper's phone number displayed.

She flipped the phone open. "Tandy."

"Kristen, it's Sam Cooper. I'm at the Sycamore Inn in town with Norah. How soon can you get here?" The tension in his voice made her stomach hurt.

"I'm about five minutes away. What's up?"

"I was just talking to Norah about some of my old cases and I think we may have something."

He was talking to Norah about old cases? Had he forgotten she was still a suspect? Tamping down her annoyance, she asked, "What kind of something?"

"A damned good motive for someone to use Maddy to hurt me," Sam answered.

"His name is Enrique Calderon," Sam told Kristen the minute she entered Norah's room, eager to get her input. "His son, Carlos, was here on a student visa six years ago when he raped and murdered a fellow student at Georgetown University. Two weeks ago, while serving twenty to life in a Maryland state prison, he was murdered by another inmate."

He told her about the case, how he'd prosecuted Carlos Calderon despite his father's multiple attempts to buy off judges and intimidate witnesses.

She listened carefully, her expression darkening. "And since you put Carlos in jail in the first place, you think Calderon wants revenge?"

"Absolutely."

Kristen glanced at Norah. "Were you around at the time of the trial?"

Norah nodded. "I heard about Carlos Calderon's death soon after it happened, but since Sam was down here by then, I thought he might not have heard about it."

"How lucky for him that you had," Kristen murmured. Sam didn't miss the skepticism in her voice.

Neither did Norah. "What are you suggesting?"

"It's a place to look that we didn't have before," Sam said firmly, drawing Kristen's attention back to him.

"You said Enrique Calderon lives in Sanselmo," Kristen pointed out, shooting another glance at Norah. "That's quite a long reach."

"He's a man with a very long reach," Sam countered. "Calderon is one of the most powerful criminals in a country with its share of powerful criminals. He's behind much of the corruption that kept Sanselmo poor and dangerous for decades. He's probably funding half the terror attacks El Cambio and other rebel groups are carrying out in Sanselmo right now."

Kristen's brow furrowed. "And he's taking time out of trying to destabilize a whole country to kidnap Maddy?"

"Do you have a better theory?" Norah asked coolly.

"Maddy said the assailant was Caucasian," Kristen added.

"Maddy wouldn't know the difference between white and Hispanic," Sam said.

Kristen looked a little annoyed, but she gave a brief nod. "Okay. I'll look into his current whereabouts."

"We've already got feelers out," Sam said. "Norah has friends in the State Department."

Kristen looked up at him. "We'll go through our own channels," she insisted. If she was bluffing, it didn't show. Maybe she really did have her own channels, although he found it hard to believe a small-town Alabama police department could possibly have better intel than Norah's friends at State.

"Were you the lead prosecutor?" Kristen asked.

"Yes," he answered.

"So he would be likely to remember you by name, I suppose."

"And with his son dying just a couple of weeks ago—"

"The timing is interesting," Kristen conceded. "I'll go call this in, get the ball rolling." Tucking the folder under one arm, she pulled her phone from her pocket and walked across the room to make her call.

Sam watched her as she spoke into the phone, her voice too low for him to make out words. She looked tired, he thought, her face a little pale. Dark circles bruised the skin beneath her eyes, bringing to mind her earlier reaction to the phone call she'd received at his parents' house.

The memory pinged his curiosity. Who had been on the phone? What had she heard to knock her so off-kilter?

He hoped it hadn't been bad news. She'd had enough bad news in her life.

"Quite the poker face." Norah's voice was low and amused.

He drew his gaze away from Kristen to meet Norah's bright green eyes. "Detective Tandy's or mine?"

Norah smiled. "The sweet young detective, of course. You're an open book, my love." She nodded toward

Kristen. "Her own channels? As if a little cop shop like hers could possibly know anything about an international crime lord."

"You think we don't have our own share of big-time crime in Alabama?" Sam murmured, not sure why he felt the urge to defend Kristen Tandy when he'd had his own doubts about the usefulness of her connections. "A Mexican drug cartel carried out a series of gang executions south of here not long ago. It's a global economy, even for the bad guys."

"That doesn't mean Elly Mae Clampett over there can make a phone call and find out where Enrique Calderon has been for the last five days," Norah scoffed. "She just doesn't want to look like an idiot in front of you. It's kind of sweet."

Sam pressed his lips together, irritated by Norah's constant stream of insults. "Kristen Tandy is not an idiot. She's got good instincts, and she's putting herself on the line more ways than you know to protect my daughter—our daughter. There are things you don't know about her—"

As soon as the words escaped his mouth, he knew he'd made a mistake. Norah's eyes lit up with wicked interest.

"What things?" she asked.

A knock on the front door saved him from having to answer. He opened the door to his brother Gabe, who was carrying Maddy on his back.

"Jake and Mariah had to take Micah to the doctor, so they left the rug rat in my care," Gabe said with a grin.

Norah smiled. "Hello, Gabe."

Gabe's smile went a little brittle. "Hello, Norah." He lowered Maddy to the floor.

"Uncle Gabe's gotta go fishing," Maddy announced as she reached up to Sam for a hug. Sam gave her a squeeze, shooting a quizzical look at his brother.

"I have a last-minute afternoon guide job," Gabe said apologetically. "We were in town for ice cream when I got the page. I called Mom to see if she could keep her down at the bait shop, but Miss Priss caught sight of Detective Tandy as we were driving past and demanded to come here instead. I saw your Jeep and figured you must be here with your ex." He gave a nod in Norah's direction. "If it's a problem—"

"No, that's fine." Sam shifted Maddy to his hip. "It's about time I take her home for her nap anyway."

"No, don't wanna nap!" Maddy protested.

"If you don't take a nap now, you'll have to go to bed early tonight. And I have big plans for tonight, let me tell you." He made a face at his daughter, knowing she couldn't resist a tease like that.

Maddy cocked her head, her eyes bright with curiosity. "Like what?"

He lowered his voice. "It's a secret."

Maddy gave a long, frustrated growl. "I hate secrets!"

"You love secrets," he insisted.

She sighed deeply and gave him a look that made his heart curl into a helpless knot. "Okay, Daddy." She gave him a hug. He hugged her back, trying not to squeeze too tightly.

"I guess I'd better get going then," Gabe said, nodding politely to Norah, then to Kristen, who'd apparently finished her phone call. He headed out the door.

"Quite the charmer," Norah said drily.

"You'd be surprised." Sam looked at Kristen. "Detective Tandy? Were you able to put out any feelers to your contacts?"

Ignoring Norah's soft huff of skepticism, Kristen lifted her chin and met his gaze steadily. "Foley's brother is an FBI agent whose area of focus is the identification and interdiction of South American drug cartels trying to set up shop in the states. Foley's calling him to see if he can figure out Calderon's movements over the last four days."

Sam glanced at Norah for her reaction. Her expression was a mixture of disbelief and annoyance.

"Well, I'm going to get Maddy home for her nap. Detective Tandy, didn't you want to ask Norah some questions?"

"Oh, terrible time for that," Norah said firmly, grabbing her purse from the writing table. "I'm afraid I made an appointment with Limbaugh Motors just down the street to obtain a rental car while I'm here in town. Give me a call later and I'm sure we can arrange something." She handed the room key to Sam. "Do lock up for me, Sam. I'll pick up the key later this afternoon." She breezed past them on a trail of Chanel No 5.

"Son of a b—" Kristen sputtered.

"Small ears," Sam warned.

She looked up at him, her eyes ablaze. "I'm not through with that woman," she warned, pushing past him through the door Norah had left open on her way out. Sam watched her go, enjoying the view of her denim-clad backside a little more than he should.

The next couple of days might turn out to be a lot more complicated than he'd anticipated.

CHAPTER SEVEN

"How did a Sanselmo drug cartel get mixed up in this anyway?" Jason Foley asked Kristen later that afternoon when she dropped by the office to see if his brother had called back.

"Apparently Sam Cooper was involved in several high-profile cases in D.C., including the conviction of a drug lord's son." Kristen explained what she knew about the Carlos Calderon case. "Junior ticked off a fellow inmate and ended up dead a couple of weeks ago."

"And Cooper thinks Papa C. has decided nabbing the Cooper kid will exact some sort of vengeance?" Foley looked skeptical.

"It was Norah Cabot's idea, actually." Kristen tried not to let her dislike show. "But it's certainly a motive worth investigating," she added grudgingly.

"What did you think of the former Mrs. Cooper?" Foley asked in a tone suggesting he already knew the answer.

Kristen tried to be fair. "She's smart, beautiful and sophisticated, befitting a high-powered corporate attorney. Seems to harbor no ill will toward Cooper."

"How'd she interact with the kid?"

Kristen thought about how she'd phrased it earlier to Carl. "She's kind to Maddy, and seems to like her. But

I just don't get any sense that they connect like you'd think a mother and child would."

"And your theory about the fiancé's Senate run?"

"I still think that probably explains why she hopped a plane and flew down here so fast, but I can't really see where it supplies a motive for trying to kidnap Maddy from her father's home. Sam Cooper is open to Norah seeing more of Maddy, so why break the law when she could accomplish the same thing through normal, legal means?"

"So we mark her off the list?"

With a sigh, Kristen nodded. "Probably."

Foley chuckled. "Don't sound so disappointed."

"I'm not." She had to smile. "Well, not much. But if that woman looks at me like I'm some inbred hick idiot one more time—"

The phone rang, keeping Foley from saying whatever he was clearly itching to say. His wry grin faded immediately. He listened to whoever was on the other line for over a minute, jotting notes on the pad in front of him. Finally, he put down his pen and looked up at Kristen. "Thanks, Rick. I'll tell her what you found."

Kristen's gut tightened as he hung up the phone. "Was that your brother? Does he know something about Enrique Calderon?"

Foley nodded. "He found out where Calderon was the night of the attack on Sam Cooper's niece and daughter."

"SAM COOPER, A GOURMET CHEF. Who'd have believed it?" Norah lifted the lid and sniffed the savory aroma rising from the stew pot. She'd arrived at the guesthouse a half hour earlier, driving a shiny red Mercedes convertible with a Limbaugh Motors sticker and dealer plates. Sam suspected Mike Limbaugh had rented Norah his personal car, since the small dealership wasn't known for its luxury vehicles.

"It's just chicken-vegetable soup," he said aloud, mildly amused by Norah's hyperbole. "You chop a few vegetables, add some chunk chicken, water and seasonings and let it all simmer together. You should try it. It'll knock Junior's socks off."

She made a face at him. "I'm just surprised you turned out to be such a good hausfrau. You were always a take-out menu sort of man back in the day."

"Perhaps because you were always a take-out menu sort of woman." Sam stirred the soup. "I'm working fewer hours these days, and I have a child to feed."

As he reached for the pepper mill, he heard footsteps on the stairs outside. Automatically he went tense, reaching for the knife lying on the chopping board nearby and wishing his Glock 9 mm wasn't hidden in a box at the top of his closet.

Norah looked up with alarm. "Sam?"

A knock on the door eased his tension only marginally. Keeping the knife in his right hand, he crossed to the door and looked out. It was Kristen Tandy. He relaxed, reaching for the door handle.

Behind him, Norah's cell phone rang. He heard her answer as he opened the door and greeted Kristen.

"I have news," she said tersely, not waiting to be invited inside.

Sam closed the door behind her and followed Kristen into the room. Norah joined them, her eyes bright.

In unison, both women blurted, "Enrique Calderon is dead."

The twinge of disappointment Sam felt upon hearing the news that one of their best leads had dried up gave way to amusement as Norah and Kristen stared at each other in disbelief.

"How the hell did you know that?" Norah asked Kristen. "My contact at State called me the second he found out."

Kristen smiled placidly. "My contact called a half hour ago with the news."

"When did he die?" Sam asked.

Both women turned to look at him as if suddenly realizing they weren't alone in the room. Kristen answered first. "The last time anyone saw him alive was five days ago. The FBI's source within the cartel confirmed Calderon's been dead at least four of those days—he saw the leader's body himself. The cartel's inner sanctum has been keeping things mum while they jockey for position in the leadership stakes."

Sam glanced at Norah to see if she had anything else to add. She looked annoyed but didn't contradict anything Kristen had said.

"Well," he said, before the tension in the room blew up in his face, "I guess we can mark Calderon off the list, then."

Kristen nodded. "But I think your case history is probably a good place to keep looking," she added. "There are bound to be others like Calderon in your past."

"Does this mean you're taking me off the suspect list, Detective?" Norah asked drily.

Kristen turned to Norah, her gaze narrowed. "I can't see where you'd have any motive to try to harm Maddy or Sam. They've made it clear that you're welcome to have a part in their lives, so you'd have no reason to take extreme measures to be with your child."

"Well, hallelujah. The Gossamer Ridge Constabulary takes me off the most-wanted list." Norah feigned relief.

"Perhaps you'd prefer we skip steps and leave stones unturned in our quest to protect your daughter," Kristen responded quietly.

Norah's expression went serious. "No. I would not prefer that, Detective."

"I think I hear Maddy stirring from her nap," Sam interjected. "We didn't discuss dinner, Detective Tandy, but there's plenty for everyone. Unless you have other plans?"

Norah spoke before Kristen could answer. "Actually, Sam, would you mind terribly if I took Maddy out for dinner tonight? The Sycamore Inn has a lovely little French café on the first floor. I thought Maddy and I could eat there and get a little better acquainted. Just the two of us."

Sam's gut twisted at the request, catching him by surprise. He had thought he would be happy to see Norah take an interest in their daughter, but the idea of handing Maddy over to the mother she barely knew suddenly held no appeal for him.

"I'm not sure it's safe, given what's been happening," Kristen interjected. Sam flashed her a grateful look.

"Oh, please. We won't be walking down Main Street flashing a 'come and get us' sign," Norah scoffed. "I just want a little alone time with my daughter at a perfectly safe little inn in downtown Gossamer Ridge." She put her hand on Sam's arm. "You always say I can see Maddy whenever I want, no conditions. I want to take her to dinner. Please trust me to do that."

Sam glanced at Kristen, wondering if she'd come up with another argument. "I don't think someone will go after her in a public place," Kristen said, her watchful gaze batting the ball back into his court.

With a sigh, he turned back to Norah. "Her bedtime is eight-thirty. I'll go see if she's up from her nap."

Sam moved reluctantly toward the bedroom door, half expecting a fight to break out the second his back was turned. But both Norah and Kristen remained silent as he opened the door and slipped into the darkened bedroom.

He crossed to the bed and turned on the small bedside lamp. Pale gold light illuminated his daughter's sleepy face. "Is it time for my surprise?" she asked, her voice hoarse from the nap.

Trust his little girl to have a sharp memory when it came to promised treats. The surprise he'd promised was the batch of peanut butter fudge his mom had made the night before and packed up for him earlier when they were at his parents' house, but now he had a different surprise. "How would you like to go to dinner with just your mommy tonight?"

"Mommy?" Maddy sounded a little doubtful, as if she had expected to wake to find Norah already gone.

Sam's heart spasmed. "Your mother wants to take you to the inn where she's staying to have dinner. Just the two of you. Wouldn't you like that? A girls' night out?"

Maddy's forehead wrinkled. "Just Mommy and me?"

Sam nodded. "It'll be fun. I bet she'll even buy you some chocolate ice cream for dessert." He made a mental note to make sure Norah did just that.

"Well, okay," Maddy said after a moment. "Can I wear my purple dress?"

He smiled, relieved he'd thought to pack it. "You betcha." He went to the closet and pulled down her favorite purple sundress, the one with the bright yellow sash and the enormous sunflower right in the middle. Maddy loved to wear it for special occasions like birthdays and parties. Maybe it was a good sign that she was excited enough about dinner with her mother to think of the purple dress.

As he helped her into the dress and brushed her hair, he found his mind wandering away from the idea of Norah and Maddy out on the town together and into the dangerous territory of dinner alone with Kristen Tandy. Would she agree to stay for dinner, without the buffer of Maddy between them? Did she even feel the same tension he felt every time they were alone together?

"Ready to go, baby?" he asked Maddy when he'd finished putting her hair up in a neat ponytail.

"Come with us, Daddy."

"I can't, sweetie. Your mama wants to take you to dinner all by herself. And besides, if I go, Miss Kristen will have to eat dinner all alone. You don't want that, do you?"

She looked inclined to argue, but he hurried her out to the living room, where he found Kristen and Norah standing about as far apart as they could manage.

Norah smiled at Maddy. "You look so pretty, Maddy," she proclaimed, although Sam could almost see her mind clicking off a list of ways she'd have dressed Maddy differently. He hoped she'd keep her constructive criticism to herself around Maddy.

He resisted the temptation to walk Maddy and Norah

out to the car, appeasing himself by watching them drive away through the front window, his heart in his throat.

"I think she'll be fine with your ex-wife," Kristen said softly. Her voice was close; when he turned to face her, he found her standing only a foot or so away.

"I know. I'm being an idiot." He managed a smile. "You know, the dinner invitation stands. I have a big pot of chicken soup and nobody to share it with. Do you have dinner plans?"

She shot him a wry smile. "No plans."

He held out his arm. "Your table awaits, madam."

She cocked her head, surprise tinting her expression. But she slipped her hand into the crook of his arm and smiled up at him, letting him walk her over to the table.

She didn't sit immediately when he pulled out her chair. "Don't you need help in the kitchen?"

"Are you impugning my culinary skills?"

"No, of course not." She sat when he waved his hand insistently at the chair, but her voice followed him into the kitchen. "But I could at least get some ice in the glasses."

He turned to look at her, amused by her obvious unease at being waited on. "Let me do this for you. Consider it a thank-you for what you're doing for Maddy."

She looked as if she wanted to argue but finally gave a nod of assent and settled in the chair, her hands folded primly in her lap. She looked nervous—adorably so, like a teenager on her first formal date. Well, except for the teenager part. There was nothing girlish in the way her curvy body filled out her faded jeans and fitted gray blouse.

He spooned soup into two bowls and carried them to

the table. "Today's chicken soup includes a dash of sea salt, a delicate sprinkle of chicken bouillon powder and a bold, ambitious canned vegetable blend."

She grinned up at him. "Don't you hate when waiters do that? Like it's going to make the entrée taste better if you know the mushrooms were grown in the basement of a tiny monastery in France."

He grinned back at her, pleased she got the joke. "Especially when you know they were probably grown accidentally in the leaky basement beneath the restaurant."

"Exactly!"

He returned to the kitchen for the iced tea, still smiling. Maybe this evening would turn out even better than he had hoped.

AN HOUR LATER, Kristen had finally let herself relax. Sam was a funny, entertaining dinner companion, seeming to instinctively steer clear of touchy subjects during the meal. Instead, he told her stories about his time in the JAG corps, with himself as the butt of most of the jokes. By the time they moved to the living room for the whipped cream and strawberry dessert, Kristen had begun to wonder why she'd felt so nervous about sticking around.

"My mother grows strawberries in a little garden beside the house," he told her, setting the bowl of fruit and cream in front of her. "She has an amazing green thumb. The garden is tiny—maybe twenty feet long by six feet wide, but she gets the most out of the soil. Strawberries, blueberries, turnip greens, green beans, tomatoes—one year she even grew corn."

"I always wanted a garden," Kristen admitted. "I tried once, when I was about ten. I wanted to grow flowers—daisies and irises and roses. Our neighbor down the street, Mrs. Tamberlain, had the most beautiful rose garden. One day she gave me a cutting and told me how to get it to root in water so I could plant it myself." She smiled at the memory. "When the roots started to sprout from the cuttings, I was so excited I started jumping around like I'd won the lottery or something."

"Did it grow?"

Her smile faded. "Mama got angry at me about something—I don't even remember what now. She threw the glass holding the roses at the refrigerator. It smashed all over the place. And she just stomped over the roses to make me cry." She pressed her lips to a tight line, anger and hurt bubbling up from a place deep inside her, a place she thought she'd shut down a long time ago. "But I didn't cry."

She felt his gaze on her, knew what she'd see if she looked at him. Pity. Maybe horror. Probably both.

She cleared her throat and picked up the bowl of strawberries and cream, even though her appetite was long gone.

"You don't talk about your childhood much, I imagine," Sam said. He didn't sound pitying or horrified, just curious. She dared a quick look at him. He met her gaze almost impassively.

"No, I don't," she admitted.

"I should warn you, I talk about mine all the time. Growing up here by the lake was any kid's dream come true." He took a bite of dessert. "I know I'm lucky."

"You are." She took a bite of the strawberries and cream, as well. The flavor was the perfect blend of sweet and tart, and the appetite that had fled with her memories came roaring back with a vengeance. "These strawberries are amazing."

"Told you." He gave her a light nudge with his elbow. "Next time we're up at the main house, get Mom to show you her tomatoes. She might give you a cutting so you can grow some of your own."

"Nowhere to grow tomatoes at my apartment."

"Not even a sunny balcony or porch?"

She did have a small, sunny patio at the back of her apartment, facing the grassy courtyard of the apartment complex. "I guess I could grow them in large planters."

"That's the spirit. You'll be a gardener in no time." Sam set his empty bowl on the table in front of him. "Sometimes you don't get exactly what you want in life, you know. But if you're creative and maybe a little brave, you can usually get pretty damned close."

He wasn't just talking about gardens anymore, she knew. But he was talking as someone who'd had a pretty good life. Maybe his first marriage hadn't worked out, but he had the kind of family background that made it easy to pick himself up and move on to the next challenge.

She didn't have that kind of foundation. She didn't even know what a normal life looked like.

"You and Maddy seemed to be having fun when we got here." Sam reached across the coffee table and picked up the drawing Kristen and Maddy had been working on earlier. "I guess you're developing a little resistance to your kid allergy, huh?"

"I don't have a kid allergy," she replied. "They just—"

"Bring back bad memories?"

She looked up at him. "Yeah."

He nodded, his expression solemn but mercifully devoid of pity. "I figured it might be something like that."

She didn't want to talk about her childhood, but the emotions roiling inside her chest were clamoring to get out, and she was tired of fighting them. Sam Cooper would understand, she realized on an almost visceral level. He'd keep her secrets if she asked him to.

"I was all my brothers and sisters really had, in the end." She had to push the admission past her closed throat. "Mama wasn't herself at all by then. She—she didn't exist in the same reality as the rest of us."

"You were a teenager by then?"

"Thirteen. Barely." She'd felt much older by then, however. Ancient. "It was like juggling a million flaming clubs all at once, while wolves were snapping at your heels. Trying to keep everyone fed and clothed, trying to get them to school on time, trying to keep social services from finding out our situation, trying to keep the little ones from understanding how far gone Mama really was—" She ran her hands over her face, nausea flicking at the base of her throat. Maybe she should have let DHR—the Department of Human Resources, the state's social service agency—know what was going on in her household. She'd been terrified that they would separate her from the other children, but in hindsight, intervention would have been so much better than what had actually happened.

"You know what?" Interrupting her bleak thoughts, Sam reached across and took her hands in his. His palms were warm and slightly calloused, pleasantly rough against hers. "You don't have to talk about this tonight if you don't want to."

"You don't think I need to get it all out?" she asked

wryly. "Won't I feel all better if I spill my guts about my tragic past?"

"Probably not." His grip on her hands tightened. "But if you want to tell me about your not-as-tragic life afterward, I'd love to hear about that."

She smiled at him, almost limp with grateful relief. "That would bore you to death."

He let go of her hands. She tamped down a sense of disappointment. "Have you heard anything new about your niece?" she asked after searching her mind for new topics. In her haste to hurry back here to tell Sam about Calderon, she'd forgotten to ask Foley for an update on Cissy Cooper's condition.

"I ran by the hospital to check on her before I picked Norah up at the airport. She's still in a coma, though the doctor says he's more optimistic she may not have lasting brain damage once she comes out of it."

"That's good news, isn't it?" Impulsively, Kristen squeezed his arm, her fingers digging gently into the hard muscle of his bicep.

His gaze dropped to her hand, then slowly lifted to meet hers. The air between them supercharged immediately, making her fingers tingle where she touched him. She felt a hot tug deep in her belly, drawing her closer.

This was why staying for dinner was dangerous.

She should pull her hand away. Pull away and put distance between them, before she did something stupid and irrevocable.

But she couldn't move.

His gaze slid down to her lips, and she parted them helplessly, a whisper of breath escaping her throat. She saw the vein in his neck throbbing wildly.

Her whole body vibrated as the trill of a cell phone ripped through the tense atmosphere.

Sam jerked away, reaching in his pocket for his phone. "Cooper." He listened a second, his eyes widening with alarm. "When? How?"

Kristen's stomach tightened as she saw terror fill his eyes. When he spoke again, his voice was strangled. "Stay right where you are. I'm on the way."

He was halfway to the door before Kristen could react. She jumped up to keep pace with him, her heart in her throat. "What is it?"

He paused for half a second at the door to look at her, his eyes dark with fear. "That was Norah. Maddy's missing."

CHAPTER EIGHT

NORAH MET THEM at the door of the Sycamore Café, fear and guilt battling in her expression. Inside the small ground floor restaurant, the scene was pure chaos, everyone from diners to staff abuzz with interest and concern. A couple of Gossamer Ridge police officers mingled among them, taking statements.

Sam took Norah's arm and led her to a quiet spot to one side of the room, trying to keep from panicking. He slanted a quick look at Kristen, just to assure himself that she was there with him. She gazed back at him, her eyes fathomless. He grounded himself in their depths and turned back to Norah. "Still no sign of her?"

Norah shook her head, her lips trembling. "Nobody saw her leave, but—" She raked her red-tipped fingers through her hair, spiking it in a dozen different directions. "I had to take the call, Sam. I have a case going to trial in a couple of weeks. I couldn't seem to get reception in the bathroom, and Maddy told me she was fine, so I went outside for just a minute. I told her to stay there till I got back." Her face crumpled. "It was only a few minutes. It took longer than I thought, but I swear, Sam, it was only a few minutes."

Sam looked at Kristen again, struggling hard against a gathering storm of despair. Her expressive eyes were dark with worry, but she seemed otherwise calm, far more focused than he felt at the moment. She laid her hand on his arm, her fingers warm and strong, and he felt some of his fear ease away. He covered her hand with his, giving it a grateful squeeze.

After a moment, Kristen slipped her hand from Sam's grip and turned to face Norah. "What did you and Maddy talk about before she went to the restroom?"

The question caught Norah by surprise. "T-talk about?"

"Could you have said something to Maddy that would make her run away from you?" Kristen asked.

Sam experienced the first glimmer of hope he'd felt since he'd answered Norah's call. "You think she ran away?"

"Kids run and hide when they're afraid," Kristen answered, looking at Sam. "Remember the closet?"

Norah cleared her throat, and he turned his attention back to her. "Why would she be afraid of me? We just talked about her preschool, how she likes living in Alabama and about—" Norah stopped short, giving Sam a horrified look.

Sam's gut tightened. "What?"

"I told her maybe I'd take her back to Washington. I meant for a visit, of course, but—" Norah turned suddenly to Kristen, closing her long fingers over the other woman's arm. "Could she have thought I was going to take her away from Sam?"

"She might have misunderstood." Kristen turned to look at Sam. "Call her name, Sam."

His heart pounding like a piston, he called out, "Maddy? Are you in here?"

The patrons, staff and policemen alike turned to look at him, the hum of low conversation stopping, then ramping up to a steady buzz. Ignoring their stares, he moved through the tiny restaurant in search of any place a four-year-old might hide.

Kristen joined the search, taking the opposite side of the restaurant. "Maddy, it's Miss Kristen. Are you playing hide-and-seek?" The two Gossamer Ridge officers followed her lead, spreading out to cover the other areas of the café.

Sam grabbed the arm of a waiter. "Where are the bathrooms?"

The startled man pointed to an alcove off the kitchen. Sam headed that way and found himself in a narrow, dimly lit hallway. The men's and women's restrooms were to his left, clearly marked. To his right were two unmarked doors. He tried the first one. Locked.

The handle of the second door turned easily in his hand. Inside, he found a small storage closet. Boxes and bins took up almost every inch of the space.

"Maddy?"

The small, muffled voice that answered him sent such a powerful shot of relief through his veins that his knees nearly buckled. "I'm not going with Mommy!"

"You don't have to, baby."

A small box near the back of the closet shifted, and Maddy's tear-streaked face stared back at him from the void. "Daddy's honor?"

He grinned. "Daddy's honor."

She squeezed out of the tight hiding spot and threw herself in his arms. He hugged her tightly, flattening his hand against her back until he could feel her heartbeat against his palm.

"Is she okay?" Kristen asked just behind him.

He eased his grip on Maddy and turned to look at her. Her eyes were soft with relief, and he reached for her instinctively. She didn't resist as he pulled her into his arms and buried his face in her hair.

She smelled good, like the woods after a rain, and where her cheek brushed his, her skin was as soft as a whisper. Relief faded into something darker and hotter, and he wondered if she could feel the sudden acceleration of his heartbeat as it hammered in his chest.

"Sam?" Norah's voice broke through the heated haze settling over his brain. He felt Kristen push gently against his grasp, and he let her go, turning toward the sound of his ex-wife's voice. Norah stood at the end of the narrow corridor, her expression tentative.

Maddy tightened her grip on Sam, burying her face in his neck. "No, Daddy!" she whispered.

Norah didn't miss their daughter's reaction. Her face crumpled, and she hurried out of sight.

"Ah, hell," he muttered.

Kristen laid her hand on his arm. "Take Maddy home. I'll make sure Norah's okay."

The offer surprised him. "You sure you want to do that?"

Her lips curved in a wry half smile. "I think I'm probably the most uniquely qualified person to do that. You know, being an expert on really bad mothers."

His gut twisted in a knot. Until he'd seen his own daughter's terrified reaction to Norah's unintentional gaffe, his understanding of what Kristen had gone through as a child was mostly academic. But if something as simple and harmless as a misunderstanding could reduce his normally happy-go-lucky child to a terrified, quivering mess, how much worse must it have been for Kristen Tandy, living day in and day out with a mother like hers? And to witness the murders of her sisters and brothers, barely escaping her own death at her mother's hand—how had she survived it?

No wonder she was so guarded with her emotions, so reticent about her inner life.

He walked with her into the main dining area, staying close enough to feel her warmth against his arm. The patrons and staff stared for a second before breaking into applause. Kristen's face went red with embarrassment as the restaurant manager came over to offer his congratulations—and dinner on the house.

Sam thanked him but declined. "I just want to get Maddy home to bed." As the manager returned to his post at the front, Sam leaned his head toward Kristen. "How am I supposed to get back to the lake? You drove."

"I'll get one of the officers to drop you off." She smiled at Maddy, who'd finally loosened her death grip on Sam's neck. "Maybe you can sweet-talk the nice officer into running the siren!"

"Don't give her any ideas," Sam warned with a smile.

Kristen grabbed one of the uniformed officers, murmured a few words to him and brought him over to where Sam and Maddy stood near the door. "This is Officer Simmons. He's going to drive you back to the lake."

As Sam started to follow Simmons out the door, Maddy tugged sharply at his collar. "Wait!" she insisted, and twisted her body in his grasp, holding her arms out toward Kristen.

Kristen stared at her a moment, her expression hard to read. Sam held his breath, wondering if she'd rebuff his daughter's offer of affection. He might better understand the difficulty she had relating to Maddy now, but he couldn't explain those nuances to a four-year-old. Maddy would feel rejected no matter what he told her.

Kristen's lips curved into a big smile and she opened her arms, wrapping Maddy in a quick but genuine hug. "Make your daddy read you *two* stories tonight," she murmured, her tone conspiratorial. Maddy grinned with delight.

Kristen's gaze slid up to meet Sam's. He could see the pain lurking there in their blue depths, and his heart broke a little for her, but for the first time, he also saw the spark of genuine affection for his daughter. "Thank you," he said, reaching out to touch her arm.

Her mouth tightened, and she turned away from him quickly. "Talk to you later," she tossed gruffly over her shoulder, and then she was gone, weaving her way through the crowd in search of Norah.

Sam watched her go, regret settling low in his gut. Tonight's events might have broken down a few of the walls Kristen Tandy built around herself, but there were still plenty left in place. It might take a whole lifetime to tear them all down.

Did he want to devote his life to such a task or drag Maddy along on that kind of roller-coaster ride? Wouldn't it be better to just step back and regain some distance from Kristen and her problems?

At this point, however, he wasn't sure stepping back was even possible. Maddy was crazy about Kristen, flaws and all. And despite his clear-eyed understanding of just how difficult a woman she might be to care about, he found himself becoming more and more entangled in her life.

It wasn't likely, at this point, that any of them would leave this case unscathed.

"GO AWAY, DETECTIVE." Norah Cabot's voice was muffled and weary behind the door to her room at the inn. "We can talk in the morning."

"I think we should talk now," Kristen said firmly, even though a part of her wanted nothing more than to go home and bury herself under the covers of her old four-poster bed.

"Are you enjoying this?" Norah asked faintly.

"No, I'm not," Kristen replied. "Believe it or not, I'm here to help you."

There was a brief pause, then a rattle of the latch. The door opened and Norah stood on the other side, clad in a red silk robe that nearly matched the color of her tear-swollen eyes. "Here to help me. I've heard that before."

"I brought tissues." Kristen held out the small travel-size tissue box she'd picked up at the gift shop downstairs before heading up to the guest rooms.

Norah released a huff of laughter and took the box from Kristen's outstretched hand. "You think of everything."

"May I come in?"

Norah seemed to consider the question for a moment, then gave an indifferent shrug. "Why not? It's not like my night could get any worse."

"Believe me, it could," Kristen murmured.

Norah ignored her and crossed to a small credenza along one wall of the small but pretty room. "The inn was kind enough to send up a complimentary bottle of sparkling water. I would have preferred champagne, but I suppose this is one of those dry counties you Southerners are so fond of."

"If you want to get liquored up, I could drive you to the next county over."

"Couldn't you just direct me to the nearest moonshine still instead?" Norah tossed a couple of ice cubes in a glass with excessive vigor. She set the glass down with a clatter and drove her long fingers through her hair, tousling the already unruly curls. "I'm sorry. I can be a total bitch."

"But at least you're self-aware," Kristen said.

Norah slanted a look at her and gave a short laugh. "Yes, I suppose that's a plus." She held out the glass of sparkling water. "Can I interest you in a drink?"

Kristen shook her head. "I just came to make sure you're okay. Can I get anything for you?"

Norah's brow furrowed. "Why would you care?"

Kristen knew what she was asking. Norah hadn't exactly done anything to garner Kristen's sympathy since her arrival. But it didn't change the fact that she'd been through an emotionally wrenching couple of hours. "I just thought maybe you could use someone...neutral. To hear your side of things."

Norah arched one perfect eyebrow. "Neutral?"

"Well, more neutral than your ex-husband, anyway."

Norah shook her head. "Sam must think I'm a complete idiot. Not even thinking how what I said might have sounded to Maddy—so stupid."

"You didn't mean to frighten her."

"But I did." Norah's gaze met hers, fierce and angry. "I'm very good at my job, Detective. I have companies trying to hire me away from my firm every day. Senators and congressmen who want me on their staffs. When a question arises at the office, you know who they look to for answers? They look to me. And I'm always right." She laid the glass of sparkling water on the credenza. "But I haven't done a single thing right for my daughter since the day she was born."

"That's not true," Kristen said. "You gave full custody to Sam. That was the right thing to do."

Norah paused with her hand on the glass, turning to look at Kristen. "Come now, surely you think I'm heartless and cruel for abandoning my flesh and blood, don't you? That I'm selfish and thoughtless for not even checking to see how she's been doing all these years?" Norah sank against the edge of the credenza, her expression bleak. "Guilty as charged."

"You're just not cut out to be a mother," Kristen said. "Sam has told me that you made it clear to him from the beginning that you didn't want children. You didn't lie or pretend to be anything you're not."

"But I should have wanted to be a mother as soon as I saw my daughter!"

Kristen thought of her own mother and tamped down a shudder. "Wanting to be a mother isn't the same thing as being a good one. You knew the life you wanted wouldn't accommodate motherhood, and you'd never be good at it. Why drag your child into a life that would be miserable for both of you?"

Norah looked up at her, eyes narrowed. "I guess you of all people would know about bad mothers."

Kristen hid a flinch.

"I know what your mother did to you and your brothers and sisters," Norah added when Kristen didn't respond.

Kristen squelched the familiar rush of shame and anger, feeling even more certain of the decision she'd made earlier that day. She couldn't go visit her mother, as the woman had requested. No way was she ready yet. "Who told you? Sam?"

"Of course not. Sam's the soul of discretion." Norah's smile was almost apologetic. "See, I'm not the sort of woman who abides having my life pried into without returning the favor. As soon as Sam hinted that you were more complicated than you look, my curiosity wouldn't rest until I did some checking. So I asked around about you when I went to rent the car. Seems you're quite notorious around these parts."

Kristen looked down at the scar on her hand, resisting the urge to beat a fast retreat. After all this time, she should be used to people knowing all the ugly details of her tragic history.

"My mother should never have been a parent," Kristen admitted aloud. "So I do have some respect for your decision not to inflict yourself on Maddy."

"Thanks—I think," Norah answered wryly.

"You could do more harm than good by hanging around and mothering her if you're not cut out for it. Sam's a great father. He's done a wonderful job with Maddy by himself. If you know you'd end up disappointing them both if you tried to start playing Mommy now—"

The sparkle of tears in Norah's eyes caught Kristen by surprise. "I would. I hate that that's how things are, but I don't have it in me to change who I am at this point in my life."

"Then don't let your fiancé's aspirations push you into doing something that will hurt both Maddy and you."

Norah scraped her hair out of her eyes. "Graham doesn't want kids, either. But he knows it's hard for people to understand, and God knows Halston Stevens will hammer him about it. 'What kind of man would marry a woman who abandoned her beautiful little child? Do you want that kind of man for your Senator?'"

"The right thing to do isn't always the easy thing to do. Matter of fact, it's usually not."

"Thank you, Obi-Wan Kenobi."

Kristen smiled. "You gonna be okay?"

Norah nodded. "I guess I should call Graham and tell him what's happened." She walked with Kristen to the door. "I know I've been a pain since I arrived—"

"It's part of your charm," Kristen said, still smiling.

Norah returned the smile. "Like prickly and defensive is part of yours?"

Kristen nodded, realizing she'd finally made Norah recognize her as an equal. "Exactly."

Norah's expression grew serious as she opened the door. "Protect my daughter. Find out who's trying to use her to hurt Sam and make them pay. Will you do that for me?"

"Yes," Kristen answered. "I'll do everything I can to protect them both."

"Good." Norah managed a weak smile and lifted her hand in a goodbye salute. She closed the door, leaving Kristen alone in the narrow hallway.

When she reached her car, Kristen called the office to see if anyone was still in the detective's office. The Gossamer Ridge Police Department wasn't large enough or busy enough to field a twenty-four-hour detective's division, but there was usually a night detective on duty until 11:00 p.m.

In this case, she got Jason Foley on the phone. "What are you still doing there?" she asked. "Gina finally come to her senses and kick you out of the house?"

"Ha. She and the kids are visiting her folks in Huntsville for the night, so I thought I'd review some of the neighbor interviews from Mission Road, see if I missed any clues."

"Did you?"

"Of course not. I'm a seasoned law enforcement professional," he answered glibly. "Heard you had a scare tonight with the Cooper kid."

"Yeah, but it had a happy ending."

"Gee, Tandy, two days on babysitting duty and you've already lost the kid once," Foley said, clicking his tongue. "That's not gonna look good in your personnel file."

She made a face at the phone. "Need me to come in and help you go through the interviews?"

"Is your life really that pathetic? You're twenty-eight and single, Kristen. If you don't want to go back to kidsville at the moment, go pick up a guy at a bar or something."

"You're just full of good advice. I'm so lucky to have you as my partner." She made another face at the phone. "I'm heading back to Cooper's place. Call me if you need me."

"Wait a second." Foley's voice went serious, setting Kristen's nerves instantly on edge.

"Found something?"

"Maybe." He sounded a little hesitant. "New interview—Carl put a couple of uniforms on the beat to cover more of the area faster, and this one came in this afternoon. Interview with a neighbor about two doors down from the Cooper house—Regina Fonseca. Her daughter goes to preschool where Maddy does. I know we're keeping the photos quiet for now, but the uniform thought to ask her if she'd noticed anyone paying special attention to Maddy."

"Did she?"

"Not Maddy per se. But apparently she got to talking about how hard it is these days to know who can be trusted and who can't. Said she'd freaked out when she saw a guy taking pictures of the preschool playground a couple of weeks ago—thought it might be a pedophile—until she recognized him as the photographer who does the class photos for the school."

"That doesn't automatically rule him out as a suspect," Kristen said, a little buzz of excitement building in her veins.

"No, it doesn't…."

"Good catch. I'll check it out in the morning." She rang off and started the car. The clock on the dashboard of the Impala read 10:15 p.m. She hoped Sam wouldn't be in bed yet. She wanted to get his take on what Foley had uncovered.

And, if she were honest, she just wanted to see him again before she settled down for the night in the guest-house's spare bedroom. Her body still hummed from their earlier embrace, as if her skin had memorized the sensation and kept playing it over and over like a favorite record.

As crazy and dangerous an idea as it was, she

wanted more, and her usual self-control seemed to have left town.

Parked outside the guesthouse, she cut the engine and sat in the dark, wrestling with her reckless desires. Beyond the ethical and procedural problems inherent in getting involved with a crime victim, she was as wrong for Sam Cooper—and his daughter—as Norah Cabot ever thought of being. She had bad mothering in her genes, for God's sake. Her mother hadn't always been a nutcase—what if having kids drove Kristen to the same deadly extremes? She couldn't really know, could she?

And yet—she'd been a good mother to her brothers and sisters when her own mother couldn't. The little ones had secretly called her Mommy, going to her when they skinned knees, wanted a cup of milk or needed a bedtime story read. Didn't that count for something?

Across the darkness in front of her flashed an image of her two youngest siblings, sprawled across the hardwood floor of their bedroom, covered in their own blood. Kristen squeezed her eyes shut, trying to force the image away, but the truth remained. She'd failed them in the end, no matter how good her intentions.

Was she going to fail Maddy Cooper, as well?

A knock on her car window made her jerk. She looked up wildly to find Sam Cooper standing outside the car, his face illuminated by the pale blue glow of a quarter moon overhead.

She rolled down the window, feeling foolish.

"Something wrong?" Sam asked, concern in his voice.

She pasted on a calm smile. "Just trying to talk myself out of this nice, comfortable car. It's been a long day."

"I set up the spare bedroom for you. There are fresh towels in the bathroom if you want a shower." Sam's hand settled on the car door, his knuckles brushing lightly against her upper arm. Awareness rippled through her, even though a layer of cotton separated her skin from his.

It had been such a bad idea to agree to stay here with Sam and his daughter, she thought. But it was too late to back out now.

It was too late for a lot of things.

CHAPTER NINE

SAM SETTLED DEEPER into the welcoming cushions of the sofa, worrying through what Kristen had just told him. It didn't seem likely that the school photographer could be the man who'd been stalking his daughter. "Surely the school vetted him before letting him get anywhere near the kids," he said aloud.

"Probably," Kris agreed. "But people fall through the cracks of background checks all the time. And besides, the photos notwithstanding, since this guy is really targeting you, not Maddy, he's likely not a pedophile."

"So a background check wouldn't flag him as a risk."

"Probably not. I'm going to check with the school in the morning to get the photographer's name." She reached for the cup of decaf he'd poured for her, closing her fingers tightly around the mug. He saw her hands tremble.

"Are you cold?" He reached behind her to grab the knitted throw from the back of the sofa. As he did so, his chest brushed against her shoulder, and he felt her whole body jerk as if she'd just touched a live wire. Coffee sloshed onto his leg, not quite hot enough to burn.

"I'm so sorry!" Kristen twisted away from him, setting the coffee mug onto a corkwood coaster on the coffee table. She pushed quickly to her feet, a look of mortification on her face as she gazed down at him.

"It's okay. These jeans have seen worse." He wasn't as sure about his mother's cream-colored sofa, although many more days of Maddy Jane Cooper and the sofa wouldn't have escaped unscathed anyway.

"I'll get a towel." She hurried out of the room toward the bathroom just off the kitchenette, returning with a fluffy green towel. "I'll pay for the sofa to be cleaned. If it can even be cleaned." Her brow furrowed. "I'll buy you a new sofa."

He laughed softly. "My mother will know how to clean it."

To his surprise, she looked as if she was on the verge of tears. "My mother used to get really angry at us when we spilled things. I'm usually so good at being neat and careful."

Something inside him seemed to break open, spilling sympathetic pain into his chest. "Kristen." He stood, taking a couple of steps toward her until they stood facing each other, only a few inches of space between them.

Her gaze lifted to meet his, and he saw a battle going on behind her dark blue eyes. But he couldn't tell what parts of her were at war, or which side was winning.

"I should go to bed now," she said, but she didn't make a move toward the spare room.

The tone of longing in her voice seemed to echo inside his own head, a match for the restlessness pacing the center of his chest like a hungry wolf. The overwhelming need to touch her eclipsed the myriad reasons why he should step away and let her go, and he reached up to slide a strand of golden hair away from her cheek.

She closed her eyes as his fingers brushed against her skin. Her lips parted, a soft, trembling breath escaping.

When he trailed his thumb over the curve of her jaw to settle against her bottom lip, her eyes flickered open.

Fire burned there, out of control. It seemed to draw out the fierce flames coursing through his blood, until his whole body burned with hunger. He wrapped his hand around the back of her neck and drew her to him, covering her mouth with his.

Her response wasn't tentative or shy. She wound her arms around his waist, pressing her body hard against his. Her mouth moved wildly, matching his passion until his head spun from the sensation.

He ran his hands down her back, tracing the curves and planes, drawing a map of her body in his mind and memorizing the landmarks—the lean, hard muscles of her back, the dipping valley of her waist, the sweet swell of her buttocks.

This is crazy, he thought, but he couldn't bring himself to care, not when her breasts pressed against his chest and her hands moved restlessly over his rib cage, setting off fires everywhere she touched.

He tasted coffee on her tongue, dark and rich, with just a hint of sweetness. Lifting one hand to the back of her head, he held her in place so he could deepen the kiss, drinking in the taste and feel of her. She answered, kiss for kiss, sliding her hands up his chest, gathering bunches of his cotton T-shirt in her trembling fists.

She dragged her mouth away for a moment. "I can't—" She didn't finish before she rose to her toes and kissed him again, threading her fingers through his hair and drawing him closer.

"Daddy!" Maddy's voice, tinged with panic, broke through the heated haze overtaking his brain. He felt Kristen's body jerk against his, as if the sound of his daughter's voice had hit her like a bucket of cold water. She scurried away from him, nearly tripping over the coffee table. She caught herself and moved toward the door to the spare bedroom.

"Good night," she said, her voice strangled.

He didn't want to leave things like this between them, not with the stricken look of horror on her face. But Maddy called for him again, a rising tone of distress in her voice.

"Don't go to bed yet," he urged Kristen, and hurried to his daughter's room, switching on the overhead light.

Maddy sat upright in her bed, blinking at the sudden flood of brightness. He could tell she was only half-awake, gripped by whatever nightmare had dragged her out of her peaceful sleep.

He sat on the bed beside her, and she crawled into his lap, wrapping her little hands tightly around his neck. "Don' wanna go with Mommy," she whimpered.

"It's okay, baby. You're staying right here with me, you hear me?" He kissed her moist cheek, his heart twisting inside. He'd thought it would be good for her to have Norah in her life, but maybe they'd left it too late. So soon after the attack on Cissy, having her mother come to town had been just one more disruption in her life at the worst possible time.

She settled against him, already drifting back to sleep. When he felt her grip on his neck loosen and her breathing grow slow and even, he laid her back against her pillows. Standing, he tucked her blanket firmly around her and stepped back, looking down at his sleeping daughter with his heart trapped firmly in his throat.

The last few days had turned their lives upside down,

but one thing hadn't changed: he would do anything in his power to protect his child, whether it was from a mystery assailant or her absent mother.

Or a mercurial, enigmatic police detective with a troubled past, he added silently, the phantom touch of Kristen's mouth still lingering on his lips.

He closed the door quietly behind him and headed back to the living room, bracing himself to have a long, honest and almost certainly uncomfortable talk with Kristen Tandy.

But she was nowhere to be found.

STUPID, STUPID, STUPID.

Kristen stopped her car at the intersection with the main highway, pressing her hot forehead against the cool curve of the steering wheel, the last five minutes of her life running through her mind like a recurring nightmare.

How could she have let Sam Cooper kiss her? Hadn't she just been warning herself about the danger of entanglements with crime victims she was trying to help? It broke every rule of ethics in the book, and that wasn't even taking into consideration the extra-special problems that Sam Cooper and his motherless daughter posed.

No way in hell could Kristen ever let herself get involved with a man with a kid. She had figured out a long time ago that she was a bad risk for motherhood. Her genetics alone, with her crazy, homicidal mother and her deadbeat, absent father, would disqualify her from procreation. And what kind of mother could she be to someone else's kid when she hadn't even been able to stop one crazy woman from killing her brothers and sisters?

She should have protected them. She hadn't. The end.

She didn't deserve to have children of her own. And she sure as hell wasn't going to inflict herself and her nasty baggage on someone else's kid.

She rubbed her burning eyes and turned right on the highway, heading for the office. If she went to the office, she could at least pretend she was still doing her job, trying to protect Maddy Cooper instead of running away like a scared teenager who'd gone too far on her first date.

And wanted to go further still, a traitorous little voice whispered in the back of her head. Her body still felt hot and restless from her encounter with Sam.

Maybe Foley would still be around the office. She could help him go through the files again, see if there was anything else they'd missed. Work was the best distraction. It always had been.

She dialed his cell number. He answered on the second ring, his voice weary. "What are you doing calling at this hour, Tandy?"

"Just checking to see if you were still in the office."

"After midnight? I'm dedicated, but not that dedicated."

She looked at the dashboard clock. Almost half past twelve. She hadn't even thought to look. "I'm sorry. I lost track of time."

"Where are you?"

"In the car."

"I thought you were at Cooper's place tonight."

"I was there earlier. I just thought I'd head into the

office for a bit, do a little catch-up." She grimaced, knowing the excuse sounded lame.

"After midnight?" Foley clearly agreed.

"Forget it. Sorry I called so late." She rang off and shoved her phone back in her jacket pocket, squirming with shame at her own cowardice.

She turned the car around and headed back to the lake.

The porch light was on when she arrived, but the door was locked already. Rather than knock and risk waking Maddy, she let herself in with the spare key Sam had given her.

Inside, all the lights were dimmed. Sam had apparently gone to bed already.

She locked the door behind her and walked quietly down the short hall to the spare bedroom. Flicking on the light, she looked around the room, noting that Sam had put away the bags she'd brought with her and turned down the bed. Fresh-cut daisies in water sat in a clear glass vase on the bedside table, a feminizing touch in the otherwise utilitarian room.

Kristen sat on the edge of the bed, fingering the delicate petals of the daisies, tears burning her eyes. Such a thoughtful gesture, the flowers. Sam had gone out of his way to make her feel welcome, even though her presence had to be a disruption in his already-up-ended life.

It made her wish she was a different kind of woman.

But she wasn't a different kind of woman. She was Kristen Tandy, with a homicidal mother and scars that ran deep, inside and out. That wasn't going to change, no matter how much she might wish otherwise.

"HIS NAME IS DARRYL MORRIS." Gossamer Ridge Day School director Jennifer Franks looked up at Kristen, curiosity bright in her green eyes. She shifted her gaze to Foley, who stood at Kristen's side. "Has Darryl done something wrong?"

Kristen darted a look at her partner, who sat beside her in a bright yellow chair in front of the desk in the director's office. Judging by the room's decor, the preschool bought into the idea that exposure to a plethora of bright primary colors was good for developing young minds.

They just gave Kristen a headache.

"We're hoping he might have seen something the other day when he was here taking photos," Foley told the director.

Jennifer's brow furrowed. "He was here taking photos recently? Are you certain?"

"One of the parents mentioned seeing Mr. Morris here a couple of weeks ago," Kristen said. "She thought the school had hired Mr. Morris to take photos of the grounds."

Jennifer shook her head. "We don't have any upcoming projects that would require his services. Perhaps she saw someone else and just thought it was Mr. Morris."

"Someone else on the grounds during school hours, taking pictures?" Kristen asked skeptically. "With the children around?"

Jennifer's frown deepened. "No, certainly not."

Kristen exchanged glances with Foley. One of his dark eyebrows notched upward.

"Do you have Mr. Morris's contact information?" he asked.

The director reached into her desk drawer for a vinyl

business card folio. She flipped pages and withdrew a plain white business card with the inscription, Darryl Morris, Photographer and a toll-free phone number.

Kris jotted the information into her notebook. "Thank you, Ms. Franks."

"Is he a danger to our students?" Jennifer Franks asked, her tone urgent.

Foley handed her his business card. "We have no reason to think so at this point. As you said, the witness may have been mistaken."

"We just want to talk to him," Kristen added. "Meanwhile, if you think of anything you've seen or heard in the last couple of weeks, anything that seemed out of the ordinary, please give Detective Foley or me a call at the number on that card."

She followed Foley out of the school office, sidestepping a boisterous kindergartner who'd broken free from the line of five-year-olds marching down the hall toward the playground. Foley reached out and snagged the little boy's shirt, tugging him gently to a halt.

"Slow down, cowboy," Foley chided mildly.

The boy turned and flashed a sheepish, gap-toothed grin at Foley before his teacher took him by the hand and led him back into line.

Foley was still smiling when they reached the car. "Gina's pregnant again," he said.

Kristen stopped short, looking at him over the roof of the Impala. "Congratulations."

He smiled at her. "Thanks. It was a surprise. We'd always figured we'd stop at two."

Kristen wasn't sure what to say. Foley's mood was usually easy to gauge, but his out-of-the-blue announcement had her feeling off balance.

Not that she didn't have a million reasons of her own to feel off balance, starting with her unfinished business with Sam Cooper.

He and Maddy had both been up and dressed by the time Kristen finished showering and dressing that morning. Sam's mother was there, as well, having brought breakfast muffins for everyone. She'd stayed until Kristen had to leave to meet Foley at the preschool, her happy, motherly presence providing a welcome buffer between Kristen and Sam. Sam had looked a bit frustrated, but Kristen couldn't feel anything but relief.

She wasn't ready to talk to Sam about what had happened between them the night before. Not yet.

Maybe not ever.

"Is something wrong?" Foley asked when she didn't make a move to open the car door.

She meant to shake her head and get in the car, hoping the subject would drop. So she was surprised to hear herself blurt, "How did you know you were good parent material?"

Foley stared at her, puzzlement written on every inch of his face. "What?"

Ignoring the nagging voice at the back of her mind ordering her to shut up and get in the car, she answered, "When you and Gina decided to have your first child, how did you know you'd be any good at it?"

Foley's bark of laughter caught her by surprise. "We were young and stupid. That kind of question never occurred to us." He nodded toward the car. "Get in and I'll tell you all about my first year as a father. We'll call it 'Nightmare on Main Street.'"

Kristen slid into the passenger seat and buckled in, kicking herself for bringing up the subject in the first place. She didn't mind hearing Foley's tales from the dark side of fatherhood, but she knew that her out-of-character curiosity was bound to stick in her partner's mind, long after he'd exhausted his store of anecdotes.

The last thing she needed was a fellow detective trying to ferret out the motives of her sudden interest in parenthood.

Her cell phone rang in the middle of a faintly horrifying story of Foley's first experience with projectile vomiting. She grabbed the phone quickly, grateful for the interruption—until she saw Sam Cooper's name on the display window.

She stared at the ringing phone, her heart in her throat.

Foley shot her an odd look. "You gonna answer that?"

She braced herself with a deep breath and answered. "Tandy."

"It's Sam. Anything on the school photographer?"

His voice was businesslike. Annoyingly normal. Comparing his calm tone to the nervous flutter in her stomach, Kristen grimaced. "We have a name. Darryl Morris."

"Darryl Morris?" The calm tone in Sam's voice disappeared. "I know Darryl Morris. And now that I think of it, he just might think he has a damned good reason to hurt me."

CHAPTER TEN

EXCITEMENT PUSHED ASIDE any lingering unease Kristen felt. "Detective Foley's with me. I'm putting you on speaker." She pushed the button. "How do you know Darryl Morris?"

"About eight months ago, his teenage son was killed in a traffic accident. The other driver had been distracted by his kids, hadn't seen the light change to red, and he slammed into Charlie Morris's motorcycle. The kid didn't have a chance."

"What does that have to do with you?" Foley asked.

"It was one of my first cases when I joined the Jefferson County D.A.'s office. I was assigned to assess the case and see if any criminal charges should be filed."

"And you didn't file any charges," Kristen guessed, beginning to understand.

"Not criminal charges," Sam answered. "We worked out a plea deal—the other driver pleaded down to reckless endangerment, was put on probation and did several hours of community service as well as taking a remedial driving course."

Kristen thought that sounded fair, given the circumstances. But she wasn't the father of a dead kid. "Morris didn't think it was enough, right?"

"His only kid was dead. I don't think anything would have been enough." There was a hint of bleak understanding in Sam's voice, and Kristen knew he was thinking about Maddy.

"Did Darryl Morris ever threaten you? Send you any angry letters?" Foley asked.

"He was definitely upset when we told him about the plea deal. There might have been an angry letter or two—I'll have to check my files. But I don't remember ever feeling as if he were any kind of real threat to me."

"Can you meet us at your office?" Kristen asked. "I'd like to take a look at any letters Morris might have sent."

"I'll have to bring Maddy. I don't feel like letting her out of my sight today."

She glanced at Foley. "That's okay—Foley can use the extra babysitting practice."

Foley made a face at her. "I'd better track down Morris, make sure he's not making a Mexico trip or something."

"I could do that," Kristen said quickly.

"Actually, Detective Tandy, I need to see you about another matter anyway," Sam interjected.

Kristen ignored Foley's curious look, heat rising up her neck. "I can be in Birmingham in about an hour," she said, knowing that further protest would only pique her partner's interest more.

"See you then." Sam rang off.

"Are you blushing?" Foley asked.

She frowned at him. "What?"

He looked ready to tease her further but stopped himself. "I'll drop you back at the station to pick up your car."

She spent most of the drive to Birmingham dreading her arrival, worrying over the "other matter" Sam wanted to talk to her about. Was he going to want to do an extensive postmortem of her behavior the night before? She already knew she'd thrown professionalism out the window. And his willing participation didn't change the fact that she was the one with the ethical constraints, not him. She was the cop. She was the one who should have behaved better.

The worst part was, she wasn't sure she regretted it enough. The memory kept creeping up on her when she least expected it, whether at a preshift meeting with Carl and Foley or listening to a preschool principal give her a new lead on the case. Even now, with the air conditioner running full blast and the police radio squawking now and then, she felt Sam Cooper's warm lips moving with slow, devastating skill over hers as surely as if it had just happened.

She gripped the steering wheel tightly, trying to drag her focus back to the case. She reached for the phone clipped to her waistband, thinking Foley might have had time to locate Darryl Morris by now. But before she even had a chance to flip it open, the phone rang, making her strained nerves jangle.

The number on the display was unfamiliar, an Alabama area code but not local. She flipped the phone open. "Tandy."

"Detective Tandy, this is Dr. Victor Sowell with Darden Secure Medical Facility. I'm the psychiatrist in charge of your mother's case."

"How did you get my number?" she asked bluntly. If Carl had given the facility her number, she was going to kill him.

"Your mother gave it to me."

Kristen felt the blood drain from her face. "How the hell did she get it?"

"I'm not certain. It's one reason I thought I should call you."

Kristen checked her mirrors and pulled over on the highway. She didn't want to have this conversation while navigating traffic. She put the car in Park and hit the blue light on the dash to flash. "Tell me what happened. From the beginning."

"I can't really discuss the details of your mother's treatment," Sowell answered. "I can only tell you that she's been allowed some privileges recently. Visitors now and then. We allow her to make phone calls on a limited basis, and we monitor them to make sure she's not harassing anyone."

"And is she?"

"Not that we've been able to ascertain. But she has had a visitor recently. A man showed up yesterday, introducing himself as a lawyer interested in offering her representation pro bono. He said he was with an organization that represents the mentally ill in criminal cases."

Kristen pulled out her notepad. "Did you get a name?"

"Bryant Thompson. But that's really why I called," Dr. Sowell said, his voice troubled. "We had someone check Thompson's credentials and that of his organization, Humane Justice, just to make sure he wasn't trying to pull some sort of scam. The organization exists, absolutely. There's even a Bryant Thompson who works as an attorney with the group."

"But?"

"But the guy who came to see your mother was definitely not the same Bryant Thompson."

"DADDY, WHEN'S MISS KRISTEN gonna get here?"

Sam looked up at the sound of his daughter's plaintive voice, realizing he'd been staring at the same page in the file for the last twenty minutes. Too easily, he'd let his mind wander from the case at hand to the memory of Kristen Tandy's warm, strong hands moving urgently over his body.

He cleared his throat. "Anytime now, baby." Kristen had called back thirty minutes ago to let him know she'd gotten held up and would be there as soon as she could.

She'd sounded odd. Troubled. Probably upset about the lines they'd crossed the night before. He supposed he should be, too, but he couldn't bring himself to worry about ethical lapses when every cell in his body wanted to give it another go.

He just hoped he'd have enough self-control to wait until Maddy wasn't watching.

He distracted himself by dialing the number of the ICU waiting room at the hospital where Cissy was being treated, asking to speak to someone with the Cooper family. His brother J.D. came to the phone.

"It's me," Sam said. "Just wanted to check on Cissy."

"She's moving around," J.D. said. He was trying to keep his voice calm—self-control was J. D. Cooper's defining characteristic—but he couldn't mask an undertone of excitement. "The doctor says it may be a sign she's coming out of the coma."

Sam felt a massive weight lift from his shoulders. "That's great news!"

"The doctor's not sure how much she'll remember, if anything, so I don't know if she'll be able to help you catch the guy who did it," J.D. warned.

"All that matters is getting her well." A knock

sounded on his office door, and Maddy jumped to her feet at the noise. "Go tell her that Maddy and I are rooting for her."

"Will do," J.D. said.

Apparently tired of waiting for Sam to get off the phone, Maddy went to the door and opened it, throwing herself at Kristen Tandy with a squeal of excitement. Kristen's wince, though quickly suppressed, made Sam's stomach knot.

"J.D., someone's at the door. I'll call you later." Sam rang off and hurried to the door to peel his daughter off Kristen's legs, swinging her up to his hip. "Sorry about that."

Kristen shook her head. "Just caught me by surprise."

"Miss Kristen, come see what I drawed!" Maddy held her hands out, her fingers wiggling with excitement, as if she could draw Kristen to her through sheer force of will.

Kristen pasted on a smile and caught one of Maddy's flailing hands. "Slow down, cupcake."

"Why don't you finish it up while Miss Kristen and I talk? Then when we're through, you can show it to both of us." Sam put Maddy down on the floor again.

Maddy looked ready to argue, but he gave her a gentle nudge toward the coffee table where she'd been filling a couple of his spare legal pads full of squiggly drawings. With a long-suffering sigh, she picked up one of the highlighter pens he'd given her to draw with and went back to work with renewed zeal, the tip of her tongue peeking through her cupid's bow lips.

"Sorry about the delay." Kristen settled into the armchair he indicated. He pulled up the chair's twin and turned it to face her, unwilling to have the bulk of his large oak desk between them.

"Everything okay?" he asked. She looked distracted.

"I'm not sure." She shook her head. "Doesn't matter. Nothing to do with this case. Did you find any letters from Darryl Morris?"

"A couple." He handed her the letters he'd culled from his files. "The first one is pretty straightforward. Morris asks me to reconsider the plea deal. His tone is urgent but not particularly hostile."

"I see that." She set that letter aside and picked up the second one. "This one's not quite as...diplomatic."

"No." In the second letter, Morris had informed Sam in angry language that he'd contacted the mayor to lodge a formal complaint against Sam and the district attorney's office for their decision to make the plea bargain. He also informed Sam that if the D.A.'s office didn't reverse the decision, he'd contact the media, as well.

"Did he contact the media?" Kristen asked.

"Probably. But Charlie Morris was a seventeen-year-old kid who'd already been pulled over twice for speeding and who had just dropped out of high school because he 'didn't like all that school stuff.' The driver of the other vehicle was a devoted father and husband who ran a popular pizza restaurant and volunteered at a homeless mission. Honestly, the media wouldn't have touched the story with a ten-foot pole."

"And he never wrote you again?"

"There's nothing else from him in the files."

Kristen's brow furrowed. "I guess we at least bring Morris in to tell us why he was taking photos of the kids at the preschool. Maybe if we keep him talking long enough, we'll find out if he still holds a grudge against you." She held up the letters. "Can you make me copies of these?"

"Those are the copies. I thought you might want them." He gave her the file to hold the letters. "Any chance I could take a look at the interrogation video when you're done?"

She shot him a wry look. "I think you overestimate the technological savvy of the Gossamer Ridge Police Department."

"You do record audio, at least?"

"We do. I'll ask Carl if it's okay to let you take a listen." Kristen stood up, tucking the folder under her arm. Sam was about to remind her of Maddy's request when she turned to Maddy on her own and said, "Now, Miss Maddy, you had something to show me?"

Maddy beamed at Kristen as she crouched beside her at the low coffee table. "It's me and Uncle Gabe, see? He taked me fishing. I catched a big catfish, see?"

"I see," Kristen said, sounding impressed. "Did your daddy clean it and cook it for you?"

Maddy looked up at Kristen in horror. "Cook it?"

"We haven't told her where fish sticks come from yet," Sam said quietly.

Kristen gave him a "now you tell me" look and turned back to Maddy. "I'm sorry, did you say catfish? Of course you don't cook catfish! So, that's you in the green dress, right?"

Maddy nodded, pointing her stubby little finger at some more squiggles on the page. "That's Uncle Gabe, and that's Rowdy—"

"J.D.'s dog," Sam supplied. "Mom and Dad are keeping him, along with Mike, at the lake while J.D.'s up here at the hospital with Cissy."

"And that's Uncle Jake in his boat," Maddy continued, pointing at a speck just above the patch of blue that Sam supposed was the lake, "and that's you and daddy." She beamed up at Kristen.

Kristen turned and gave Sam an odd look. Bending closer, he saw why. The stick figures Maddy had identified as Kristen and him were standing on the pier, holding hands.

"That's a beautiful picture, baby," Sam said. "Why don't you draw us another one?"

Maddy grinned up at him and went to work on a fresh page of the legal pad.

Kristen pushed to her feet and turned to Sam, keeping her distance, "no touching" written all over her body language. "I'm going back to the station to pass all this by Carl and get the go-ahead to bring Darryl Morris in for questioning. I'll see you later, Maddy, okay?"

Maddy looked up at her, frowning. "Don't you wanna see my picture?"

"You can show it to me later at the house. Make it pretty!"

"Okay!" Maddy turned back to her drawing.

Sam hurried after Kristen, catching up at the door. He laid his hand on her arm to stop her from leaving. "We need to talk."

Her chin went up, but her eyes didn't quite meet his. "I'll call to let you know how the interview goes."

"That's not what I meant and you know it."

Her jaw squared a bit more and this time she met his gaze, her eyes defiant. "You're not going to go all squishy on me about a stupid kiss, are you? Because if I'd known you were going to be such a girl about it—"

"You're projecting, Detective." He leaned closer, smiling a little as her lips trembled in response. "You don't want to admit how much it got to you, do you? So you pretend I'm just imagining that pulse in your throat fluttering like a butterfly."

Her throat bobbed and her eyelashes dipped to shield her eyes from his gaze. "Whatever last night was, it's not going to happen again. We're clear about that, right?"

His smile widening, he opened the door for her. "Let me know how the interview with Morris goes."

Not looking at him, she slipped out the door and disappeared down the hall.

Sam's smile faded as he walked slowly back to his daughter's side. It might have been fun seeing just how far he could get under Kristen Tandy's prickly skin, but she had a point. Sure, when the case was over and done, there'd be no ethical reason why he and Kristen couldn't see where their attraction would take them. But there were other reasons not to entangle himself with her, beyond the ethical questions.

Kristen was kind to Maddy, and Sam had no doubt that she'd give her own life to protect his daughter, but that didn't mean she was good for Maddy in the long run, did it? Kristen had been up front about her issues with children, even more than Norah had. Her reasons might be understandable, but they didn't change the fact that she didn't want to be a mother. And Sam couldn't pretend it didn't matter. He wasn't some young stud Marine ready for action with any woman willing. He had Maddy to consider.

Maddy already had a mother who didn't want to be saddled with children in her life. She needed stability, not more of the same.

He checked his watch. Almost lunchtime. He'd promised Norah he'd bring Maddy by the inn for lunch to try to repair some of the damage done the night before.

"Maddy, remember when I told you we were going to go have lunch with Mommy today?"

Maddy's little brow furrowed. "Do we hafta?"

He nodded. "We hafta. Remember, we talked about how Mommy didn't mean to scare you. She's not taking you anywhere without me, right?"

"Right," Maddy said, although she didn't look entirely convinced. "Can Miss Kristen come, too?"

"Miss Kristen has to work."

"Can't we go see Miss Kristen work?"

"Not today," Sam said firmly, though in the center of his chest he felt a flicker of unease. He already saw all the signs of a Maddy-sized fixation. He wondered how much worse it would get over the next few days, with Kristen living with them at the guesthouse.

A soft knock on the door pulled him out of his musings. Had Kristen come back? When he found a clerk standing outside, holding a manila envelope, he felt a twinge of disappointment.

"A courier dropped this off at the front desk a few minutes ago, sir."

Thanking her, he carried the envelope to his desk, relaxing a little at seeing a return address on the front of the envelope for a law firm he'd crossed swords with before. He opened it to see what it was about.

But inside, he didn't find a letter, legal brief or anything else he might have expected.

Instead, he found a stack of color photo prints. The top image was a close-up of Maddy and her mother, sitting at a table for two in the small dining room at the Sycamore Inn.

His heart in his throat, Sam fished in his pocket for a handkerchief. He used the cloth to handle the photos, flipping through the small stack of images, alarm swiftly giving way to a fierce and growing rage until he reached the last photo in the stack, a picture of Maddy cradled in Sam's arms after he'd found her in the storage closet.

Arrogant son of a bitch had been right there in the restaurant the whole time.

He turned the photo over, knowing even as he did so that he'd find nothing. The wily bastard wouldn't have sent the photos if he'd thought he could be incriminated by them.

But Sam was wrong. There *was* something on the back of the last photo—a message scrawled in firm, black felt-tip pen that made his heart freeze solid in his chest.

Your child for mine.

CHAPTER ELEVEN

KRISTEN'S PHONE RANG as she was belting herself behind the wheel of the Impala. "Tandy."

"Where are you?" It was Sam. He sounded tense.

"What's wrong?"

"Are you still in the courthouse complex area?"

"I just got in the car. What's going on?"

"Did you see anyone as you left the building wearing a tan windbreaker jacket and a blue baseball cap?"

"No, I didn't see anyone like that. Now tell me what the hell is going on."

"I got another packet of photos. It was just delivered. The staffer who took it described the person who left the package as a man in his mid-forties, brown hair, wearing a blue baseball cap and a tan windbreaker." Sam's voice tightened further. "The son of a bitch made a threat."

"I'll be right up."

"Meet me at the reception area. I'm trying to get a look at whatever surveillance video might be available."

Kristen retraced her steps back to the District Attorney's office, where she found Sam in the lobby, holding Maddy tightly on his hip while he conferred with a couple of Jefferson County Sheriff's Deputies.

"Any luck on the video?" she asked.

Sam introduced her to Griggs and Baker, the two deputies who were apparently part of the office's security detail. "Baker printed a screen grab." He handed her the grainy photo of a man in a light-colored jacket and dark cap with a blurry cursive *A* on the front. "We think it's a Braves cap."

Kristen stared at the photo, remembering with growing excitement the picture she had helped Maddy color the day before. Maddy had chosen a dark blue crayon and said there was an "ABC" on the front of the cap.

"Could this be Darryl Morris?" Kristen asked Sam.

"Maybe. The photo's not great so it's hard to be sure."

Kristen's cell phone rang. It was Foley. "Excuse me a second." She stepped a few feet away and answered. "Tandy."

"It's me. I've got a bead on Darryl Morris."

"You mean you're looking at him right now?"

"Yeah—had to drive all the way to Birmingham to do it, too," Foley answered.

"Where are you now?"

"Parked outside the shipping company where he works. He just walked in. Did you get a look at the letters he sent Cooper? Do we have probable cause to pick him up?"

"What was he wearing?"

Foley was silent a second. "Why do you ask?"

"Just tell me what he was wearing."

"Jeans, a tan jacket, blue Braves cap—"

Kristen looked over at Sam and Maddy, anticipation surging into her veins. "Oh, yeah," she said with a broad grin. "We have probable cause."

"Detective Tandy really thinks he's the one?" Norah asked Sam later when he met her for lunch in town. She glanced at Maddy, who clung to Sam like a little leech.

Sam coaxed Maddy into one of the chairs lining the sandwich shop window. "He fits the description of the man who left the photos at the office earlier today. The police were already looking at him because of the angry letters he sent me after his son's case was settled. We think he's the one."

Norah took the seat across from him, careful not to encroach on Maddy's space. "Then maybe this is really over."

"It won't really be over until Cissy wakes up and is okay," Sam said soberly, thinking about the way his niece had looked the last time he'd visited her hospital room.

"Of course," Norah said with a sympathetic nod. "But Maddy is safe, at least."

He hoped so. After the scares of the past couple of days, he wasn't quite ready to let her out of his sight.

"I have to go back to D.C. I'd only taken a couple of days off to go to the Hamptons, and I've had a case blow up on me that I really need to attend to." Norah waited for the waitress to bring water to the table before she continued. "I've already arranged for the nice people at Limbaugh Motors to take me to the airport this afternoon. You don't need to worry about it."

"That wasn't necessary—"

"I think it was," Norah said gently. "I made a decision four years ago because I thought it was the right thing for everyone involved. I still think it was."

He looked down at Maddy, who was playing with the colorful place mat on the table, oblivious to their conversation. At least he hoped she was. "So, back to how things were before?"

"Yes." She leaned a little closer, her eyes full of regret but also determination. "I'll never be what she needs. We both know that. It makes no sense for me to disrupt her life every once in a while just because of biology. She won't understand why I always leave again. She'll think it's something she's done when it really has nothing to do with her at all."

Sam would never understand how Norah could walk away from her daughter, but he also believed she was sincere in saying she didn't want to cause Maddy harm.

It was time to let Norah go completely and move on. No more hopes for something changing.

Norah wasn't going to change.

"I would like frequent updates, however," Norah added. "To know how the two of you are getting along."

"I'll e-mail you."

The waitress approached with menus. Sam took one and bent to show Maddy what the children's menu included. As she weighed the merits of a peanut butter and jelly sandwich versus chicken fingers, Sam glanced at Norah and found her smiling.

"I was right," she said. "You were meant to be a father."

On that, he thought, they could agree.

"Are you going to sit in on the interrogation?" Norah asked later, after the waitress had brought their orders.

"Detective Tandy wouldn't let me."

Norah smiled. "She's quite the little authoritarian."

"She's right. It would be a conflict of interests."

"But she'll whisper the details in your ear later, no doubt."

Sam tried not to react to Norah's sly tone. She was clearly fishing for information about his relationship with Kristen, and since he didn't know how to define it himself, playing Norah's game would be folly.

"If she's as good at interrogating suspects as she is at interrogating innocent people like me, Mr. Morris should break in no time." Norah settled back in her chair with a wry smile.

Sam hoped she was right. Because if Darryl Morris wasn't the person who'd tried to kidnap Maddy, then Sam and the cops were back to square one.

"THIS IS YOU in the surveillance video, isn't it?" Kristen reached into the manila envelope lying on the table, pulled out the screen grab the deputy had supplied and slid it toward Darryl Morris.

Morris looked down at the photo, his complexion shiny with sweat. Morris had grown increasingly unnerved since the Birmingham Police had transferred him over to her custody. The interview room she'd placed him in wasn't air-conditioned, by design, but it wasn't hot enough to warrant the perspiration dripping down the man's sallow cheeks. He looked queasy, well aware he'd been caught red-handed.

"That could be anyone."

"Anyone wearing a tan windbreaker and a Braves cap."

"Exactly." Morris looked at Foley, who'd remained quiet to this point. "There's gotta be a lot of guys out there with Braves caps."

"Who also happened to send angry letters to Sam Cooper?" Foley asked reasonably.

"And took pictures at Maddy's preschool while Maddy was in attendance?" Kristen added.

"I'm a part-time photographer. Big deal."

"Apparently a courier, as well." Kristen tapped the photo.

"Jeez, okay. I dropped off a package at the D.A.'s office. Is that some sort of crime?"

"A terroristic threat comes to mind," Kristen said to Foley. "Wouldn't you agree?"

"I'd think that's fair."

Morris's eyes widened. "Wait a second—terroristic threat? Sure, I wrote the jerk a couple of letters, but I didn't make any threats."

Kristen pulled a piece of paper from the envelope and placed it on the table in front of Morris. It was a full-size photocopy of the handwritten threat on the back of the last photo.

"What does that say, Mr. Morris?" she asked.

He stared at the words. "I didn't write that."

"That was in the envelope you delivered to Sam Cooper."

"I didn't know what was in the envelope."

"Why not?" Kristen prodded.

"Some guy paid me ten bucks to deliver it."

"You needed ten bucks that bad?" Kristen asked, skeptical. "Come on, Darryl. You don't really expect me to buy this."

"'Your child for mine.'" Foley read the phrase written on the paper aloud, letting his tongue linger over each word. "You lost your son in a terrible accident."

"He was murdered."

"Sam Cooper didn't see it that way," Foley said.

"Wasn't his kid!"

"But Maddy Cooper is." Kristen leaned closer, dropping her voice a level. "Must be hard for you, watching

Maddy Cooper running around the playground, so full of life and promise."

"No," Morris said, shaking his head. "I think her father's a bootlicking political hack, but I'd never hurt a kid."

"How about a teenager?" Foley nodded at Kristen.

She pulled out another photo and laid it on the table in front of Morris. It was a photo taken at the crime scene of Sam Cooper's niece Cissy lying unconscious and still, her face wet with blood from her head wound.

Morris recoiled. "You think I did that?"

"Where were you this past Tuesday night?" Kristen asked.

Morris looked at her suspiciously. "At home."

"Anybody there with you?"

He looked down at his hands. "No."

"Nobody saw you at home?"

"I live up in Pell City, near the river. Not a lot of neighbors around."

"You took these photos of Maddy, didn't you?" Kristen pulled out the photocopies of the pictures Sam had received, both the more recent batch and the set from two days earlier.

He looked down at the photos again. She saw his eyelids flicker, and she knew she had him.

"Why did you take the photos and send them to Sam Cooper? Why did you tell him, 'your child for mine'?" Kristen pulled up the chair across from Morris, settling down to look him in the eyes. "He denied you the justice you needed, and yet there he was, with his perfect, happy little child. It wasn't fair, was it? That he could go home to his kid while the best you can do is go see a headstone."

Morris's eyes welled up with tears. "Charlie didn't deserve to die. Yeah, he had some trouble, but he didn't deserve to die!" He wiped his nose with the back of his sleeve. "Sam Cooper didn't think his life was worth crap, or he'd have tried that stupid son of a bitch who ran Charlie over!"

"You wanted to give Sam a taste of his own medicine." Kristen kept her voice low and soothing. "Because he should know how it feels to lose his kid."

Morris froze. "No, I didn't say that—"

"Why did you take the photos, Darryl?"

"The guy paid me to."

"What guy?"

"The guy who gave me the envelope. He was right outside the courthouse—didn't your cameras catch that, too?"

Kristen slanted a look at Foley. He shrugged.

"What did the guy look like?" she asked, deciding it wouldn't hurt to play along.

"I don't know—average. About my age. Blondish hair, going gray, maybe, what there was of it. Not short, not tall." Morris's face twisted with frustration. "Go look at the video."

Kristen glanced at Foley again. He gave a little nod and slipped out of the room.

Kristen remained silent for a few minutes, deciding it wouldn't hurt to let Morris sweat a little more. She wasn't really buying his story about another man— what were the odds that there were two men, both with an axe to grind with Sam Cooper, collaborating on the threats against Maddy?

But might as well be thorough. Foley would check with Jefferson County Courthouse security and be back with the answer. Meanwhile, she could toy with Morris a little more, see if she could coax a confession out of him.

"You don't believe me, do you?" Morris broke the silence after a couple of minutes.

"Don't you think it's a bit of a coincidence that a guy who has it in for Sam Cooper managed to find the only other guy in town who feels the same way?"

"Maybe he heard about my son's case."

"And just knew you'd go along with his plan to terrorize Cooper?"

"I didn't know what he was going to do with the photos."

"Then why did you take them?"

"He said he was working for Cooper's old lady."

"His old lady?"

"Yeah, the kid's mother. Said she was looking to take the kid away from Cooper, and if I'd take pictures of her at the day care it would prove he just pawned her off every day to other people to take care of."

Kristen frowned. "Maddy Cooper's mother is not seeking custody of Maddy."

Morris looked confused. "She's not?"

"No, she's not."

He pressed his lips into a tight, thin line. "Then he lied to me about what he was up to."

"Isn't it more likely that you decided to pick this excuse for your own behavior without knowing the real situation between Sam Cooper and his ex-wife?" Kristen asked gently. "It's understandable, to assume Maddy's mother wanted custody. Most mothers do."

"You're trying to twist me up and make me cop to something I didn't do," Morris protested. "I didn't touch that kid. Or that girl, either." He pushed away the photo of Cissy. "I wouldn't do that."

Foley came back into the room. She looked up. He gave a small shake of his head.

"The camera outside the courthouse didn't pick up anyone else with you, Mr. Morris," she said aloud.

Morris looked up at her, alarmed. "He was there!"

"The camera didn't see him."

"I'm telling you—"

Foley pulled up a chair next to Darryl Morris, crowding close. "Mr. Morris, what say we start over from the beginning?"

"Is Mommy really gone?" Maddy asked Sam that afternoon as he fed her a snack of peanut butter, banana and crackers.

He paused, his heart breaking a little for his daughter, who seemed more confused than saddened by the question. "She went back to Washington. That's where she lives, just like we did for a while, remember?"

Maddy licked a stray dollop of peanut butter from her fingers, blinking at him. "And she's not coming back?"

"Maybe now and then to visit. I don't know." He handed her a slice of banana. "Does that make you sad, baby?"

Maddy shook her head. "Now Miss Kristen can be my mommy, can't she, Daddy?"

He stared at her, nonplussed. "Miss Kristen isn't your mommy, Maddy Jane. You know that."

"But she can be, right? If I want her to?"

"I don't think it's that easy. Miss Kristen may not want to be your mommy."

The look of puzzlement on Maddy's face would have been comical under other circumstances. "Why not?"

"She may want to wait and have a little girl of her own."

"She don't have to wait."

"But maybe she wants to."

The light of determination in Maddy's green eyes reminded him of his younger sister, Hannah, who'd never taken no for an answer without a fight. "You do it, Daddy. You tell her to be my mommy."

He couldn't help but laugh at the thought. "I *know* that won't work."

She reached out and cradled his face between her sticky hands, her expression serious. "Try, Daddy."

He swept her up into his arms, cracker crumbs and all. "Tell you what. Why don't you take a nap and we'll talk about this when you wake up?" He tickled her gently to distract her.

She squealed in his ear, half deafening him, but at least she dropped the subject of Kristen after that. The last couple of days with Norah had apparently taken some energy out of her, for she settled down to her nap without protest, drifting off before he'd finished half of *The Cat in the Hat.*

He tucked her in, his mind still worrying with her question about Kristen. Of all the women in the world, why had Maddy decided a kidphobic cop with a bleak and tragic past was the best candidate for motherhood? Hell, why was he himself thinking about taking their already-complicated relationship into dangerous new territory?

Anytime now, Kristen could call with the news that

Darryl Morris was the guy behind the attack on Cissy. Then it would all be over.

Maybe instead of thinking so much about how to make their relationship with Kristen last beyond the end of the case, he should be thinking about how to close the book on the Kristen Tandy chapter of his life for good.

"JEFFERSON COUNTY'S BOOKING HIM," Carl Madison told Kristen after another fruitless hour of interviewing Darryl Morris. "We only have the threatening message to hold him on, and that happened in their jurisdiction."

Kristen didn't answer, frustration bubbling deep in her gut. He'd admitted to almost everything except the attack on Cissy and the threat, and he hadn't wavered a bit from his story about a mystery man pulling the strings. The story seemed crazy, but if Morris was lying, he was lying consistently.

"We'll tie him to the attack," Foley added when she remained silent. "He's got to be the one."

She wanted to believe it. Then Maddy Cooper would be out of danger and safe to return to a normal, happy life with Sam and the rest of his family.

And she could get out of their lives before anyone got hurt.

Carl pulled her aside as they walked down the hall toward the detective's office. "Dr. Sowell from Darden left a message for you. He asked if you were still planning to visit the facility this afternoon."

Damn. She'd forgotten about her planned drive to Tuscaloosa. She glanced at her watch. Almost three o'clock. If she left now, she could be there by five-thirty.

On her way down to the parking lot, she called Dr. Sowell to make sure someone would be there to talk to her about the mysterious "Bryant Thompson." He promised to stick around until she arrived, so he was waiting for her when she got to Tuscaloosa. He guided her through the security checkpoint, where she had to relinquish her Ruger P95 pistol to the guard before following the doctor to his office.

Sowell pulled a grainy black-and-white photo from the top drawer of his desk and handed it to her. "This is the man who introduced himself as Bryant Thompson. Do you recognize him?"

She looked at the image. The surveillance camera apparently covered the small visitors' area from a position high on the wall, giving her a bird's-eye view of the entire room but not much in the way of details about anyone in the frame.

There were only three people in the photo—the mysterious Bryant Thompson, a uniformed guard standing nearby and a thin, frail woman dressed in a white gown and a darker robe, her hands folded in her lap.

Kristen's stomach gave a sickening lurch as she realized the woman in the photo must be her mother.

She was almost entirely unrecognizable, no longer the woman Kristen remembered. Though hospitalized for only fifteen years, she looked decades older, her formerly dark red hair now a dull gray bird's nest twisted up in a messy knot atop her head. Her cheeks were thin and sunken, her body stooped and frail.

Tears burned Kristen's eyes, catching her unprepared. She blinked them away, steeling herself against a flood of devastating memories.

Just look at the photo, she told herself firmly. *Study the man. You already know the woman.*

She forced her attention to the man sitting across

from her mother. He had light-colored hair—blond? Gray? Hard to say, given the photo was in black and white. He seemed to be sitting very still, his hands on his knees. He wasn't leaning forward into her mother's space, as she might have expected from someone claiming to be there to help her. If anything, he seemed to be keeping a careful distance.

Beyond that, she could see only small, unimportant details about the mystery man. He wore light-colored slacks, not jeans, and a jacket that might be corduroy.

"What do you remember about the man?" she asked Dr. Sowell.

"Very little, I'm afraid. I saw him only in passing, as I had been called to an emergency elsewhere. The guard on duty may be the best person to ask, but he works the day shift so he left earlier. I can give him your phone number and ask him to call you if you like."

She frowned at the photo, impatient. She didn't want to wait for the guard to call her. She wanted this mystery over with now, so she could put it behind her and never have to come back to this place again.

"Did you ask my mother about the man who visited her?"

Sowell seemed surprised by the question. "No. I didn't think it would be appropriate to interrogate her when she'd done nothing wrong."

"At least not this time," Kristen muttered.

Sowell gave her a pitying look. "Of course."

Dread crept over her, greasy and pitch-black, as she realized the best way to get the answers she needed about Bryant Thompson was to go directly to the source. She'd avoided this moment long enough. Time to face the demons head-on.

"Dr. Sowell, I'd like to talk to my mother."

CHAPTER TWELVE

KRISTEN WAITED, HER heart racing, for the guard to bring her mother out to see her. The interview room was cold, the chair uncomfortable and the atmosphere utterly bleak. Appropriate, she thought, a bubble of hysterical laughter knocking at the back of her throat.

The door to the room opened with a loud rattle and the guard entered first, his bulk filling the doorway. Right behind him, her bony wrist encircled by the guard's beefy hand, Molly Jane Tandy shuffled into the room. Someone had cut and combed her hair since her earlier visit with the mystery man calling himself Bryant Thompson. It was almost completely gray now, chopped to chin length and hanging in stringy, frizzy strands.

A pale pink, shapeless gown covered her body from throat to shins, a dark green terry cloth robe draped over her thin arms and shoulders to combat the hospital's chilly air. No belt, of course.

She was forty-seven years old. She looked closer to sixty-seven, her haggard face dry and lined. The bright blue eyes that had once danced with wicked charm were now rheumy and restless, darting about the visitor's room before finally settling on Kristen's face. Her mouth dropped open in a silent O and her eyes widened.

"Kristy," she said, her voice a hoarse creak.

The urge to run was almost more than Kristen could control. She wrapped her fingers around the edges of the chair seat beneath her, gritting her teeth until she found the control to speak. "Hello, Mother."

Molly hurried forward, her arm outstretched. Kristen felt her whole body recoil and almost collapsed with relief when the guard caught Molly's arm and halted her approach. He was gentle but insistent as he settled her in the chair across from Kristen.

It hadn't been obvious in the photo, but in person, she saw that the patient's chair was a safe distance from the visitor's chair, well beyond arm's reach. The chair's legs were bolted to the floor, and the guard bent to slide a leather cuff around her mother's right leg, keeping her safely secured to her seat.

The burly guard took a step back, flashing Kristen a sympathetic look. She supposed he knew all about Molly's crime and could guess just how hard it was for Kristen to be here.

Normally, she hated pity, but this time, she found the guard's kind look to be a comfort. It made her feel less alone.

Less vulnerable.

"Mother, Dr. Sowell told me that a man came to visit you the other day. He called himself Bryant Thompson."

"A lovely man," Molly said distractedly. "He spoke very well of you, Kristy."

"He spoke of me?"

Molly smiled. "Oh, yes. He told me that you're very important now. A policewoman." Her eyes brightened, the look in them almost beatific.

Kristen glanced at the guard. His eyes were on her mother, watchful and full of pity.

"Mother, did Mr. Thompson offer to do anything for you?"

"No, he only wanted to show me the picture."

"What picture?"

Her mother slowly reached into the pocket of her robe. Immediately the guard moved forward, stepping between Kristen and Molly. But his watchfulness was unnecessary; all Molly pulled from her pocket was a folded piece of paper. The guard took it from her, unfolded it, then handed it to Kristen.

It was a clipping from the *Chickasaw County Herald* newspaper, dated two days earlier. The article was about the break-in at Sam Cooper's home and the injury to his niece. There was a photograph accompanying the article, a telephoto shot of Kristen, Sam and Maddy in the chairs at the hospital. There must have been a reporter there with a digital camera, she realized, or a staff member who'd seen the chance to sell a newsworthy photo to the local rag.

"Mr. Thompson said you're watching out for that sweet little girl, Kristy. Is that true?"

Kristen dragged her gaze from the newspaper clipping. "Why would Mr. Thompson bring this to you?"

"He said it would be good for my recovery to know that you were doing so well," Molly answered. "And you know, I think it is. I feel so much better now, knowing that I have a chance to start over again."

Kristen narrowed her eyes, not following her mother's logic. "Start over again how?"

"With the little girl, of course," Molly said. Her tone of voice sounded calm and reasoned, though the light shining in her blue eyes was sheer madness. "Now that you're taking care of the little girl, you can bring her to see me."

Kristen stared at her in horror, realizing what her mother was suggesting. "No—"

"I could help you take care of her. I could teach you how to be a mother. I miss my own sweet babies so."

The guard made a low, groaning sound deep in his chest. Kristen looked up to find his face contorted with sheer horror.

Her own stomach had twisted into a painful knot, bile rising to the back of her throat. She pushed out of her chair, throwing a pleading look at the guard.

"Outside to the right, third door on the left."

She bolted down the hall to the restroom, barely making it inside one of the stalls before she threw up.

She wasn't sure how long she remained in the bathroom stall, gripping the side of the toilet as she waited out the last of the dry heaves. Apparently it was long enough for the guard to have returned her mother to her room and contacted Dr. Sowell, for a few minutes later there was a knock on the door, and Dr. Sowell's concerned voice sounded through the heavy wood.

"Are you all right, Detective Tandy?"

She pushed herself up and flushed the toilet. "I'm okay," she called hoarsely, staggering slightly as she went to the sink to wash her hands and face. The woman staring back at her in the mirror looked like a war survivor, pale and haunted.

When she emerged from the restroom, the psychiatrist was waiting for her outside, his expression full of concern. "Hastings told me what happened. I'm sorry. I had no idea she'd ambush you that way."

Kristen shook her head. "I knew seeing her would be difficult after all this time. I'm fine."

"Is there someone I could call for you?"

"No, I'm okay. I just—I need to get out of here."

He walked her out to her car. He reached into his jacket pocket and pulled out a photo print. "You almost forgot this."

It was the photograph of the mysterious Bryant Thompson, sitting in the interview room with Kristen's mother. Kristen had left it on Dr. Sowell's desk, planning to return there before she left the facility.

She put it in her coat pocket with the clipping she'd taken from her mother. "Thank you. Let me know if my mother receives any other visits from this Bryant Thompson character."

"I will."

She settled behind the steering wheel of the Impala, breathing deeply to calm her still-ragged nerves. Her mouth tasted bitter; she dug in the glove compartment for a pack of breath mints she kept there and popped one in her mouth. As she started the car, she pulled the newspaper clipping from her pocket. Earlier, she'd noticed something bleeding through the back of the clipping. She turned it over now and found a ten-digit phone number written in black ink.

Her own cell phone number.

She rubbed her burning eyes, her mind spinning in a million different directions. Who was this man who called himself Bryant Thompson? What did he want from her mother?

And how the hell had he gotten her cell phone number?

SAM HAD JUST put Maddy to bed around eight-thirty that
evening when he heard a knock on the guesthouse door.
He finished tucking her in and dropped a kiss on her
cheek. "Sleep tight, Maddycakes."

Already drowsing, she made a soft murmuring noise
and rolled onto her side.

He went to the front door, opening it a crack to find
Kristen Tandy on his doorstep, looking pale and tense.

"What's wrong?" he asked, letting her in. "Why
didn't you just let yourself in with the key?"

She made an attempt to straighten her face. "Forgot I had a key." She sat on the sofa hunched forward,
her elbows resting on her knees as if she was winded.

He sat beside her, alarmed by the obvious distress
she was trying to hide. "I talked to Detective Foley a
couple of hours ago. He said Morris hasn't confessed
to the attack yet."

"He still looks good for it," she said, but he sensed
a little hesitation underlying her words.

"But?"

She shook her head. "I don't know. It's—it's stupid.
Every perp nabbed red-handed tries out the same lame
excuse—'I didn't really do it. You have the wrong guy.'"

"Foley said he admitted most of it."

"He admitted delivering the envelope. He admitted
taking the photos. But he said someone paid him for
them, and he didn't know what they were for. He also
swears he didn't write the threatening note on the back
of the photo."

"Do you believe him?"

She paused, the furrow in her brow deepening.
"Morris admits holding you responsible for dropping
the charges against the man who hit his son's motorcy-

cle. He cops to the taking the pictures. But we're supposed to believe someone else asked him to take them and deliver them to you? It's crazy." Her voice firmed up. "It's unbelievable. He's got to be the guy."

"So it's over?" Sam was afraid to believe.

"I think so," she said after a pause.

"Who's booking him? Chickasaw County or Jefferson?"

"All anyone can book him on at the moment is the threatening note to you. That happened in Birmingham, so Jefferson County's going to file the charges for now. But we're still trying to tie him to the attack on Maddy and Cissy."

"They won't let me near the case." He smiled wryly. "You'll probably have to give me all the updates."

She slanted a look at him, her expression almost pained.

"Okay, that's it," he said. "What's wrong?"

She looked away. "Nothing."

"It's not nothing."

She pushed to her feet. "It's been a long day and I could use a shower and some sleep. Let's table this until morning."

He stood, closing his hand around her upper arm. She looked up at him, her eyes wide and dark with pain.

He eased his grip on her arm. "You're scaring me."

She looked away. "It's nothing to do with Maddy or this case. It's personal."

He moved his hand slowly up her arm, over her shoulder, finally settling his fingers gently against the soft curve of her cheek. He lifted his other hand to cradle her face between his palms, forcing her to look at him. Her lips trembled as she visibly fought for control.

"Tell me what happened," he said in a quiet but firm voice.

She closed her eyes. "Sam, please. Just let it go, okay?"

He let go with reluctance, stepping back. She opened her eyes, gave him a halfhearted smile and went down the hall to the bathroom, leaving him to lock up for the night.

He checked the doors and windows, tiptoeing into Maddy's room to double-check the window by her bed. Outside, the moon had risen high in the cloudless sky, surrounded by a million stars. He'd forgotten, living in D.C., what the night sky looked like when there weren't a lot of city lights around to pollute the view.

He heard the shower kick on down the hall, and he left Maddy's room quietly, his mind returning to the disturbing encounter with Kristen. What had set her on edge that way? Knowing what he did of her past, he imagined it would take something pretty terrible to shake Kristen Tandy's control.

He suddenly remembered her shaken reaction to the phone call she received the day before. What had he heard her say to the caller?

Tell her no.

Tell whom no? Had to be her mother, didn't it? Who else could send Kristen into such an emotional tailspin?

It's none of your business, Cooper.

The case was nearly over. Morris was in jail, waiting for arraignment. With any luck, the judge would deny bail and Sam and Maddy could go back to a normal life, while Kristen Tandy went on to whatever case came her way next. It was better for everyone that way, he told himself.

But he knew letting Kristen walk away wasn't going to be anywhere near that simple or easy.

A hot metallic odor permeated the air as Kristen bent over the trash can in the kitchen and tried to throw up, though her stomach was empty after a long night's sleep. She welcomed the pain of the dry heaves, needing something to crowd out the pictures imprinted on her brain.

Blood everywhere, smeared on the walls and floor, spread over the bedsheets and the pajamas and nightgowns of her younger brothers and sisters—the images burned into her brain. Kristen had found Tammy first, her nine-year-old sister's small body stretched out on the floor in the hall outside Kristen's bedroom, half blocking the door. She'd crouched by her sister, her mind rebelling against what she was seeing, only to realize there was more blood. A lot more blood.

Four bodies. Julie. Tammy. David. Kevin. All beyond help. And her mother was nowhere to be found.

The dry heaves ended and she slithered to the floor, tears sliding silently down her cheeks. She tried to think. What should she do? Who should she call now?

"Kristy?" Mama's voice was soft and bewildered.

Kristen looked up. Mama stood in the kitchen doorway, still in her pale blue nightgown. Blood painted a grotesque abstract pattern across the nylon fabric. She held a large chef's knife at her side. Blood dripped from the blade to the linoleum in slow, steady drops.

Kristen's heart slammed into her rib cage.

Mama walked past her to the sink. She laid the knife on the counter and reached for the paper towels hanging on the wall by the stove. On one of the eyes, a pot of oatmeal was boiling over, making a mess on the stovetop.

Mama wet a couple of paper towels under the tap and wiped up the overflow. Pulling open the utensil drawer, she pulled out a steel serving spatula, shaped like a diamond with a fleur-de-lis cutout in the middle, and started stirring the oatmeal.

Kristen stared at the spatula, her overloaded brain latching on to that one small incongruity. Why would Mama use a cake spatula to stir oatmeal? That was crazy.

Mama turned to look at her, her eyes widening as if she were surprised to see Kristen. "When did you get up, baby?"

Kristen stumbled backward. "I need to go get dressed."

"Have breakfast first." Mama scraped the spatula on the edge of the pan. "It's almost ready. Go get yourself a bowl."

Afraid to disobey, Kristen crossed to the cabinet next to the stove, her knees shaking, and retrieved a plastic cereal bowl. She started to set the bowl down beside her mother, but Mama grabbed her hand, leaving a smear of blood on Kristen's wrist.

"Hold it still while I scoop." Mama's voice was

unbearably calm. Kristen's hand shook as Mama scooped up hot oatmeal with the spatula. Chunks of hot cereal spilled through the fleur-de-lis cutout, splashing on Kristen's hand.

"Ow!" She tried to jerk her hand away but Mama's grip tightened.

"Why are you such a big baby?" Her mother's voice rose hysterically. She shoved the pan off the eye and set the spatula down over the flame. Oatmeal caught fire and burned to carbon, blackening the spatula.

"Mama, no—"

"Miss Kristen?"

The tiny voice caught her by surprise. She looked away from the madness in Mama's eyes and saw Maddy Cooper standing in the kitchen doorway, dressed in blue Winnie the Pooh pajamas and carrying a battered gray stuffed raccoon.

"Maddy—" Terror gripped her, crushing her heart until she could barely feel it beating. She had to get Maddy out of here, away from Mama, before—

Pain seared the back of her hand. She cried out and turned to look at Mama. But Mama was looking at Maddy, a gleam of excitement in her mad blue eyes.

"You brought her to see me, Kristy. Just like I asked."

Kristen pulled her aching hand away and grabbed for the knife. But Mama reached it first.

Kristen threw herself in front of Maddy, covering the child with her whole body.

"No, Mama. Please!"

Maddy wriggled against her. "Miss Kristen, wake up!"

KRISTEN JERKED AWAKE, her heart scampering like a jackrabbit in her chest. A shaft of light poured in from the half-open door, illuminating the dim room.

And her arms were wrapped tightly around a flailing Maddy Cooper.

CHAPTER THIRTEEN

KRISTEN LOOSENED HER GRIP, and Maddy looked up at her, a comical look of surprise on her face. "You squeezed too tight!"

"I'm sorry, sweetie." She stroked Maddy's hair, relief washing over her in enervating waves. "I must have been dreaming. What are you doing here?"

Maddy cuddled close, her sweet baby scent enveloping Kristen, as tangible as a touch. "I heard you crying. I brought Bandit to make you feel better." She held up the well-worn plush raccoon that was her favorite toy, as Kristen had quickly learned.

Kristen kissed the little girl's warm forehead, closing her eyes against the lingering images of her nightmare. She could still feel the bone-deep pain of the burn on the back of her hand, but she ignored it. It was a phantom, long gone.

Right here, right now, she was safe. And so was Maddy.

Footsteps sounded in the hallway, and Sam Cooper's tall, broad body filled the doorway. He wore only a pair of black silk boxer shorts and a white T-shirt that he'd apparently just thrown on, if the twisted fabric was anything to go by.

"Everything okay?" he asked, his blue eyes dark with worry.

"Everything's fine," she assured him.

He entered the bedroom. "Maddycakes, time to get back in your bed."

"Let her stay a little longer," Kristen blurted, as surprised by the words as Sam seemed to be.

"Are you sure?"

"I'm sure." Maddy was already starting to get drowsy-eyed. She'd be asleep in no time, and Kristen could take her back to her bed. Right now, however, she needed to feel Maddy's warm little body tucked safely next to her to drive away the last, lingering wisps of her nightmare.

"I'll take her back to her bed when she falls asleep," she added softly when Sam made no move to leave the bedroom.

He hesitated a moment longer, his gaze appraising. "Okay," he said finally. "Night again, Maddycakes."

"Night, Daddy!" Maddy snuggled closer to Kristen.

Kristen watched Sam leave, understanding his reluctance. She hadn't given him much reason to trust her maternal instincts, and he had to be worrying that Maddy would get hurt in the long run.

Kristen had worried about that herself, knowing that the child was already becoming attached to her. But the case would be over soon—possibly was over already, if they could tie up all the loose ends of the case against Darryl Morris. Then she'd move to another case and be out of Sam's and Maddy's lives for good.

Hot tears hammered at the backs of her eyes at the thought of saying goodbye to them, but she fought the emotion, knowing a clean break was the right thing to do, no matter how painful. If her visit with her mother had done anything, it had convinced Kristen that she'd been right all these years to avoid motherhood as though it was a disease.

Except *she* was the disease, not motherhood. She was the one with insanity in her genes and a maternal role model wretched enough to make the very notion of having children an unbearably bad risk.

"Miss Kristen, do you know any songs?" Maddy's sleepy voice pulled her out of her bleak thoughts.

She pasted on a smile. "I'm not much of a singer. Why don't you start, and if I know the song, I'll sing along."

"Okay!" Maddy smiled and propped herself up against Kristen's arm. She thought a moment, then started singing "Old McDonald Had a Farm." By the time they got to the sillier farm animals, Kristen found herself laughing as hard as Maddy.

"Okay, next one's gotta be a lullaby, bug," she told Maddy as the little girl's giggles finally subsided. She put her arm around Maddy and tucked her close. A tune from the distant past drifted into her mind, a reminder of a simpler, sweeter time. As Maddy snuggled against her, she started singing.

"River rolls closer, near the green hills. Reaches for the moon, but the moon stands still. Moon stands still while the river runs, waiting in the dark for Mr. Sun."

Maddy's eyes closed as Kristen repeated the same verse, the only one she could remember. It had been a silly song she'd made up to sing Julie to sleep. She'd forgotten it until just now, maybe because she'd spent so much time trying to forget the horrors of that last day with her brothers and sisters that she'd buried the good memories, too.

Maddy drifted off to sleep just as a flood of emotions

started to break through the fortifications Kristen had built up in her mind over the last fifteen years. A hundred images swam through her thoughts, for the first time in a long time more sweet than bitter. Blinking back tears, she picked up Maddy and carried her back to her room, settling her under the covers.

Maddy turned over, her sweet face burrowing into her pillow. Kristen felt a smile breaking through her sadness as she slipped from the room, closing the door behind her.

"She asleep?"

Sam's voice, emerging from the darkness of the hallway, was a shock to her system. She pressed her hand over her chest, acutely aware that she hadn't even bothered to throw on a robe over the tank top and silk shorts she'd worn to bed.

"Yes," she answered, starting to sidle past him to her room. But he caught her arm, keeping her in place. Sparks ignited along her spine, radiating out from where his big, warm hand closed over her bare arm.

"Good," he said. "Because we need to talk."

She eyed him warily. "About what?"

"About where you went this afternoon." Sam caught her chin, forcing her gaze up to meet his. "You went to see your mother, didn't you?"

Her heart skipped a beat. "What makes you think that?"

"Carl Madison called to check on you while you were in the shower. He was worried he couldn't get you on your cell phone and wondered if seeing your mother again had been too much for you." Sam ran his thumb over the curve of her chin. "Was it?"

Kristen glanced at Maddy's bedroom door. "Do we have to talk about this tonight?"

He dropped his hand. "Not if you don't want to."

She threw him an exasperated look, hating how much she wanted to tell him everything she'd been through that day. Right now, a pair of warm, strong arms wrapped around her seemed like the most necessary thing in the world.

She settled for admitting, "I didn't think I wanted to."

"But now you do?"

She made a growling noise deep in her throat and walked away, heading for the darkened living room. Her shin made contact with the end table by the sofa, sending pain shooting up her leg. She uttered a quiet, heartfelt curse and fumbled for the lamp switch. A twist of the knob later, lamplight flooded half the room, illuminating the sofa.

With a sigh of surrender, Kristen turned to look at Sam. "A couple of days ago, my mother's doctor called Carl, asking for me. He told Carl my mother wanted to see me."

"And Carl called you," Sam guessed correctly. "That was the call you took the day Norah arrived, right? The one that had you so upset."

She briefly considered arguing with him about his assessment of her mood that day, but he was right. The call had scared the hell out of her, among other things.

She slumped onto the nearest sofa cushion, wrapping her arms around herself. "I told Carl I didn't want to see her."

"I remember."

She licked her lips. "But the doctor called me today."

Sam sat beside her, careful to leave her plenty of

space, she noticed bleakly. Apparently she was giving off major "don't touch" vibes.

"Is it the first time you've seen her since she was committed?" he asked gently.

She met his curious gaze, her lips twisting in a wry smile. "Yeah. Probably the last, too."

"Why did you decide to see her after all this time?"

She supposed it wouldn't hurt to tell him about Bryant Thompson. She reached for the jacket she'd left draped over the arm of the sofa and pulled the clipping from the pocket. "Because of this."

Sam frowned as he took in the article. "I thought you said it wasn't related to the attempted kidnapping."

"I don't think it is. Someone visited my mother yesterday, out of the blue. He brought her this photo."

Sam looked puzzled. "Who would do that? And why?"

"That's what I'm going to have to find out." She took back the clipping and put it in her pocket. "But that's my mystery, not yours." The last thing she wanted to do was involve Sam in her life any more than he was already, not when she was on the verge of walking away for good.

A clean break would be better for everyone, right?

"You helped me with mine. Maybe I could help you with yours," he offered.

She had to smile at the offer. "How do you plan to do that, Sherlock?"

He brushed a lock of hair away from her cheek. Her smile faded, replaced by a tremble in her lips that had nothing to do with fear and everything to do with the crackling heat simmering low in her belly. "Maybe we could start with why seeing your mother after all this time bothered you so much," he murmured.

She grimaced, trying not to lean any closer to him. "That's not really a mystery, is it?"

"Do you ever talk about what happened to you?"

She shook her head. "Not if I can help it."

"But you still think about it."

"Every day." She sighed. "Look, Sam, I appreciate what you're trying to do here. But there are some things I can't—" She broke off with a wince, unable to find the words.

In his eyes, she saw his internal struggle. He wanted to help her—she saw the urge so clearly that she found herself feeling sorry for him. Poor Sam, trying to break through a decade and a half of walls she'd built to protect herself, she thought. She loved him a little bit for it, even though she wasn't sure she'd ever let those walls fall completely.

Silence stretched between them, taut and uncomfortable. Kristen closed her fingers around her knees, squeezing tightly as she struggled against the tears burning behind her eyes. She felt words hammering the back of her throat, struggling to find a voice, but she had no idea what to say.

When she finally opened her mouth and let the words spill out, they were the last thing she expected. "My mother asked me to bring Maddy to see her."

"What?"

She turned to look at him, hating herself for putting that look of horror on his face. "Forget it. It doesn't matter. I'm not going to see her again."

"Why did she want to see Maddy? Why did she think you'd ever do such a thing?"

Kristen scraped her hair away from her face. "She's crazy, Sam. She looked at that newspaper clipping and that's what she got out of it. That I had access to your four-year-old daughter and I could bring Maddy by to see her."

She could see Sam floundering for a response to such madness. "How—what—?"

She gave a huff of brittle, mirthless laughter. "Yeah, my thoughts exactly." Her laughter died in her throat as the nightmare of her past swooped in like a vulture, feeding off her pain. "She said she missed her little ones so much."

Sam looked sick. "My God."

The tears she'd been fighting reached critical mass, spilling over her lower eyelids and trickling down her cheeks in hot streaks. "She thought—" She had to stop, swallowing hard before starting again, her voice low and choked. "She thought I'd bring Maddy there to her because she missed her babies. The babies she stabbed to death and left bleeding where they lay." She broke off with a soft, bleating sob.

"Oh, honey." Sam wrapped his arm around her, pulling her close. She turned, burying her face against his throat, needing the warm, solid strength of his body against hers more than she'd expected.

She cried wordlessly a few seconds, then pulled back, wiping at the tears with her knuckles. "I don't know how much you know about what happened—"

"Just a few things people told me," he admitted.

"She'd always been, I don't know...scattered. Not very dependable. I don't really remember if she was always that way or if it just started after my father left us. I just know I was eight years old and suddenly I was the mommy of the household." She'd been so scared, as the days turned into weeks and she realized that her mother's little "spells" weren't going to go away. "I made lunch for the little ones, and if there were dishes to be washed or clothes to be laundered, I did most of that, too. Mama would do things if I asked her to, but she never seemed to think of them herself."

Sam made a low, murmuring sound of encouragement. "That must have been so hard for you."

She pushed her hair back from her damp face. "She kept telling me that I had to help her keep things together or the government would take us all away from her and split us up."

"There was nobody to look out for you and your brothers and sisters?" Sam asked, his voice unspeakably sad.

"My grandparents on my mother's side were dead, and I never had anything to do with my father's parents. I couldn't even tell you their names." She unclenched her fingers, flexing them in front of her. They felt cold and numb. "I did everything I could to keep the neighbors and our teachers from finding out how bad it was, because I was terrified the social workers would separate us." She gave another soft, defeated sob. "I should have let them. We'd all still be alive."

He shook his head. "You were a kid. You didn't know how bad it would get. Apparently nobody did."

"I should have gotten help for us. I should have—" She ended on a little noise of frustration, just as she always did when she thought about the past, about the mistakes she'd made. "I should have done something."

"You did. You took care of your brothers and sisters when nobody else did."

"I didn't protect them from the one thing I should have," she whispered. "I didn't protect them from her."

Sam took her hand in his, squeezing her fingers gently. "Whenever someone you love dies unexpectedly, you wonder what you could have done differently."

She shook her head, frustrated. "It's not the same—"

"Isn't it? My sister-in-law died eight years ago. Murdered. J.D. was in the navy at the time, away at sea. I know he wonders if being here instead would have changed things. My brother Gabe was late going to check on her when she called him with car trouble. He got there a few minutes after she was killed, just in time to find her body. He's still working through his guilt about that."

"They didn't know someone was going to kill her. But I knew my mother was insane."

"Insanity and murder are two different things, Kristen." He cupped her chin, his touch gentle but firm. "Your mother didn't abuse you physically, did she?"

She shook her head. Until the day she snapped, Molly Tandy's crimes against her children had been emotional rather than physical.

"Then how could you have known?"

"I just should have." She pulled away from his touch, not ready to be comforted. She'd spent too many years going over and over that day in her mind to be easily mollified by Sam's reasonable words. She stood up, rubbing her tired eyes. "It's late, Sam, and we've had a long day. Can't we table this for later?"

Sam looked inclined to argue, but she didn't give him a chance, heading down the hall toward the bedroom before he could speak. She closed herself inside the darkened room, pressing her ear to the door until she heard Sam's footsteps in the hall.

For a moment, the urge to fling the door open and invite him inside for the night was so tempting that she dropped her hand to the doorknob, making it rattle softly. Outside, Sam's footsteps halted, and she wondered if he'd heard the noise.

She heard the faintest sound, as if Sam had placed his hand on the other side of the door. She leaned her head closer and imagined she could hear him breathing.

Was he leaning against the door the way she was? Did he want to come in as much as she wanted him to?

After a moment, she heard his footsteps move down the hall. His door opened and closed, and she slumped against the door, releasing a pent-up breath.

The one thing she couldn't afford was false hope for a life forever out of her grasp. Hot, sweaty sex with Sam Cooper might take her mind off her problems for a couple of hours, but nothing—and no one—could make her past disappear for good. Not even Sam and his beautiful little daughter.

The sooner she brought this case to an end, the better.

CHAPTER FOURTEEN

KRISTEN WAS DRESSED and on the phone when Sam walked into the guesthouse living room around 6:00 a.m. the next morning. She waved at the coffeepot on the counter and continued her conversation. "No, I agree. The evidence is pretty solid."

Sam poured a cup of coffee and leaned against the breakfast bar, taking advantage of a rare opportunity to watch Kristen without her paying attention. Though it was early Saturday morning, she was already dressed for work in a pair of charcoal trousers and a pale blue tailored blouse that did nothing to hide her sleek curves. As she turned to reach for a bowl in the cabinet by the sink, he caught sight of her waistband holster with her Ruger tucked inside.

The combination of feminine beauty and deadly fire-power was unspeakably sexy, he thought with a grin.

Kristen tossed a glance over her shoulder, gesturing to the bowls in the cabinet. He nodded, and she pulled another one down for him.

"I'll be in the office around seven-thirty. See you then." Kristen closed her phone and dropped it in her trousers pocket.

"Foley?" Sam asked.

She nodded, handing him one of the bowls. "We're going to hand Darryl Morris over to the Birmingham

Police this morning. A detective should be here around eight to transport him back to the city."

"Then I guess that means Maddy can go back to pre-school Monday morning," he said, his relief palpable.

Kristen's brow furrowed. "I suppose that would be okay."

Her frown gave him an uneasy feeling. "You're not having doubts about Darryl Morris's guilt, are you?"

"No. He took the photos. He delivered them to your office. He's admitted that."

"And what about the man he claims paid him to do it?"

"There's no evidence such a man even exists," she answered firmly. "Morris has a grudge against you, and the things he's admitted to are pretty damning."

She was right. He knew she was. He was just leery about taking any chances with Maddy's safety.

But they had to start living a normal life again sooner or later. Putting Maddy back into preschool was a good first step. She'd be happy to see her friends again, he knew; she talked about them all the time.

He opened the cabinet under the cutlery drawer and peered at the cereal choices. His mother had stocked the pantry with entirely too many sugary choices, but he supposed that's what grandparents did with their grandchildren. In the back, he found a box of toasted wheat flakes. Reasonably nutritious.

He poured himself a bowl and flashed a questioning look at Kristen. She nodded and he poured a bowl for her, as well, before getting the milk out of the refrigerator.

"So now that you're about to go off bodyguard duty, what comes next for you?" he asked.

He heard a slight hesitation before she answered. "Foley will be continuing with follow-up on this case. He'll want to keep trying to tie Morris to the attack on Cissy. Maybe when she wakes up, she'll have more information."

"Foley? What about you?"

Kristen looked away, licking her lips. "Actually, I'm thinking about asking Carl to assign me to a different case."

A hot ache settled in the pit of Sam's gut. Even though he'd known she'd be going back to her own place sooner rather than later, he hadn't realized she was thinking about handing over the investigation to someone else.

"Why?" he asked.

She darted a quick look at him. "It's time to move on."

He didn't miss her meaning. "From Maddy and me, you mean."

A queasy expression darted across her face. "Don't you think that's for the best?"

"This is about the kiss, isn't it?"

She slanted another look at him. "You're fixated on the kiss, Sam. It was nothing. Hormones and stress."

"What about the rest of it?"

She pushed aside her untouched bowl of cereal with a growl of frustration. "The rest of what? What exactly do you think has been going on between us? We've known each other—what? Three days?"

"Sometimes that's all it takes," he said quietly, realizing how crazy he sounded. Why was he even arguing with her about this? Hadn't he already proved his judgment about women was pretty damned suspect? He'd been certain he and Norah were meant to be together, and look how well that had turned out.

"People like me don't get happily ever afters," Kristen said just as quietly, pain darkening her blue eyes.

It wasn't the response he'd expected. He'd figured she'd stick with how short a time they'd been acquainted, maybe toss in the fact that high-stress situations sometimes magnified emotions that wouldn't otherwise make a blip on a person's radar. They were good, sound arguments.

But she'd gone straight to the heart of the problem. She didn't believe they had a chance together because of her past. That's what it all came down to, wasn't it?

Well, he couldn't accept that argument. He couldn't accept that she was doomed to solitude because of her mother's sins. It wasn't right or fair.

He pushed aside his own cereal bowl, welcoming the surge of frustration that drove out the hurt he'd felt a few seconds earlier. "I know you had a horrible childhood. Your recent history probably hasn't been the greatest, either. But I don't think life picks winners or losers, Kristen. I think we choose that ourselves—if we have the guts to."

She stared at him, shaking her head. "You think the problem is that I'm afraid of being happy?"

"Yeah, I do."

She threw up her hands. "Believe me, I don't want to live alone the rest of my life. I don't want to freak out every time I'm around kids. I love kids! I used to be great with kids. I used to dream about growing up and having children of my own."

"Then do it."

She shot him a glare as he took a step toward her. He backed off.

"I would love to jump into a relationship with you and see where it goes. What woman wouldn't? You're sexy, successful, funny...." She drew a long, shaky breath, blinking hard to hold back the tears. "But I'm a bad risk, Sam. Not just for you but also for Maddy. My mother wasn't always crazy, you know. For all I know, what happened to her was genetic. It could happen to me, too."

"You can't know that."

"And you can't be sure I'm wrong," she countered.

He wanted to argue, but she was right. He couldn't be sure. He knew nothing about her mother's situation, what had caused her madness and whether or not Kristen's own mind was a ticking time bomb. "Have you never asked anyone what caused your mother's mental break? Her doctor, maybe?"

Her expression was bleak. "No."

"Maybe you should."

Her lips flattened with frustration. "I need to leave now. Before Maddy wakes up."

Sam swallowed hard, fighting the urge to touch her, to try something, anything to make her reconsider walking out of their lives this way. He could tell there was nothing he could say right now to change her mind.

He wasn't even sure he should try.

He stepped away from her, jamming his restless hands into his pockets. "Maddy will be hurt if you leave without saying goodbye, Kristen."

She grimaced. "It's been only three days, Sam. She'll forget me sooner than you think."

He wasn't so sure. Maddy had apparently reached

the age where having a mother seemed important, and with her own mother heading back to D.C. and out of the picture, Maddy had picked Kristen to fill the void, just as she might have picked a new puppy at the pound.

Maybe Kristen was right not to make a big deal out of saying goodbye. Perhaps the best way to handle Maddy's certain disappointment would be the same way he'd handle saying no to a new puppy—blatant distraction tactics.

"I think you're right," he said evenly, even though a heavy ache had settled right in the center of his chest. "No big goodbye. I'll have my folks keep her busy today and tomorrow while I finish readying the house for us to move back, and Monday she'll start back to preschool, which she'll love. It'll be okay."

Kristen nodded, although he saw worry in her eyes. It was more than he'd seen in Norah's eyes when she left, he realized. All he'd seen in his ex-wife's expression as she headed for her gate at the airport were equal parts guilt and relief.

"This is for the best, Sam." Kristen reached for the bowl of now-soggy cereal sitting on the counter, starting toward the garbage disposal.

He caught her arm, stopping her. She gazed up at him, her lips trembling slightly.

It would be so easy to kiss her, he thought. Just a soft, sweet kiss goodbye.

But he forced himself to let her go, taking the bowl from her unsteady hands. "I'll take care of this. You should go now, before Maddy wakes up."

The stricken look in her eyes almost unraveled his resolve. But she moved away quickly, before he could falter, grabbing her purse and jacket and heading out the door at a clip.

Sam forced himself to empty the two bowls of cereal into the garbage disposal and wash up, needing the activity to take his mind off the strange, empty feeling that had hollowed out his insides the second the door had closed behind Kristen.

"WHEN I GET HOME, can we go see Miss Kristen?" Maddy asked as Sam unlatched her safety seat Monday morning.

Sam sighed, lifting her out of the Jeep and setting her on the ground. "Miss Kristen is very busy at work now, Maddy. Don't you remember, we talked about this last night."

Maddy's little face scrunched up with displeasure. "I wanna see Miss Kristen!"

So much for his daughter being easily distracted. She'd been asking about Kristen for two days straight. "Tell you what, this afternoon, when Aunt Hannah picks you up from school, maybe she'll take you out fishing." He made a mental note to check with his sister to see if she already had a client lined up that afternoon. Surely she'd give herself a day or so to get settled back in from her trip to Arizona and wouldn't mind some one-on-one time with her youngest niece.

He saw warning signs that Maddy was gearing up to argue, so he took her hand and tugged her gently up the walkway to the front entrance of Gossamer Ridge Day School, where the director, Jennifer Franks, was greeting children that morning. When she caught sight of Sam and Maddy, her expression shifted quickly to regret.

"I was horrified to read about Mr. Morris's arrest," she said earnestly. "I'm so sorry I hired him—we had no idea—"

"Nobody did," Sam assured her. "There was never any indication in his background that he'd be any sort of threat. You couldn't have known."

"Still, we take these things very seriously. We've hired guards to patrol the grounds during the day so parents can feel secure about leaving their children with us." Jennifer waved toward a young man in a blue uniform standing a few steps away. "One here at the front entrance and another in the play area."

Seeing the guard did ease Sam's mind a bit. He supposed the bad publicity about Morris had forced the director's hand.

Maddy caught sight of one of her friends and tugged her hand out of Sam's, dashing away with a squeal of delight. Sam watched her go with a smile, though mild anxiety tugged at his gut. Over the past few days, he'd gotten used to having her close, protected by himself or people he trusted implicitly. It was hard to let go of that control, but he couldn't keep her wrapped in cotton padding and stored under glass.

"She'll be fine," Jennifer said.

"She asked me to put her favorite stuffed toy in the bag," Sam warned the principal. "I know you have rules about bringing toys to school, but she's had a rough few days. I made her promise to give the backpack to the teacher as soon as she got in the classroom and not to bug Miss Kathy about taking Bandit out of the bag during class."

Jennifer smiled sympathetically. "I suppose we can look the other way just this once."

Sam thanked her, turning to watch Maddy until she disappeared into her classroom down the hallway. With a tugging sensation in the middle of his chest, he returned to his car to make the long drive into Birmingham for his first full day back at the office.

Sam was smart enough to know that any interference from him might jeopardize the District Attorney's case against Darryl Morris, and the last thing he wanted to do was provide Morris with any sort of get-out-of-jail-free card. So he resisted the temptation to snoop around the office's newest case, instead spending the morning buried under the backlog of cases he'd had to put on hold the week before while he dealt with the threat to Maddy, sorting through what cases could be easily pleaded out and which ones would require actual court time.

By the time his cell phone rang that morning around eleven, he was bleary-eyed and grateful for the interruption. "Cooper."

"Sam, it's J.D. Cissy's awake."

"JUST STICK WITH it a few more days," Foley cajoled, following at Kristen's heels as she checked the fax machine to see if anything had come in overnight. She turned quickly, and Foley almost barreled into her, grabbing the file cabinet at the last second to stop his momentum.

"Stop following me around like a puppy," she ordered.

"Stop being a scaredy cat."

"Oh, that's mature." The fax machine tray was empty, so she edged around Foley and returned to her desk.

"It's not like you to turn your back on a case that's

still active." Foley settled on the edge of her desk, in her way.

She shooed him off. "Park your backside on your own desk. And how would you know whether or not it's like me to turn my back on an open case? This was my first case as a detective."

Foley made a face. "You know what I mean. I saw how you tackled this case. You must want to see it through to the end. So why ask for reassignment? Unless you and Cooper—"

She glared at him. "Mind your own business, Foley."

He opened his mouth to respond, but the trill of his desk phone stopped him midsound. He slid off Kristen's desk and crossed to answer. "Foley."

Kristen straightened her desk blotter where Foley's hip had knocked it askew, wishing her fellow investigator wasn't quite so good a detective. He probably knew exactly why she'd asked Carl to assign her to a different case. And unlike Carl, who'd at least had the kindness to keep his comments to himself, Foley was likely to make her next few weeks miserable with his endless attempts at armchair psychoanalysis.

"We'll be there." Foley hung up the phone and picked up the folder in front of him. "Grab your jacket, Tandy. You're going to get to be in on the end of this case after all."

"What's going on?"

Foley stopped in the doorway, flashing a smile. "Cissy Cooper's awake. And she's talking."

"Everything seems to be in proper working order," J.D. told Sam as they waited outside Cissy's hospital room for the nurse to finish taking her vital signs. "No neurological deficits or anything like that. She even remembers the night of the attack. When I told her the police had a suspect in custody, she said she thinks she can identify him if the police show her a photo."

Sam clapped his hand on his brother's arm, happy to see J.D. looking so relieved and excited. "This is the best news, huh? Did you call the police?"

"He did." Jason Foley walked up, followed closely by Kristen. Sam tried to make eye contact with her, but she kept her gaze on J.D.'s face, her expression impossible to read.

So that was how she thought she was going to play it, huh?

Like hell.

The nurse emerged, smiling at J.D. "You'd never know she was out for four days. She's doing really great, Mr. Cooper."

J.D. beamed at the nurse and headed back into Cissy's room. Foley and Kristen followed, and Sam brought up the rear, trying not to stare too obviously at Kristen's slim, curvy backside. Just two days away from her, and he felt like an addict twitching for the next hit.

Cissy looked good, Sam was relieved to see. She grinned weakly at him. "How's Maddy? Daddy said she didn't get hurt, but is she really okay?"

"She's fine," Sam assured his niece, squeezing her hand.

"Your father told us you remember the attack." Kristen moved closer to the hospital bed.

Cissy looked up at her. "I do."

Sam let go of Cissy's hand. "Cissy, this is Detective Kristen Tandy of the Gossamer Ridge Police Department."

He could see from the shift in his niece's expression that she recognized the name. But she didn't say anything, just held out her hand to Kristen. "Nice to meet you."

"I'm very happy to finally meet you, too," Kristen said with a smile. "This is Detective Foley. We've been investigating what happened to you. We picked up a suspect a couple of days ago—can you take a look at this picture?"

Kristen pulled a photograph from her notebook and handed it to Cissy, who brought the photo closer to her face.

Sam realized he was holding his breath. He let it go slowly, glancing from his niece to Kristen, whose expression was as tense as he felt.

Cissy handed the photo back to Kristen, her expression apologetic. "I'm sorry, no. That's not the guy."

Sam felt his chest contract into a painful knot. Kristen turned to look at him, her eyes bright with alarm.

"Where's Maddy?" she asked urgently.

"At school," Sam answered, his heart pounding.

"I'll drive," she said, and hit the door at a jog.

OUTSIDE TIME WAS Maddy's favorite time of all. She liked coloring and singing and all the things she did with the teacher inside the school, but outside time was perfect. Just perfect.

Sometimes the teachers played games with them. Miss Kathy was the best at kick ball, and she laughed a lot. Maddy liked to hear Miss Kathy's laugh. It was a big, booming laugh, straight from her belly. Maddy sometimes tried to laugh just like that, although it came out kind of silly sounding. But that was okay. Daddy said it was okay to be silly sometimes.

Thinking about Daddy made her think about this morning, when he'd told her that Miss Kristen was at work. Miss Kristen was a detective, Daddy said, and her work was Very Very Important. Maddy wondered what was important about being a detective. In fact, she wondered what a detective was, anyway.

She only knew that she liked Miss Kristen. She liked how Miss Kristen didn't try to treat her like a baby since she was a big girl now. She liked the sound of Miss Kristen's voice. And she liked Miss Kristen's smile, even though Miss Kristen didn't smile nearly as much as Aunt Hannah or Grandmama. Maddy wondered why she didn't smile as much. *Maybe she needs a little girl to love,* Maddy thought. *Like me.*

Across the playground, a little girl screamed, and Maddy looked up with surprise. She saw Cassie Price jumping up and down shrieking, and a couple of the boys in her class had bent over to look at something in the grass.

Maddy saw Miss Kathy and Miss Debbie hurry over to see what was going on. She started across the playground, too, but a big hand reached out and stopped her.

She looked up and saw a tall man in a blue uniform standing just behind her. Her heart gave a little lurch of surprise.

"There's a snake over there," he said. Maddy thought his voice sounded familiar. He looked familiar, too, but she didn't know why. He had a big, bushy mustache and wore a pair of silvery sunglasses. She could see herself in the glasses, she realized with a little smile.

"Come with me, Maddy. I'm taking you to your daddy."

Was he Daddy's friend? He had a uniform sort of like her Uncle Aaron's. Was he a policeman? "I'm not afraid of snakes," she said. Aunt Hannah had taught her how to handle the little green snakes that played around Grandmama's garden. She liked to feel their dry, scaly bodies wriggle through her fingers.

"But that's a poisonous snake," the man said firmly, taking her hand. She saw he had her backpack in his other hand. She could see the ringed tail of Bandit, her stuffed raccoon, hanging out of the zippered pocket.

The man saw her looking at the tail. He reached into the pocket and gave Bandit to her. She said thank you— Daddy said always say "please" and "thank you"—and hugged Bandit close, not liking the feel of the man's big hand around hers.

"Where's my daddy?" she asked aloud.

"He's waiting for you inside my van." The man pulled her toward the side gate of the playground fence. They had gone around the side of the school building, and Maddy couldn't see the other kids on the playground anymore.

The man opened the gate and gave her a little nudge to go through. He closed the gate behind them and pulled her hand.

Maddy looked at the van parked at the end of the small parking lot. It was green and looked old. There were two windows up at the front but no windows in the side. She didn't see Daddy inside.

"Where's my daddy?" she repeated, starting to feel scared.

The man opened the door of the van, picked her up

and put her inside. He didn't even have a special seat for her, like Daddy did. Her legs dangled over the seat, and she felt hot tears on her cheeks.

"Where's my daddy?" she screamed, but the man had already closed the door. She saw him put something in her backpack and toss it into the bushes at the side of the building.

Maddy tried to open the door of the van to run away—Daddy said when you got scared, it was okay to run and find a grown-up you trusted—but she couldn't get it to open.

The man in the uniform opened the front door and pulled himself into the seat behind the steering wheel. He spoke to her, his voice firm. "No crying, Maddy. You have to be a big girl now, okay?" He pulled a cap from the dashboard and put it on. Maddy's eyes widened.

Now she knew why the man in the uniform looked and sounded familiar. He was the bad man.

The bad man who hurt Cissy.

CHAPTER FIFTEEN

SAM CLUTCHED THE cell phone more tightly as Kristen swerved around slow-moving traffic on I-59. He was on interminable hold, waiting for the preschool's principal to come on the line. He'd made a call as soon as they got outside the hospital, but the principal had been out of the office and he'd had to leave a message. He'd spent the next twenty minutes certain that Jennifer Franks would return his call at any moment.

When she didn't, he called again. The principal still wasn't in her office, but this time, he told the secretary that he wasn't hanging up until he talked to her boss.

"Still nothing?" Kristen asked, sounding as annoyed as he felt. "You've been on hold forever."

Just then, there was a click on the other end of the line and Jennifer Franks's breathless voice greeted him. "So sorry, Mr. Cooper. We've had a bit of an uproar I've been trying to get under control."

Sam's stomach twisted. "What kind of an uproar?"

"One of the children found a rather large snake on the playground a little while ago. We're still trying to find out whether or not it's harmless, and several of the children are very upset. We've had to call some parents."

Sam tamped down his impatience. "I left a message with your secretary twenty minutes ago—I'm trying to locate Maddy. Did you get that message?"

"No, I'm sorry—my secretary just told me. Maddy's class was outside for recess when the snake incident happened, but Maddy wasn't one of the children involved."

"Where is she now?"

"I assume she's back in her classroom with her teacher."

"You assume?"

Across the seat, Kristen muttered a profanity under her breath.

"I'll check right now. Hold on a moment."

"I'm on hold again," Sam muttered.

"For God's sake!" Kristen jerked the wheel, taking the Impala around a slow-moving coal truck at breakneck speed. "How hard is it to find one four-year-old?"

"Mr. Cooper?"

The fear he heard in Jennifer Franks's voice made Sam's blood freeze. "Tell me you found her safe and sound," he said.

"I'm sorry. We don't know how it happened."

"What happened, damn it?"

Kristen shot him a look full of unadulterated terror.

"She didn't return with the rest of her class after recess," Jennifer answered, sounding sick. "We don't know where she is."

"Get your security guards to start searching every inch of the grounds."

"I've already sent my assistant out to do just that. I don't think we should panic yet, Mr. Cooper. It's possible that she was there for the snake incident and ran away to hide because she was scared."

He wished he could believe that, but he knew that snakes didn't scare Maddy. He'd actually had to give her a lesson on not touching snakes unless a grown-up was there to supervise, for fear she'd end up trying to befriend a ground rattler or one of the bigger copperheads that roamed the woods near the lake.

"Please call me back with any news. I'm on my way."

"Should we contact the police?"

"I'll handle that," Sam answered, ringing off only long enough to dial his brother-in-law's cell phone number. A few moments later, Hannah's husband answered. "Deputy Patterson."

"Riley, it's Sam. Maddy's missing from her preschool and I'm about thirty minutes out. I need you to go there and supervise the search if you can."

"Of course. What can you tell me?"

He outlined for his brother-in-law what Jennifer Franks had told him. "You know Maddy—a snake wouldn't have scared her away. I'm afraid the man who tried to take her before may have gotten to her this time."

"I thought Jefferson County had the guy in custody."

"They have Darryl Morris in custody—but Cissy just woke up from her coma. She said Morris definitely isn't the guy who attacked her."

"Son of a bitch," Riley growled. "Did she give you a description of who we *are* looking for?"

"I left as soon as I heard Morris wasn't the guy. Detective Foley with the GRPD is still there taking her statement. Right now, we're just looking for Maddy."

"I'm about five minutes away from the preschool," Riley said. "I'll call you in a few." He rang off.

Sam snapped his cell phone shut. "This isn't happening."

"This is my fault," Kristen muttered, white-knuckling the steering wheel through the interstate traffic. "I knew in my gut Morris was too easy an answer, but I wanted to believe it was over."

"We all did," Sam said firmly. The last thing Kristen needed to do was second-guess herself now, when she needed to focus. "Don't kick yourself. The evidence was there. We just didn't know there were missing pieces."

"Except Morris told us all along there was someone else involved," Kristen said, her tone full of disgust. "I should have looked deeper."

"You will now."

She released a shaky breath, and for the first time Sam realized she was hovering on the edge of tears. "I'm so sorry, Sam. I never should have agreed to let Carl put me in charge of protecting Maddy. I knew it was a bad idea."

"If you'd still been with Maddy, she wouldn't be missing," Sam replied. "You wouldn't have taken your eye off her for even a second. So stop blaming yourself. We all thought she was out of danger." He touched her shoulder. "I need you with me on this. I need your focus. Tell me you can do that."

She spared him a quick look. "I can do that."

They had reached their exit on the Interstate. They'd be at the school in ten minutes. Sam tried to keep his mind away from worst-case scenarios. The snake might not have scared Maddy, but she'd shown a hearty self-protective streak over the past few days, hiding first from the kidnapper and then from her mother when she'd felt threatened by Norah's careless comments.

"Could she be hiding?" Kristen asked, her mind moving in tandem with his. "I know the snake wouldn't have scared her, but maybe all the commotion spooked her?"

"Maybe." He was afraid to hope. His gut was telling him it wouldn't be that easy. Not this time.

Kristen killed the sirens about a block from the preschool. "The kids'll be freaked out enough as it is."

He slanted a look at her, wondering how she could possibly believe she wasn't mother material. Even with all the uncertainty about Maddy's whereabouts, Kristen had enough presence of mind to worry about the other children.

He hadn't even given them a thought.

Riley Patterson was waiting for them at the front of the school, easy to spot thanks to his signature pearl-gray Stetson, a legacy of his native Wyoming. Sam could tell by the look on his brother-in-law's face that the news wasn't good.

"We've found her backpack in the bushes near the side gate." Riley's voice was tight. "And one of the security guards is missing."

"Missing?" Sam frowned at Riley. "You think someone got rid of him to get to Maddy?"

"We're not sure," Riley said. "There's no sign of a struggle, no blood or anything like that—"

"Where's the backpack?" Kristen asked. She'd already pulled on a pair of latex gloves.

Riley gestured for them to follow. "I wanted to wait until you got here to take a look at it. You'd know what's missing, if anything." He led them around the side of the building, where a yellow barrier tape flapped lazily in the warm midday breeze. A handful of people from the neighborhood had gathered outside the fence, watching curiously as Sam, Kristen and Riley approached the backpack lying on its side near the bushes.

Sam felt moisture burning his eyes as he saw Maddy's name written in faded denim letters stitched to the side of the backpack. Hannah had made those letters for Maddy out of a pair of old jeans and let Maddy help her stitch them to the bag.

His whole family had pitched in when he returned home to Alabama with his little girl, knowing how much harder her life was going to be without a mother there for her full-time. If something had happened to his baby—

Kristen's warm hand slipped into his. He looked down at her and found her gazing up at him with scared blue eyes. But her jaw was squared and mingled with the fear was a bracing double shot of determination.

"Focus on the evidence," she said. "You packed the bag for her this morning, right? Tell me if something's missing."

He squeezed her hand, grateful for her calming presence. He hunkered down with her as she crouched beside the backpack, watching her carefully open the bag to look inside.

"Bandit's missing," he said aloud, noticing the stuffed raccoon's absence immediately. Maddy's favorite toy had taken up most of the space in the bag.

"Her stuffed raccoon," Kristen explained when Riley gave Sam a querying look. "She's very attached." She pulled the zipper down farther. There was a small gold change purse inside—empty, since Maddy had no concept of money. She only liked the little purse because of its shiny color.

Kristen picked up the purse, looking at it, her eyes

damp. Sam put his hand on her back, and she shot him a grateful look. Putting the purse down, she opened one of the outside pockets. "Commander Patterson, do you have tweezers or something like that?"

"What is it?" Sam asked as Riley reached into his pocket and brought out a slim, leather-bound tool kit.

"It looks like a piece of paper." Kristen took the tweezers Riley gave her and reached into the zippered pocket to withdraw a small piece of paper folded into four sections. Using the tweezers and the very tip of her gloved finger, she nudged the paper open.

There was writing inside, blocky letters just like the ones Sam had found on the back of the photos Darryl Morris had delivered to the D.A.'s office.

"'Let's make a deal,'" Kristen read aloud, her voice shaking. "'Your life for hers.'"

Riley muttered a soft string of curses.

"What kind of sick game is this guy playing?" Kristen dropped the note into the clear plastic bag Riley had produced from his jacket pocket and started going through the other pockets with greater urgency, as if hoping she'd find something that would contradict the message she'd just discovered.

"I don't think it's a game," Sam said thoughtfully, his initial fear beginning to subside. At least he could be pretty sure his daughter was still alive, if the man was talking about a trade. The fact that Bandit was missing also gave him hope; only someone who cared about Maddy's emotional state would have bothered dragging the stuffed toy along with them.

Whoever had taken Maddy wanted her alive, as a pawn in his game, not as a victim. It wasn't great news, but Sam would take it. It was a hell of a lot better than finding his daughter's body under the bushes instead.

Riley put his hand on Sam's shoulder. "I'm going to call this in and get a few more deputies down here. I'll see if the DEA can spare Aaron, too."

Sam stood and shook Riley's hand. "Thanks, man. Call Hannah, too. She needs to let the rest of the family know what's going on."

As Riley went to make the radio call, Sam turned to Kristen. "Was there anything else in the backpack?"

Kristen shook her head. "That was it."

"So he's going to find a way to get in touch with me."

Kristen pulled her gloves off and planted herself in front of him. "You're not making a trade, Sam."

"You can't stop me."

She moved even closer, her gaze locked with his. "If you try to make the deal, you're just playing his game."

"It's the only game in town, Kristen." He laid his hands on her shoulders, running his thumbs gently over the curve of her collarbone. "I will do anything for my daughter. Including die for her, if it comes to that."

"I know that. But we can't be stupid about this."

"What am I supposed to do?" He felt some of his control begin to slip. "That man has my daughter. He holds all the cards here. We're practically at square one now that Cissy's eliminated Morris as a suspect."

"No, we're not." Kristen closed her hands over his, her fingers warm and strong. "Cissy is giving Foley a description as we speak. And, you know, Darryl Morris may have been telling the truth about his accomplice. We may be able to get more information from him."

Something that had been niggling at the back of

Sam's mind since he'd arrived at the preschool snapped into focus. "The missing guard," he said.

Kristen's brow creased for a second, then smoothed with a look of understanding. "The guard took Maddy."

Sam nodded, his mind racing. "I've taught her about being wary with strangers, but she knows that someone in uniform is a person who can help her when she's in trouble."

"He used the snake situation as a distraction," Kristen added. "Maybe he even engineered it himself."

"And he was already in place, in a position of trust. Nobody was going to think twice about a security guard leading Maddy away from the confusion." Sam shook his head. "How did he ever get a job here?"

"Maybe he doesn't have any sort of record." Kristen looked around, catching sight of Riley returning to the taped-off crime scene. "Deputy, can you keep an eye on the scene? We need to talk to the teachers and kids."

Riley slipped under the tape. "Sure. I've got some men on the way. Aaron's out of pocket," he added, speaking to Sam, "but I left a message with the DEA for him."

"Thanks," Sam said, hurrying to catch up with Kristen, who was already halfway to the school entrance.

"HERE'S A PHOTOCOPY of his driver's license," Jennifer Franks said, looking about ten years older than she had the last time Kristen had seen her, the day she'd answered questions about Darryl Morris. She handed the paper to Kristen.

"Grant Mitchell," she read aloud, studying the grainy photo. Driver's license photos were almost never flattering, and this one was no exception. The man in the photo was in his late forties or early fifties, with short-cropped brown hair and a handlebar mustache that made him look like a throwback to the Civil War era. The photocopy wasn't the best quality, so it was impossible to make out much about the man's eyes, nor could she read anything in his expression that might give her a clue to the man inside.

Though she was sure she'd never met the man before, he seemed vaguely familiar to her. She showed Sam the photocopy. "Anyone you know?"

He studied the paper, his brow creased with concentration. After a moment, he released a disappointed sigh. "No, I don't think so." He looked across the desk at Jennifer. "Is this photo a good likeness?"

"Drivers' licenses never are," Jennifer said. "But yes, I'd say that's what he looks like, more or less."

"This doesn't make sense," Sam muttered.

Kristen laid her hand on Sam's shoulder. "Maybe we're wrong about Grant Mitchell. He could be a victim here, too. Or maybe he just decided guarding preschoolers isn't for him." She took the photocopy from Sam and looked down at the driver's license. "We could try his address—"

She stopped, rereading the address listed on the license. 1240 Copperhead Road. She slumped in her seat. "This address doesn't exist," she told Sam, showing him the photocopy. "There's no 1240 Copperhead Road. Addresses on that road only go to the 900s."

"What does that mean?" Jennifer asked.

"It means this license is a fake," Sam answered.

AFTER ANOTHER HOUR at the school listening to Kristen, Riley and the rest of the officers and deputies who'd arrived on scene interviewing the other students and teachers, Sam had a much better idea of what had transpired that morning.

Kristen's theory had proved right; at least three of the other students and one of the assistant teachers had noticed the guard leading Kristen away from the playground. Nobody had thought anything about it, assuming Maddy had become upset and the guard had decided to take her away from the commotion to calm her down.

"This guy knew just how to pull this off," he murmured to Kristen later at his house. She'd suggested that they go there after they stopped at the police station to drop off the evidence and make extra copies of the security guard's fake license. Kristen figured Grant Mitchell or whoever he really was would probably call Sam there with further instructions.

She sat on the sofa beside him, studying the photo. The Chickasaw County Sheriff's Department had offered their services setting up a tap on the phone in case the kidnapper called, so there wasn't much left for either of them to do but sit and wait to hear from the man who had his daughter.

"I keep thinking I've seen this guy before," she said distractedly. "I don't think I've met him, though. Just—seen him. Like maybe a photo or—" She stopped short, her brow furrowing. "I wonder—" She started to dig in her pockets of her jacket, first the left, then the right.

"What are you looking for?"

She came up empty-handed. "I may have left it in my other jacket at home. It was a photo that Dr. Sowell gave me—he's the doctor who's treating my mother at Darden. Anyway, he gave me a copy of a screen grab from the surveillance cameras at the facility, a picture of the man who visited my mother the other day—the one who took her that newspaper clipping about the attack on Cissy and Maddy."

Sam felt the first niggle of hope he'd had in a couple of hours. "Could it have been the same man?"

"I'm not sure. He didn't have a mustache, and I don't think his hair was as dark as the guy calling himself Grant Mitchell." She gave a little growl of frustration. "Where is that damned photo?"

"Could it be in your car?" Sam suggested.

"I'll go look." She jumped up from the sofa and ran out the door.

Sam picked up the photocopy and stared at the phony driver's license, trying to picture the man with lighter hair and no mustache. A memory danced around the shadowy edges of his mind but wouldn't come out into the light.

His cell phone beeped, the signal for a text message. He pulled his phone from his pocket and punched a couple of buttons. Five words showed up in the display window:

BELLEWOOD MFG 730 2NITE ALONE.

Sam's heart stuttered, then began to race.

Kristen burst through the front door, slightly out of breath but grinning. "Found it." She crossed the room in a coltish bound and dropped onto the sofa beside him.

He quickly tucked his phone into his pocket. Alone, the message had said.

No one else could know.

"Any news?" Kristen asked, following his movement with her sharp blue eyes.

He shook his head, trying to look calm even though his insides had turned to ice. "Nothing. Is that the picture?"

She showed him the grainy photo. The photo showed only the side of the man's face, but it was enough. The elusive memory that had been nagging him for the past few minutes crashed into full view, bringing with it both enlightenment and a heavy, crushing sense of despair. He knew the man in the photo. And now he understood the meaning of "Your child for mine."

Ten years ago, at a snowy staging area in Kaziristan, Sam had killed this man's son.

CHAPTER SIXTEEN

THE LOOK ON Sam's face made Kristen's blood freeze. "You know who he is, don't you?"

Sam looked up at her, his expression bleak. "His name is Stan Burkett. I killed his son."

"You killed—how? When?" The ice flooding her veins spread to her skin, raising goose bumps on her arms and legs. Her hand shook as she reached for Sam's hand.

He eluded her touch, rising from the sofa. Apparently he'd found the nervous energy that had just drained out of her; he kept moving as he spoke. "It was ten years ago, in Kaziristan." He stopped pacing long enough to look at her. "There'd been an earthquake, and we'd sent in the Marines to help with the search and rescue, carry emergency supplies—you know the drill."

She nodded. "I remember that."

He went back to pacing. "I was there because I was assigned to the humanitarian mission as a legal liaison. Some of the kids who went over there were fresh out of boot camp at Parris Island. This was their first overseas assignment. Richard Burkett was one of them. Nineteen, with a chip on his shoulder. He got crossways with his CO, a real tough guy—Captain Kent Sullivan." Sam's lips curved slightly. "Sully was hard but fair. Most of the other Marines respected that, but Burkett was convinced Sully was picking on him specifically. Burkett had a temper. And a weapon."

"Burkett fragged Sullivan?" Kristen asked, guessing ahead.

Sam stopped and looked at her. "He tried to. I stopped him with my service weapon." He seemed to have run out of steam, dropping heavily into the armchair across from her. "He was a second away from blowing off Sully's head with an M16 rifle. I didn't have a choice."

"But Burkett's father didn't see it that way?"

"I was cleared by a JAGMAN investigation. I had acted within reason. But Burkett yelled cover-up, claimed the investigation cleared me because I was one of them. He raised a stink but it never went anywhere." Sam ran his hand over his face, his palm rasping against the beard stubble darkening his jaw. "He went away after a few months. I thought that was the end of it."

Kristen crossed to the chair and crouched in front of him, taking his hands in hers. "Not exactly the break in the case you wanted, huh?"

He squeezed her hands, his gaze meeting hers, dark with fear. "If he's been nursing this grudge this long, he's dangerous. And he has Maddy."

"But it's not really Maddy he wants, right? The note in the backpack said it's you he's after. So he's not going to hurt her while there's a chance to use her to get to you. He's going to be in touch again soon, and then we can figure out how to catch him and get Maddy back."

Sam dropped his gaze to their hands. "Yeah."

She felt the tension in the room rise a few notches, reminding her of the furtive way Sam had tucked his phone in his pocket a few minutes earlier. What wasn't he telling her?

Had he already heard from Burkett?

"Sam, has he already contacted you?"

There was the faintest hesitation before he spoke. "No."

Now she knew he was lying. He'd been holding the phone when she came back in the house, as if he'd just rung off. She'd figured it was one of his family, or maybe Riley Patterson.

What if it had been Burkett?

"Kristen, can you do me a favor?" Sam finally looked up, meeting her gaze. "I need to stick around here, in case a call comes in, but we could really use a little more background information on Burkett. Find out where he's been the last few years, what he's been up to. You have resources at the police department, and I trust you to be thorough. Will you do that for me? And see if Foley's gotten anything out of Darryl Morris."

He might be lying, but the plea she heard in Sam's words was genuine. He was right, too—looking into Stan Burkett's recent activities would be helpful. It might help them figure out where he'd be keeping Maddy, for one thing.

But deep down, she knew that Sam really just wanted her to leave him alone for a while so he could do whatever it was Burkett had told him to do.

She knew confronting him would be useless. If he thought meeting Burkett's demands would save Maddy, he'd do it and lie to God Himself about it.

And she'd lie to save them both.

"I'll do that," she answered finally, rising to her feet.

She reached out her hand. "Go take a shower or something while I'm gone. It'll help you relax."

"I don't think anything can do that," Sam said bleakly, but he took her hand and let her pull him to his feet.

She tugged at his suit jacket. "Give it a try anyway."

He let her pull his jacket off. She draped it over her arm and turned him toward the hallway. "Go. I'll let myself out."

"Call if you learn anything," Sam said.

"And you call if you hear anything from Burkett."

"I will," Sam lied over his shoulder as he headed toward the bathroom down the hall. Kristen heard a hint of regret in his voice. She supposed she could find a little comfort in knowing he didn't enjoy lying to her.

Suddenly, he turned around and strode back to her, wrapping his hand around the back of her neck. Pulling her to him, he bent his head and kissed her, hard and hungry, his fingers threading through her hair to hold her still while he drank his fill. He drew away, finally, resting his forehead against hers, his breath fast and warm against her cheeks. "I know you wanted off this case, but thanks for staying with it. It means a lot."

For a moment, she thought about nothing but the feel of his body against hers, warm and powerful, yet vulnerable to her touch. It made her feel guilty for what she was about to do—but not guilty enough to change her mind.

He dropped a last, soft kiss on her forehead as he let her go. "I'll see you tomorrow."

"Go take your shower," she whispered.

After he'd disappeared down the hallway, she unfolded his coat, reached into the breast pocket and pulled out his cell phone. The most recent activity had been a text message:

BELLEWOOD MFG 730 2NITE ALONE.

She stared at the message, her heart racing. Bellewood Manufacturing had once been a textile mill on Catawba Road, out past the old dam bridge. No longer in business, the abandoned mill was secluded, well away from prying eyes. By seven-thirty tonight, darkness would have fallen, giving anyone lying in wait at the mill an extra advantage. And Sam believed he'd be going there to meet Burkett alone.

Like hell.

Kristen put the cell phone back in Sam's pocket and draped the coat over the arm of the sofa, wondering what to do next. Wait for him to come out of the shower and confront him with what she knew? Threaten to take him into protective custody to keep him from trying to go out there alone?

One thing she wasn't going to do was let Stan Burkett lay a trap for Sam to walk into.

She let herself out of Sam's house, reaching into her pocket for her cell phone. Carl Madison answered on the first ring. "Madison."

"Carl, it's me." Kristen slid behind the wheel of the Impala. "I need your help."

SAM DIDN'T THINK Burkett would leave another message before the meeting that evening—the one succinct message he'd sent had been sufficient to set Sam's nerves on permanent alert, which he suspected had been Burkett's intention. But he couldn't take chances, so he checked his cell phone as soon as he got out of his shower.

As he'd expected, nothing from Burkett. But his sister Hannah had left a message. "I'm on my way over." He glanced at his watch. He barely had time to dress before she would arrive.

He let her in after the first couple of bangs on the door and staggered beneath the force of her tackle-hug.

"Tell me what you want me to do," Hannah said without preamble, grabbing his hand and dragging him to the sofa. She was five months pregnant and, thanks to hormones, had two speeds these days, high and supersonic.

"There's nothing to do. The police are all over this, including your cowboy cop. I'm just waiting like everyone else for news."

Hannah's eyes narrowed. "That's a load of bull manure."

"Riley is rubbing off on you."

"No way you're just waiting around for news, Sam Cooper. You're up to something." She scooted closer. "What is it?"

"If I had a supersecret plan, do you think I'd tell you, the biggest blabbermouth in the family?"

"That was twenty years ago," she protested. Her eyes widened suddenly. "You've heard from the kidnapper! What did he do, break in and leave a note under your pillow? I know he didn't call the house or Riley would already know about it. Oh! Your cell phone. He called your cell phone!"

Sam stared at his sister, wondering why she wasn't the cop in the family. "I have no idea what you're talking about."

"You can't go by yourself," she said firmly. "I'll call Riley. He can back you up—"

He caught her hand before she could pull her cell phone from her jacket pocket. "No, Hannah."

She shot him a fierce look. "You're not meeting that bastard alone, Sam. And don't even try to tell me that's not what you have in mind, because you never were any good at lying." Her expression softened. "You're the white knight, Sam. This family needs a white knight. You can't go get yourself killed."

He felt his control beginning to crumble. "He has my baby, Hannah. What else am I supposed to do?"

"Let Riley back you up."

"I can't risk it. Stan Burkett is a former cop—"

Hannah's eyes widened again. "Stan Burkett? The guy whose son—"

"Yes," he interrupted.

"My God." Hannah's expression grew instantly grim. "That explains the note—'your child for mine.'"

Sam nodded. "He'll be looking for signs of police presence. He knows how that works. I can't chance it, not even with Riley. You get that now, don't you?"

He could see that his sister wanted to argue, but she finally nodded. "What time are you meeting him?" she asked.

"I can't tell you that."

She sighed with frustration. "Can you at least tell me if it's today?"

"If you don't hear from me by midnight tonight, you can tell Riley what's going on."

"But we won't know where to look for you."

"I'll leave a message for you. What to do in case you don't hear from me." It wasn't a bad idea, really. If something went wrong, he'd want people to know where to look to get back on Burkett's trail. He could use a free text message scheduling service to leave messages for Kristen and his family. Just to be safe.

Hannah looked as if she still wanted to argue, but she kept her protest to herself, instead pulling him in for a hug. He felt her pregnancy bump against his stomach and smiled in spite of his tension.

"Please be careful," she said.

"I promise, I will. I'm all Maddy has, you know."

But that wasn't true, was it? Maddy had her grandparents, her aunts and uncles. She even had Norah, in a pinch.

And she had Kristen, whether the stubborn detective was ready to admit it or not.

Hannah stayed with Sam a little longer, distracting him with chatter about all the local gossip and goings-on he'd missed during his years away from Gossamer Ridge. Of all his brothers and sisters, Hannah seemed the one most wedded to their hometown, to the beauty of the mountains and the bounty of Gossamer Lake.

When she'd fallen in love with the cowboy cop who'd saved her life when her Wyoming vacation had gone horribly wrong, there had been little discussion about where they'd end up once they said "I do." Riley had sold his property to his friend Joe Garrison, loaded his two horses in a trailer behind his truck and headed south to Alabama and a new life with his bride.

Sam wished he could tell Riley what he was doing, he reflected later after Hannah had left. Hell, he wished he could tell Kristen. Lying to her about the text message had bothered him a hell of a lot more than keeping it a secret from the rest of the police. She'd put herself on the line for him and Maddy, more than once. She deserved his trust.

She deserved the truth.

But he couldn't tell anyone what he had planned. Not until he had Maddy safely back in his arms.

CARL MADISON GOT into the passenger seat of Kristen's Impala and reached for the seat belt. The dashboard clock read seven o'clock on the nose.

"The perimeter's in place." Carl told her. "We're using tracker teams who know the lay of the land. Burkett won't have a clue they're there."

"He'd better not," Kristen answered, her neck already beginning to ache from the unrelenting tension. After passing most of the afternoon working up background information on Stanhope Burkett, she was worried that Sam's decision to go it alone might have been the right one after all.

For one thing, Sam's nemesis was a former St. Louis police officer who probably knew quite a bit about setting traps—and avoiding them. He'd quit the force not long after his son's death and had spent most of the past ten years off the grid, if the lack of a paper trail was anything to go by.

For a while, he'd popped up here and there, speaking to antiwar groups about what he called the "Kaziristan cover-up"—officers getting away with "friendly fire" murders of the enlisted by blaming the victims. But that paper trail had gone cold four years ago after the embassy siege in Kaziristan had changed public sentiment in favor of more military involvement in the area, not less.

The most recent mention of Stan Burkett she'd found

was the one that troubled her most, however. The FBI had noted in passing, on a report regarding possible antimilitary activity among some of the more anarchistic antiwar groups, that a man named Stanhope Burkett had been offering survival training to some of the groups for free.

There was no telling where Stan Burkett was keeping Maddy or how easily he might see through Carl's carefully positioned perimeter. She had no idea what he'd do if he spotted the trackers or suspected the police were watching.

And worst of all, Sam Cooper was thirty minutes away from walking right into the middle of the whole mess.

She glanced at the clock again. Five after seven. Time seemed to be creeping.

"You holding up okay?" Carl asked.

She nodded. "Just worried."

"You've grown attached to the kid. And her father."

She didn't answer, her mind full of the reasons she'd given Sam for walking away. With Maddy in danger and Sam putting his life on the line, she wasn't nearly as sure now that she was doing the right thing. What if she was turning her back on her best chance at happiness? At a real family?

"Carl," she said aloud, "what do you know about my mother's condition?"

Carl gave her an odd look. "Her condition?"

She forced the words out. "Her madness. Why did she go crazy? Was it a genetic condition?"

He hesitated a moment. "I thought you knew."

She turned to look at him. "Knew what?"

"It was part of her court proceedings. They assessed her condition to see if she could be treated."

She looked down at the scar on the back of her hand, which glowed faintly in the light from the dashboard. "I've never read the case file. I guess I was afraid to." She forced herself to meet Carl's gaze. "What was wrong with her?"

"She had encephalitis a couple of years after Tammy was born. You must have been around eight. She'd have been in the hospital a week or so—do you remember?"

She nodded. That had been a couple of years after her father had left the family for good.

"The encephalitis apparently caused irreparable damage to the part of your mother's brain that controlled her impulses." Carl's expression was gentle. "She probably started losing her mind immediately, a little at a time."

Kristen felt her whole body begin to tingle as relief washed over her like floodwaters. Encephalitis, not genetics.

Carl reached across the car seat and touched her cheek. "I thought you knew, kitten. Have you been worrying all this time that you'd turn out like your mama?"

She blinked back tears, her throat constricted with emotion. She just nodded.

"Oh, baby."

The radio crackled. "Team Two, in position." A second later, Team One repeated the call-in.

Carl looked at Kristen. "Game on."

She nodded, still trying to process what he'd told her about her mother's condition. She wasn't going to go mad the way Molly Tandy had. And whether or not she could be a good mother was up to her alone.

It changed everything, she realized. The life she'd thought she could never have was a possibility once more.

But not if something happened to Sam Cooper or his daughter.

BELLEWOOD MANUFACTURING'S GOSSAMER Ridge mill had been out of business almost ten years, and as abandoned buildings do in a small town where nothing exciting ever happened, the old mill had fallen prey to vandals and thieves. Sam spotted the building's time-worn, graffiti-riddled facade as soon as he rounded a curve in the packed-gravel track that had once been the mill's main drive.

He had parked his Jeep a few yards from the main road, near enough that he could make it back quickly if the need to grab Maddy and flee arose, but not so close or so exposed that his car was an easy mark for sabotage. He was playing by Burkett's rules, for the moment, but he wasn't an idiot.

The sun had set about a half hour earlier, days growing longer as June and the hot Alabama summer approached. A half-moon gazed down in cool blue dispassion, hidden more often than not by silver-edged storm clouds gathering in the western sky, heavy with the threat of rain. When the moon disappeared, the path ahead grew as dark as a cave, the lights of civilization too distant and few to temper the gloom of nightfall.

Sam picked his way carefully through the high-growing grass that had once been the mill's front lawn. Broken liquor bottles and cigarette butts littered the ground beneath his feet, a blighted obstacle course on his path to the mill. He cursed as his foot hit the curve of one bottle, twisting his ankle. He bent to rub the aching joint, taking advantage of the chance to double-check the Glock tucked in the holster tied to his ankle.

He'd come alone, as Burkett said.

But he'd also come armed.

The interior of the mill was even darker than the outside, and smelled of dust and old beer. He pulled a small penlight from his pocket and switched it on. The weak beam illuminated only a few feet ahead of him. He saw the broken hulk of a curved wooden reception desk ahead, tumped onto its side, boards missing and gouges dug out of the wood.

Sam turned off the light and listened a moment. He knew he might be walking into a trap, but he'd had no choice. He just wished that whatever Burkett had planned for him, he'd get on with it. He was tired of waiting.

He decided to try the direct approach. "Burkett? Are you here?"

Silence greeted him, thick and cold.

He turned on the penlight again and started a methodical tour of the mill, going from room to room, trying to keep a map of where he'd already been firm in his mind.

He had reached the main floor of the shop, an enormous area littered with the stripped skeletons of what machinery the mill hadn't been able to sell when it closed up shop. It looked eerily like an industrial abattoir, strewn with metal limbs torn from their mechanical bodies and electrical wires disemboweled from their metal husks.

A low hum against his hip made him jerk. He'd left his phone on vibrate in case Burkett had sent him any last-minute text messages, though he'd put all regular calls on automatic forward to his voice mail.

He pulled the phone from his pocket and flipped it open. The display panel lit up. One text message.

His heart in his throat, he accessed the message.

COPS IN WOODS. YOU DIDNT LISTEN.

Sam stared at the words, his body going cold and shaky. Cops in the woods? Had Hannah broken her promise?

He weaved through the mill's maze of hallways and rooms, emerging a few minutes later through the front door and out into the cool evening air. The moon was peeking through the clouds at the moment, shedding pale silver light over the mill and the surrounding woods.

Sam turned a slow circle, looking for movement in the woods. The woods were usually alive at night, birds and small animals rustling leaves and disturbing the underbrush. But the woods around him seemed unnaturally still, as if the animals were lying low and watchful.

Aware of human intruders in their habitat, Sam thought, anger pouring into his body, driving out his earlier fear.

Stealth was pointless now. Burkett was long gone.

"You scared him off!" he shouted as strongly as he could, wanting to be sure whoever was lurking in the woods heard him loud and clear. "Did you hear me? He spotted you. He's not coming. I want to talk to whoever sent you out here. Now!"

There was a long, silent pause, though Sam thought he might have heard a faint burst of static from a radio somewhere in the deep woods. He remained where he was, his heart hammering in his chest, driven by equal parts anger and fear, while his mind raced frantically for some idea what he should do next.

He prayed for another buzz from his cell phone with another chance to meet Burkett's demand, but the phone remained stubbornly still. The number Burkett had texted from was blocked from receiving messages. Sam supposed, in time, the police might be able to trace his messages back to their source,

But he didn't think Maddy had that much time.

Headlights sliced through the gloom, headed slowly up the access road. He heard the hum of the engine, the hiss-pop of tires on the gravel surface, and then the car came into full view. It was a Chevrolet Impala, and Sam knew before the car door opened who he'd see.

But it still hurt like hell when Kristen stepped out and into the headlight beams.

"You read the text message on my phone," he said as she closed the distance between them. He was surprised by how betrayed he felt. "You surrounded this place with cops when Burkett said for me to come alone. Do you have any idea what you've done?"

"Yes," she said. He heard tears in her voice.

"He could kill Maddy."

Kristen froze a few steps away from him. When she spoke, her voice was broken and raw. "I know."

He didn't know what to say to her now. He didn't even know what he felt anymore.

He just knew he couldn't stay here one minute longer.

With one last look back at the abandoned mill, he started walking down the road to his car.

CHAPTER SEVENTEEN

KRISTEN POUNDED SAM's front door, sick with regret and fear. "Let me in, Sam!"

She could feel him on the other side of the door, his anger and his despair, and the knowledge that she was the one who'd done this to him was almost more than she could bear. She'd felt so hopeful just a little while ago, knowing that her fate was in her own hands. But now, every doubt she'd had about taking this case crashed down around her, mingling with her own terror about what might be happening to Maddy right now.

Blood everywhere. Four little bodies, strewn about the house, lying where Mama had left them...

She choked back a sob and slid to the porch, what little energy she had left draining from her in a flood of despair.

She'd done this. Whatever happened to Maddy now, she owned it. She didn't know how she could live with this one. The pain in her chest felt as if her heart were being shredded apart, strip by strip. She could never piece it back together again.

Behind her, the door opened. The wooden porch floor creaked as Sam walked onto the porch and stood beside her.

She couldn't look up at him. She should never have

come here in the first place. Apologies were pointless. What she'd done tonight could never be forgiven.

Sam crouched down beside her. "You shouldn't have gone behind my back. I knew what I was doing. If you figured out I was keeping something from you, you should have trusted that I had a good reason."

She forced the words from her aching throat. "I didn't want you to walk into a trap alone."

"I know you were trying to protect me." She felt his hand on her head, his fingers tangling lightly in her hair. "But she's my daughter. I had the right to take that risk for her."

She looked up at him, her heart full of feeling she couldn't contain. "I love Maddy, too, Sam."

A bubble of joy, out of place in the middle of so much fear and dread, caught her by surprise. A watery laugh erupted from her throat as the full weight of emotion crashed over her.

Sam's gaze locked with hers, and she saw that he understood her jumble of emotions, maybe more than she understood them herself. He caught her hands in his. Rising, he pulled her to her feet and wrapped his arm around her shoulder, leading her into the house and over to the sofa. He made her sit, pulling a crocheted throw from the back of the sofa and wrapping it around her. Only then did she realize she was shivering.

"I'm angry with you," Sam told her, his expression tight.

"You should be." Her teeth were chattering a little.

"You're not supposed to agree. You're supposed to argue back." Sam raked his hand through his hair, his movement rapid and agitated. His voice rose. "You're supposed to tell me I was a stupid fool to go out there by myself and you're the cop and you know better. And then I'm supposed to yell at you that you don't know what you're talking about."

She stood up on wobbly knees to face him, understanding. He needed to feel something besides bone-freezing terror. It was the least she could do for him. "He could have been waiting to kill you the minute you walked in that mill, Sam."

"With me dead, he'd have no reason to keep holding Maddy." Sam's gaze lowered, his voice dropping to a hush, as if confessing something he hadn't even admitted to himself before now. "Burkett would have no reason to hurt her, because doing so would no longer hurt me."

"If he'd killed you, I'd have hunted him down for the rest of my life," she answered in a tone just as hushed. "I wouldn't rest until I found him."

Sam's eyes lifted to meet hers. She could see that he understood what she was really admitting. His throat bobbed and he took a hesitant step toward her, his hand outstretched.

But he stopped, an odd look coming over his face. He reached into his pocket, his face a chaos of emotions, and pulled out his cell phone. Kristen could hear the faint buzz of the vibrating phone now, and her heart froze in place.

Sam's shaking fingers punched a couple of buttons. Kristen watched his face grow slack for a second. Then his gaze flew up to meet hers, and she saw the light of hope blazing from his dark blue eyes.

"He wants to meet again."

Kristen didn't ask where or when. She wasn't going

to ruin things for Sam a second time. "I should leave, then."

She started toward the door, but he caught her hand, tugging her back around to face him.

"No," he said firmly. "I'm not playing his game his way this time."

She frowned, not understanding. "What do you mean?"

He touched her face with the lightest brush of his fingertips. "This time, Detective, you're gonna have my back."

"I'M NOT SURE how he's finding all the abandoned buildings in Chickasaw County," Sam said later as he and Kristen went over the plans. It was almost ten o'clock, a half hour before the next rendezvous with Burkett. Old Saddlecreek Church hadn't seen a congregation through its doors for six or seven years, according to Kristen, who knew more about the town's recent history than he did. The congregation had merged with another church closer to town, and attempts to sell the building hadn't met with much success.

Kristen had called the pastor of the new church and gotten the phone number of the former pastor at Saddlecreek, figuring that if anyone knew the layout of the building, he'd be the one. She'd gleaned enough information that they now had a rough but workable floor plan for the main sanctuary, where Burkett's message had directed Sam to come.

"I'll have the text message set up to send," Sam said, programming the message into the phone so that all he'd have to do was punch one button and the message would go to Kristen's phone. "When you get the message, it will mean I have a visual on Burkett and can distract him while you head into the sanctuary through the back."

"I'm going to make my approach on the organ side," Kristen said, pointing to the organ pit on the right side of the floor plan sketch. "Brother Handley said they were able to sell the piano, but the organ was in such disrepair they haven't been able to unload it. It'll give me some cover. Just make sure he's facing the front of the church."

Sam nodded as he put the cell phone back into his pocket. "Ready to go?"

She looked terrified, but also determined, and if Sam had had any doubts about including her in this plan, that one look would have driven them away. Whatever happened, he knew he'd made the right choice in trusting Kristen.

With his daughter and with his own life.

When this was all over, and Maddy was back with them, safe and sound, his next big project was going to be convincing Kristen they could trust each other with their hearts, as well. And not just for Maddy's sake.

He couldn't bear the thought of telling Kristen Tandy goodbye.

She was silent on the drive through town, her profile like cool white marble tinged with blue from the dashboard lights. He felt her nervous tension all the way across the cab of the Jeep, but he didn't know how to ease her fears when he was a bundle of nerves himself.

Just do your part, Cooper. You know Kristen will move heaven and earth to do hers.

He reached across and touched her hand where it lay

on the seat beside her. She gave a little jerk, then relaxed, turning her hand over to twine with his.

"I don't know whether to hope he has Maddy with him or not," she admitted.

He gave her hand a squeeze. "I know. I've decided it'll be easier if she's not there. Then he can't use her as a pawn."

"But what if he won't tell us where she is?"

He released her hand, needing both hands to steer into a sharp curve. "We'll get it out of him."

The approach to Saddlecreek Church was a narrow, winding blacktop road. Sam supposed Burkett had chosen the meeting place for just such a reason—easy to see cars—and people—approaching. As he made the turn onto the access road, Kristen unbelted herself and slid down in the floorboard of the Jeep, out of sight. She would stay there until she received the text message signal.

Sam parked about fifty yards from the front of the church and cut the engine. "Showtime."

"Be careful."

Sam patted his ankle holster. "I will."

He leaned over the seat toward her, until his face was inches from hers. "Be careful, too." He kissed her cold lips, felt them tremble beneath his. Backing away, he met her anxious gaze. "See you soon."

He exited the Jeep and walked the track to the front of the church. A large chain dangled, snapped in two, from the doors of the church. Under closer examination, the cut in the chains looked fresh. And what he'd thought was the reflection of faint moonlight on the dusty blue stained glass windows was actually a light flickering within the building.

Was Burkett inside already?

Sam pulled the door open. It gave a loud creak and a rattle of the chains, so stealth was out of the question. Not that it mattered. Burkett wouldn't have chosen the old church if he'd thought there was a chance Sam could sneak up on him.

The interior of the old sanctuary was dusty and smelled of rotting wood and fabric. A mouse scuttled across Sam's path, giving him a start, but he kept his cool, scanning the open room to get a quick lay of the land.

Rows of pews lined the sanctuary, a few missing here and there, either scavenged by thieves or sold by the church. The hymnal racks were empty, and on some of the remaining pews, mice, rats or other vermin, including perhaps the human variety, had torn some of the blue velvet seat pads to shreds.

At the front of the sanctuary, the altar table remained, covered by a tattered purple altar cloth with a gold cross stitched in the middle. Atop the altar cloth sat a hurricane lamp with a flickering flame that filled the room with pale gold light and a dozen writhing shadows.

Sam took in all of this in the matter of a couple of seconds, which was all the time he needed to realize a man was sitting on the front pew, just a few feet from the altar.

His heartbeat skyrocketed.

Slowly, the man in the front pew rose. He took his time as he turned around to face Sam.

It was Burkett. And he was holding Maddy tightly in his arms, a knife blade pressed against her throat.

"Daddy?" Maddy croaked. The man squeezed her to him more tightly, and her cry cut off.

"Son of a bitch!" Sam yelled, forgetting about anything but the sight of his daughter in a madman's arms.

"Not one step farther." Burkett's firm voice carried across the distance between them.

Sam froze, his eyes never leaving his daughter's terrified face. "I'm stopped."

"Take your hand out of your pocket."

Sam realized he still had his finger on the cell phone button. And Burkett had his back to the organ pit.

With the slightest flick of his finger, he pushed the message button. Then he slowly drew his hand from his pocket and lifted it into the air, along with his other one.

And prayed Kristen got the message.

CROUCHED IN THE FLOORBOARD of Sam's Jeep, Kristen felt one leg starting to go to sleep, a cool tingle setting in. She shifted her position to return some circulation to the limb, but almost immediately she felt her other leg start to tingle.

How long had Sam been gone? It felt like an hour, though she knew it couldn't have been more than a few minutes.

She lifted her cell phone, checking the time on the display. Only ten-thirty-five. He'd been gone less than ten minutes. But if Stan Burkett was punctual, they might be standing face-to-face this very moment.

"Text me, Sam," she muttered at the stubbornly silent phone. As if in direct response, her cell phone began vibrating, startling her so much that she dropped it between her folded legs and had to contort her body to pick it up again.

She read the message. It was one word.

Go.

Heart pounding, she opened the car door from her crouched position and slipped outside into the cool night air. She allowed herself a stretch, keeping alert for any sign that Burkett might have an accomplice watching from the woods. They'd considered that possibility, and while they'd both agreed he was almost certainly acting alone, she'd had enough training to take care as she circled through the woods to the back of the church building.

There was a small education annex behind the main church building. It was connected to the sanctuary, probably so that churchgoers wouldn't have to cross from their Sunday school classes to the worship service in the cold or the rain. She checked the clip of her Ruger, then made her way into the education annex through a broken window and flicked on the small flashlight she'd stuck in the pocket of her jeans.

The flashlight beam revealed a long, grimy passageway, filled with litter, a few old beer bottles and soft drink cans. *Kids today,* she thought grimly, making her way as silently as she could through the obstacle course of detritus.

She heard the faint sound of voices somewhere ahead. She followed the sound around a corner and found herself in front of a doorless archway. From inside, a faint glow was visible.

Kristen turned off the flashlight. It took a few seconds for her eyes to acclimate to the darkness, but when her vision settled, she entered the archway and found herself in a small anteroom. Across from her stood a set of heavy wooden doors.

The organ-side entranceway to the sanctuary.

To the right of the double doors, another door stood open. It was from this open door that the faint, flickering light came, casting dancing shadows across the anteroom.

Choir loft, she thought. She'd been in the church choir as a kid, an enthusiastic if not particularly talented alto.

She crossed to the open door and looked inside. A set of five carpeted steps led up to an empty choir loft. Standing in this doorway, she more clearly heard the voices coming from the sanctuary.

"You had to know it would end this way sooner or later." That must be Burkett's voice, a low growl full of barely tempered pain. Kristen would have preferred a more dispassionate voice, she realized. The man's old and nurtured anguish made him deadly.

She padded silently up the carpeted steps to the choir loft and paused at the edge of the panel wall that had once hidden the choir from the view of the congregation as they filed into the loft. She dared a quick peek around the edge.

She saw Sam immediately, standing with his hands slightly raised. If he spotted her, he gave no indication. His attention was focused on the front of the altar area, where another man stood with his back to the choir loft.

"I didn't want to kill your son, Mr. Burkett. I did all I could to talk him down. But he was going to pull that trigger."

"Lies!" Burkett's cry was that of an animal in pain. "You hated him for not being a good little soldier and killing on your orders. You slaughtered him for his conscience!"

Just over the top of the man's shoulder, Kristen spotted a head full of dark curls.

Maddy.

She ducked back out of view, leaning against the panel wall. She closed her eyes and breathed silently but deeply.

Now or never, Tandy.

First, a quick change of plans. Going through the double doors and using the organ would ultimately gain her no advantage. Even if the doors didn't creak when she opened them, Burkett would spot her through his peripheral vision before she got anywhere near him. If she wanted to stay behind him until the last minute, she'd have to go through the choir loft.

"I don't care what you do to me, Burkett. If you think I'm guilty, I'll take your punishment. But Maddy didn't do anything to you or your son. Let her go. Let her go right now and I'll do whatever you want."

The desperation in Sam's voice broke Kristen's heart. She knew he'd say the same thing—and mean it—even if he didn't know she was waiting to make her move.

Daring another quick glance around the edge of the wall, she spotted the small door set into the wooden rail separating the choir loft from the raised preaching dais. It was half-open already, she saw with a quick spurt of excitement. That would make slipping through it soundlessly that much easier.

"She's the only thing you care about, isn't she?" Burkett said just as Kristen made her swift, silent move out from the shelter of the wall panel and onto the main floor of the choir loft. She lifted the Ruger at the ready, treading lightly as the carpeting ended at the edge of the choir loft. She would have to cross a short span of worn vinyl tiles to get to the low door from the loft to the carpeted dais.

"I'll confess what I did," Sam said quickly, his voice rising. He took a couple of steps toward Burkett, giving Kristen her opportunity to make it through the door and onto the dais without Burkett noticing.

Sam didn't even lift his gaze to look at her, his attention laser-focused on Burkett and his small hostage. "I'll tell the truth about what I did. About what we all did. Just let my daughter go. No more innocents need to die."

"I didn't mean to hurt the girl, you know." Burkett took a step toward Sam.

Kristen froze, holding her breath.

"I just wanted to tie her up so that she wouldn't stop me from taking your daughter."

"She's going to be okay. She can tell the authorities that you didn't mean to hurt her."

Kristen eased to the edge of the dais, by the pulpit. In front of the altar table, with its purple velvet cloth and the flickering hurricane lamp was where she wanted to be. It would put her in the perfect position to jump Burkett at the first chance.

"I want my Daddy!" It was the first time Maddy had spoken since Kristen arrived. She sounded hoarse, as if she'd been crying a lot. Kristen felt a surge of pure rage at Burkett for putting Maddy through this nightmare, and she barely restrained the urge to launch herself at Burkett this very second.

"I'm right here, baby," Sam answered his daughter, taking a couple of steps toward her.

"Stop, Cooper."

"You stop, Burkett. Stop tormenting my child."

"Now you know how it feels."

Maddy started wriggling in Burkett's arms, forcing him to tighten his grasp on her. Maddy cried out in pain.

That was it for Kristen. For Sam, as well, for just as she leaped from the dais, she saw Sam flying up the aisle toward Burkett at a dead run.

Kristen's leg hit the hurricane lamp as she jumped, knocking it onto its side. The flame guttered out, plunging the sanctuary into utter blackness just as Kristen landed on her feet only inches behind Burkett.

She heard Maddy screaming, the sound of grunts and blows landed. She groped in the dark until she felt her fingers tangle in short, coarse hair. Burkett's hair, not Sam's. Sam's hair was softer and a little longer.

Grabbing a handful of hair in her fist, she pressed the butt of the Ruger against the back of his head.

"Give Sam his daughter," she said in a low, deadly tone.

She felt movement, and Sam called out, "I've got her."

Kristen let go of Burkett's hair long enough to reach in her pocket for the penlight. But the second Burkett felt her hand move, he whirled around, catching her off guard. He slammed her into the altar with a bone-jarring thud. One of his hands circled her wrist, forcing her gun hand back against the wooden table with a sharp crack.

She tried to keep her grip on the Ruger but her fingers went briefly numb, and the weapon slid from her grasp. She heard it bounce across the altar table and hit the carpeted floor with a muted thud.

"Kristen!" Sam called out.

"Get Maddy out of here!"

She felt a sudden, sharp pain in her side and realized Burkett still had the knife. As he hauled back for another stab, she shifted right and brought her knee up into his groin.

Burkett reeled away, and she scrambled away from his grasp, her side burning as if it was on fire. Her foot connected with something on the floor. The Ruger. She dropped to her knees and found the pistol. Rising quickly, she pulled the penlight from her pocket and switched it on, illuminating the front of the sanctuary.

Burkett staggered toward her, knife in hand. Sam was right behind him, ready to pounce.

"Gun beats knife," Kristen barked, raising the Ruger steadily in front of her, though it took every ounce of waning strength she had. She felt blood spilling from the wound in her side, a hot, wet stream moving over her hip and down her leg.

Sam grabbed the knife from Burkett and threw it into the pews. "Stay back there, Maddy!" he called over his shoulder as he subdued Burkett with the set of plastic flex cuffs Kristen had given him before they left the house.

"You're hurt," he said to Kristen, his eyes wide with fear as he took in the blood pouring from her side.

"I'm okay," she said, but her voice barely registered. Her knees gave out, and she sank to the floor.

The penlight must have broken, she thought as the world went dark again. She thought she heard Sam's voice again, but it was faint and faraway.

Had he left her? Had he taken Maddy and gone far, far away? She struggled to sit up, to find her feet again. She had to go after then. She couldn't let them leave her. She needed them both so much.

Then even sound abandoned her, and she sank into a deep, silent darkness.

WHEN SOUND AND sight returned, they arrived in a ca-
cophony of raised voices and frantic motion. It took
Kristen a second to realize she was in a hospital emergency room bay, surrounded by green-clad doctors,
nurses and technicians poking, prodding and dragging
her out of the peaceful darkness.

"There she is," one of the doctors said, smiling at her.
"BP's coming back. She's stabilizing nicely." He bent
closer to her. "You're in the Chickasaw County Medical Center, Detective Tandy. Can you talk?"

Kristen's voice came out in a croak. "Where's Sam?"

"Mr. Cooper's just outside. Let us get you all hooked
up and settled down here and we'll bring him right in."

Looking down, she saw that she was naked, her
clothes lying in strips on a nearby equipment table.
Her left side was a screaming ball of agony, but the
doctor assured her they had stopped the bleeding and
once the blood transfusion was finished, she'd be feeling better in no time.

They covered her with a sheet, finally, and brought
Sam into the emergency bay. He was bone-white and
looked as though he'd just walked through the pit of hell,
but when he locked gazes with her, his face spread into
a smile as bright as a clear June morning. He caught her
hand in his, lifting her knuckles to his lips for a quick
kiss. "You sure know how to make an impression on
a guy, Tandy."

"Where's Maddy?" she asked. "Is she okay?"

"She's fine. The doctors just finished checking her
out and now she's with my folks in the waiting room.
I'll bring her to see you once you're in a room."

"Is someone watching her?" she asked, anxious.

"Riley's playing bodyguard, but it's over now. Burkett's in lockup." Sam stroked her hair, his smile widening. "Half the Gossamer Ridge police force is guarding him. The other half is out in the waiting room, driving the nurses crazy. You have quite an admiration society going on there."

She shook her head. "I blew it back there. I heard Maddy cry out and I lost my head."

"So did I." He stroked a stray lock of hair away from her damp face. "It's what parents do."

Tears pricked her eyes. "I had to protect her, whatever the cost."

"I know."

"I would have done that for my brothers and sisters, Sam. If I'd had an idea what my mother was going to do——"

Sam touched her lips with his fingertips. "I know that, too. You were always too hard on yourself about that."

She pressed her lips to his fingers in a light kiss. "You sound like Carl."

"Carl's a smart man," Sam replied with a smile. "He was smart enough to love you."

She heard the vow hidden in his words. She saw the emotion shining in his eyes. It was crazy, really, to feel so much after such a short time, but she knew it was true.

She felt it herself.

"When you get out of here, we need to talk," Sam said.

She managed a weak smile. "If by 'talk' you mean you're going to tell me how things will be between us from now on, I should warn you I already have a few ideas about that."

He ran his thumb over the curve of her chin. "Really."

"Yeah. Like daily foot rubs. And who gets to drive."

"Daily foot rubs, huh? For you or for me?"

"I suppose it could be a mutual thing," she answered, feeling a little silly being flirtatious while she was lying naked and wounded under a little bitty sheet on a gurney.

"Deal," he said, bending to give her a passionate kiss that made her woozy head reel until the doctor came into the room to shoo him out.

Kristen watched him leave, her heart so full of joy she could hardly breathe. Maddy was safe. Burkett was in custody. And she was crazy in love with a wonderful man just crazy enough to love her back. Had she actually died back there in the abandoned church and gone straight to heaven?

If so, there was nowhere else she'd rather be.

EPILOGUE

Six months later

THEY HAD DECIDED against a big, fancy wedding, opting instead for a smaller lakeside ceremony, with just family and close friends in attendance. The whole Cooper clan was there, except for Sam's brother Luke, who seemed to be the prodigal son. On Kristen's side, there were Carl and Helen, of course, and Jason Foley was there with his very pregnant wife.

"She's promised she won't go into labor during the ceremony," Foley assured Kristen when he found a minute alone with her shortly before the ceremony. "I told her if her water breaks, move closer to the lake and she'll be fine."

"God, you're gross," Kristen said with a grimace, but she gave him a hug anyway. "Thanks for coming."

"Wouldn't miss it, Tandy. I can still call you Tandy, right?"

"For the next twenty minutes." Sam's voice was close to Kristen's ear. She pulled back from Foley's embrace and beamed up at her husband-to-be.

"Don't you know it's bad luck to see the bride before the wedding?" she teased.

He smiled back. "Looking at you could never be bad luck."

"Ugh. Newlyweds," Foley muttered. He winked at Kristen. "Enjoy this phase while it lasts. Dirty dishes and laundry are just around the bend." He shook Sam's hand, his expression growing serious. "Be good to her."

"I will," Sam promised. He turned back to Kristen after Foley left. She saw that he was holding a box in his left hand. He gave it to her. "I brought you a prewedding gift."

She examined it. It was a sturdy cardboard box, unwrapped. About the size of a tissue box. Whatever lay inside was heavy.

"Don't shake it and don't drop it," Sam warned. "Need my help opening it?"

"I can do it," she said, even though her hands were shaking a little. Prewedding jitters, she supposed, although after six months of courtship by both Sam and Maddy, she was finally sure this marriage was the right thing for all of them.

The box opened easily from the top. Inside, she found a clear jar filled with water and a small cutting from a rosebush. Her bittersweet childhood memory came rushing back, more sweet than bitter for the first time.

She looked up at him through a film of tears. "I can't believe you remembered that story."

He grinned at her, clearly pleased with himself. "Your neighbor still lives in the same house, you know. She still has the same rosebushes."

She stared at him. "You got this from Mrs. Tamberlain?"

"She was happy to hear you were getting married and sends her best wishes." He leaned closer. "Do you like it?"

She felt tears spill down her cheeks, probably ruining her makeup, but she didn't care. "It's perfect."

"I thought about buying you a brand-new bush," he admitted, pulling out his handkerchief and wiping the tears away, "but I decided I wanted to give you something that showed you how much faith I have in you. In us."

She didn't need proof of that, of course. He'd shown his faith in her when he'd asked her to be part of his and Maddy's lives. But she understood what he was telling her with this beautiful, unique gift.

He was entrusting her with something delicate and fragile, just like the rose cutting. Something that would need nurturing, attention and care.

He was entrusting her with Maddy. And with his own heart.

"I love you," she whispered, rising on tiptoe to brush her lips against his.

He tugged her close, his arms wrapping tightly around her waist. "Love you back," he murmured against her ear.

Behind his back, she lifted the jar of water holding the rose cutting to look at it again. Sunlight slanted through the windows of the room, making the water sparkle like diamonds.

And at the bottom of the cutting, she saw with delight, the first little root had begun to sprout.

* * * * *